POSEIDON'S ACADEMY AND THE OLYMPIAN MYSTERIES

BOOK 4

SARAH A VOGLER

GREEK MYTHOLOGY PRONUNCIATION GUIDE

(Note: this is a general guide only. Certain names have varying pronunciations.)

THE GODS

Anemoi: uh-nem-o

Aphrodite: afro-die-tee

Apollo: uh-pol-o

Ares: air-eez

Artemis: ar-tuh-miss

Asclepius: as-kleh-pee-uhs

Athena: uh-thee-na

Chione: key-own-knee

Demeter: deh-mee-tur

Dionysus: dio-nice-us

Hades: hay-deez

Hebe: hee-bee

Hecate: hek-uh-tay

Hephaestus: huh-fes-tus

Hera: hair-uh

Heracles: hair-uh-cleez

Hermes: her-meez
Hypnos: hip-nos
Persephone: per-sef-uh-nee
Poseidon: poh-sigh-den
Protogenoi: pro-toe-jen-oy
Thanatos: than-uh-tos
Tyche: ty-key
Zeus: zoos

NYMPHS
Naiad: ney-ad
Nereid: neer-ee-id
Oceanid: oh-see-uh-nid

MONSTERS AND CREATURES
Arachne: uh-rak-nee
Chimera: ky-meer-uh
Cyclops: sigh-clops
Erinys/Erinyes: e-rin-es/e-rin-eez
Harpy: hahr-pee
Lamia: lay-me-uh
Lycaon: lie-kay-on
Medusa: meh-doo-sa
Minotaur: min-uh-tor
Nemean Lion: nee-me-un lion
Siren: sigh-ren
Sphinx: sfingks

PLACES
Acheron River: ack-er-on river
Elysium: e-lee-zee-uhm
Olympus: uh-lim-pus
River Styx: sticks
Tartarus: tar-ta-rus

PROLOGUE

'Praise Hermes. Praise the messenger of the gods. Please accept our offering as a sign of our gratitude for all you do. We ask that you continue blessing our city with good trade,' five worshippers begged as they fell to their knees in front of a stone statue of Hermes that towered eight feet above them.

Frankincense wafted around the small stone temple, filling the air with a woodsy scent peppered with spices. Hermes inhaled it, smiling as he stood in the temple's doorway, watching the worshippers bow their heads to the marble floor. *Yes, worship me. I am your god. I...* Rage as hot and bright as Zeus's lightning shot through Hermes when he saw what was in the basket the worshippers had placed at his statue's feet.

'ARE THOSE GRAPES?'

The worshippers' heads snapped around. Their jaws dropped as they saw who was standing behind them. 'Her-rmes. You hon-n-our us with your p-presence,' one of the men stammered, twisting his body around to bow before the Olympian.

'Grapes!' Hermes roared. 'Your offering insults me. I am not Dionysus, the god of wine!' He held his hand out. A fireball as grey as the temple's stone walls materialised in his palm. He drew his hand back, and that's when he felt it. The tiniest drain. Like his powers were leaking from a hole the size of a pinprick. The fireball flickered, its flames dying for a moment before burning back to life. 'What the...?'

HERMES! He cringed as Zeus's voice roared in his head.

'Be grateful I am sparing your lives,' Hermes hissed at the cowering worshippers. He clicked his winged sandals together and disappeared in the blink of an eye.

He materialised in the entryway of Olympus's palace. Sunlight streamed down from the glass ceiling high above, making the diamond floor sparkle with rainbows. Marble pillars ran down the length of the open space, and between them the palace stretched out in different directions. Hermes strode straight for the end of the entryway, heading for the gold double doors between two curving staircases.

He pushed the gold doors open with a thrust of his hands. Zeus was waiting, standing in the centre of the thrones that circled the round room. Lightning sparked on his fingertips, hinting at the rage burning inside him.

'You summoned me,' Hermes said, walking to stand in front of the King of the Gods.

'Did you feel it?'

So I wasn't the only one to feel the drain... 'My powers waned, only for a moment. Do you know why?'

'The humans,' Zeus growled, turning his back on Hermes and pacing away. 'To affect us like that, even for a moment, means that a large group have ceased worshiping us.'

'What? Why would they be so foolish? They know we will destroy them for such insolence. Is that what you have summoned me for? Would you like me to gather the other gods and destroy the Iron Race?'

Zeus turned back, lightning still sparking on his fingertips. 'Let's not be hasty. First find out what is happening among the humans. In the meantime, I will summon the other Olympians here.'

Hermes nodded. 'I will return shortly.' He clicked his heels together and reappeared in the temple he'd been in before Zeus had summoned him. The five worshippers were still there, bowing before his statue.

'Please forgive us. Please show us mercy, Hermes,' they begged as they stretched their hands out to touch his statue's feet.

'I will forgive you, but first I require information.'

The worshippers gasped, turning their bodies to face Hermes. They bowed even lower. 'Thank you, Hermes. You are most kind to return and offer us a chance of forgiveness,' the same man who had spoken to Hermes the first time said, keeping his eyes on the marble floor.

'You're lucky I'm feeling magnanimous today,' Hermes said, his eyes glancing to the basket by his statue. The grapes were gone, beaded bracelets and necklaces having taken their place. *Much better.* 'Tell me, what humans have stopped worshipping my kin and me?'

The worshippers' heads remained bowed, none of them daring to look upon the god. But Hermes saw the shudder that ran through all five of them at his question.

'Someone did come here, to our city,' the man said. 'They spoke slanderous things of the gods. They said all who wish to be free should go to the birthplace of Zeus.'

Hermes ground his teeth. *How dare they! We gods created humans. And this is how they repay us? By rebelling? Ungrateful vermin!* A fireball ignited in his hand—his rage come to life.

'I am loyal to you, Hermes, and the other gods. Always and forever,' the man said, a slight quiver in his voice.

'If you were truly loyal, you would have killed the blasphemer.' The fireball flew from Hermes's hand, hitting the basket of jewellery by his statue's feet.

The worshippers leapt up, running to put out the flames with their sandals, Hermes dematerialising before the smoke could waft towards him. He reappeared in a plain at the bottom of Mount Dicte. Rocky mountains surrounded the enormous field of dirt and dying grass. Hermes expected to find a thousand humans—maybe two thousand—but tens of thousands surrounded him. Their armour shone in the sunlight, and their swords, axes, and spears glinted. Horses whinnied and neighed, and elephants stomped their feet. They were ready for war. Hades was so taken aback by the army that he didn't notice the man approaching him through the crowd until he was right in front of him.

'I knew it would only be a matter of time before they sent you,' the man said. A round shield was strapped to his left arm, and he held a spear with his right hand.

'Who are you to address me in such a manner?' Hermes spat. The human was even looking him directly in the eye. His rage burned, and a fireball materialised in his hand.

'I am Nikolai,' the man said, sparing only a quick glance to the grey fireball burning on Hermes's palm. 'You can kill me if you want, but another will take my place.' His voice was steady. Calm. 'Humans will worship the gods no more.'

'We created you,' Hermes growled, resisting the urge to hurl the fireball at the insolent human. *Patience. Gain as much information as you can first, and then slaughter him.* The other humans watched, their metal armour clinking as they shifted and fidgeted. *Plus the rest of them will attack if I harm this one. They are not worth the effort it would take to slaughter them all—or the mess their blood will make of my tunic.* Hermes took a deep breath, pushing his anger down. 'You will worship us. That is your purpose.'

'No more.' Nikolai slammed the bottom of his spear on the ground. 'We will no longer be your slaves.'

Cheering erupted, and metal clanged as soldiers banged their fists against their armoured chests.

Fools. Death is staring them directly in the eyes and they are too daft to even notice. 'We will destroy your race like we did your ancestors,' Hermes said, looking straight at Nikolai. 'We will create another race—one who knows their place as our slaves.'

Nikolai waved his left arm, and the crowd's cheers and banging cut off, silence descending over the plain. 'I am aware that is within your power. But I would like to make a proposition. We ask that the gods battle us.'

Hermes scoffed. 'I am immortal, as are my kin. You cannot defeat us.'

'We would like to battle for our freedom none the less,' Nikolai said. 'It is our right.'

'You have no rights. We created you. And we can end you.' Hermes's rage flared, and he drew his arm back, his fireball's grey flames growing, hungry to claim a life. He'd gained enough information now. And he knew exactly what he had to do—kill them all.

HERMES! Zeus's voice boomed in his head.

Hermes ground his teeth together, crushing the fireball at the same time, wisps of smoke escaping between his fingers as he dropped his arm. 'Tyche has smiled upon you and granted you a few more moments of life. I suggest you use them to beg us for our clemency, and perhaps we'll be merciful enough to slaughter you quickly.'

Nikolai's defiant face disappeared from Hermes's view, the entryway of Olympus's palace replacing the rocky plain. He strode towards the throne room, already imagining the different ways he and the other Olympians could kill this human race—*poison every stream in the world, kill every plant that grows upon the earth, send a plethora of tornadoes...*

Hermes pushed through the doors to the throne room. The other Olympians were already there, sitting on their thrones.

Their eyes locked on to him, fury burning in their gazes. *I almost pity the humans. My kin look like they'll gladly tear every last human apart, limb by limb.* Hermes stopped in front of Zeus. The King of the Gods was on his throne—a lightning cloud that Hecate had spelled into the shape of a highbacked chair.

'Well, what did you learn?' Zeus demanded.

'There is a rebellion.' Saying the word aloud only fuelled Hermes's rage more. 'At least fifty thousand humans are waiting at Mount Dicte to battle us. They say they will worship us no more.'

'I'll give them a battle.' Ares launched to his feet, pulling a sword from the sheath on his back.

'Wait, Ares,' Zeus growled. 'We must discuss this first. Sit down.'

Ares glowered, holding Zeus's gaze for a moment before tossing his sword to the floor with a clang and dropping back onto his black throne. Spikes stuck from the sides of it like spears, waiting to impale anyone unfortunate enough to get too close.

'I believe our only option is to destroy the Iron Race and create another,' Hermes said, his gaze still on Zeus.

'Agreed,' Hera said. She sat to the right of Zeus, her ivory throne decorated with peacock feathers as blue as the gown she wore.

'Agreed,' voices echoed around the room as the other Olympians voted.

Lightning flickered in Zeus's throne. 'We cannot.'

'Why?' Poseidon demanded from his glass throne, the sapphires, aquamarines, and tanzanite sparkling in it. 'We destroyed the previous races for far less. I'll happily drown every last human on this earth.' A tremor shot through the ground as his grip tightened on his gold trident.

'Believe me, I desire nothing more than to burn them all to ashes.' Lightning sparked between Zeus's fingers as he gripped his throne's armrests. 'But we cannot… because of the prophecy.'

Hermes cocked an eyebrow. 'What prophecy?'

'The one that says if a fifth race is ever created, they will destroy the gods.'

'No such prophecy exists,' Apollo said from his gold throne, which had tiny suns engraved over it. 'I am the god of foresight, if such a prophecy had been foretold, I would know of it.'

'It was told before your time.' Zeus didn't bother glancing at his son. 'A millennia or so ago, when I first approached Prometheus about creating the first humans—the Golden Race—Prometheus had a vision. The prophecy foretold was this… *If a fifth race is ever created, they will steal the powers of the gods and use them to defeat us.* I never believed we would come anywhere near creating a fifth race, so I paid no mind to the prophecy. That is why I never told anyone of it—I didn't feel there would ever be a chance for it to transpire.'

'Father, if you knew of this prophecy, why did you wipe out the other races?' Athena asked. She clutched her spear as she leaned forward in her throne, which was made of leather-bound tomes.

'I have a temper,' Zeus admitted. 'It got the best of me.'

'So what do we do now? The Iron Race is the fourth race,' Hermes said, disappointment clutching at him. He'd been so looking forward to wiping them all out. To personally going back down to kill the one named Nikolai. But now, because of a ridiculous prophecy, this race of traitorous vermin would get to continue living their blasphemer lives. *Pain and death, that's what they deserve… Maybe Zeus will let me wipe out half the world's population. At least that will be something.*

Zeus drummed his fingers on his throne's armrests. 'We require humans to worship us—their worship feeds our powers, so without it we will die. We cannot risk creating another race though,' he stated the facts of their predicament. 'We have no choice but to battle them. If we slaughter all those who oppose us, then that will hopefully end this little rebellion. But if things do not go in our favour, there is another way for us to survive.'

'How?' Hera asked.

Zeus leaned back, lightning sparking in his throne. 'When we created the fourth race, I knew there would be no more races. If this one ceased worshipping us, we would have to find another way to survive. I was confident we could control this race, but just in case, I wanted a contingency plan. I went to Hecate and asked her to create a spell that would allow us—the Olympians—to survive, should the humans be foolish enough to rebel against us.'

'But we won't have to do that, will we, Father?' Athena asked. 'If we kill these ones that will be enough, won't it?'

'I hope so,' Zeus said. 'But if it is not, we must be prepared. Hermes, go to the Underworld. Get the spell from Hecate. The rest of us will enter the battle.'

1

PANIC MODE

The world spun around Hailey in melting and merging colours. Swirls of blue wrapped around her as she materialised in her bedroom. She froze for a second, listening. Silence… No screaming. No cracks of thunder. She blew out a long breath. *The gods haven't come here yet. There's still time.*

'Mum!' Hailey shouted, water dripping from her wet uniform onto the wooden floor. Normally when Hailey arrived back home from the Academy, Evonee would be sitting on Hailey's bed, waiting. This time she wasn't, since Hailey had only left for Poseidon's Academy a couple of hours ago and wasn't supposed to be back home for months.

But things had gone wrong. Horribly wrong. Hailey's mind reeled, trying to make sense of everything that had happened. How Poseidon had strode into the main hall and flooded the Academy with bombarding waves. *How is he alive? Are the other gods back too? Where are the teachers? Amathia? None of them got swept into the sea. Is Pandora okay? Did Poseidon catch her when she went back to the palace?*

Hailey shook her head. *You need to focus. You need to pack and get to Alec's house. Who knows how much time we have. The other gods could show up at any second.* Hailey pushed away the questions swirling around in her head and stripped off her soaked uniform. 'Mum!' she shouted again while throwing on a pair of shorts and a t-shirt, and pulling on runners.

'Hailey?' Evonee's voice called out in a panic, quickly followed by footsteps running up the stairs. Evonee flew into the room, leaving behind a trail of purple paint. Judging by the splotches of paint in her mum's auburn hair, and over her overalls, Hailey guessed she'd just run from the art studio. 'What are you doing back? What's wrong?'

Hailey reached for the overnight bag stashed at the top of her wardrobe. Her suitcase, and most of her clothes, were back at the Academy. 'You need to pack.'

'What? Why? Hailey, tell me what's happening. Are you okay?'

Hailey ripped open her dresser drawers and began shoving the few clothes she had left into the bag. 'You need to pack. We need to get to Alec's house.'

Evonee grabbed Hailey's arm and spun her around, her blue eyes wide with panic. 'Hailey, what is going on? You're scaring me.'

Ugh, she didn't have time for this. 'If I tell you now, you'll never believe me. Can you just trust that I need you to pack and come to Alec's house? Please. There isn't time to explain.'

Evonee chewed her lip, her eyes growing wider and wider by the second. 'Okay. But I expect a full explanation when we get there.'

'I promise.'

'I'll get my suitcase.'

'Don't forget the travelling necklace,' Hailey called after her as her mum rushed from the room, leaving behind purple footprints.

Hailey threw the last of her clothes into the bag and raced down the stairs. She burst into the kitchen. Bowls, plates, spilt flour, and egg goo covered the kitchen bench. The sweet buttery smell of pancakes still lingered in the air from the pancake lunch her, her mum, and Pandora had had. *Was that really only a few hours ago?* She'd been laughing with her mum and Pandora, and now the world was very possibly about to end. *How can so much have changed since then? Focus. You need to focus. You can freak out later.*

Hailey dropped her bag on the ground and threw open the pantry door. Half-empty bags of flour, sugar, and pasta, and opened boxes of cereal and crackers were sparsely spread across the top two shelves. 'We'll need a lot more than that,' Hailey muttered, her attention turning to the middle shelf, where a 7-inch white screen glowed on the back wall. The words *The Demeter Conjurer 3000* filled the screen, and beneath it stretched a slit wide enough to fit an envelope.

Hailey grabbed the notepad and pen from the shelf and scribbled down a list of food…

5 x cans baked beans

5 x packs of granola bars

2 x jars of peanut butter

10 x cans of tuna

10 x bottles of water

Hailey looked at the list, and then at her unzipped bag on the floor. 'I don't think I'll be able to fit any more than that in.' She tore the shopping list from the notepad and pushed it through the slit. The writing, *The Demeter Conjurer 3000,* disappeared from the screen, Hailey's shopping list appearing in its place, with prices listed beside each item.

'Total for order will be twenty-three drachmas,' a robotic voice said from the screen. 'You currently have thirty-seven drachmas in your account. Do you wish to process your order?'

'Yes,' Hailey said. *Hurry up. Hurry up.* At any second she expected to hear an explosion, or screaming. She didn't want to be anywhere near the gods when they reappeared.

'Please close the door to complete your order. Have a nice day.'

Hailey closed the pantry door, opening it again almost immediately. Tins of baked beans and tuna, boxes of granola bars, jars of peanut butter, and bottles of water now filled the middle shelf. Hailey grabbed the items, cramming them into her bag. *Are the gods already here? Maybe a city over, raining down fireballs?*

'Tartarus,' she cursed when she tried—and failed—to zip up her bulging bag. She tossed out a few bottles of water and tuna. 'I can come back for more. I hope.' She pulled the zip closed and hauled the bag over her shoulder, grunting against the weight of it, before dashing into the lounge room and turning on the TV.

She held her breath, waiting to see a news report about how the gods were on the loose and wreaking havoc—washing away entire cities with tidal waves, making the sky rain lava, and about a hundred other awful things.

Hailey's breath came out in a gush when she saw an episode of *Ninja Warrior: The Ares Edition* playing. 'If the gods had shown themselves, their return would be featured on every channel. We still have time to get to Alec's and work out a plan.'

Thud. Thud. Thud. 'Okay, I'm packed,' Evonee said, the wheels of her suitcase thumping on the stairs as she walked down them.

'Did you pack the healing kit?' she asked her mum as she met her at the bottom of the stairs. She wasn't sure what good a few healing plasters and pain-relieving bandages would be if they did cross paths with the gods, but it was something.

Evonee nodded. 'I packed our toiletries as well. Can you please tell me what's happening?'

'Not yet.' Hailey switched the TV off. 'We need to go. Where's the travelling necklace?'

Evonee pulled a bronze necklace with a winged pendant from her trousers—she'd changed out of her paint-smeared overalls, but paint still speckled her auburn hair. She slipped it over her neck and gripped her suitcase with one hand and Hailey's hand with the other.

The room spun, the furniture swirling into a mixture of colours, before everything reformed. Hailey and Evonee stood outside London Station. People materialised around them and bustled along the car-less street, going about their day like the world wasn't about to end. Hailey wanted to shout at them to get somewhere safe. That the gods were on the loose and it wouldn't be long before they attacked. But she doubted anyone would believe her—and if her mum knew that was the reason why they were "on the run", then she'd want answers now. Hailey didn't have time to explain things, not yet.

'Nicole,' Evonee called, waving at a woman wearing a blouse covered in cats; she'd just materialised a few feet away. Demi was beside her, her brown wavy hair blowing in the light breeze.

Nicole smiled with relief and hurried towards them. Demi followed behind her, an overstuffed backpack on her back. 'Thank the Tyches you're here, Evonee. Do you have any idea what's going on? Demi refuses to tell me anything, except that we needed to leave.'

Evonee shook her head. 'Hailey won't tell me either. She ordered me to pack and come with her.'

'Where's your sister and dad?' Hailey asked Demi as people continued to materialise around them, with most heading through the doors to London Station.

Demi swallowed. 'I tried to convince Mum to get them, but she wouldn't—she refused to even pack a bag.'

'I'm not going to drag them away from school and work when I have no idea what's going on,' Nicole argued. 'And I can't just pack up and leave—I have a house of pets to care for.'

'I'll go back for them after we get to Alec's,' Demi said, the slightest trickle of panic in her voice, as if she feared it would be too late by then.

Hailey adjusted her bag's strap, her shoulder aching from where it was digging into her skin. 'We need to go.' She led the way into the station, ignoring her mum's pleas to explain what was going on.

She headed straight for the wall of automatic ticket machines, fiddling with her necklace—a gold heart pendant engraved with her name. Her dad had used his Hephaestus powers to make it for her eighth birthday. He'd died shortly after giving it to her. *Come on, hurry up!* Hailey wanted to say to the three people in front of her. She didn't have time to wait in lines. The gods could appear at any moment. Her gaze flicked around the station for any signs of them, but all she saw were hordes of people coming and going through the archways on the opposite wall, which had platform numbers painted above them. Nothing out of the ordinary, and she really doubted the gods would show up at London Station to announce their big return. *Surely they'd pick somewhere more prominent like the Eiffel Tower or the Colosseum.*

'Your turn, Hailey.' Demi nudged her in the back.

Finally. Hailey stepped up to the machine, typing in Manchester for her destination and feeding ten drachmas into the coin slot. The machine spat out a ticket with a pair of gold wings printed on it, and the words *Manchester Platform 7*.

Hailey moved out of the way so her mum, Demi, and Nicole could buy their tickets. She glanced up at the screen displaying platforms and departure times. The next tube to Manchester was coming in two minutes.

'Let's go,' Demi said.

The four of them shoved their way towards Platform 7, dodging around the people streaming into the station and towards the archways. Hailey pinched her ticket between her fingers, the gold wings on it glowing brighter as she stepped through Platform 7's archway, and then the ticket disappeared, as if it had never existed. The platform was basically a giant empty hall with a few seats spread about. Only a dozen people were inside, standing behind the yellow line that stretched down the length of the platform.

'The tube doesn't come for another minute,' Evonee said, stopping behind the yellow line. 'Can you please give us a hint as to why we're going to Alec's with packed bags. Or at least why you're not at school. Did something happen with Alec's family?'

'No, his family is fine,' Hailey said; her eyes drifted to the giant clock hanging from the ceiling. *Thirty-five seconds until the tube gets here. Come on.* 'I can't explain everything in less than a minute, and it'll only make you freak out more.'

Evonee gulped. 'I wish you hadn't said that. Now I'm *really* freaking out. What happened to the school? Another attack? Oh, I knew I shouldn't have let you go back there. That school was cursed from the start. I should have taken you out the second they let you run off to an island and almost get eaten by monsters.'

Whoo, whoo, a whistle cut off Evonee's rant. The air in front of the yellow line shimmered like heat waves rising from the road on a hot day. A train popped into existence in front of them, a pair of gold wings spelled with transportation magic— just like the travelling necklace Hailey and her mum had used to get to the station—painted on all twenty carriages.

'Manchester,' someone called. 'All aboard for Manchester.'

'Please, just trust me,' Hailey said to her mum before piling onto the tube, which consisted of empty space and hanging handles—no seats.

Hailey dropped her bag between her feet, rolling her aching shoulder, and grabbed a handle. Beside her, her mum looked very pale, as though she might be sick at any second. Hailey had no idea what was going through her head, but she doubted the gods having returned had crossed her mind. Nicole was pestering Demi now, trying to get the truth out of her.

Demi shook her head. 'Wait. We have to get to Alec's first.'

'Just tell me,' Nicole pleaded, 'or I'll ground you for a month —and that means no TV.'

'None of that matters.'

The conductor's voice cut Nicole off from replying: 'The tube to Manchester will depart in 10, 9, 8, 7, 6, 5, 4, 3, 2, 1.'

Whoosh. Hailey's body exploded in tingles as the tube, and everyone on it, swirled into a mixture of colours. A heartbeat later, the tube rematerialised, its doors sliding open.

'Manchester Station,' the conductor announced.

The four of them hurried from the tube, bustling down a set of stairs into an underground space bursting with people, cafes, convenience stores, and a few buskers. They headed straight for the wall of automatic ticket machines, where there was one machine free. Hailey typed in Alec's address: 5 Herodotus Place, Perseus Estate. She dropped two drachmas into the coin slot.

A pair of gold wings appeared on the screen. 'I'll explain everything when we get there,' Hailey told her mum before touching the wings. Pins and needles pricked at her fingertips, the tingling sensation sweeping up her arm and swarming her entire body.

The world swirled around her again, and this time when it reformed, she was standing in front of a set of gold towering gates. On the other side was an acre of yard decorated with statues leading up to a mansion.

'Wow. I don't think I even noticed how big this place was when I came here last time,' Evonee said, materialising beside Hailey. 'All I wanted to do was get to you—after Alec's mum said you'd fought off a robber with your friends. Alec's parents must be so rich.'

'They're not,' Hailey said, walking up to the speaker by the gate. 'The TripleAS owns the place.'

'Oh my word, their mansion is bigger than I remember it being.' Nicole gawked.

'We're here,' Hailey said into the speaker.

'Hurry,' was the reply before the gates creaked open.

'The TripleAS owns it apparently,' Evonee told Nicole.

Nicole scratched her head. 'What's a TripleAS?'

'The Artefacts Ancient Archaeology Society,' Demi explained, materialising.

Hailey would have laughed under different circumstances. 'It's actually The Archaeological Ancient Artefacts Society.' She walked through the gates and along the pathway.

'How do you get a job with them?' Nicole mused, following with Demi and Evonee. 'I wouldn't mind living in a place like this.' She admired the grounds, the green grass dotted with hundreds of statues, which ranged from Theseus wrestling the original minotaur, to men and women dressed in Grecian robes posing. 'Our ponies would love to run around here.'

Hailey shuddered as she stared at the statues; flashbacks of her confrontation with Stetho swarmed her mind. Students and teachers had vanished from Poseidon's Academy at the start of the year, and no one could work out why. It turned out that Poseidon had a gorgon for a daughter who he'd hidden in a secret part of the palace. The nereids had let her loose to cull the human population.

'They give me the chills too,' Demi said, walking beside Hailey. 'But they don't have that sparkle that Stetho's statues did, so these aren't people. Just statues.'

'I know.' Hailey pushed the memories from her mind as she neared the white mansion, which reminded her of an ancient temple, with a row of towering columns out front and a pediment.

She ran up the four steps, finding the double doors already open.

'The entryway could fit our entire house in it,' Evonee

marvelled, gazing around the enormous room with its wide marble staircase and white polished columns.

'The ceiling is so pretty.' Nicole stared at the gold-leaf ornate patterns decorating the towering ceiling.

'Where's Alec?' Demi said. 'I thought he'd be waiting for us. ALEC,' she yelled.

'Weapons room,' a voice yelled back.

'Weapons?' Nicole gasped. 'I wouldn't have let you come to a house with weapons lying around in it.'

'They're not real,' Demi protested, leading the way off to the left, where they passed through a hallway lined with ancient vases and pots. 'They're replicas.'

Technically, they were real, but only the TripleAS and Alec's dad were supposed to know that. It was a way to protect the artefacts if anyone tried to steal them from museums—they'd only be stealing fakes.

As Hailey neared the weapons room, she heard arguing.

'Don't touch that! Alec, what's wrong with you? You know you can't touch the artefacts.'

'Dad, I told you, we need weapons. We have to defend ourselves.'

'Sweetheart, please, you're going to hurt yourself.'

Hailey, Demi, Evonee, and Nicole piled into the weapons room, which reminded Hailey of the Ares room at Poseidon's Academy, having everything from swords to bows hanging from the walls, or encased in glass cabinets. Alec gripped a double-headed axe, the blade looking sharp enough to chop someone's head off. His arms were so skinny that Hailey would have wondered how he possibly had the strength to hold it, if she hadn't already known he was gifted with the strength of Heracles. His blond hair was usually neat and perfectly styled, but it was currently unruly and damp, giving him the appearance of someone a little unhinged. His parents—Alaric and Amelie—reached their hands towards him, pleading.

Evonee cleared her throat. 'So sorry to interrupt.'

Alaric and Amelie swung around. 'Oh, ah, I'm sorry about the scene,' Alaric said, pushing his glasses up the bridge of his nose. 'You must be Evonee and Nicole. Alec did mention you were coming.'

'It's a pleasure to finally meet you.' Amelie walked towards them, her red Grecian dress flowing behind her; she reminded Hailey of a nymph, with how gracefully she moved. 'Normally I would take you out on the terrace for drinks, but I'—she glanced back at Alec, who was still clutching the axe—'I really don't know what's going on.'

'Neither do we,' Nicole admitted.

'We were promised an explanation when we got here,' Evonee said, shooting Hailey a pointed look.

'We'd like one too,' Amelie said, crossing her arms and turning back to Alec.

Alec gulped. 'I don't even know where to start.'

'The gods are alive,' Demi blurted.

'WHAT?!' everyone exclaimed, turning on Demi.

Demi shrugged. 'The gods are alive. The short version is that the Olympians found a way to go into stasis or something, and they've been trapped on Olympus since the Great Battle. The nereids who live in—' Demi's words twisted into a choking gasp for air.

'The spell that keeps us from talking about what's in Poseidon's Academy won't let you tell them,' Alec said, still gripping the axe.

Demi cleared her throat. 'Forgot about that. Anyway, let's just say someone found a way to free the gods. Poseidon broke into the palace and kicked us all out on a giant wave. Now we need to go into hiding before the rest of the Olympians show up.'

No one said anything. Evonee's, Nicole's, Alaric's, and Amelie's faces were completely blank.

'I know this is a lot to take in.' Hailey broke the silence. Her bag thudded to the floor as she dropped it from her aching shoulder. 'But it's true. We've been protecting the world from the gods since we started at Poseidon's Academy. I don't know how they managed to get free, but they are, and it's only a matter of time before they attack.'

Evonee finally blinked. 'I don't understand. This is a joke. It has to be a joke. The gods are dead.'

'It's not,' Alec said. 'Mum and Dad, you have to believe us. You wrote a paper about the prophecy foretold after the gods' demise. You said that you believed they were out there some-where, waiting.'

Hailey jerked at the mention of the prophecy. It had haunted her since the day she'd first heard it: "The gods will one day return to claim back their thrones. Only the one born with the powers of Zeus, who can shoot lightning from their hands, will be able to defeat them." Hailey was the only Zeus in the world. Everyone would look to her to stop the gods. But she was only fifteen; she couldn't take on the Olympians. She'd barely survived her confrontation with Hades. Plus she couldn't shoot lightning from her hands—no Zeus had ever been able to do that—so obviously she wasn't the Zeus the prophecy spoke of, but she doubted that would stop the world from forcing her to face them. She'd spent her whole life running from that prophecy, and now it was coming true.

'Well, uh, yes, we did write a paper about that,' Alaric stammered. 'But we didn't think the gods would actually return—not in our lifetime.'

'Alec, sweetheart,' Amelie said, putting her hands on his shoulders, 'promise me you're telling the truth.'

Alec's grip tightened on the axe. 'I promise. They're back.'

Amelie turned around, a mask of determination washing away her confusion. 'All right, we need to get ourselves organised.'

'What?' Nicole gaped. 'Like that you believe them? This is ludicrous. The gods are dead. Come on, Demi, we're going.' She grabbed Demi's wrist.

Demi pulled her arm free. 'No. It's the truth. Do you remember when we vanished in first year and Amathia told you we got trapped in a room? That was a lie. I stole a wand from a griffin's nest, and then we accidentally read a spell that woke up Hades, Persephone, and the Erinyes. When all those people started vanishing from around the world that was the Erinyes taking them to the Underworld. We figured it out and went there to stop them, and that's when we discovered Hades was planning to bring back the Olympians. We kicked his butt before he could.'

Nicole shook her head. 'No, you were trapped in a room. That's what Amathia said. That's the truth. Why would you lie about something like that?'

Demi gripped her mother's shaking hands. 'I'm not lying. It happened.'

Tears streamed down Nicole's face. 'No. You couldn't have been in the Underworld, not in that horrible place, alone. No.'

Demi hugged her mother. 'It's okay. I got out. I'm okay.'

'Hailey, is that true?'

Hailey gulped and faced her mother, who looked ready to join Nicole in her mental breakdown. 'Yes. But in my defence, I did tell you the truth and you laughed.'

Evonee's jaw dropped. 'What?! You told me the truth? You think I'd believe that my daughter found her way to Tartarus and took on the King of the Underworld?'

Hailey dropped her eyes. 'No.'

'ALEC?' someone yelled.

'Weapons room,' Alec called back.

Footsteps rushed down the hallway, and Aaron burst into the room. He looked like a soldier, dressed in black cargo trousers and a t-shirt—there was even a knife strapped to his utility belt. His mum was next to him, dressed the same, the both of them looking like they were about to charge into battle.

'What are you all doing standing around?' Aaron snapped. 'You should be getting as many weapons as possible.'

'Our parents are having a hard time grasping the truth,' Demi explained. Her mother had managed to stop crying; her face was blank now, like her brain had shut down.

'Well, we don't have time for that. The Olympian Mysteries know this is where the TripleAS keep the real artefacts hidden. They, or the gods, could show up here at any second.'

Alaric's eyes widened. 'The Olympian Mysteries? They're supposed to be harmless.'

'What's the Olympian Mysteries?' Evonee asked. 'How much have you been keeping from me, Hailey?'

The look of betrayal her mum gave her sent a dagger through Hailey's heart. 'They're a cult who want to bring back the Olympians.'

'We don't have time for this,' Aaron interrupted. 'We need to clear this place out. We can't risk the Mysteries getting a hold of anything.'

'I think what my son is trying to say,' his mother said with a censorious glance to Aaron, 'is that we understand this is a shock, but now is not the time to discuss things. We need to move as fast as possible, and then we can find out everything our children have been hiding from us—Oh, and I'm Natasha, by the way. It's lovely to meet you all.' The remnants of a Russian accent tinged her words.

Evonee took a deep breath. 'What do you need us to do?'

'Alaric can tell you what things to grab—anything powerful that can be used to fight the gods,' Aaron said. 'Not sure that axe will be any good, Alec.'

'It's a conjuring weapon.' Alec spun the axe. Within the blink of an eye, it transformed into a sword. He spun it again and was suddenly holding a spear. 'It can become any weapon.'

'Okay, that's cool,' Aaron admitted. 'Now, Alaric, what should we grab?'

Alaric rubbed his chin. 'Oh, well, that's a tough one. There's hundreds of artefacts in here. Perhaps the apple of discord? Although that won't work on the gods, only the Mysteries.'

'This isn't a time for babbling, husband,' Amelie cut in. 'I know one thing we'll need—the cornucopia.' She dashed from the room, her dress flowing behind her.

'I'll help,' Natasha said, darting after her.

A high-pitched screech exploded.

Hailey's hands flew to her ears. 'We're too late. Someone's already here.'

2

PERIMETER BREACH

'What in Tartarus is that?' Nicole yelled over the blaring. 'A screecher alarm.' Demi pressed her hands tight to her ears.

'Mute alarm,' Alaric called. The screeching cut off, leaving Hailey's ears ringing.

'It wasn't me. I didn't touch anything… this time,' Demi said, dropping her hands.

'Show the breach,' Alaric said.

The room's white walls flickered like a TV screen, and suddenly a video of the front yard appeared on them, showing ten people garbed in black marching towards the mansion.

One of them was a woman with long auburn hair a few shades lighter than Hailey's. Hailey gripped the heart pendant on her gold necklace as her stomach twisted. She knew exactly who that was: the intruder who had tried to steal Perseus's sword at the start of the year—she was part of the Olympian Mysteries. *But she's meant to be in jail. How is she here?*

'What is happening?' Evonee demanded, staring at the people in black getting closer and closer to the mansion. 'Who are those people?'

'The Olympian Mysteries,' Aaron answered. 'We're too late.'

'Here it comes!' the woman with auburn hair yelled on the screen.

A nine-headed monster double Hailey's height slithered into the camera's view on a serpent tail, screeching and launching itself at the Mysteries. The Mysteries jumped into fight mode, swinging swords, firing arrows, and throwing fireballs.

'What is that thing?' Nicole gasped, her voice barely a whisper.

'Circe,' Amelie explained, coming back into the room with Natasha, an overnight bag hanging from her shoulder. 'She's our guard hydra.'

'Poor Circe,' Demi said, watching as the Mysteries slashed their swords at the monster's snapping heads.

'Only adamantine metal—like Perseus's sword—is strong enough to cut her skin. She'll be fine,' Alaric assured her.

'What's the plan?' Natasha asked.

'We call the police.' Evonee's voice shook. 'People are trying to break in. People with *weapons*.'

Alaric swallowed. 'They should have been here by now. If anyone climbs over the gates, it sets off a silent alarm that summons the police—it was a security update added after the invasion at the start of the year.'

'The police, at least some of them, are working with the Mysteries.' Aaron pointed to the wall, where the auburn-haired woman and two others were making a run for the mansion, while the other seven members ducked and weaved Circe's heads. 'That woman should be in jail. If she's out, it means someone let her out.'

'So what do we do?' Nicole looked ready to faint. 'Is there a back entrance we can leave through?'

'The mansion is in lockdown.' Alaric rubbed the back of his neck. 'There's only one way out.' He looked at Amelie.

She nodded and ran off.

Circe screeched.

Hailey's gaze flicked to the wall. A cloud of gold dust sprayed over the front yard like an explosion of glitter. Circe's heads swayed from side to side, her eighteen eyes drooping closed a heartbeat before she lolled backwards, knocking over a statue of a woman holding a giant vase, smashing it to pieces.

'A sleep spell,' Hailey muttered.

'That's not good.' Aaron stated the obvious. 'We need to get ready to fight.'

Bang. Bang. Bang.

'We can't let them in,' Alaric said, watching as the video on the walls changed to show the front of the mansion. The Mysteries fired fireballs and exploding potions at the front doors. 'The artefacts in here are too dangerous to fall into enemy hands.' He pressed his thumb onto the face of his wrist watch. 'Activate back-up protocol.'

'Fingerprint confirmed as Alaric Parker's,' a voice spoke from his watch. 'Self-destruct initiated. Thirty, twenty-nine, twenty-eight.'

'WHAT?!' Evonee and Nicole both shrieked.

Demi's eyes were wide. 'You can't self-destruct this place. We're *inside!*'

Hailey gripped her necklace tighter. She didn't want to die at the hands of the Mysteries, but she also didn't want to get blown up.

'Nineteen, eighteen.'

'Got them.' Amelie ran back into the room. 'Put these on.' She handed Evonee, Nicole, and Natasha a white gold travelling necklace, putting the last one over her own head. 'These will get us out of here, but there aren't enough for all of us. We need to hold hands to amplify the necklaces' magic.'

'Thirteen.' A bang shook the mansion.

'Come out, come out, wherever you are,' a voice taunted.

'Ten, nine.'

'We need to go,' Alaric urged.

Hailey hauled her bag back over her shoulder as footsteps ran down the hallway towards them.

'Seven, six.'

Everyone gripped hands.

The Mysteries swarmed into the weapons room. The auburn-haired woman sneered. 'Found you.'

'Three, two.'

The world swirled around Hailey, and a second later she was standing in a windowless room the size of her bedroom. Light streamed down from the ceiling like sunlight. 'Where are we?' The room was completely bare, with not a single piece of furniture.

'The TripleAS headquarters,' Alaric explained. 'Those travelling necklaces'—he nudged his head to the necklaces as everyone took them off and handed them to him and Amelie —'are the only things capable of bringing anyone here.'

'Dad, I can't believe what you did.' Alec shook his head, leaning into the spear gripped in his hand, like it was the only thing keeping him from collapsing. 'You blew up all those artefacts. Why would you do that?'

'Not to mention you killed those Mysteries people,' Demi added.

'And almost killed us.' Evonee's face was red with fury. 'How dare you put us in such danger. One more second and we all would have been dead.'

'Whoa, whoa, whoa.' Alaric put his hands up. 'I didn't blow up any artefacts, or any people. I can't believe you would think I'd destroy pieces of history like that, Alec.'

'So it was a ruse?' Aaron gaped. 'So the Mysteries now have access to everything in your mansion? All of those weapons and magical items?'

Medusa, we are *screwed. The Mysteries will take the artefacts to the Olympians, who are already unstoppable enough. But with magical items like Circe's staff and the Ring of Gyges, they'll be beyond unstoppable.*

'They don't have anything,' Alaric said. He exchanged an unsure look with Amelie, who nodded, as if giving him permission to explain. 'The truth is that the TripleAS installed a self-destruct after the break-in at the start of the year. They didn't want any artefacts getting into the wrong hands.' Alaric swallowed. 'But I couldn't stand the thought of pieces of history being destroyed, so Amelie and I found a Hecate to alter the self-destruct. The Hecate overrode the explosion with a spell instead—one that would freeze anyone inside, and make it appear to anyone outside that the mansion had blown up. If we went back there now, we'd see a pile of rubble. But the mansion is still there, with all of the artefacts safely inside. I promise.'

Alec breathed a giant sigh of relief, like he'd just been told the gods' reappearance was a false alarm and everything was okay.

Thank the Tyches the Mysteries didn't get anything.

'No one else knows the truth about the self-destruct,' Alaric went on. 'You have to keep—'

The door in the wall across from them flew open—Hailey hadn't even noticed it—and a man marched in. An insignia with three "A"s interlocking in the shape of a triangle was stitched onto his dark blue robe. *He's with the TripleAS. We're safe here.* Hailey sighed.

'Oh, Lionel, thank the Tyches,' Alaric said. 'I was beginning to think this castle had been infiltrated when you didn't show up right away.'

'Castle?' Demi gaped. 'We're in a castle?' She looked around, as if expecting a window to have suddenly appeared.

The man, Lionel, gazed around, confused. 'Alaric, who are these people? This location is top secret, you know that.'

'I didn't have a choice. The Mysteries were storming the mansion. This was the only way to get everyone out.'

'The Mysteries?' Lionel scratched his grey head of hair. 'I didn't receive any notification that the mansion had been breached.'

'Someone tampered with the silent alarm. I think someone in the police, at the very least, is working with them.'

'Oh my, that is not good. Did you activate the self-destruct?'

Alaric nodded.

Lionel's shoulders dropped. 'Oh.' He looked as if Alaric had just told him the sun would never rise again. 'Well, I suppose it's a good thing. We set up the self-destruct to insure no artefacts got into the wrong hands, so I guess it worked.'

'Where is everyone else?' Alaric stared behind him to the empty doorway. 'Why are you the only one here?'

'They're a little tied up with something at the moment.'

'Um, excuse me,' Nicole said, standing between Demi and Evonee. 'I'm sorry to interrupt, but um, you see, I didn't exactly believe my daughter when she told me I needed to get my family to safety, so I left behind my husband and other daughter —and all of my pets. I need to go back and get them. How do you get out of this castle?'

'Oh, I can arrange to have them brought here for you,' Lionel said. 'This is the safest place in the world. You don't want to be wandering around out there with the gods on the loose.'

Aaron stood on Alec's left. 'Hang on.' He narrowed his eyes. 'How do you know the gods are on the loose? Have they shown themselves?'

'No,' Lionel said quickly. 'I just assumed that's what had happened when you mentioned the Mysteries storming the mansion. They wouldn't do that unless it had something to do with the gods.'

'Why would the Mysteries grouping together mean that the gods had returned?' Amelie asked from beside her husband. 'We've always believed the Mysteries were nothing more than worshippers and had no way of resurrecting the gods, so why would your first thought have been that the gods had risen again?'

Lionel waved his hands. 'I don't know. It does seem like a rather odd leap to make, now that you mention it.' His gaze shifted to the bag on Amelie's shoulder, and the spear in Alec's hand. 'You managed to pilfer some items I see. Well, I'll take those and keep them safe.' He reached for the spear.

Aaron stepped in front of Alec, blocking him from Lionel. 'I don't think so. Something doesn't feel right here.'

'I agree,' Hailey said, her fingertips tingling in warning, her powers already sensing danger. *Something is definitely off. Why is this Lionel guy being so weird? Are the gods already here?*

'Where did you say the other members were?' Alaric asked. 'It's protocol for everyone to return once there's been a breach. You should have alerted them to come back the instant we all materialised.'

Sweat trickled down Lionel's forehead. 'Um, they're… well.' He blew out a breath. 'Fine. You win. I don't see the point in this charade. I'm in the Mysteries—so many more perks, especially now that the gods are back. While the rest of the world suffers, I will live in luxury. The other members are in the dungeon—too stupid to see they're on the losing side. So I'll take those artefacts now.' He held out his hands. 'And then you can join them in the dungeon.'

Demi laughed. 'Are you serious? There's one of you and nine of us. We're taking this castle.'

Lionel smirked. 'You can come in now,' he called.

A dozen people dressed in black swarmed the room.

The tingling in Hailey's fingertips intensified, but she couldn't exactly use her powers without the sky.

Aaron's hands flew up. The air in front of him shimmered slightly as his force field activated. The Mysteries rammed into it, stumbling back a step as they steadied themselves.

'Destroy the barricade,' Lionel ordered, standing to the side of the group. 'Throw everything you have at it.'

Fireballs soared towards Aaron's force field. Potions exploded against it. Knives stabbed into it. Each blow sent a ripple across it, like a lake someone had thrown a stone into.

'This isn't going to be easy to hold,' Aaron said through clenched teeth. 'Those exploding potions feel like a cyclops's pounding fist.'

Hailey's eyes darted around the room, desperately searching for something—a pane of glass, a crack in the wall—anything that would give her access to outside. But there was nothing. Not a single shred of sky for her to call upon.

'I can't believe the Mysteries infiltrated the TriplaAS.' Alaric shook his head, looking crestfallen rather than terrified, like there wasn't a psychotic group of people currently trying to kill them. 'This was meant to be the location that everyone came to if something like the gods returning happened—it's impenetrable, and inescapable. There's nowhere else. We're trapped.'

Aaron grunted, his hands shaking as the Mysteries continued to bombard his force field.

'No, we're not.' Alec pulled a gold travelling necklace from his pocket. 'We still have the travelling necklaces from Poseidon's Academy. We can use them to get out of here.'

'That's a great idea,' Hailey said, her chest untightening just a little. The necklaces would take them to Poseidon's Island. No one knew where it was, so the Mysteries wouldn't be able to follow them there. She grabbed her own necklace from her bag, Demi doing the same.

'In – my – pocket,' Aaron puffed to his mum. His force field rippled as fireball after fireball blasted into it—a few of the Mysteries had even started kicking and punching the invisible wall.

Hailey gulped. The only way they could use the necklaces was if they all joined hands, since there weren't enough to go around. For that, Aaron would have to drop his force field, and the Mysteries would overtake them before they'd even had a chance to grab hands. 'How are we supposed to use the necklaces? They'll swarm us the second Aaron drops his force field.'

'I'll take care of that,' Natasha said. 'I'm a siren—but my powers work a little differently to other sirens,' she added when everyone frowned at her. 'Get in position.'

Hailey, Demi, and Alec put the necklaces on and joined hands with their parents as Natasha lowered Aaron's necklace over his head.

'Best you surrender,' Lionel said, still standing to the side of the firing squad. 'Otherwise I can't promise a stray fireball won't hit you.'

'Go to Tartarus, you turncoat,' Alaric spat back.

'Now!' Natasha yelled.

Aaron dropped his hands, hunching over to catch his breath. The Mysteries surged forward, devilish grins on their faces as they reached out to grab Hailey and the others. And then a scream as loud as the screecher alarm at Alec's mansion ripped through the air. The Mysteries froze, their hands flying to their ears.

Natasha stepped towards them, her mouth wide open as she screamed even louder, so loud that the Mysteries flew backwards and crashed into the wall, with some of them even flying through the open door.

Something warm and wet dribbled from Hailey's ears—blood, she was guessing—as Aaron grabbed her hand. 'Get ready,' he said.

The scream cut off, leaving Hailey's ears ringing. Natasha joined their circle, gripping hands with Nicole and Alaric. 'Let's go.'

Tingles swept through Hailey's body, but that was it. The world didn't swirl into colours. She didn't appear anywhere else. She was still in the castle, with the Mysteries lying on the floor, starting to twitch and move.

'What's happening?' Demi asked. 'Why isn't it working?'

Alec gulped. 'Too many people.'

'But the other necklaces worked,' Demi argued.

'They were different necklaces,' Alaric said, his voice flat. 'These ones must only allow an extra person. There's one too many of us.'

The Mysteries lumbered to their feet, groaning.

'Um, Natasha, you might need to use your scream on them again,' Nicole said.

Natasha shook her head. 'It's too soon. My powers are drained.' Her voice sounded like gravel.

Amelie shifted the bag she was carrying to Alec's shoulder. 'I love you, my sweet boy.' She kissed him on the forehead.

'Take care of each other,' Alaric said.

'No!' Alec cried, but it was too late. His parents broke from the circle and launched into the Mysteries, kicking and punching.

Aaron grabbed Alec when he tried to run to them. 'We need to go. Otherwise we won't be able to come back and save them.'

Tears gleamed in Alec's eyes as he watched the Mysteries wrestle his parents to the ground. He turned away from them and took hold of Aaron's and Natasha's hands.

The room swirled out of view.

3

REFUGEES

Poseidon's Island swirled into existence around them. Usually it was bright, with the sun beaming on the lapping sea, making the water shimmer like emeralds, sapphires, and aquamarines. Students would normally be sitting under the coconut trees, laughing with their friends while they waited for Master Anderson to summon the whirlpool that would take them to Poseidon's Academy.

That happy scene was gone, replaced by a grey sky pouring rain that turned the white sand mushy. A hundred or so tents were scattered around. *Guess everyone had the same idea about bringing their families to Poseidon's Island.*

Hailey swiped her hand at the sky. Warmth rushed up her arm and shot from her fingertips like heat rays. The rain vanished in an instant, with the grey clouds speeding out of sight. Hailey didn't need a mirror to know that her grey eyes had brightened to azure blue to match the sky.

Heads poked out of tents as the beaming sun glowed.

'Hailey! Demi!' someone cried in an Australian accent.

Hailey saw a brief glimpse of blonde hair streaked with pink before a girl launched on her, wrapping her arms around Hailey and Demi. 'It's good to see you, too, Kora,' Hailey said when they broke apart.

'I'm so glad you're okay.' Tahlia joined their group, her long black hair gleaming like satin. 'What's the matter, Alec?'

Alec sniffed. 'My parents,' was all he managed to say, his voice thick.

Evonee put an arm around him, hugging him to her side. 'They're going to be okay.'

'What happened?' Kora asked. 'Why did it take you so long to get here? I thought you would have been the first ones.'

'We had to make a stop.' Hailey dropped her bag on the wet mushy sand. She wasn't sure what else to say.

Everything had happened so fast. The Mysteries had appeared out of nowhere. At the start of the year, when she'd been worried about them, everyone had told her they were harmless. *They were so wrong. The Mysteries found a way to free the Olympians. How? How did they do it?*

And Alec's poor parents...

Someone cleared their throat.

'Oh, these are our parents,' Kora said, turning to the four people standing behind her and Tahlia.

'They're still coming to terms with everything,' Tahlia added.

'Us too.' Nicole was biting her nails and looking seconds away from a nervous breakdown. 'I need to get Annabelle and your father. And make arrangements for the pets. Demi, I need to go back.'

'I'll come with you,' Demi said.

'No.' Nicole shook her head. 'I want you to stay here where it's safe. If the gods really are back, it's too dangerous to be anywhere in the open.'

'But I don't want you to go alone. I can protect you if something happens,' Demi pleaded.

'I'm the parent—it's my job to protect *you*, not the other way around. I'm going alone, and that's that.' Nicole's voice was final. 'Give me your travelling necklace, please.'

Demi pressed her lips together, fighting the urge to keep arguing. She pulled the necklace from around her neck and held it out to her mum.

'You can have mine too,' Hailey said, holding out her own necklace. 'You'll need at least two to bring the three of you back here.'

'Thank you,' Nicole said, slipping the extra necklace into her pocket before pulling Demi into a hug. 'I love you so much. But I'm still really angry. We're going to have a very big talk when I get back.'

Demi squeezed her mum. 'I love you too.'

'I'll take care of Demi until you're back,' Evonee promised as Nicole and Demi broke apart from their hug.

Nicole wiped away a stray tear. 'Thank you.' She gazed around the island, her face dazed, as if she were trying to decide if this was reality or a horrible nightmare. 'See you soon.' She popped Demi's travelling necklace over her head and swirled into a mixture of colours before vanishing altogether.

Demi gulped. 'I wish she'd let me go with her. I don't like not knowing what's happening. What if the gods have come out of hiding now and are attacking? She's just a Hestia. She won't be able to defend herself. I have to check.' Demi pulled her phone—a circle of glass with a pair of gold wings printed on it—from the pocket of her shorts. She rested it in the palm of her hand. 'Show me the news.' She touched the pair of gold wings. Gold light shone up from the symbol and morphed into a 15-inch screen that showed a video of a woman sitting behind a desk.

'Wasn't that a touching video of a Nemean lion raising a lamb. Hopefully it's not saving the lamb for a snack.' The woman chuckled. 'Now, in other news, Dionysuses are competing at the Italian Wine Festival to see who can produce the best wine.'

'They're still not back. Good.' Demi touched the gold wings again, and the video disappeared.

Aaron cleared his throat. 'Um, I think now might be a good time to discuss some things,' he said to Hailey, Demi, Alec, Kora, and Tahlia. 'So how about all the parents talk while we have our own discussion.'

Evonee grabbed Hailey's arm. 'I don't want you to leave my sight.'

'I won't. I'll only be a yard away, over there by that coconut tree.' She squeezed her mum's hand. 'I'll be okay.'

Evonee's hand slipped from Hailey's arm as Hailey wandered over to the coconut tree with her friends.

'Your parents are going to be okay,' Demi reassured Alec, rubbing his back. 'They're smart, and they seem pretty important, so I don't think that Lionel person will do anything to them—they're more valuable alive.'

Alec sniffed and nodded.

'What happened?' Tahlia asked, her crystal blue eyes turning rheumy as she looked at Alec's pained face.

Hailey was still trying to understand everything that had happened herself. 'Um, we ran into some trouble while we were...' She didn't know if she could mention the fact Alec's home held most of history's ancient relics. 'Um, getting reinforcements. There's this cult called the Olympian Mysteries who want the gods back in power, and we crossed paths with them. Alec's parents... well, they, uh, fought them off so we could escape.'

Tahlia squeezed Alec's arm. 'I'm so sorry.'

Alec swiped at his eyes.

'I know you're going through a lot right now,' Aaron said, putting a hand on Alec's shoulder, 'but we really need to focus.

The gods are on the loose, and the Mysteries are helping them. We need to get a plan in action.'

'Isn't that something your dad and his team should be taking care of?' Demi said. 'Or like some other SWAT team. I know my powers are pretty awesome and all, but I don't think they'd do well against Demeter herself.'

'My dad's team are,' Aaron assured her. 'The first thing I did when I got back home was call my dad. I told him everything— the truth about what happened last year when he couldn't remember why he was at the Academy.'

'How did he take that?' Demi asked.

'It's something we'll be discussing later.' Aaron dragged a hand through his hair, his shoulders dropping a fraction. 'Anyway, we think the palace follows the same path through the sea every year. When I was collecting information on the palace in first year, I charted the star constellations every night that the palace was above water. My dad is going to use those to try and track the palace.'

'So why do we have to come up with a plan then?' Hailey said. *By the sounds of it, "the problem" is being handled.* 'If PET is taking care of everything and dealing with the gods, then we don't have to worry, right?' She was desperate for him to say yes, that his dad would take care of everything and the gods would be dead or gone by the end of the day.

'I really hope so. But you always need a Plan B, just in case.'

'So what's the plan?' Kora asked.

'We get everyone on the island to write letters to everyone they know from the Academy, telling them to pack bags, grab their family, and meet here.'

'But the travelling necklaces only allow an extra person. No one will be able to take all their family,' Tahlia pointed out.

'They'll just have to make multiple trips back and forth,' Aaron said simply.

'What if the Mysterious or gods find out where we are?'

Hailey's eyes darted around the island, searching between the tents for anyone who might be an enemy. 'If they get a hold of one of the letters, they'll know exactly where we are.'

Aaron shrugged. 'That's a chance we're going to have to take.'

'We can get a Hecate to spell the letters as well.' Alec's voice was quiet, his eyes on the shell-dotted sand. 'They can cast a spell or brew a potion so that the letters disintegrate as soon as they're read.'

'That's a great idea, Alec.' Tahlia squeezed his hand. 'I'll go look for one. Come and help me, Kora.' They both ran off.

'I hope the Tyches have our backs on this.' Demi chewed her lip as she stared at the spot her mum had vanished from. 'Otherwise, we're all screwed.'

Three hours later, the island was packed. Just about every square inch of it was scattered with tents and people roaming about.

Hailey was standing back at the coconut tree with Alec and Aaron, while Demi was a few feet away squeezing her family, who had just arrived.

'Demi,' Aaron called. 'We need to start organising some things.'

'Coming.' Demi released her little sister, Annabelle, from a hug and rushed over.

'Is everything okay?' Hailey asked. 'Did your mum say why it took so long to get back?'

'It took her a while to find somewhere for the animals—Dad had to convince her not to bring them here. They're all checked in to Artemis's Sanctuary now, so they're safe.'

'So nothing about the gods appearing?' Aaron pressed.

Demi shook her head. 'Nope. Everything was normal.' She glanced around the island, her eyes combing over the five hundred-plus people there. 'Should we be worried Jayden's not here yet?'

'He'll come.' Like everyone else, Hailey guessed it would take him a little while to convince his family to pack up their things and follow him to Poseidon's Island. 'Even though he wasn't at school when Poseidon attacked, we've been through enough for him to trust us when we tell him the gods are back and to meet us here.'

Demi chewed her lip. 'Yeah, you're right.'

'Aren't you worried about your boyfriend, Jackson?' Aaron asked.

'His name is Brax,' Demi corrected. 'And he said he'll be here soon—he's still trying to convince his parents.'

Hailey gazed around, trying to spot as many of her friends as possible in the crowd. Kora and Tahlia were with Tanzy and Lexa… and Brennan. She blew out a breath when she spotted him, and the knot in her stomach unfurled the tiniest amount. She hadn't even realised she'd been worried about him. His eyes met hers, and she smiled awkwardly as she waved. *Why am I being so weird?*

'Why don't you go and talk to him.' Demi nudged her. 'You two are so gaga for one another.'

'Are not.' Hailey's cheeks burned. 'We're friends.'

'That's enough,' Aaron snapped. 'We've got more important things to worry about than high school crushes. We need to make an announcement. Most of the parents here have no idea what's going on—and even the other students don't know the full story.'

'I've got this.' Demi reached an arm towards the coconut tree beside them. A shudder tore through it, and a few coconuts shook loose as the tree shrunk down. Its lowest branch now touched the sand.

'Demi, wait,' Aaron pleaded, reaching to grab her.

Demi leapt onto the lowest branch before he could grab her

and raised her hand up. The coconut tree shook again, and this time it shot into the air, soaring up two storeys.

'Demi Penelope Evans, what are you doing?' her mum demanded. 'Get down from that tree right now before you break your neck.'

'It's fine, Mum.' Demi gripped the branch above her head to keep her balance. 'If I fall, I'll get the branches to catch me.' She turned her gaze to the rest of the island. 'Listen up,' she shouted. The people closest to the tree stopped talking and looked up, but everyone on the island's outskirts paid no attention. 'A little help, Hails,' she called down.

Hailey lifted her hands towards the sky. Warmth flowed up her arms and shot from her fingertips. A breeze whipped past her, blowing out her auburn air. 'Okay, go,' she said, sending the breeze flowing over the island.

'Listen up,' Demi shouted again. The breeze carried her voice across Poseidon's Island, and this time everyone stopped to stare at her. 'I know you're all freaking out. I mean, Poseidon showing up at school and almost drowning us was a bit of a shock. And I get that the adults here are having a hard time believing the gods are back, but it's true.'

'Where's the proof?' someone called out. 'If the gods were back they would be attacking somewhere right now.'

'Maybe they need to rest or something first to get their strength back,' Demi replied. 'Coming back from the dead would probably be exhausting. That explains why Poseidon attacked the school—he wanted to go to bed.'

'Oh, Medusa.' Aaron shook his head. 'She really has no idea what she's talking about.'

Yep, Hailey had to agree Demi was being a little bit imaginative, but the important thing was that she got the point across: the gods are alive and they'll be showing up soon.

'How is this possible?' a woman standing a few rows behind

Hailey asked. 'How can the gods be back? We've lived centuries without them showing up, so what changed?'

Demi tightened her grip on the branch above her as she stared down at the woman. 'I have no idea—and don't ask me about how we can have their powers if they didn't die, because I don't know the answer to that either,' she quickly added before anyone could ask. 'But what I can tell you is that two years ago my friends and I discovered Hecate's wand in a griffin's nest—yeah, we took on a griffin and won.' Her chest puffed up. 'Anyway, there was a spell attached to it and we kind of read it, and it woke up Hades and Persephone—oh, and the Erinyes. They were the ones making people disappear.'

Everyone gasped, a few people calling out that that wasn't possible.

Evonee shot Hailey a censorious look that told her their conversation regarding the Underworld was far from over.

'It was an accident,' Demi quickly said.

Aaron slapped his palm against his forehead. 'This is a nightmare.'

'Anyway, so Hades was going to wake up the Olympians, but we stopped him, so he never got a chance—you're welcome. But it looks like someone—I'm guessing the nereids—found a way to wake up the Olympians after all.'

'Who are the nereids?' a voice asked from the crowd.

'The psychotic sea-nymphs living in—' Demi's words cut off as she coughed. She rubbed a hand on her throat. 'They're psychotic sea-nymphs who have a mission to bring back the Olympians.'

'Why should we believe any of this?' a woman with crossed arms asked.

Demi sighed, frustration creeping into her features. 'Because it's true. You're safer here than you are back home—the gods haven't shown up yet, but they will.'

'And then what?' the same woman asked. 'What do you expect us to do?'

'Um…' Demi looked down to Hailey and Aaron for help.

'The Government is already aware of what's happened,' Aaron called out. Warmth poured from Hailey's fingertips as she shifted the wind to carry Aaron's voice across the island. 'They currently have a special ops team working on it. All we have to do right now is stay calm and let the professionals sort it out.'

4

THE MOVE

Hailey stood on the beach, inhaling the salty sea-air as she watched the sun rise, painting the sky a mixture of pinks and oranges that reflected in the endless sea before her. Ninety percent of the island's population was still asleep in their tents. There were only a few early risers sitting around dying bonfires, warming themselves or watching TV on their phones, waiting for the breaking news alert that the Olympian gods had returned to destroy them all.

Waves lapped at Hailey's feet, their icy chill making her shiver. She barely noticed the coldness, too caught up in her thoughts as she stared at the glowing orb of light pushing through the sky. *Why haven't the Olympians shown up yet? What's their plan? Are they in Olympus right now plotting the human race's demise? Are fireballs about to rain from the sky? No, they still need humans to worship them; they can't kill us all... unless they're planning on creating a new race.* Hailey gulped. Hiding on this island wouldn't save them if that's what the gods decided.

You need to stop, she told herself. *Stop freaking out. The Government would have to have had a plan worked out if the prophecy ever did come true. Maybe they've already dealt with the Olympians.*

Maybe that's why the gods haven't shown up—because they're dead or locked up. Aaron's dad is probably going to materialise here soon to let us know it's safe to go home. Please, please, please, Tyches, let that be it!

Something nudged Hailey's back, pushing her forward half a step. She spun around and smiled. A pegacorn stood in front of her, its snow-white fur sparkling, and its gold hooves, tail, and mane glimmering. Feathered wings hugged its side, and a gold horn protruded from its forehead.

'Good morning, Rain,' Hailey said, rubbing her hand down the bridge of the pegacorn's nose. Hailey and her friends had rescued her from becoming a griffin's lunch back in first year. She'd been living at the Academy since then and had escaped with them when Poseidon had attacked the school. Normally when Hailey was freaking out about something, she'd sneak down to the Academy's stable and talk to Rain, but the shore of Poseidon's Island was as good a place as any. 'I know the gods haven't shown up yet, but I think that might actually be worse than them not making a move, because we have no idea what they're up to,' she began, launching into all of the things that were worrying her.

'I don't know how this is all going to work out,' she said once she'd finished unburdening herself, 'but I'm really scared.'

Rain whinnied and licked her arm, which Hailey interrupted as *Everything will be fine.*

'I really hope you're right.'

'I didn't know you were an Artemis as well as a Zeus.'

Hailey looked past Rain, her heart skipping a beat when she saw who was walking towards them. *Brennan.* 'I'm not,' she said, her cheeks flushing a little. 'Rain's just a really good listener— talking to her always makes me feel better. Well, usually,' she added, her stomach still feeling as knotted as a fisherman's net.

'Do you want to talk about it?' Brennan asked, stopping in front of her. Despite being the same age as Hailey, he looked older, and was so tall she had to crane her neck to look up at him.

'I think you can guess why I'm a little stressed out—same reason as everyone else on this island,' she said, turning around to gaze at the sparkling sea.

He stepped up to her side, sending a shiver through her body. 'What are you scared of most?'

'That we'll lose our world.' She continued to stare at the endless water. 'That we'll become the gods' slaves. Or that they'll wipe us out from existence altogether.'

'And what else?'

'Isn't that enough?' She finally looked at him, her stomach lurching as her eyes met his. There was so much sympathy in them, so much caring.

'I think there's something more,' Brennan said. 'You can trust me. I won't tell anyone.'

The knot in Hailey's stomach twisted tighter. She'd been trying not to think about the real reason she was so scared, because if she didn't think about it, then maybe it wouldn't come true. Maybe nobody else would remember exactly who she was. Rain snorted behind Brennan, nodding her head, like she was telling Hailey it was safe to admit her greatest fear.

Hailey blew out a breath. 'I'm afraid that when the gods eventually show up everyone will look to me to stop them, because I'm the only Zeus in the world, and you know what the prophecy says about a Zeus defeating the gods. Everyone will expect me to fight them. I already went up against Hades and almost died, and he wasn't even an Olympian. I won't have any chance. And what if Zeus or the other Olympians find out about the prophecy and decide to hunt me down and kill me?' A tear streamed down Hailey's cheek. 'I don't want to die. I also don't want to fight in a war against the gods. I want someone else to fix this entire mess.' She swiped at her tears. 'Sorry for being such a mess.'

Brennan put a hand on her shoulder, the woodsy scent of his body spray tickling her nose. 'Don't apologise. You have every right to be scared. But I'll make you a promise right now. If anyone tells you it's your job to fight the gods, I'll evict them from this island—I'll take them back home. And if an Olympian comes for you, I'll defend you with my life.'

Hailey's heart skipped a beat. 'Do you mean that?'

Brennan nodded. 'You're my friend.' His hand dropped from her shoulder to her hand and squeezed. 'I always protect my friends.'

'I—'

'There you are, Rain.'

Hailey jerked her hand away from Brennan's as she spun around to find Kendra, with her thick golden-brown hair, coming towards them, along with Isla—the girl she'd materialised in with last night.

'Hey, Hails. Hey, Brennan,' Kendra said with a grin. 'Hope I'm not interrupting anything.'

'No,' Brennan said quickly, his cheeks flushing. 'We were just admiring the sunrise.'

'Well, I'm going to admire it with my girlfriend from the sky,' she said. 'Rain, do you mind taking Isla and me for a ride?'

Rain whinnied and nodded before tucking her legs under her and lowering her belly onto the sand.

'So this is the kind of cool stuff you get to do at Poseidon's Academy while I'm stuck at Artemis's School for the Gifted Artemises?' Isla said as her and Kendra climbed onto Rain's back.

'Pretty much.' Kendra smiled. 'Let's go, Rain.'

Rain pushed back up to her hooves and shot down the beach, galloping at full speed, before spreading her wings and leaping into the air.

'They make a cute couple,' Brennan remarked, watching

Rain soar higher and higher. 'And so do Demi and Brax,' he added, glancing back at Hailey.

Her stomach lurched as she stared into his eyes, her cheeks burning. He started to lean down, sending Hailey's heart racing as fast as Rain's galloping hooves. *He's going to kiss me!*

'You two are up early.'

Hailey and Brennan whirled around. Aaron was jogging towards them, wearing shorts, a tank, and runners.

'Are you really exercising?' Hailey asked, hoping Aaron wouldn't notice her red cheeks, or how close her and Brennan were standing to each other.

'Yep,' he replied, jogging on the spot, standing far enough back that the lapping waves didn't wash over his runners. 'With the gods on the loose, I need to stay in shape more than ever— just in case I have to join the fight.'

'Is there any news from your dad?' *Please say that the military has everything under control and there's nothing to worry about—or, even better, that it's all taken care of and safe for everyone to go home now.*

Aaron shook his head. 'Nope. Nothing yet.'

Hailey's shoulders slumped.

'No news is good news, right?' Brennan said.

'Yeah, the gods haven't shown themselves to the world yet, so there's a chance Dad managed to stop them but hasn't let me know.' Aaron stopped jogging and wiped away the sweat dripping down his face. 'But we really should be smart and move to a different island, just in case things aren't under control.'

Hailey cocked an eyebrow. 'What do you mean move?'

'Well, for starters, it's too small for everyone here.' He waved his hand towards the tents. There had to be at least five hundred, all of them crammed together, leaving barely any room to manoeuvre between them. 'I also think it's too dangerous to stay here. For all we know, the nereids know exactly where the travelling necklaces take students. They'll tell the gods that they can probably find a bunch of humans here to slaughter or enslave. It's safer for us to find somewhere else.' He turned his gaze on Brennan. 'I was actually hoping you'd help with that.'

Brennan nodded. 'Sure. What do you want me to do?'

'Gather up all the dematerialises and meet Alec at his tent. He's got a book of sea maps. I want all the islands on them checked out to see which would be best for us to move to—preferably forest free. The last thing we need is monsters hunting us.'

'Sounds good. I'll start rounding up the dematerialisers.' Brennan's eyes briefly met Hailey's, only for a second, and then he walked off towards the tents.

'How is Alec?' Hailey asked, waves washing over her feet as she dug her toes into the wet sand. He'd barely said a word since they'd arrived on the island yesterday, and he'd vanished into his tent last night the moment the sun had set.

Aaron shrugged. 'I think it's important to keep him busy.'

'Yeah, good idea,' Hailey agreed, not even being able to fathom what he was going through right now, not knowing if his parents were dead or alive, or if they were being tortured. She shuddered.

'They'll be okay, Hails. They're more valuable alive than dead.'

'I hope you're right,' she said, turning her gaze back to the sea as she clutched her heart pendant.

* * *

'Aaron, we can't move yet,' Demi protested, grabbing his shirt and trying to tug him back down to sit with her, Hailey, Alec, and Brax. They were on the shore, sitting around a small bonfire, its flames warming Hailey's skin against the afternoon's cool breeze.

'Demi, every minute we stay here it gets more dangerous,' Aaron tried to reason. 'We've already waited longer than we should have—it's been over twenty-four hours.'

'But Jayden isn't here yet,' Demi pleaded, refusing to let go of Aaron's shirt. 'We can't leave him behind.'

'Maybe we can give him another hour?' Hailey said, offering a compromise. She didn't want to leave her friend behind either. She had no idea why he hadn't turned up yet, but if there was a chance he was on his way, she didn't want him coming to a deserted island.

'We've given him long enough.' Aaron crossed his arms. 'How many letters have you sent him telling him to come here asap?'

Demi dropped her head. 'Five.'

'He's not coming,' Aaron said, voice resolute. 'I'm sorry. I don't know why. But if he wanted to be here, he would have come when you sent the first letter.'

Demi dropped her hand from Aaron's shirt, her shoulders slumping. 'I just don't understand.'

Brax wrapped an arm around her. 'Don't worry, babe. He obviously found somewhere safer than here to hide.'

'I hope so,' Demi said, hugging into him as she watched the flames flicker.

'Well, I need to inform everyone about the move.' Aaron aimed his hands down. The sand beneath his shoes shimmered ever so slightly, and then he rose into the air as if he'd gained Lexa's power to levitate. 'Can you help me, Hailey?'

She pushed to her feet; Aaron stood in the air a foot above her, balancing on his force field. She raised her hands to the blue sky, warmth flowing from her fingertips as a breeze whipped past her and gusted over the island.

'Everyone listen up,' Aaron called out; the wind carried his voice around to the thousand-plus people sitting outside their tents, or around bonfires on the shore. Silence descended over the island as everyone stopped to listen. 'You all need to start packing. This island's not safe—too many people know about it, and someone might have leaked its whereabouts to the Mysteries or the gods. The dematerialisers have already located a new island for us—a bigger one—and are going to start transporting people there in the next ten minutes. We need to be off this island before the sun sets.'

'This is ridiculous,' a man shouted, his arms crossed as he stood in front of a tent, only ten yards from Hailey and her friends. 'We're letting our teenage kids boss us around. I, for one, am sick of it. I'm going home. This is all nonsense!'

Mumbles of agreement followed, and heads nodded.

'I don't care if you believe me or not. If you value your life, you'll do what I say and pack.'

'No!' the same man shouted. 'I'm not taking orders from a fifteen year old. Now tell us where you put the travelling necklaces so we can get off this damn island.'

'You can't leave,' Aaron said.

'Fine, we'll find them ourselves.' The man who'd been speaking stormed to the nearest tent and ripped out all of its contents—pillows, suitcases, and lanterns—before moving to the next tent. Other adults began doing the same, tearing tents to shreds in an effort to find the necklaces.

'Stop!' Aaron yelled, still standing in the air on his force field. His voice echoed around the entire island, but no one paid him any attention.

A scream as loud as a screecher alarm ripped through the air, forcing Hailey to drop her hands to her ears. The adults who'd been tearing the tents apart froze, blocking their own ears—a few even fell to their knees.

'That's enough!' Natasha stood beside Hailey, gripping a chest of travelling necklaces. Hailey's ears rang as she lifted her hands back to the sky and summoned the wind again. 'Aaron might only be fifteen, but he is more qualified to give orders than anyone here. His father, my husband, is the leader of a special ops team who is currently trying to contain the gods,' she said, Hailey's wind carrying her voice across the island. 'Every single word my son and his friends have spoken is true. The gods are alive, and it's only a matter of time before they make their presence known. Your chances of survival are far higher if you stay with us. But this isn't a prison, so if you want to return to your homes and face possible enslavement or death, then we won't stop you.' She threw the chest to the ground, travelling necklaces spilling onto the white sand and glittering in the sunlight.

Some of the adults who'd been ransacking the tents grabbed them and vanished with their families, but eighty percent of the island's population didn't move an inch.

'Is that everyone who wishes to leave?' Natasha asked. 'Because anyone who stays will be listening to my son.'

No one moved.

'Good,' Natasha said. 'Start packing,' she ordered.

Aaron relaxed his hands and dropped through the air, softly landing on the sand. 'Mum, you completely undermined me. No one is going to take me seriously if I need my mum to stand up for me.'

'Aaron, I love you, and I have every confidence in you. But what that man said about you is true—you're fifteen. Would you be happy if you had to take orders from a seven year old?'

'If they knew what they were talking about I would,' Aaron huffed, crossing his arms.

'I doubt that.' Natasha cupped a hand on his cheek. 'You're doing great, sweetie, but as your mother, it's my job to defend you, and that will never change, no matter how old you are.'

'Your mum is a badass,' Demi said as Natasha walked away.

Aaron shrugged. 'I guess so.'

'I wish my mum was that cool,' Brax agreed. 'Come on,

Dems, let's get packing before Aaron's mum yells at us again.' He snickered.

'I better get packing too.' Hailey walked towards the tents, slipping inside the one she shared with her mum—it was small compared to a lot of the other tents, only being big enough to fit two single beds, with a little extra room to move about in. Her mum was scooping clothes—the ones Evonee had worn yesterday—off the floor and stuffing them into a bag.

'This is all really starting to scare me,' Evonee said when Hailey walked into the tent, the fabric floor crinkling under her feet.

'You're only just getting scared *now?*' Hailey said, shoving her own dirty clothes into her bag, as well as the tins of food that had spilled onto the floor.

'I think I was in shock yesterday, more than anything.' She sunk onto her bed. 'We could die. We could really die.'

Hailey dropped down beside her, hugging an arm around her mum's shoulders. 'Jake and his special ops team will sort it out. And I'm sure the Government sent other teams with them too. They're trained to deal with this kind of thing. We're not going to die,' she promised her mum, and herself.

'I hope you're right, kiddo.' She sighed, and then jumped back up. 'I guess I can freak out later; right now we need to pack up the tent and get off this island.'

Hailey lifted her bag over her shoulder, the strap digging into her skin, and ambled outside with her mum.

Evonee pointed a rectangular remote control, which was about as big as a box of matches, at the tent. *Click.* She pressed the button in the centre of it, and the tent vanished in the blink of an eye. 'Thank the Tyches for conjuring tents. Otherwise we'd have had to pack it up the old-fashioned way,' Evonee remarked, looking towards the few families that had "old-fashioned" tents and were trying to disassemble them as quickly as possible.

'Can I give you a lift?' Brennan asked, walking up to Hailey.

Evonee raised an eyebrow. 'And you are?'

Brennan blushed. 'Oh, I'm, uh, Brennan—I, um, go to school with Hailey.'

'I see,' Evonee said, the slightest grin on her lips as she glanced at Hailey, who wanted to melt into the sand she felt so awkward. 'Well, I'm Evonee, Hailey's mum. And we would love a lift.'

'Grab on.' Brennan held his hands out.

Hailey hesitated, her eyes searching through the crowd of people packing up their tents. *Where are you, Jayden?* If she took Brennan's hand, that would be it. They'd be leaving him behind, and anyone else who hadn't made it here yet. *Maybe Jayden and other students are still trying to convince their parents to come here. Maybe they just need a little more time. But if Aaron's right, and the nereids do know where this island is, then we might only have minutes before the Olympians, or the Mysteries, show up here.*

'Hailey.'

Brennan's voice called her back. *Please, Tyches, look after Jayden and everyone else who didn't make it to the island.* Tingles swept up Hailey's arm and flooded her body the second she touched Brennan's hand. The island swirled into a mixture of colours, and then everything reformed. She was standing on another island now. This one looked very similar to the one she'd come from, but was twice as large, and the sea around them shimmered a sparkling blue, as if it were full of sapphires. Coconut trees were spread around in clusters, offering plenty of shade. Thankfully there wasn't a forest, which meant she didn't have to worry about an arachne, or any other monster, sneaking up on her in the middle of the night for a late-night human snack.

'Oh, this is much better,' Evonee said. 'Thanks for the lift, Brennan. Once you're finished transporting people, maybe you and Hailey can catch up.'

Brennan's cheeks turned an even brighter red. 'Sounds nice.' He briefly met Hailey's eyes before saying, 'Well, I have about another fifty trips to make, so I better go back.' He vanished.

'He's cute.'

'We're just friends,' Hailey said, chewing her lip.

'Well, either way, friend or more-than-a-friend, I like him. Now, let's pick a good spot before anyone else gets here.'

5

THE GAME

Aday had passed since the move to the new island, and they hadn't wasted any time in making it "homey". Long tables stretched down one section, with the cornucopia Alec's mum had taken spilling bread, fruit, and vegetables onto one of the tables. Hammocks swung between coconut trees. Bonfires burned between tents, with people sitting around them, roasting marshmallows, despite the humidity hanging heavy over the island. Other people sprawled out on sun lounges, soaking up the sun's rays. In the middle of it all was a soccer field, complete with grass freshly grown by some of the more powerful Demeters.

Hailey stood by her tent, watching students from Poseidon's Academy run up and down the soccer field as they tried to score a goal. *How can they be so carefree? The gods are on the loose.* Aaron's dad hadn't shown up yet to tell them it was safe, so she could only assume they were still out there. *Where? Why haven't they attacked yet? Where's PET? Did they find Poseidon's palace? And what happened to the teachers? To Pandora? Did Poseidon take them as prisoners? Is there any hope left?* Hailey would give anything to be able to know what was happening at the palace right now.

'Hails, we're playing in the next game,' Demi said, coming to her side with Brax.

Hailey narrowed her eyes. 'What? You want to play sports? What's wrong with you?'

'I'm bored. I'm not used to sitting around waiting while someone else saves the world—that's usually our job.'

Hailey shook her head. 'I've got too much on my mind—I mean the world could end at any moment.'

'Come on, Hailey,' Aaron said, joining their group. 'We all deserve a break from worrying about the gods.'

Hailey's frown deepened. 'You too? You're the one who's always saying we need to be on high alert, and now you want to play a game of soccer?'

'It's been three days, and the gods haven't made a move; I think we should be safe for the next hour,' he said. 'And there's plenty of people not playing who can jump into defence mode if something happens. Come on, we need this.'

'And we're playing too,' Tahlia said, walking over with Alec and Kora.

'Really, Alec?' Hailey couldn't keep the shock from her voice. Under normal circumstances, Alec never would have stepped foot onto a soccer field, and now, when his parents were gone and the world was possibly going to end, he wanted to play.

'Yeah, Tahlia thinks being distracted for a little while will be good for me.' His voice was flat.

Tahlia squeezed his hand. 'Everyone deserves a little fun.'

'You can go straight back to holding the weight of the sea on your shoulders after the game, Hails,' Demi said.

Is there any point in saying no? It wasn't like her refusing to play would change anything—or more like *stop* anything from happening. *A distraction would be nice...* 'Okay,' she gave in, and followed her friends to the edge of the soccer field, where students cheered their friends on as they kicked the ball back and forth down the field.

'Are you playing in the next one?' someone asked from beside her.

Hailey smiled at the gangly guy standing to her left. 'Oh, hey, Riley. Yeah, I am.'

'I'm Riley. That's Charlie,' someone said from her other side.

Hailey smiled at the real Riley. 'Sorry. I have no idea how to tell you apart.'

'I'm the more handsome one.' Charlie grinned, standing up taller.

'You're an exact replica of me,' Riley argued. 'I'm the handsome one—you're just the cheap knockoff.'

Hailey couldn't help but smirk as the twins bickered about who was the better version. She glanced around for Ava, since she usually broke up the twins when they were like this, but she couldn't see her. 'Where's Ava?' she asked, interrupting the twins' arguing.

'Walking around somewhere with her parents,' Riley said, waving his hand in no particular direction.

'Where's Jayden?' Charlie asked. 'I haven't seen him at all hanging out with you guys.'

Hailey gulped, fiddling with her necklace. 'I don't know. He didn't come back to school after our break—and he never responded to any of the letters Demi sent him about coming to Poseidon's Island.'

'Weird.' Riley dragged a hand through his hair, messing it up. 'I've heard that happened with a few students—they just disappeared after the gorgon attack.' He shrugged. 'Maybe they're in denial about the gods being back.'

'Maybe.' An uneasy feeling settled in the pit of Hailey's stomach.

It seems like the students who didn't come back to the Academy are the same ones who didn't make it to Poseidon's Island, despite us sending them travelling necklaces. Why? Hailey could understand that their parents hadn't wanted to send them back to a school that had had a gorgon turning people to stone. But that didn't explain why the students hadn't come to Poseidon's Island with their families after Hailey and the other students had sent out letters explaining what had happened. *It was probably harder for them to convince their parents, since they didn't pop back home from school two hours after leaving, but still... they should have at least come to the island alone to check it out—especially Jayden, who knew the truth about the gods more than anyone.*

A whistle pierced Hailey's train of thoughts. 'That's time,' the ref—someone's dad—called from the other side of the soccer field. 'Next players in.'

'That's us,' Demi said with an excited squeak, dashing onto the field with Brax.

Everyone else mingling on the sidelines followed and split into teams. Hailey's team consisted of Demi, Alec, Aaron, Kora, Tahlia, Tanzy, Lexa, and Brax. Riley and Charlie had joined the other team, which was a mixture of older students she didn't know—except for Amber: the twins' crush.

'You're one short,' the ref informed Hailey's team. 'You need to find an extra player to make the teams even.'

'I'll play.'

Hailey's heart lurched when she locked eyes with Brennan. He smiled at her before averting his gaze to the grass and standing next to Aaron.

'First team to score three goals—or last team to have players left on the field—is the winner. As soon as a player leaves the field, they're out of the game—so no dematerialising your opponents off the field and then re-entering the game,' the ref instructed, adding that last bit to Brennan. 'Ball in play,' he said, throwing the soccer ball into the centre of the field.

Both teams sprinted for it, Riley managing to reach it first and kick it over everyone's heads. The ball flew towards the goal, only to collide with an invisible barrier and bounce outside the soccer field. Aaron grinned from beside the goal, holding his hands up.

'Come on, that's not fair,' Riley whinged to the ref. 'He can't create a force field in front of the goal. How are we meant to get the ball in?'

The ref shrugged. 'That's your job to figure out—all powers are legal in soccer.'

Riley kicked the grass. 'Unfair.'

'Ball back in play,' the ref said as someone on the beach threw it towards them.

Lexa levitated, her long layered brown hair flying out as she shot above everyone's heads and kicked the soccer ball before it hit the ground. The ball soared towards the goal, bursting into flames just before it reached the net.

The opposition's goalkeeper smirked as a fireball flickered in his hand. 'You can try, but you won't score.'

'New ball,' the ref called, holding his hands out. One second they were empty, and the next he was holding a brand new soccer ball. He threw the freshly conjured ball back into the field.

The teams jumped into action, battling to kick it towards their goal. Sleep dust exploded from Tahlia's mouth, hitting three of the opposition's players in the face and sending them sinking to the ground.

Demi used the distraction to lunge for the ball, kicking it through the crowd and towards their goal. She was only a few yards shy of it when she fell through the grass. 'Hey!' Demi roared as sand rose up from the grass to swallow her up to her shoulders. 'Let me out!'

The ball had escaped the quicksand and was sitting just in front of Demi's face.

'Not a chance,' a girl who looked old enough to be a fifth year said. She lined her foot up with the ball and kicked it back towards the opposition's goal.

The ball barely made it halfway down the field before it vanished.

'I'll take that,' Tanzy said, wearing her usual purple ribbon in her dark hair. She clicked her fingers, and the ball popped back into existence in front of her. She drew her leg back and kicked her foot forward, sending the ball speeding down the field. It exploded into flames a heartbeat later.

'New ball.' The ref conjured another ball.

The opposition got to it first, with the girl who'd created quicksand to swallow Demi kicking the ball around players as she headed for the goal. One second she was running at full speed, and the next she was moving slower than a sea-snail. Brax grinned and ran for the ball, kicking it away from the girl. The ball burst into flames again.

'You'll never get a score on me,' the fireball thrower mocked, juggling two fireballs in his hands as he danced about in front of the goal.

'We'll see about that,' Hailey muttered, deciding it was time she actually started participating in this game instead of standing around. 'You need your eyesight to aim your fireballs,' she said quiet enough that no one would hear.

Warmth flowed down Hailey's arms and into her hands. She spun around in a circle, stretching her fingers out. The hairs on her arms stood on end as the temperature dropped; fog rolled in like a cloud of smoke, concealing the entire soccer field.

Hailey swiped her hand at the fog in front of her. It blew away like mist, forming a narrow path towards where she'd last seen the ball.

'What's going on?' someone asked from the fog.

'I can't see anything,' she heard Charlie say.

'Ouch,' Riley yelped. 'Who just bumped into me?'

Gotcha. The ball was a few feet away now; Amber stood beside it, staring around as people called out in the fog. As quiet as a nymph, Hailey snuck towards her and nudged the ball away with her foot.

'Hey!' Amber cried out, but Hailey had already vanished.

Hailey cleared away the fog up to her ankles so she could see the ball, and then slowly pushed through the fog towards the goal. The goalkeeper's legs moved from side to side as he tried to cover the goal while he, no doubt, squinted through the fog.

Hailey gave the ball a gentle nudge with her foot. 'Got one!' she hollered, waving her hands to clear the fog so the ref could see that she'd scored.

'No you didn—' The goalkeeper's words fell away as he turned to see the ball inside the net. 'Hey, that's not fair! My vision was impaired.'

'It's all fair,' the ref said. 'Team A scores one point,' he confirmed.

'Woohoo, go Hailey!' Demi hollered from her spot in the quicksand.

'Dimitri,' the goalkeeper yelled, throwing the ball at a player with hair to his shoulders. Dimitri leapt into the air, leaning his head and shoulders backwards as his right leg kicked up, bicycle kicking the ball and sending it shooting down the field. It arced towards the goal, and then rebounded as it collided with Aaron's force field.

Hailey caught a glimpse of Riley shaking his head in frustration before whispering something in Amber's ear. She smiled and nodded before moving to stand beside Aaron.

'You'll never get past my force field,' Aaron told her. 'I've held it up against a cyclops before, and a few other monsters. I can keep it up all day if I have to.'

'We'll see about that,' she replied in an Irish accent.

The opposition kicked another goal at Aaron's force field; it bounced off as well.

Tahlia zoomed in and took possession of the ball, dribbling it towards the goal, where the goalkeeper waited with a fireball in his hand. 'Go, Alec!' she called when she was halfway down the field, kicking him the ball.

He continued dribbling it towards the goal, his movements uncoordinated and jerky, like someone who was playing soccer for the first time.

'Running into me isn't going to help,' the goalkeeper said, drawing his arm back when Alec was only a yard away. 'I'll hit *you* with the fireball instead of the soccer ball.' His arm arced forward, the fireball flying free and heading straight for Alec's chest. Alec's body blurred like an out-of-focus photo, and the fireball passed straight through him, landing on the grass, singeing it, before puffing into smoke.

Alec ran straight through the goalkeeper with the ball, scoring.

'Team A scores a second goal,' the ref said. 'That's two to zero.'

The fireball thrower gritted his teeth. 'You won't get another one past me.'

'We'll see about that,' Demi retorted from the quicksand while Tahlia jumped around with Alec, celebrating his goal.

Riley nodded at a player with dreadlocks. The player nodded back and sucked in a breath. He exhaled it straight at Alec, standing a yard away.

'Ahhh!' Alec cried out, flying backwards as a gale of wind ploughed into him like a tornado.

'Alec!' Aaron called, running a few feet out of the goal.

Amber slipped behind his force field and touched the back of his neck. Ice spread over his skin like a shell as he froze in place.

'Woo! Great work, Amber!' Riley cheered.

'Sorry for using my Anemoi powers on you, dude,' Dreadlocks said as he helped Alec up, 'but we needed to score a goal, and that required distracting your goalkeeper.'

'Uh,' was all Alec could manage to say; he looked seconds away from vomiting.

'Don't you ever touch him again!' Tahlia blew a puff of sleep dust into Dreadlocks's face.

'Peanut butter toast,' Dreadlocks mumbled, swaying on his feet before dropping to the ground and snoring softly.

Tahlia helped Alec limp off the field, Kora rushing after them to heal his injuries.

'Team B scores a goal,' the ref announced as Charlie kicked a goal past Aaron's frozen body.

'Can we swap goalkeepers?' Brax asked the ref.

'Nope. Your goalkeeper is still in play while he's on the field, so you can't swap.'

'But he's frozen,' Brax protested.

The ref shrugged. 'Work it out—but stay a yard clear of the goal.' The ref threw the ball back into play, and the opposition kicked a second goal almost immediately.

'We need someone to protect the goal,' Brax said, continuing his argument with the ref.

'Unless your goalkeeper is off the field that's not going to happen.'

'I'll take care of it.' Brennan vanished for a heartbeat, and then reappeared beside Aaron. He touched Aaron's frozen shoulder; beads of water dripped down Aaron's arm as the sun slowly melted his ice shell. Hailey blinked and they were both gone. Brax bolted into the goal as Brennan rematerialised with Aaron on the sidelines, where Alec, Tahlia, and Kora now watched the game from.

Thank the Tyches our goal is defended again, Hailey thought, watching Brax spin his finger anti-clockwise. The approaching soccer ball slowed to a stop before it reached the goal, and Brax kicked it away.

'Woo! Go, babe!' Demi hollered from the other end of the

field, where she was still stuck up to her shoulders in the quicksand.

Their team only needed one more goal to win, and Hailey knew exactly how to get it. 'Get ready to score,' she called to Lexa, who was dribbling the ball towards the opposition's goal.

Warmth poured down Hailey's arms and she threw her hands forward, aiming her fingertips at the goalkeeper three yards in front of her. The wind hit him like a charging minotaur, throwing him against the goal's net. The fireball in his hand slipped free, lighting the net on fire as Lexa lined up the soccer ball.

The goalkeeper shrieked, stumbling out of the flaming goal as Lexa kicked her foot forward and scored.

'Team A are the winners,' the ref announced, Hailey and her teammates cheering and jumping around, celebrating their victory. 'Can someone put the fire out please,' he added.

Someone standing on the shore lazily waved their hand towards the burning goal, as if they were swatting away a fly; a wave rose from the sea, charging towards the goal and crashing over the flames.

Salt prickled Hailey's tongue as water sloshed against her face from the crashed wave.

'Next game,' the ref called, conjuring a new goal as Tanzy clicked her fingers to make the burned one disappear.

'Good game,' Amber said, coming up to congratulate Hailey.

'I feel like you cheated,' Riley griped. 'I mean you almost set Tyler on fire.'

Amber elbowed him.

He huffed. 'Yeah, good game,' he said through gritted teeth.

'Thanks,' Hailey said, not caring that he didn't mean it. She'd won—well, helped her team win. *At least my powers are good for something.* 'You guys played really well too.'

'That was amazing!' The wet grass squelched under Demi's runners as she raced up to them, finally free from the quicksand. 'It sucks I missed out on all the fun, but it was awesome to watch!'

'I think we made a pretty good team,' Brax agreed. 'You were a great cheering squad, if nothing else,' he told Demi, leaning down to kiss her.

'Um, see you later,' Hailey said, walking off to give them some privacy, and bumping straight into Brennan. 'Oh, sorry.' Her cheeks flushed. 'Um, thanks for helping with Aaron—and for filling our team.'

He smiled. 'I'm always happy to help you out.'

Her blush deepened. 'Thanks.'

His eyes dropped to his feet as he chewed his lip. 'Um, did you maybe want to, uh, get lunch?'

Hailey opened her mouth to answer when she spotted Kallie over his shoulder skimming rocks across the sea. An idea suddenly popped into her head: one so obvious that she couldn't believe she hadn't thought of it before. 'There's actually something I have to do.' Brennan's shoulders slumped. 'But dinner?' she added.

His face lit up. 'Okay.'

'Talk later,' she said, and practically ran towards Kallie. Just this morning she'd been begging the Tyches to let her know what was happening at the Academy, and now she knew exactly how to find out and didn't want to waste a single second.

6

THE PLAN

'Hey, Kallie.'

Kallie flicked a white pebble from between her chubby fingers; it skipped across the sea, rippling the sapphire blue water. 'Hey, Hailey,' she said, turning to face her. 'I saw some of your game—pretty cool what you did with the fog.'

'Thanks. Um, I kind of wanted to ask you a favour.'

'You want me to take you to a parallel world again, don't you? To try and see what the future might hold, right?'

Hailey shook her head. While the thought had definitely crossed her mind, she didn't want to risk entering a world that the gods were seconds away from destroying, or where the Mysteries might grab her and bring her before the Olympians. She was terrified enough of dying in her own world, let alone in someone else's. Besides, this year had taught her that while their world was similar to other worlds, things happened differently here, so all going to a parallel world might achieve was risking her life.

'Not exactly. Your powers can take you anywhere in a parallel world as long as you've been to that place before, right?'

Kallie nodded.

'Well, I was hoping you could take me to Poseidon's Academy in a parallel world and then to our own Poseidon's Academy.'

Kallie's eyes widened. 'Why would you want to go back there? Poseidon is there. He'll kill us if he sees us.'

'Look, I know it's dangerous, and if you don't feel comfortable with it then I won't ask you to do it,' Hailey said. 'It's just killing me not knowing what's happening—and what happened to the teachers. I feel like I have to make sure they're okay. It's a dumb idea, I know,' she admitted, dropping her head.

Kallie put a hand on her shoulder, the flecks of glitter in her purple nail polish sparkling in the sunlight. 'Dangerous, not dumb,' she corrected. 'I'd like to make sure the teachers are okay too.'

Hailey met her gaze, her eyes hopeful. 'Really?'

Kallie nodded. 'Yeah.'

'Thank you.' Hailey said, hugging her, the knot in her stomach loosening the tiniest bit at the thought of actually getting off this island and gathering some information on what the Tartarus was going on. If she went to the palace and saw Jake's team in control, or even them battling Poseidon, then she wouldn't have to worry so much about the world ending at any moment.

'Who else is coming?' Kallie asked, looking towards the soccer field. Demi was still rubbing her victory in Riley's and Charlie's faces, jumping around them, grinning, while Aaron sat next to a bonfire, shivering, and Alec walked around the island hand in hand with Tahlia.

Hailey would have loved to have them as backup, but there was too much risk. She didn't want to endanger anyone's life but her own—and Kallie's, but that was only because she was the only one who could help her. She would have asked Brennan to take her instead, but a spell blocked dematerialises from materialising at the Academy—plus Brennan had to know exactly where the palace was to materialise in it, and it was always moving.

'No one. The more of us there are, the higher the risk of us being spotted.'

'I agree,' Kallie said. 'Let's find somewhere to open the portal away from everyone else so no one sees.'

They headed for the other side of the island, the sand squeaking beneath their shoes as they walked towards a thick cluster of coconut trees and shrubs.

'Ready?' Kallie asked as they trekked through the shrubs to hide behind them.

Was she ready? They were about to walk into Poseidon's home. What if he was still in control and sensed them when they arrived? Would he kill them? Would he take them to the other Olympians? But this was the only way to find out what was happening. She couldn't just sit around anymore waiting for Aaron's dad to show up. And if Poseidon—or a nereid—did spot them, Kallie could get them out straight away. They'd just take a peek, and then they'd leave.

'Read—'

A branch snapped, the bushes rustling. 'What are you doing?'

Hailey whirled around, her heart sinking when she saw her mum standing right behind her, arms folded. 'We were, um…'

'Going to climb for coconuts,' Kallie jumped in, pointing at the coconuts at the top of the trees around them.

'Oh really? You walked through bushes to climb for coconuts when there are coconuts trees all over the rest of the island, not to mention coconuts lying on the ground?' Evonee kicked a fallen coconut with her sandal.

'Yes,' Kallie squeaked.

Hailey sighed. 'I asked Kallie to take me to the Academy,' she admitted; there was no lie she could tell her mum that she would believe, so she didn't see the point in trying. Plus she'd already lied to her mum so much; she didn't want to do it anymore.

Evonee shook her head, looking beyond disappointed. 'How could you be so stupid, Hailey? This isn't a game, but you and your friends seem to think it is—oh, let's just pop off to the Underworld and fight some gods... how about we take on a gorgon.' She shook her head again. 'Don't you understand you could die? And if you did, it would destroy me.'

'I'm sorry, Mum.' Guilt tightened Hailey's chest. 'I just want to know what's happening, and if the teachers are okay—and Hope. They were still in the palace when we left. I need to know they're alive.'

Evonee didn't say anything for a long time. She just stood there, disappointment and fury radiating from her like heat radiating from a fire.

'Um, should I go?' Kallie asked, looking like she wanted to melt into the sand from awkwardness.

'I'm coming with you,' Evonee finally said.

'Wh-what?' Hailey stammered.

'I want to know what's happening too. And Hope stayed with us over the break, so I feel responsible in making sure she's safe.'

'Really?' Hailey was dumbfounded. Her mum had busted her about to do something dangerously stupid, and instead of grounding her to the tent, she was asking to go with her. *This has to be a trick.*

Evonee nodded. 'Yes. Let's go.'

'Okay,' Hailey said, sounding unsure. She nodded at Kallie to open the portal, fully expecting her mum to start yelling that she couldn't believe Hailey would be so stupid to think she was being serious about going.

Kallie clapped her hands together and drew them apart, inch by inch, as she blew out a long breath. A white sphere formed between her palms, growing bigger and bigger until it was the size of a soccer ball. She threw it forward, the white sphere exploding into a vortex of swirling lights the colour of a rainbow

'Medusa,' Evonee gasped. 'That's incredible.' She reached her hand out, her fingers disappearing into the swirling lights. 'So this takes us to a parallel world?'

Kallie nodded.

'Amazing.' Evonee's eyes grew wider and wider.

So far her mum hadn't freaked out, so Hailey started to believe that she was being serious about coming with them. 'Come on, Mum,' Hailey said, not wanting her mum to change her mind. 'Follow me.' She stepped into the portal. Wisps of red, green, yellow, and blue swirled around her like mist, and then vanished as the sharp scent of salt rushed up her nostrils.

The grounds looked exactly the same as the grounds in her own world. Sea-anemones and coral formed bright gardens of pinks, purples, blues, and greens. Between them trees with coral trunks grew, each blooming different types of jewels every colour of the sea—there were emerald trees, aquamarine trees, blue opal trees, and so many more. Other trees grew big bunches of pearls, and some trees were draped in seaweed, resembling weeping willows, with sea-shell flowers dotting them.

Evonee's jaw dropped as she walked up beside Hailey, her eyes drinking in every inch of the grounds, and the palace, which sparkled like a diamond as imitation sunlight glinted off its crystal turrets and spires. The sea stretched over everything like a dome of water, multi-coloured fish darting about, and even a dolphin swimming in the sky of water above. 'Ah bah...' was all Evonee could say.

'Welcome to Poseidon's Academy, Mum.'

'It's... It's... I... Wow,' Evonee stammered.

'Ready for the second trip?' Kallie asked, the portal closing behind her as she came through.

'Yes, but can you take us to our common room? I doubt the nereids or Poseidon are hanging out up there.'

Kallie nodded and drew her hands apart, reforming the sphere of white light and throwing it forward.

'Time to go inside the palace,' Hailey told her mum, pulling her through the vortex of lights.

Hailey half-expected to find the common room destroyed, with nothing but torn pillows and broken chairs left, but it was untouched. *Maybe Poseidon never had a chance to unleash his rage here. Maybe PET got to him first.* Scallop-shell chairs, polished-coral desks, and a bookcase crowded with thick tomes filled one half of the room. The other half had sofas, armchairs, and floor cushions spread around. Blue flames crackled in the fireplace. Normally students would be crowded in front of the fire or lounging on the sofas, laughing and chatting to their friends. But the common room was silent and empty.

'Oh,' Evonee said, her features sagging a little. 'This isn't as spectacular as the outside. Do you think we could go back out there? I'd love to collect some of the jewels for a painting.'

'Maybe later, Mum.' Collecting jewels for her mother's artwork was the last thing on Hailey's mind.

'Where should we go?' Kallie asked; the portal shrunk behind her, closing in on itself until there was nothing left.

'Well, the main hall was the last place we saw everyone, so maybe there?'

'And what if we run into Poseidon?' Evonee asked, her voice low.

'Kallie will portal us straight out,' Hailey said. 'You can stay up here if you like.'

Evonee shook her head. 'I'm not letting you out of my sight.' She gripped Hailey's hand. 'We're glued together from now on until we get back to the island.'

Hailey smirked. 'Okay, Mum.'

They snuck onto the crystal staircase, Hailey listening for

drifting voices before quietly venturing down it. She paused when she reached the second floor and peered over the crystal railing. A glass statue of Poseidon stood in the centre of the entryway, between a pair of crystal staircases that curved their way up to the second floor.

Hailey's ears strained as she listened for voices and footsteps. Silence pressed against her, sending a chill down her spine. She'd never heard the palace so quiet before; it was unnerving, like it had been abandoned. *Does this mean Poseidon's gone? Did PET get rid of him and the other gods? Don't get excited yet,* she cautioned herself. 'Come on,' she whispered to her mum and Kallie, and slunk down the right staircase, descending into the entryway.

Three archways were carved into the jewel and sea-shell encrusted frosted crystal walls: one in the left wall, one in the right, and one in the wall between the staircases. She headed through the middle one, entering the main hall.

Normally, over a hundred mother-of-pearl tables stretched across the vast space. Gold plates, goblets, and cutlery would usually cover them, glimmering under the light cast by the glowing orbs that floated beneath the ceiling. Whenever Hailey had walked into the main hall it had been filled with chattering students, and a mixture of smells that ranged from coconut-infused rice to spicy buffalo wings as students conjured a variety of foods on their plates.

She barely recognised the main hall now. Tables were tipped on their sides; scallop-shell chairs scattered and broken; plates, goblets, and cutlery spread over the floor.

Kallie picked up a plate from beside a chair that was missing one of its legs. 'These will be good to take back to the island,' she said in a low voice, collecting a few more.

'It looks like a bomb exploded.' Evonee's voice was barely a whisper.

'More like a tidal wave,' Hailey remarked.

What had happened in here once everyone had washed into the sea? What did Poseidon do to the teachers? Is Pandora still in the palace? Where are the nereids? Did Jake and his team arrest them? But if he did, then where is he? This place would be swarming with the military, wouldn't it?

'Where to now?' Kallie asked, holding a dozen plates and tucking a couple of goblets under her arms.

'The Underworld,' someone hissed.

Hailey whipped around, catching a glimpse of Nemertes before a vial shattered on the floor. Gold liquid leaked over the pearls and then exploded into a shower of gold dust that rained over the room like an explosion of glitter. 'Don't breathe it i–' Hailey's eyelids drooped closed, and she fell into darkness.

7

CAPTURED

'Wake up! You need to wake up! Open your eyes!'

Hailey's eyelids fluttered open.

'Good, you're finally awake.'

Hailey's jaw dropped when she saw who was sitting across from her. *No, it can't be. This can't be happening.*

'How did you get here?' Aaron's dad, Jake, asked.

She couldn't form words. Jake was meant to be fighting the gods—or, better yet, keeping watch over them in some top secret facility that had prisons strong enough to hold the Olympians. He wasn't meant to be tied to a chair in Poseidon's palace. All of PET was beside him—thirty men and woman garbed in black tied to chairs—their eyes closed and their heads lank. *If they're tied up down here, that means the gods are still free.* The knot in Hailey's stomach pulled tighter, and then she saw her mum and Kallie tied to chairs beside her. They weren't moving.

'Mum!' Hailey tried to reach for her, but Hailey's hands were tied behind her back, trapping her in the scallop-shell chair.

'Shh,' Jake hissed, his eyes darting up to the open hatch in the ceiling. 'You'll bring her back.'

'Are they…' Hailey couldn't finish the sentence. She couldn't face the possibility that her mum and Kallie weren't going to wake up.

'They're alive,' Jake quickly said. 'I'm guessing you got hit with a sleep spell. You're Aaron's friend, right? I remember you from when my team and I were suddenly here—I mean the palace—and had no idea how we'd gotten here.'

Jake and his team had originally invaded the palace with the intention of handing its location over to the Government. The only way to save the school had been to use a *watwdaom atpkonaskdao*—a memory extractor—which had taken all of PET's memories about the palace.

'Yeah, I'm Hailey.' She stared at her mum's chest, sighing when she saw it rise and fall. She was alive.

'I'm Colonel Jake Wynton. Now, I need you to tell me how you got here.'

Hailey glanced around to work out where *here* was. Orbs of light floated beneath the ceiling, casting the empty space in a dim glow. The room's walls were transparent, revealing the sea outside, where fish darted through coral reefs. *It's like a giant fish tank.* 'This isn't possible,' she mumbled. 'A sea-monster destroyed the dungeon last year.'

'Poseidon rebuilt it.' Hailey's gaze snapped to the crystal staircase to the right of her. Nemertes's thin pale blue dress flowed behind her as she descended the stairs. 'The palace needs somewhere to keep filthy humans until they die,' she hissed as she stepped onto the squishy bluish-green grass that covered the floor. 'He has not acquired a constraining anemone yet, though, so seaweed rope will have to suffice until then,' she added.

'Where is Poseidon?' *Please don't say he's on his way down here.* Hailey was pretty sure she would pass out from terror if she ever saw him again.

'That is not your concern.' Nemertes stopped in front of Hailey, leering down at her with venomous green eyes.

'Where are the teachers? Where's Hope—I mean Pandora? Where's Amathia?' she asked, remembering the main reason she'd come here.

'You should be more concerned about your own fate.' She trailed a slender finger across Hailey's throat. 'What I would give to kill you myself, the human who thwarted so many of my plans. In the end your attempts were futile.'

Light glinted off the blue glass teardrop hanging from a thin chain around Nemertes's neck. Hailey's jaw dropped. *Amathia's necklace! If Nemertes is wearing it, does that mean...* 'Is Amathia dead?' Hailey's voice shook as she asked the question, her throat burning, anticipating the answer.

Nemertes tapped a finger against the teardrop, a poisonous smile spreading across her face. 'Oh, she's still alive... for now. But I daresay she is wishing for death. As I said, though, you should be more concerned with yourself. Poseidon will return shortly, and when he does, he'll let Zeus know that he's captured the human prophesised to destroy the gods.'

Hailey flinched, the knot in her stomach squeezing as tightly as a boa constrictor crushing the air from a golden hind's lungs. *No! It's starting. They know about the prophecy. They know about my powers. They won't care that I can't shoot lightning. They're going to kill me.*

'You've toyed with her enough,' Jake said from behind Nemertes, his voice steady. 'Let her and the other civilians go.'

Nemertes's head snapped around, her dark wavy hair fanning out. 'Do not order me about, human. You are only alive because Poseidon likes to keep his dungeon occupied. It soothes him to know there are humans down here suffering.'

'What did you come down here for?' Jake's face showed no fear.

'To see if the new arrivals were awake yet.' She grinned like a ravenous arachne about to devour its prey. 'Poseidon only wishes you to be alive when he arrives,' she said, turning back to Hailey. 'He said nothing about you needing to be unharmed.' Her grin widened. 'Oh, we will have much fun.' Her green eyes glittered with the promise of terrible things.

Show no fear. Don't let her win, Hailey told herself, willing her heart to slow and her hands not to tremble.

'I'll let my sisters know you're awake—they would like to have some fun with you themselves.' She slithered back up the stairs.

Bang. The hatch slammed shut behind her.

'How did you get here?' Jake asked Hailey again.

She didn't hear him. Her mind was reeling. Poseidon was coming here, for her. Would he take her to Olympus? Would Zeus strike her down with a lightning bolt? Would it be quick? Would it hurt?

'Hailey, I need you to focus. How did you get here?'

Hailey swallowed around the lump in her throat. 'Um, with Kallie's portal.'

'What portal?' Jake pressed.

'She can create portals to parallel worlds.'

'So she can get us out of here?'

'Yes, although I don't know if her powers will work when her hands are tied.' Hailey tried to pull her wrists apart, the seaweed rope digging into her skin. *No use*. 'Did you only just get captured too?' Hailey asked, attempting to distract herself from her impeding death. The rest of Jake's team was sleeping like her mum and Kallie, so chances were they'd only recently been hit with a sleeping spell too.

Jake shook his head. 'No. We located the palace two days ago. We thought we had the upper hand—element of surprise and all that—but the nereids had traps set. A sea-urchin bomb exploded almost the second we stepped into the grounds. We woke up here.' He stared at a squid with barbs running down its tentacles as it swam past the glass. 'They have a cure for the sea-urchin's poison; they used it on us. It's a form of torture for Nemertes. She comes down here all the time to prick us with sea-urchin darts, watching as we fight the poison, before eventually giving us the cure. That's what's happened to my team—she poisoned all of them but me. She likes at least one of us conscious so we can watch the others dying.'

'That's awful,' Hailey said, noticing the sweat beading on PET's foreheads, and the tremors shaking their bodies. *They're not sleeping; they're dying.* 'If we can get them out of here, we can get Asclepiuses to heal them.' She turned to her left. Kallie and her mum were still asleep, their heads bent forward. 'Kallie,' Hailey yelled, not caring if Nemertes heard—this was her only chance of getting out, of escaping the torture Nemertes had planned for her, and escaping the gods killing her. 'Kallie, wake up!' Her voice was desperate. She was the only chance they had of getting out of this.

'Hailey?'

'Mum. I'm here, Mum.'

Evonee looked over at her, her eyelids fluttering. 'Where are we?' Her voice was groggy. 'Why are we tied up?'

'We're in Poseidon's dungeon.'

'What?!'

'I can get us out,' Kallie mumbled, her eyes slowly opening. 'I just have to open a portal... hey, why are my hands tied?'

'Do you need your hands to open a portal?' Jake asked, disappointment already creasing his face.

Kallie nodded.

'I haven't been able to break free, and I've been trying for days,' he said, wriggling.

'I can get out.'

Jake narrowed his eyes at Evonee. 'How? Are you a Heracles?'

'A Hebe,' she said, her voice turning soft and sweet as her

face stretched and contracted at the same time. She shrunk, getting shorter and shorter until she looked about six years old. The seaweed rope slipped right off her tiny wrists, and she leapt off the chair.

'When we get out of here, I'll be putting in a request for a Hebe to join the team.' Jake was beyond impressed.

'I'll take that as a compliment.' Evonee's voice deepened, her face stretching and contracting again as she grew taller, morphing back into an adult. She undid the seaweed rope around Hailey's wrists, and then began untying Kallie's hands as Hailey moved towards Jake.

The hatch slammed open.

'GO!' Jake yelled.

'NOOOO!' Nemertes roared, racing down the steps with five other nymphs as Kallie threw a sphere of white light forward; it exploded into a rainbow vortex.

Hailey spared one last glance at Jake, guilt shredding her insides as she ran from him and dove through the vortex of lights with her mum and Kallie.

8

THE RETURN

Hailey landed on her stomach. Beneath her rainbow reefs grew below the diamond ground, and fish swam about.

'What in Tartarus was that?' Evonee gasped out, pushing herself up from the ground. She stood beside a tree growing big bunches of pearls on its coral branches. 'Who was that woman?'

'That was Nemertes,' Hailey answered, standing up with Kallie. She rubbed her aching wrists, red lines circling her skin from where the seaweed rope had dug in. 'She's the leader of the nereids. She's the one who's been trying to bring the gods back since I started at the Academy.'

'And you're only telling me this *now*?'

'Yeah, that's news to me as well, Hailey,' Kallie said, drawing her palms apart to form another sphere of light.

'Amathia had my friends and I keep it a secret,' Hailey told Kallie as the sphere grew bigger. 'Mum, I couldn't tell you before because of the spell that stops you from telling people who haven't been to the palace about it. But now that you've been, I can tell you everything.'

'Oh, you'll definitely be telling me everything,' Evonee

replied as Kallie tossed the sphere forward. 'Now let's get back to the island and regroup.'

Hailey stepped through the vortex of swirling lights, returning to the thick bushes and coconut trees. She wandered from the greenery on shaky legs as she fought the urge to crumble to the sand. She'd hoped going to the Academy would make her feel better, that she would have arrived and seen the military in control and known everything was going to be okay. But it was so much worse than she could have imagined. The gods were still in control, biding their time for a big return, no doubt, and Jake... She gulped.

'I need to find Aaron,' she told her mum as she and Kallie followed her out of their hiding spot. 'I'll find you after.'

She went straight to his tent; he and Natasha were sitting outside, eating Tyche Charms straight from the cereal box. Around them people laughed from inside tents, others sat around the bonfires, roasting marshmallows, some people walked along the beach—a few even swimming in the sea—but the biggest crowd was around the soccer field, watching the latest game.

Hailey's stomach churned. *Come on, you have to tell him. He has a right to know what happened to his dad.* 'Aaron, I, um, have to tell you something, and you, too, Natasha.'

Aaron knocked the box of Tyche Charms over in his haste to stand up, spilling coin-shaped cereal over the sand. 'What's wrong? Has something happened to your mum? Demi? Alec?'

How was she supposed to tell him that his dad was locked in Poseidon's dungeon and being tortured by Nemertes? 'I, um, asked Kallie to take me to the palace.'

Aaron's jaw dropped. 'What? Why would you do that, Hailey? Do you have any idea how stupid that is?'

Hailey nodded. 'I know. But I couldn't stand sitting around not knowing what was happening.'

'Why didn't you at least tell me? I would have come with you.'

Cheering exploded from the soccer field.

'Aaron, let her talk,' Natasha said, putting a hand on his shoulder. 'What did you see at the palace?'

Hailey fiddled with her necklace, rubbing her thumb over the gold heart. 'Jake and his team.'

'My dad? So he did make it to the palace.' He blew out a breath, his shoulders relaxing. 'Did he have everything under control?'

You just have to come out and say it. There's no easy way. 'He was in the dungeon, tied up. Poseidon captured his team as soon as they showed up.'

The colour drained from Aaron's face. 'What?'

Natasha pressed a hand to her mouth. 'Oh, Jake.'

'I tried to rescue him, but Nemertes was coming, and he told me to go.' The words came out in a rush. 'I'm so sorry,' she said, guilt crushing her chest like a knoxen trying to suffocate her. 'We can go back and get him. We just need enough people to fight off the nereids.'

'No.' Natasha dropped her hand from her mouth and straightened her shoulders, the shock and grief washing from her face to be replaced with stoicism. 'We can't.'

Hailey frowned. 'Why?' She thought Natasha would have been begging them to go back.

'They'll have set a trap,' Aaron admitted in a defeated voice. 'The nereids, or Poseidon, will be expecting you to go back.' His eyes met Hailey's. 'You have to promise me you won't.'

'I can't just leave him there.' She saw Jake's face, shrouded with fear and despair, as she'd run for the portal, abandoning him and his dying team. 'What if Nemertes or Poseidon kills him?'

'Jake knew what he was getting himself into,' Natasha said,

her shoulders still high and her face impassive, like she was talking about someone she'd never met, rather than her husband. 'We'll just have to pray to the Tyches to keep him safe.'

'Please, Hailey, promise me you won't go back there.' Aaron's eyes were desperate, pleading.

Could she just leave Jake and his team there, knowing what might happen to them? If they died, she would feel responsible. But Aaron was right about the nereids most likely setting a trap to catch them if she or anyone else went back there. She'd blown the one chance she had of rescuing him. Nemertes had said Poseidon liked to keep his dungeon occupied, so Hailey hoped that meant PET would be safe—aside from the torture. 'Okay, I promise.'

'Medusa!' someone shouted.

'It's happening!' someone else called.

Hailey whipped around. It was like the entire island had frozen. Laughter cut off, and the cheers from the soccer field turned to gasps. Everyone was staring at their phones, their jaws open and their eyes wide.

'Do you have your phone?' Hailey asked Aaron, her heart pounding in her ears.

Aaron pulled a circle of glass with a pair of gold wings printed on it from his shorts and rested it in the palm of his hand. 'Show us the news,' he said, touching the wings.

Gold light shone up from the symbol and morphed into a 15-inch screen that played a video.

Fear ripped the air from Hailey's lungs as she watched the newsfeed.

A man wearing a ring of gold leaves on his head was standing in Times Square, in front of a red staircase that looked towards high-rise buildings and flashing billboards. Hailey gulped; it was Zeus.

'BOW DOWN!' Zeus roared.

Thousands of humans crowded the square. Some fled,

running between the buildings and vanishing out of sight. But most paid him no attention, acting as if he were a lunatic to be ignored.

'INSOLENT HUMANS!' Zeus raised his arms; electricity flashed between his fingertips, and then the entire sky lit up.

Hundreds of lightning strikes blasted for the square, their light as blinding as an exploding star. Hailey shielded her eyes, glancing away from the image. And then the screaming started. Hailey's legs wavered as the light cleared to reveal the carnage. Everything was on fire. Buildings 600-feet high smouldered with flames as glass, concrete, and steel rained down on the burning ground. The thousands of people who had been there seconds ago were gone. Their bodies turned to ash.

Zeus stood in the flames, which didn't so much as singe his white tunic. And then he swished his hand in an arc, and the sky unleashed a torrent of rain.

Hailey clutched her heart pendant so tightly her nails dug into her palm. *Zeus created those lightning strikes so easily, like he'd been summoning nothing more than a gust of wind. I can barely even create one lightning strike. We are so screwed.*

Zeus stepped towards the screen, eyes staring into the camera. 'Hear me, humans. This was merely a demonstration of my power. If I wished, I could burn your entire world to ash. But I am willing to show clemency, to give you a chance to make amends for what your ancestors did to us. We, the Olympians, have returned to reclaim what is ours. You will take your rightful place as our slaves. You will bow to us. You will meet our every demand. Unless you wish to share the same fate as these people here, every human will report to their nearest tube station for processing.' Lightning struck the ground, and Zeus vanished from the smouldering square.

Before Hailey could even comprehend what had happened, the image changed. This time a man dressed in a tunic that shimmered like the scales of a fish appeared on the screen.

Poseidon. Snow fell around him, clinging to his black beard as he stood at the top of a mountain. People skied and snowboarded past him, not even glancing at the god. *Why is Poseidon at a ski resort? Shouldn't he be on a beach?*

He raised his right arm, his gold trident gleaming as the sunlight bounced off it, and then he plunged the trident down. *CRACK!* A line split from where the trident was embedded in the snow and raced down the mountain, which shook with the ferocity of a volcano about to erupt. Snow and rocks shook loose, pouring down the mountain like a tidal wave as the avalanche claimed the lives of hundreds.

The next image showed the lush green landscape of Africa. Nemean lions, chimeras, sphinxes, and dozens more monsters roamed between the trees and bushes. Ten jeeps filled with tourists were mere yards away, the people on board clicking their cameras as they leaned forward to get a better look at the monsters.

'Oh wow, the monsters don't normally gather together like this,' one of the tour guides said, speaking into a microphone that amplified his voice for all the jeeps to hear. 'Oh my, is that a woman out there? Ma'am, you are in great danger. These creatures are vicious. Come towards me. Slowly.'

A woman moved into view of the camera, stepping into the middle of the herd of monsters. Hailey could only see her back; a quiver of silver arrows was strapped to it. *This has to be Artemis.*

Artemis pointed at the jeeps. 'Attack.'

The herd charged.

The image changed again, this time to a pale news reporter behind a news desk. 'I... um.' She gulped. 'It would appear the prophecy is coming true and the gods have returned. Um... there are reports of them in Asia, South America, Europe, Australia... the list goes on. As you saw from the footage of Zeus, the gods are demanding all humans report to their nearest tube station to submit to the Olympians. I...' The news reporter looked off to the side, staring at someone off-camera. 'Is the military taking care of this?'

The image turned black, and a message reading *We're experiencing technical difficulties, but we'll be back shortly* appeared.

'I guess we don't have to wonder what their plan is anymore,' Aaron said, dropping his phone into his pocket. 'They're back.'

Hailey couldn't form words. They'd finally made their reappearance. She'd known it would be bad. That they would probably be vengeful when they came back. But to actually see it... *Those poor people. How many humans are already dead? How many are dying right now because they didn't believe the Olympians could really be back? Where's the military? Why didn't they show up in any of those videos? Have the Olympians already destroyed them? Is all hope lost?*

'Where's the Zeus?' someone called out from the crowd of people gathered around their tents.

'She's over there,' someone else said, and all eyes swivelled to Hailey.

She took a step back, but there was nowhere to run to. She was surrounded by an island of people all looking to her to save them.

'This is your job.' A woman pointed her finger at Hailey. 'If the prophecy is coming true, then that means only a Zeus can stop the gods. Last I heard, you're the only Zeus in the world. So off you go. I'm sure a dematerialiser can give you a ride.'

Brennan materialised in front of Hailey, blocking her from the staring people.

'There you go. There's one to take you,' the same woman said.

'She's not going anywhere,' Brennan shouted at the woman. Hailey had never heard him raise his voice; he was always so quiet and soft spoken. 'Just because some prophecy says a Zeus will defeat the gods doesn't mean that person is Hailey.'

'Shame on you for trying to send a fifteen-year-old girl out to fight the gods,' Evonee growled, storming to Hailey's side. She wrapped an arm around Hailey's shaking shoulders. 'This is a mission for the military, not my teenage daughter.'

Hailey wanted to melt into the sand. Everyone's eyes were on her, expecting her to volunteer and say *sure, I'll go sort this all out*. Did they really think she could just pop over to Times Square and kill an immortal? Did they not see what Zeus did to all those people? How could she fight that? Zeus would shoot her down with a lightning strike before she could even lift her hand.

'And she can't shoot lightning,' Demi yelled out, joining their group, 'so that means the prophecy has nothing to do with her.'

'Maybe the gods returning has given her that power now,' someone said. 'I want to see her try.'

'Leave her alone!' Aaron boomed, stepping to Brennan's side, blocking Hailey further from the crowd. 'Even if she could shoot lightning, defeating the gods is not her responsibility.'

'The prophecy—'

'I don't care what the prophecy says!' Hailey was surprised to find she was the one who'd yelled out.

Aaron and Brennan shifted aside as they turned to look at her. Hailey set her eyes on the thousand-plus humans staring at her—parents, grandparents, aunts and uncles, students she'd been at the Academy with. Her whole life she'd been terrified of this moment: the gods returning and everyone looking to her to stop them. Now, she was furious. How dare they. How dare they put that on her. How dare they try and send her to her death.

'Just because some stupid prophecy says a Zeus will defeat the gods doesn't mean I have to do it. If the prophecy said a Dionysus with purple hair would defeat the gods, would that mean you would happily march out to face them?' she asked a teenage boy she recognised from school. His eyes dropped to the sand as he shook his head. 'So why should I have to be marched to my death? Because I can tell you right now, there's no way I would survive going against Zeus, let alone all of the Olympians. If you're so intent on defeating them, then you can do it yourselves, you cowards!' She turned on her heels and stormed away.

9

THE MILITARY

Hailey sat on her bed, staring at the tent's floor, her shoulders slumped. The rage had left her now, but she didn't dare go outside. She couldn't face those staring eyes again as everyone waited for her to do something about the gods. *Is that what the rest of the world is doing? Waiting for me? When Zeus demanded everyone go to their nearest tube station were they all thinking "no, it'll be okay. The Zeus will take care of this. She'll save us"? Well, sorry, everyone, but you're in for a whole lot of disappointment, because whoever assigns powers gave Zeus's to the wrong person.*

If she did what everyone wanted her to and went to Times Square and the other places the gods were, she'd be dead before a single drop of warmth flowed into her fingertips. Zeus had rained down lightning—set an entire city on fire. How could anyone expect her to match that kind of power? And those poor people who'd been caught near the gods. She wasn't sure what death would have been worse: incinerated by lightning, crushed by an avalanche, or torn apart by monsters. *And that was only three of the gods; what horrors had the other Olympians inflicted around the world?*

What is everyone doing right now? At some point they'll realise "the Zeus" isn't coming to save them. So they'll do the smart thing and go the tube stations, right? To be processed—what does that even mean?

'Mind if I come in?' Aaron stood in the tent's open flap, looking unsure.

Hailey shrugged. 'I guess.'

'It was really unfair of them to say that to you,' he said, the springs in Evonee's mattress squeaking as he dropped onto her bed so he could face Hailey. 'It's not your responsibility to do anything, Hailey. Everyone is just scared, that's all.'

'What are we supposed to do, Aaron? Did you see how powerful the gods are? Who can go up against *that*?'

'The military will be launching an attack, I guarantee you that much.'

'Will they be powerful enough to stop them?'

'Our weapons have advanced a lot since the gods were alive; I'm sure they'll be able to take them down,' he said, but Hailey heard the uncertainty in his voice. 'Neutralising bracelets are a thing now. If they can neutralise the gods' powers, then the military will be able to kill them—their immortality won't be an issue anymore.'

'That's true.' *It sounded simple enough—get neutralising bracelets on the gods and they'll lose their powers, but how was anyone supposed to get close enough?*

'I guess we know now why it took them so long to make their reappearance.'

Hailey narrowed her eyes. 'Why's that?'

'They were learning about our world.' Aaron leaned back on his hands. 'They knew about tube stations—it's the best meeting place, since there is one in every city. And someone taught them about video cameras—they filmed what they did so the whole world would see how powerful they are. I'd bet my powers that the Olympian Mysteries have spent the last three days teaching them about our world and how best to reclaim it.'

'Hailey! Aaron! You need to see this!' Demi's voice yelled from outside.

Hailey rushed from the tent. Everyone was staring at their phones again, faces as pale as a Thanatos's victim. Demi and Alec were a tent away, watching another video.

Hailey moved towards them, staring at the 30-inch screen projected above Alec's phone. The screen was split into ten boxes, each one playing a different video of the Olympian gods. Hailey almost collapsed to her knees in relief when she saw what was happening. The military were attacking. *Yes! Take them down.*

Tanks fired fireballs. Helicopters shot missiles. Soldiers fired bullets, and some even threw exploding potions that left crevasses in the earth. The gods fought back with all they had. Demeter raised her hands, growing a forest of thorns. Apollo and Artemis shot arrows by the dozen. Poseidon tore the earth apart with earthquake after earthquake.

It was the Great Battle all over again. When Hailey had watched Amathia's memory of it back in first year, humans had fallen by the hundreds at the hands of the gods, and that's exactly what was happening now. The military's weapons weren't doing anything. *No. This has to work. It has to. It's our only hope.*

'Look.' Aaron pointed to the screen in the bottom left-hand corner—the one showing Hermes.

He was in the desert, the pyramids of the pharaohs who had ruled Egypt after the gods' demise in the background. Hermes zipped around the enclosing military, becoming a blur as he used his super speed to mow the soldiers down—they fell before they even knew what had happened, and Hermes shot fireballs so fast it was as if they'd been fired from an invisible force. But still the military marched towards him. At least 300 soldiers advanced, a giant gold net stretched out between them, which was so long it could have stretched across Poseidon's

Island twice. The soldiers in front of the net collapsed as Hermes carved his path of destruction, and then… *Bam!*

His blurring body turned visible as he slammed into the net. It was like he'd hit a brick wall; he collapsed instantly, and the military threw the net on top of him.

'It's a neutralising net,' Alec gasped.

With speed as quick as Hermes's, a soldier ran forward and lifted the net just enough to slip a neutralising bracelet on Hermes's wrist. Hermes lay there, stunned, the camera filming all of this too far away to see the expression on his face, but Hailey was guessing it was confusion. He wouldn't understand why his powers had suddenly switched off.

'It's working.' Hailey grinned. *Yes, Tyches! Yes! The gods can be stopped.*

'Hermes, we, the human race, officially place you under arrest. If you resist—'

Hermes shot up, tossing the net off him and throwing aside dozens of soldiers in the process. 'YOU THINK YOU CAN CONTAIN ME?!'

Bullets exploded from the soldiers' guns.

Tiny dots of gold ichor peppered Hermes's skin as he hissed. *Why isn't he collapsing? He has a neutralising bracelet on; his immortality should be gone.*

'ENOUGH OF THIS!' Hermes roared, and ripped the neutralising bracelet off his wrist as if it were made of paper rather than solid gold.

Hailey's jaw dropped. *The neutralising bracelet didn't work.*

Everything turned into chaos as Hermes blasted through the military again.

And then the ten individual videos changed to one image. A woman wearing a Grecian dress and a ring of leaves on her head sat at a table, the space behind her black, concealing her whereabouts. 'Stop!' she ordered. 'I command the military to stand down now.'

'We all command it to stand down,' other voices said as the image widened to reveal five other people sitting on either side of the woman, their eyes staring straight at the camera. It was the Government. They were the people in control of the world —one dignitary from each continent. Men and women dressed in black stood at either end of the long table the Government sat behind, fireballs burning in their hands. *The Olympian Mysteries.*

Hailey gasped, her stomach churning when she noticed the empty chair, and the body lying on the floor beside it. *He must have resisted*, Hailey thought, recognising the dead man as the dignitary for Antarctica.

The image split back into ten screens. The military stood frozen. They were staring at their watches—the same watches Hailey had seen PET using to communicate with one another at the Academy.

'The Government is sending orders via the watches,' Aaron explained.

Hailey expected the gods to use the distraction to strike everyone down. But they didn't. They stood calmly among the carnage, smiling smugly when the military dropped their weapons in surrender.

The screen reverted back to the six dignitaries. They flinched as lightning struck in front of the table. Zeus materialised, staring directly into the camera. 'We asked you not to defy us, but defy us you did. We have shown clemency again by not wiping out your military. Consider it a gift that we are allowing you to keep your lives. But, be warned, it will be the last act of kindness you see from us. Anyone who defies us again will die.' Lightning flashed in Zeus's blue eyes, and he stepped back from the camera.

The dignitary for Europe—the woman who'd commanded the military to stand down—spoke again. 'Listen to him,' she said. 'If you haven't done so already, go to your nearest tube station. Submit to the gods. We, the Government, relinquish our authority as the current rulers of this world and hereby reinstate the gods to power.'

The screen went black.

Hailey's legs wavered beneath her as gasps and cries circled the island. *It's over. The military defeating the gods was the only hope we had left, and they've just laid down their weapons. No one else will fight the Olympians, not after the carnage everyone saw—no one in this world is powerful enough to contend with one of them, let alone ten. Our world belongs to the gods again.*

Hailey stumbled to her knees, the warm sand scratchy against her legs.

'Hailey, are you okay?' Evonee was beside her, rubbing her back as Hailey stared at the yellow sand, her stomach twisting, ready to throw up her breakfast.

No words came. She couldn't speak. All she could think about was the military standing down. And how the neutralising net had only slowed Hermes down for a moment—how he'd ripped off the neutralising bracelet like it was nothing. *His powers are far beyond anything our world has ever seen. How can anyone stand against him, or the other Olympians?*

'I know this looks bad,' Aaron said, pulling Hailey back to reality.

'Um, it looks a lot worse than bad,' Demi interjected. 'The military just freaking tossed their guns down and basically gave the gods free rein to do whatever the Tartarus they want. Literally the only positive thing is that we're down two Olympians, because it doesn't look like Hephaestus and Hestia came back to life, and that's a pretty small positive. We're screwed!'

'Normally I would tell you to watch your language,' Nicole said from beside Demi. 'But I think you're right.'

'Now will you go and face the gods, Zeus? 'Cos no one else is, so it's up to you,' someone yelled towards their group.

Hailey opened her mouth to say something back, but no

words came out. Her heart raced, and she gasped in tiny breaths of air, her chest so tight she could barely breathe. *This can't be real. This has to be a dream. It just has to be!*

'It is not up to her!' Evonee yelled, her voice pure fury. 'Why don't you go? Or why don't you send your child in to face them?'

'The proph—'

'I don't care what the prophecy says!' Evonee snapped, the island stunned to silence as everyone stared. 'She can't shoot lightning from her hands, and even if she could, I wouldn't let her face the gods. Shame on you for even suggesting such a thing.' Hailey had never heard her mother sound so furious before. 'The next person who tells my daughter it's her responsibility to fight the gods is getting exiled from this island. That's a promise.' Her gaze combed over the staring faces, waiting for anyone to contradict her. No one dared.

'Am I interrupting something?'

Hailey's head whipped around. A man dressed in black stood three tents away from her. What looked like a submachine gun was strapped across his chest, blue, red, purple, and yellow buttons glowing near the trigger. *He's in the military.* Hailey's stomach heaved, and her vision blurred. *He's come to take me to fight the gods.* She gulped, her mouth bitter, as she tried to keep down her breakfast.

'General Killian.' Aaron's posture turned as straight as an arrow, and his hands tucked behind his back.

'Ah, Aaron, good to see you,' the man said, moving close enough that Hailey could see the ugly scar slashed across his neck. *I know him.* She recognised him from one of PET's memories about the palace—this was the man who'd given them their mission to infiltrate the Academy. 'Although I wish it were under better circumstances,' he continued, stopping in front of Aaron, not even sparing a glance to Hailey kneeling in the sand. 'I am sorry about your father.'

Aaron frowned. 'How do you know what happened to him, sir? Actually, how did you know where to find us?'

'I sent a letter,' Natasha said, stepping up to Aaron's side. 'Jake gave me an address to send a letter to if anything ever happened to him. Thank you for coming, General Killian.'

Everyone on the island scooted closer, straining to hear the conversation.

'Um, I'd like to have this conversation in private,' General Killian said, his gaze sweeping over the hundreds of staring people. 'If you'll please follow me to somewhere we can speak openly.' He held his hands out to Aaron and Natasha.

'Sir, I'd ask that you please allow my friends to come too,' Aaron said, his posture still straight. 'You can trust them.'

General Killian's eyes glanced over Demi and Alec, and then to Hailey kneeling on the sand, fighting the urge to pass out.

He probably wants to get Aaron alone so he can ask him about me. About how to get me to go with him. Why else would he be wasting his time visiting this little island? The military had to know who she was—she was the only Zeus in the world, surely they had a record of that somewhere. They'd failed in fighting the gods, so now they were going to pin everything on her.

'All right,' General Killian agreed. 'But not their parents— only Natasha.'

'We're not letting you take them anywhere,' Nicole said, hugging Demi to her, her grip tightening when Demi tried to pull free. 'They're staying with us.'

'I will look after them, I promise,' Natasha said, taking one of General Killian's hands.

Demi pulled from her mother's grasp, turning to face her. 'Mum, it'll be okay. And you're embarrassing me,' she added with a quiet hiss.

'Hailey, you don't have to go.' Evonee squeezed Hailey's shoulder.

A large part of her wanted to run. To escape before the

general could ask her to do what she was pretty sure he was going to. But where would she go? There was nowhere to hide. And everyone would think her a coward if she ran. Could she live with their disappointment? Could she live with hearing stories of the gods wiping out entire countries because she fled from the military, unwilling to even hear what plan they might have for her to defeat the gods? It was one thing for the people on this island to ask her to battle the gods, but it was another for the military themselves to ask for her help.

She clutched a hand to her heart pendant, the warmth in it feeling like her dad's presence. *Be brave, baby doll*, his voice seemed to echo in her ears. She stumbled to her feet, sand clinging to her knees and ankles. 'I'll come.'

'Let's not waste any more time then.' The platinum travelling necklace around the general's neck gleamed in the sun.

Hailey took one of his hands, his skin as rough as sandpaper, and clasped her other hand with Demi's. The island swirled around them like a rainbow tornado, and then they were standing in a windowless room with a conference table surrounded by twenty chairs. Sunlight shone down from the ceiling, just like it had at the TripleAS headquarters.

'Where are we?' Demi asked, gazing around.

'That's need to know.' General Killian pulled his gun off and placed it on the table, the blue, red, purple, and yellow buttons glowing brighter under the sunlight. 'Please sit.' He took a seat at the head of the table. 'Out of respect for Colonel Wynton and all he risked, I wanted to let you know that while things look bleak, hope is not yet lost,' he said as they all sat down.

'The military basically threw their weapons at the gods, and the Government handed them the keys to the world,' Demi retorted. 'Hope looks pretty lost.'

'It's supposed to look that way. The gods need to believe that they have total control so that they drop their guard, at least enough for us to learn what we need to know to destroy them.'

Hailey's churning stomach eased just a little. He'd said "we", which she assumed meant the military, not her. Maybe she was wrong. Maybe they didn't want to use her. 'What are you talking about? Do you have a plan?'

'The Government has known about the Olympian Mysteries for decades. Despite the fact they appeared more of a nuisance than anything, the Government wanted to keep tabs on them, so they implanted spies within their ranks,' the general explained. 'We need to play the defeated race for now to lull the gods into a false sense of security. While we appear subservient, those spies will be doing everything they can to get close to the gods. They'll learn everything they can about their weaknesses, and when the time is right, we'll strike. PET has acquired several weapons over the years that will come in handy—unfortunately one of those isn't Poseidon's trident,' he added with a purse of his lips.

'Forgive me, sir, but why are you telling us this?' Aaron asked. 'This subterfuge mission is clearly top secret. Do you need our help? I'd be happy to offer assistance.'

'Yes, it is top secret, but I'm not telling you because I need your help,' the general said, and Aaron's shoulders dropped a little. 'I've told you because I considered—I mean, consider—Jake a friend. I didn't want to risk you losing all hope and turning yourselves over to the gods for processing. Telling you the truth was the only way I could think to protect you, as Jake would do for my family.'

'Thank you.' Natasha squeezed the general's callused hand. 'You have no idea how much we appreciate you risking so much.'

General Killian nodded. 'I'll take you back now.' He reached his hands out, and before Hailey could even frown, Demi grabbed her hand and the room swirled around her.

The sharp scent of salt rushed up her nose, and chatter filled her ears, as she materialised back on the island.

'Thank you again, sir. I'm at your service if you need me.' Aaron saluted.

'A warrior to the end, like your father.' General Killian touched a hand to the winged pendant hanging around his neck.

'Wait.' Hailey stepped towards him. She had to know if the military had a plan in store for her. She wouldn't let herself relax until she heard him say that the Government weren't planning on throwing her in front of the gods. 'Isn't there anything you want me to do?'

He cocked an eyebrow. 'Forgive my bluntness, but why would I want you to do anything?'

She swallowed, her mouth as dry as the sand beneath her shoes. Maybe this was a mistake. There was no recognition in his gaze. He didn't know who she was, but if she told him, then maybe she'd be giving him an idea. Maybe he'd decide sending the Zeus into battle was a smart plan. *I need to know.* 'Because I'm the only Zeus in the world, and I'm sure you know what the prophecy says.'

'Ah.' Understanding glittered in his eyes. 'You're the Zeus. Well, the Government, or should I say the military, don't require anything of you—only to stay safe, like everyone else, while we take care of things.'

'Really?'

'Yes. If we'd wanted you to become the ultimate weapon that faced the gods, the Government would have taken you from your parents when they first learned of your powers. You would have been raised as a soldier.'

Hailey had to keep her jaw from dropping as relief pure and bright as sunlight beamed through her. All her life she'd been worried that the gods would return and she'd get thrown in front of them, and would die on the spot and forever go down in history as the worse Zeus to ever live. But here was the head of the military telling her that that was never the plan.

'Why didn't they?' Hailey dared to ask. 'Why didn't they train me to be a soldier?'

'The Government puts no stock in prophecies,' General Killian said simply, 'especially ones that were told a millennia before our time. So any ideas you had of charging into battle to strike down the Olympians should be forgotten. Your destiny is not to defeat the gods. It is to be a normal human.'

'Thank you,' Hailey mumbled, stumbling back from him. It was as if the weight of the sky had been lifted off her shoulders. All these years she'd been freaking out over nothing. She didn't have to fight the gods. All she had to do was hide away while the soldiers took care of the Olympians. She was absolved.

'Take care of yourselves.' General Killian swirled into a mixture of colours, and then vanished out of sight.

'Are you okay, kiddo?' Evonee asked, coming to her side while her friends stood talking a few feet away.

She nodded. 'Yeah, I've never felt so relieved in my whole life. They said they don't care about the prophecy, or me. I'm free, Mum.' Tears welled in her eyes.

Evonee pushed a strand of hair from Hailey's face. 'Oh, sweetie, you didn't think they'd march you off to battle the gods, did you?'

Hailey nodded. 'Yes. It's what the prophecy says.'

She hugged Hailey's head to her shoulder. 'That must have been terrifying thinking that.' She met Hailey's gaze, tears glistening in Evonee's eyes too. 'Even if they had wanted to take you, I never would have let them. I would never let anyone take you from me, I promise you that much.'

Hailey wrapped her arms around her mum, pulling her into a hug as tears spilled down her cheeks. 'I love you.'

'Come on, Hails. We're going to debrief away from everyone else.'

Hailey pulled away from her mum. Demi was standing

outside her family's tent—the one next to Hailey and her mum's. 'Coming.'

Demi's tent was twice as big as hers, with four beds lined up against the back, and suitcases spilling out their contents over the floor.

Alec and Aaron were already inside, sitting on the bed closet to the right side of the tent. Demi's sister, Annabelle, was in there, too, spread out on her bed, strands of her blonde hair falling in front of her face as she strung shells onto a piece of thread.

'Get out, Annabelle,' Demi ordered, standing with her arms crossed by the tent flap.

'No. This is my tent too. And I want to finish my shell necklace.'

'You're a conjurer,' Demi said, speaking to her sister like she was stupid. 'You can just conjure one.'

'Like this.' Annabelle held out her palm, a plump green water balloon materialising on it.

Deja vu, Hailey thought, and jumped back from the tent, taking cover outside before Annabelle could toss the balloon.

Pop.

'Annabelle!' Demi screeched, and a second later her little sister flew from the tent, Demi hot on her heels.

'Leave her,' Aaron's voice said.

'You're so lucky you don't have siblings, any of you,' Demi huffed. 'At least I'm adopted and not related by blood to her.'

Hailey dared to walk back into the tent. Pieces of green balloon floated in a puddle of water on the tent's fabric floor—and a few had landed in the open suitcases. Demi dropped down on the bed next to the one Alec and Aaron were sitting on. Her shirt was soaked, and water dripped from her brown hair.

'At least she didn't conjure a paintball,' Aaron offered as

Hailey manoeuvred around the piles of clothes on the floor and dropped down next to Demi.

'So anyway, what are we supposed to do while the military does whatever?' Demi pulled a piece of green balloon from her shorts and tossed it aside. 'Just sit around waiting?'

'It didn't sound like they wanted our help.' Disappointment tinged Aaron's words.

'So how long do you think it will take for them to gain control back?' Alec asked. He hadn't said a single word when they were in the briefing room, or whatever it was; Hailey figured being snatched away by a general and taken to a secret location had been a little overwhelming for him.

Aaron shrugged. 'I can't imagine the gods would easily give up information about their weaknesses… so weeks, at the very least, but most likely months.'

'Months!' Demi gaped. 'I'll die of boredom.'

Aaron shrugged. 'Better than being enslaved.'

Enslaved? Of course that's what's happening to the others—to everyone who's not lucky enough to be on this island. That's what Zeus would have meant by "processing". Hailey could see it now: shaking people materialising at tube stations. *Are the Olympians there waiting for them? No, it would be the Mysteries. Are they throwing shackles on them? Are they locking them in a giant dungeon with statues of the gods to worship?*

Those poor people. It's not fair. The only reason Hailey and her friends were safe was because of Poseidon—him showing up at the Academy had been the warning they'd needed to get to safety. But the rest of the world had been taken by surprise. *Why didn't we try and save more people? We should have forced our way onto the news and warned everyone. But we'd been so scared of the gods showing up at any moment that we hadn't wanted to risk being caught out in the open.*

We should have tried. Maybe it's not too late. 'We should bring more people back here. It's not fair that we get to be safe while the rest of the world suffers.'

'Are you crazy?' Alec was staring at her as if she'd grown a second head. 'The Olympians are out there—and the Mysteries. If we get caught, they'll enslave us too.'

'So we don't get caught,' Demi said casually, like they were back at the Academy and talking about sneaking into the main hall for a midnight snack, rather than discussing risking their lives. 'If we take Brennan with us, we can pop into Jayden's house—I mean, whoever's house, and then pop straight back here.'

'And we'll be able to see what's actually happening.' Aaron rubbed his chin, thoughtful, as though already devising a plan. 'And having a dematerialiser would mean we could get out in seconds if something went wrong.'

'What is going on in here?'

Hailey's eyes shot to the open tent flap. Nicole was standing in it, Annabelle at her side, smirking like a sibling who had no greater joy in life than getting her big sister into trouble.

'Annabelle threw a water balloon at me,' Demi burst out, and then met her sister's gaze. 'You ruin everything.'

'It's a good thing she got me.' Nicole's lips pursed. 'I over-heard the end of your conversation. Please tell me you are not so foolish that you would risk your lives to go back to the main-land to rescue a boy?'

'We want to rescue more than just Jayden,' Demi pleaded. 'We want to save as many people as we can.'

'No.' The word was absolute. Hailey had only known Demi's mum to be light-hearted and kind, always running around after some animal she'd rescued. But right now fury rippled off her.

'But, Mum, it's not fair that we get to sit on a beach all day while the gods turn everyone else into slaves. You saw what they did—they *killed* people. We need to help.'

'Yes. They did *kill* people, and they'll kill you too. This isn't a game, Demi.' Nicole's gaze passed over Hailey, Alec, and Aaron. 'You are children. I'm still trying to comprehend your stupidity over the last two and a half years—how you are all still alive, I have no idea. But let me make one thing very clear right now—and trust me, all of your parents will agree—no one is leaving this island.'

10

ROGUE MISSION

'Hailey. Hailey,' someone whispered her name in the darkness.

Hailey gasped in a breath, ready to scream, but a hand over her mouth stopped her.

'Shhh, it's Demi.'

Her racing heart slowed. 'What's the matter?' She kept her voice low so she didn't wake her mum, who was asleep in the bed next to hers, her dark auburn hair shimmering in the moonlight coming in from the open tent flap.

'Get dressed and come outside—don't wake your mum,' Demi whispered before sneaking from the tent.

What in Tartarus is going on? Hailey climbed out of bed and tossed off her pyjamas, quickly throwing on shorts and a t-shirt. *Please, please, please tell me things haven't gotten worse—like the gods aren't currently destroying entire cities.* Hailey slipped her feet into sandals and snuck outside, the humidity in the air wrapping around her like a robe.

Demi was standing on the soccer field with Alec and Aaron. Elora was there, too, holding a miniature sun the size of a fire-ball, the glowing orb lighting up the soccer field enough for

Hailey to see the faces of everyone gathered—Kora, Tahlia, Kallie, Brennan, Brax, Tanzy, Lexa, Charlie, Riley, and a few other people Hailey didn't know. 'What's going on?' Hailey asked, walking up to them. She kept her voice low so she wouldn't wake up anyone snoozing in the nearby tents.

'You were right,' Aaron said, 'when you said it's not fair that we're safe here while the rest of the world gets enslaved or killed.'

Riley nodded. 'We need to kick some serious Olympian ass by taking away some of their slaves.'

'And we need to find out what happened to Jayden,' Demi added. 'And what's happening everywhere else—the news has stopped. We're in the dark.'

'And you're okay with this, Alec?' Hailey asked, surprised that he was there.

Alec shrugged. 'I think it's a stupid idea, but right now I'm willing to do anything that'll keep my mind off my parents.'

Tahlia squeezed his hand.

Brennan's eyes met Hailey's, his cheeks flushing a little. 'Aaron said you've done stuff like this before.'

Demi's chest puffed up as she smiled proudly. 'You don't know the half of it. We've battled monsters with teeth as big as your arm.'

'You're so cool.' Brax planted a kiss on Demi's cheek.

Hailey thought about all the times her and her friends had run off on some mission to save someone. They'd almost died a dozen times... more monsters than Hailey could count on one hand had tried to eat them, and then there was the Erinyes and Hades, the maze, and then all the times Nemertes had tried to kill her. Despite it all, they'd always come through okay in the end. Leaving the island to go and rescue a few people, and find out what was happening, didn't even seem that dangerous to her. They had Brennan with them; he could get them out in a second at the first sign of danger.

'Our parents will know we left the island when we come back with more people,' Kallie pointed out, chewing her lip.

'As long as we come back alive, they can't be mad at us,' Demi said matter-of-factly.

'Alive?' Alec's skin paled to the colour of the moon above them. 'Do you think it'll be that dangerous? Maybe this isn't a good idea. I'd like a distraction, but I don't want to die.'

'It's the middle of the night.' The stars twinkled in the night sky as Aaron spoke. 'The gods might be in charge, but they don't have a dungeon big enough to fit the entire world's population. Everyone should be in their houses.'

'So what's the actual plan?' a boy with spiky green hair asked. Hailey didn't know him; he looked a few years older than her—someone's older brother maybe. 'I'm all for a rogue mission, but what exactly are we planning to do?'

'Well, two of you are dematerialisers, so we're going to split into two groups.' Aaron kept his voice low. 'Each group will go to a different country—I had a Hecate cast a locator spell, and the closest places to here are New Zealand and French Polynesia, so that's where we're going. I figure the CBD of the capital city is a good place to start. I don't know what we'll be materialising into, but like I said to Alec, I think everyone will be in their houses. If that's the case, we start going door to door and asking people to come with us. We bring back as many as we can.'

'When are we going to go to Jayden's house? We need to get him too.'

'Let's see how we go with these countries first, Demi, and then we can work out how to get to England,' Aaron said. 'Don't worry, we won't leave him behind,' he added when Demi's shoulders dropped.

A whinny had Hailey turning around, just as Rain nudged her head into Hailey's shoulder. 'Hi, Rain.'

'Can we take her? I could probably fly to England on her,' Demi said, rubbing her hand down Rain's gold mane.

Rain whinnied again, nodding her head, agreeing with the plan.

'It'll take you a week to fly that far—and that's not including rest breaks,' Alec pointed out.

'And a pegacorn will attract too much attention,' Aaron added.

'Sorry, girl, you'll have to sit this one out,' Hailey told Rain, rubbing her hand down the bridge of Rain's nose. 'Thanks for offering to come though. But you should stay and watch Kendra.'

Rain snorted and nodded.

'Can we actually do this thing already?' Charlie yawned. 'I'd like to get some sleep at some point.'

'Okay, but at the first sign of trouble, we get the Tartarus out of there,' Aaron said. 'We're not risking our lives for anyone else's. We're just trying to save a few people. That's all. No one be heroes. Okay, everyone split into groups.'

Hailey teamed up with Demi, Alec, Aaron, Brax, Tanzy, Lexa, and Brennan.

'We'll take New Zealand, you guys go to French Polynesia,' Aaron told the guy with spiky green hair. 'Remember, at the first sign of trouble, you get out.' He turned his gaze to Brennan. 'Let's go.'

Hailey joined hands with Demi and Aaron. *Am I really doing this? Am I really running away from this nice safe island to jump into a Nemean lion's den? It's the right thing to do,* she reminded herself. *I wonder what it will be like. Will buildings be piles of rubble? Will people be lying dead in the streets? Will everything be on fire?*

The island swirled around her before she could freak herself out anymore. A heartbeat later, she was somewhere else. Shock as pure and crippling as a kick to the stomach hit her, and she stumbled back a step. 'What the...' she began to say before her mouth fell open in horror.

Hailey had been here once before—to Auckland CBD. She'd

walked the building-lined streets with her mum as they'd checked out clothing stores and licked their hockey pokey ice-cream cones. Everything was ash now. Hailey had been prepared for that—for the place to be destroyed, but what she hadn't expected was the enormous temple that now sat among the rubble. It was as big as Alec's mansion and made of pure marble. At least three dozen people were working on it. Glowing orbs of light like the ones in Poseidon's palace floated above the temple, lighting it enough that the workers could see what they were doing. Men and women carried huge blocks of marble, dropping them at various points around the temple. Other people touched the blocks, the marble shooting up into pillars. More people were inside the temple, covering the floor with tiles, while others pressed their hands to a hunk of rock that morphed into a statue of Apollo.

'They're forcing Hephaestuses to build them temples,' Brennan said with a gasp.

'They're regaining their power through worship,' Alec added.

'I guess that's what "being processed" meant,' Aaron said as they watched from twenty yards away. 'Being assigned a temple to build. There must be humans building them in every city.'

'Well, this one is about to lose its workers,' Demi declared, and marched straight towards the men and women.

'Demi!' Aaron hissed, reaching for her, but she was already hurrying up to the nearest person—a woman pressing her hands to the ground in front of the temple. Grass as green as Demi's eyes spread out from her palms.

'Hey, you don't have to do that anymore. We're here to rescue you.'

The woman whipped around, terror paling her skin, like Demi was a lamia about to suck the life from her. 'I am loyal to the gods,' the woman stammered. 'I don't need to be rescued.'

'What's this all about?' a man covered in marble dust asked, marching towards Demi from the temple's pillars. A few others stopped their work to stare.

'It's okay. We're not trying to trick you,' Aaron said, joining Demi, along with Hailey and the others. 'We can take you somewhere safe. You don't have to be slaves.'

'You're rebels,' the man said. 'The gods will reward us for turning you in.'

'What?' Demi gaped. 'We're trying to save you. We risked our lives coming here.'

'Demi,' Aaron warned as everyone who'd been working on the temple turned towards them, their eyes locking on to Hailey and her friends.

Run! Run! a voice in Hailey's head yelled as her fingertips exploded in tingles. They were too late. It hadn't even been a day yet, but the gods had already broken these people's spirits enough that they didn't believe there was any hope left.

'We're going,' Brennan said, holding out his hands for Hailey and the others to take.

Hailey entwined her fingers with his. The sooner they got out of there the better. She reached her other hand to Lexa beside her. A flash of orange zoomed towards them. Hailey didn't have time to react. She didn't even have time to realise what the light was. Not until the fireball slammed into Lexa's chest.

11

LOSS

'LEXA!' Hailey screamed as the fireball sent Lexa soaring backwards, ripping her hand from Hailey's. Hailey ran to her as her body slammed onto the rubble, smoke rising from her chest. 'Lexa,' she screamed again, dropping to her knees beside her.

Lexa's mouth opened, like she was about to say something, and then her head lolled to the side.

'She can't be dead! She can't be dead!' Tanzy repeated over and over again, falling to Lexa's other side, while Demi, Alec, Aaron, Brax, and Brennan stood frozen a few feet away, staring on in horror as Tanzy shook Lexa's unmoving body.

'Well, well, well, what do we have here?' A man dressed in black stood by one of the temple's pillars. A fireball burned in his hand. 'I go for a little bathroom break, and I come back to find Apollo's slaves have stopped working.' There was no mistaking him—he was an Olympian Mystery: an OM. 'Who are you?' he demanded.

'You killed her!' Demi shouted, tears streaming down her face.

'She can't be dead.' Tanzy shook Lexa's arm. 'Wake up. Wake up.'

Hailey didn't need to feel for a pulse to know she was already gone. A tightness crushed her chest like a giant's fist crushing a human's head. Smoke rose from Lexa's burned chest, and embers flickered on her singed and melted top.

'I don't know what you're so upset about,' the OM said, the fireball still burning in his hand, ready to be launched at anyone who moved. 'Zeus was very clear when he said anyone who defied the gods would die. You were trying to convince these slaves to leave with you. You are rebels. Which means you are sentenced to death.'

The fireball soared from his hand, the glowing orb heading straight for Tanzy. *Click.* The fireball puffed out of existence with a snap of her fingers. At the same time, Brennan grabbed Hailey's arm. Another fireball soared towards them, a look of absolute rage on the OM's face, and then the temple was gone. Colours swirled around Hailey, but she didn't even notice. *Lexa is dead. Lexa is dead. How? How is Lexa dead? She never even had time to scream.*

'Our mission was a total fail—' Riley began as Hailey and the others materialised back on the soccer field. He was already back, with the other eight members of his team standing behind him. His gaze landed on Lexa lying on the grass. His face drained of all colour. 'What happened? Is Lexa...' He gulped, unable to finish the sentence.

'What's wrong?' Kora asked, stepping up to Riley's side.

'Kora!' Tanzy cried with relief. 'You have to help. Please.' She was still kneeling beside Lexa, just like Hailey, who feared her legs would give out the second she tried to stand up.

Lexa's dead. Lexa's dead.

The island was quiet; everyone was still asleep in their tents, with the stars sparkling above.

'Medusa!' Kora dropped to her knees beside Hailey. She stretched her hands over Lexa's burned chest as everyone formed a circle around them, biting their nails and muttering prayers to the Asclepiuses of the world as they watched on.

Kora pulled her hands back, blood smearing her palms and tears glistening in her eyes. 'I'm sorry.'

'What are you doing?' Tanzy demanded. 'Heal her!' She grabbed Kora's hand and yanked it back onto Lexa's chest.

Kora gulped, tears streaming down her face now. 'I can't bring back the dead.'

* * *

Hailey sat on the beach, waves rolling onto the shore around her. She didn't even notice the coldness of the water soaking into her clothes. The sun was pushing above the clouds, painting everything in a pink glow. The island was finally quiet again. People had returned to their tents or were off in some corner crying. Hailey was out of tears now. The weight of Lexa's death pressed against her chest like a python squeezing tighter and tighter, determined to crush all of the air from her lungs.

'Hey.' Kallie dropped onto the wet sand beside her.

'Hi,' Hailey said, her voice raw.

'Um, I don't know how to say this, so I'm just going to say it… I'm leaving.'

Hailey's head whipped to her. 'You can't leave. It's not safe out there. You know that.'

'I'm leaving this world,' Kallie corrected.

Hailey's eyebrows shot up. 'What?'

Kallie glanced towards the sea, her eyes focused on the sparkling water. 'Lexa is dead.' Tears glistened in her eyes. '*Dead, as in never coming back.*' The tears slipped down her cheeks. 'I don't want to die, and I don't want to live in a world ruled by the gods.'

'The military will stop them,' Hailey said, the sun pushing higher in the sky. 'We just have to stay here until they do, and then it will be safe to go back home.'

'The military laid down their weapons and bowed to the gods,' Kallie argued. 'And when we tried to rescue people and bring them back here, they attacked us. The gods have already won. This world belongs to them now.'

'The military still has a plan. They haven't completely given up.' Even though Hailey trusted Kallie, she couldn't tell her the whole truth about the spies in the Mysteries—General Killian probably would have been angry at her for even mentioning that the military had a plan. But she wanted Kallie to stay. She didn't want to lose another friend. 'Please trust me on that. They're working on getting rid of the gods.'

'Well, when they do, I'll come back. I'm not staying here with them in power, not after Lexa.' She drew her eyes away from the sea to meet Hailey's gaze. 'I'm taking anyone who wants to leave with me. Will you come?'

'No,' she said automatically, not even taking a second to think about it. Yes, things were bad—beyond bad—and Lexa was dead, but this was still her world. She couldn't abandon it. 'I'm not leaving.'

'If you change your mind, I'm leaving in an hour.'

An hour later, Hailey stood beside her mum on the shore, along with Alec and Aaron, and the thousand-plus other people who lived on the island. Kallie stood in the centre of the crowd. 'I've already told everyone what's happening,' Kallie called out, talking as loud as she could. Hailey didn't have the energy in her to raise the wind to carry her voice around. Not at the moment. Not with Lexa's death still heavy on her chest. 'This world isn't safe, so I'm taking anyone who wants to leave to a different world. One where none of this has happened.'

'Can we live in a world with our doppelgangers? How will that even work if there's two of everyone running around?' someone asked. 'And where will we live?'

'I've already been to the world and have spoken to the Government there. They've agreed to take us in as refugees and place us in a different part of the world to our parallel counterparts,' Kallie explained. 'We'll never cross paths with them. And it will hopefully only be a temporary stay, and we'll get to come back here one day, when the gods are gone.' Her eyes landed on Hailey for the briefest of seconds. 'Anyone coming, say your goodbyes to those staying behind now.'

'Are you sure you don't want to go, kiddo?' Evonee asked Hailey. 'Because a world without the gods sounds pretty good to me.'

Hailey shook her head. 'No, Mum. We can't turn our backs on this world.' Her voice was flat.

'Hailey, we want to say goodbye.'

Hailey frowned at Tanzy. 'You're leaving?'

Her eyes were red and puffy. 'I'm not staying after what happened to Lexa. I don't want to live in a world where she's dead.' She sniffed.

'I'm leaving too,' Elora said from beside her. 'You should really come with us. It's not safe here.'

What would happen if she did say yes and went to this parallel world? She'd have to start her life over again, in some foreign country. All the while, she'd know that her true world—her real home—was out there, with people dying in it. It was one thing for her to hide away on this island, but it was another for her to run away to a completely different world and abandon everyone to the gods. How would she be able to live with herself knowing about the horrors happening in her world? It'd be like abandoning someone in a burning house to save herself. She couldn't live with that. Not when there was still a chance for them to win the battle against the gods. Lexa had only died because they'd left the island. As long as she stayed here, she was safe.

'I'm not leaving.'

'Well, I guess this is goodbye.' Tanzy hugged her. 'Not for long I hope.' She straightened the ribbon in her hair, quickly giving Alec and Aaron a hug, too, before walking away with Elora.

Whinnying drew Hailey's attention behind her. Rain stood with Kendra, both of their heads dropped slightly, like neither one of them was proud of what they were about to do. 'You're going too?' Tears burned Hailey's throat. *How many more of my friends are going to leave me?*

'I'm sorry.' Tears sparkled in Kendra's eyes as she finally lifted her gaze to meet Hailey's. 'My parents—Isla's too—are making us go. After Lexa…' She gulped. 'I think it's probably the smart thing to do. You should really come.'

Hailey shook her head. 'I belong here. But you're right, it would be safer in another world. You should go. And you, too, Rain.' As painful as it was for Hailey to lose so many people she loved, at least she would know they were safe. What happened to Lexa, wouldn't happen to them.

Rain whinnied, clopping an extra step up to Hailey and rubbing her cheek against Hailey's hand.

'She says she'll stay with you.'

Hailey brushed her hand over Rain's soft cheek, staring into her innocent gold eyes. 'No. It's too dangerous here. You need to go with Kendra.'

Rain whinnied again.

'She asked who will protect you if she leaves. Who will sit with you when the sun rises and listen to your dreams,' Kendra translated.

Tears slipped down Hailey's cheeks. She swallowed, holding

as many back as she could, trying to show Rain she'd be okay. 'I have my mum, and my friends,' Hailey said, continuing to pat Rain's soft fur. 'Go and protect Kendra. I'll miss you, but I'll see you again, when this world is safe.' She wrapped her arms around Rain's neck, hugging her. Rain snorted, rubbing her cheek against Hailey's.

'I wish it didn't have to be like this,' Kendra said when Hailey and Rain pulled apart. She gave Hailey a quick a hug. 'I hope we won't be gone for long. Stay safe.' Hailey watched the two of them push through the crowd, tears running down her face. *Please, Tyches, let me see them again—let me see all of my friends again.*

Everyone leaving was gathered around Kallie. She drew her hands apart as she blew out a long breath. A sphere of light glowed between her palms, growing bigger and bigger until she threw it forward.

'Whoa,' people gasped as the sphere exploded into a vortex of swirling lights.

'It's time to go,' Kallie called out.

The line was long. Longer than Hailey had imagined it would be. She'd thought most people would want to stay in their own world, but half of the island's population was stepping through that portal, one by one. Lexa's parents hugged each other, tears streaming from their eyes as they left the world that had taken their daughter from them. She could understand them wanting to go. *They'll probably track down the Lexa in this new world and try to be co-parents or something.*

'Hailey,' Demi called, pushing through the crowd to get to her, Alec, and Aaron.

'Demi, what's wrong?' Her best friend's eyes were red, tears glistening on her cheeks.

'Brax just left.' She sniffed, wrapping her arms around Hailey.

'It'll be okay.' Hailey rubbed her back. 'You've still got all of us.'

'His parents made him go,' she said, crying into Hailey's shoulder. 'I loved him, Hailey.'

'If things go our way, he'll be back,' Aaron offered.

Demi sniffed and pulled away from Hailey, her face red and her eyes puffy. 'You're right. He'll be back. He's just taking a holiday.'

Hailey squeezed her hand. 'Yeah, exactly.' *Everyone leaving will come back*, Hailey told herself as she watched the line of her friends and their families disappear through the portal. *The military will defeat the gods.* This world will be theirs again. It has to be. Because a life of enslavement was not something Hailey could even fathom.

'I didn't think there'd be so many people leaving.' Demi pushed away strands of hair clinging to her wet face.

'Me neither,' Hailey agreed.

'Not everyone is born to be fighters,' Aaron said. 'At least now we'll have more room to spread out.'

'If my parents were here, I probably would have gone,' Alec admitted, watching as the line continued to disappear through the portal.

'Really?' Demi asked. 'You should be used to this kind of stuff by now.'

'Used to people dying?'

Demi gulped, more tears glistening in her eyes. 'No, used to things looking bad.'

'I just want my parents back,' Alec said, and walked away.

* * *

Hailey stared towards the dark sea, watching the waves roll onto the beach. *Where is Poseidon right now? What poor defenceless city is he destroying?* A hand stretched from the sea as if someone were rising from the sand. Their fingers latched around Hailey's ankle.

'Get off me!' Hailey screamed, kicking, trying to break free, but the fingers gripped tighter as Nemertes rose from the shallow water. Behind her, more nereids popped up from the sea, the full moon's light falling on their snarling faces.

'Found you.' Nemertes smirked.

Hailey opened her mouth to scream for help, but before she could even gasp in a breath she was in the middle of the sea. So deep in the water that she couldn't see the surface—or what creatures might lurk down there with her in the dark.

Her eyes flew open as she woke up, and she gasped in a breath. *It's okay. I'm not drowning.* She looked across at her mum's bed; she was asleep, softly snoring. *Just a dream. Nemertes doesn't know where you are.* Her breathing steadied.

How did everything go so wrong? Before the gods came back, Hailey had been so worried about the nereids and the Olympian Mysteries being up to something. Everyone had told her there was nothing they could do to wake up the gods. *But they found a way. How? Amathia destroyed Hecate's wand, so it couldn't have been that. Did they find another wand? Hermes's, maybe?*

It doesn't matter how. They're here now.

Hailey picked her phone up from the floor, holding it in the palm of her hand. 'Show me the news.' She touched the pair of gold wings on the glass, gold light shining up from it and displaying a black screen with the words *We're experiencing technical difficulties, but we'll be back shortly* on it.

Argh. She resisted the urge to toss her phone across the tent, and instead settled for tossing it on the end of her bed. *Nothing. There hadn't been any news since the military's surrender. What is happening out there? Where are the gods? Killing people? Making it so they lose all hope and don't even take the chance to escape when it's right in front of them?*

Hailey's chest tightened with crushing pain as she thought

about Lexa. About how scared she'd looked as she'd hit the ground. *I'm sorry,* Hailey thought, a tear streaming down her cheek. *I'm so sorry.* Why didn't she wait? Why didn't they all wait? The military said they had a plan; the world could have handled being enslaved for a little bit, right? In the end, it had all been for naught. They didn't save a single person. Only learned that the gods had taken complete control. It wasn't worth Lexa's life.

How many people have the gods and Mysteries killed now? Was Jayden one of the people killed in the initial attack? Where are the teachers and Pandora? What happened to Amathia? Was Nemertes telling the truth when she said she was still alive? When will the military make their move? Hailey imagined the spies working within the Mysteries serving the gods, bowing down to them, and all the time listening for anything that would help destroy them.

What is their weakness? Obviously not being worshipped. But humans are so terrified right now convincing them to stop worshipping the Olympians won't achieve anything. Plus the Olympian Mysteries would be worshiping them. That's probably how the gods gained back so much power over the last few days. Hailey could just see the Olympians sitting on their thrones drinking ambrosia while the Mysteries fell at their feet, worshipping them.

Evonee mumbled something and rolled over.

'I can't stand this.' Hailey threw the sheets off her and snuck out of the tent. The sea-breeze brushed against her face as she walked between the tents, the sand soft beneath her bare feet. Bonfires burned, their flames dwindling slowly to embers as she walked past them.

'Can't sleep?'

Aaron was sitting on a log in front of a bonfire, ten yards away from all the tents. 'Had a bad dream,' she said, dropping onto the log across from him and staring into the dancing flames. The air was humid, and the warmth from the fire only added to it. But there was something relaxing about sitting in front of a fire, staring into the hypnotic flames. It reminded her of being on school camp, offering somewhat of a distraction from the reality of the fact she was currently stuck on an island, hiding.

'Yeah, me too. Although I never went to sleep.' He tossed a stick into the fire; the flames popped and crackled.

'Do you think we should have gone with Kallie? Was she right about this world being a lost cause?'

Aaron shook his head. 'No. We were right to stay. We have to fight for our world. We can't just let the gods come in and take it.'

'We can't fight, though, Aaron. I mean, we tried to rescue some people and Lexa died. She *died*. Just like that.' Hailey's throat burned as she held back tears. 'If we get involved again, we could all die.'

'We won't leave the island again,' Aaron promised. 'It was a stupid idea. I hold myself responsible for what happened to Lexa. I should have—'

Hailey reached out and touched his hand. 'It wasn't your fault. We all wanted to go. We didn't think—' She swallowed. 'Don't blame yourself, please.'

Aaron stared at the sand for a long time, and then finally nodded. 'We all made a choice to go. It's not a mistake we'll make again.'

'No, we won't.' Hailey drew her hand back. They'd survived deadly situations so many times now that Hailey had come to think that the Tyches would always bring them the luck they needed to escape. Lexa's death proved how wrong she'd been. This was a dangerous world, and it didn't matter who you were; you could die at any moment. 'Are you coping okay with your dad being gone?'

Aaron's shoulders straightened, his chin rising. 'He's a Wynton. We come from a long line of military members. He'll be fine. And the nereids have to keep them alive—they need PET for their trap.'

'Maybe Pandora will save him.' Hailey shrugged. 'I didn't see her, but maybe she's in that palace somewhere.'

'I—' Aaron began to say, right before the screaming started.

12

AMBUSH

Everything broke into chaos. One moment Hailey and Aaron were sitting by the fire, the nightfall peaceful, and the next screams were ripping across the island. They whipped around, towards the tents.

'Medusa!' Hailey cried, her jaw dropping.

It was still dark, but the burning fires and the moonlight lit the island enough that Hailey could see people dressed in black running into tents. They dragged out the occupants, kicking and screaming, before vanishing with them.

'The Olympian Mysteries!' Aaron gasped. 'They found us.'

'What do we do?' They were far enough away at the moment to be safe—to be unseen.

'Fight,' Aaron said, and charged towards the chaos.

Hailey ran after him. Everyone was out of their tents now. Fireballs lit the night and weapons clanged as people fought back against the Mysteries.

Just as Hailey and Aaron reached the border of the chaos, Evonee sprinted up to them with Demi, her family, Alec, and Natasha.

'Hailey! There you are.' Evonee grabbed her, her fingers

locking around Hailey's arm like she was afraid Hailey would disappear if she didn't hold tight enough. 'We need to get out of here.'

'We have to fight!' Aaron argued, his fingers twitching as his eyes glanced at the attack, only a few yards from them.

'No, son.' Natasha grabbed his arm before he could run into the fight. 'A true warrior knows when to run so they can survive to fight another day.'

Screaming. Swords clanging. More screaming.

'Where do we go?' Nicole's voice shook as she hugged a trembling Annabelle between her husband and herself.

'I—' Aaron began.

'Grab my hand,' Brennan shouted, running through the battling Mysteries and survivors to join them on the fight's outskirts. 'The other dematerialisers and me are getting people away.'

Hailey glanced behind him. The OMs were grabbing as many people as they could—adults and children—and vanishing with them, quickly returning seconds later to grab more people. Men and women fought back, throwing fireballs, blowing gusts of wind, summoning crashing waves—whatever it took to hold the Mysteries off while dematerialisers got as many people to safety as they could. But the Mysteries had powers too. Areses slashed swords and threw daggers, Demeters grew vines to slither after people like snakes and pin them to the ground, and Hypnoses blew sleep dust. There was no winning this. Not without bloodshed. Their best chance of survival was escape. Hailey grabbed Brennan's hand, her mum's fingers still tightly locked around her daughter's arm. At the same time, a man dressed in black lunged for Evonee, yanking her away from Hailey.

Tingles danced up Hailey's hand as she gripped Brennan's. 'No!' She ripped her hand from his a heartbeat before he, along with her friends and their families, blinked out of sight. 'Mum!'

she cried, and threw her arm forward, aiming it at the man dragging her mother away. Warmth shot from her fingertips like hot air. Tents flapped and fires flickered as a gust of wind ploughed into the man and her mum, knocking them to the sand. 'Mum,' Hailey called again, running forward to help her.

A hand looped around Hailey's waist and yanked her back. 'No, Brennan!' she yelled, just as the island swirled into a mixture of black and orange.

Hailey whipped around the second the world reformed. 'Take me ba—' Her words fell away as her stomach dropped. Brennan wasn't standing behind her. A balding man with knives and potions strapped around his waist was. *He's an OM! Where am I?*

Her gaze darted around. She stood in a huge hall with automatic ticket machines spread along the walls, and archways with platform numbers painted above them. *This is a tube station.* Men and women dressed in black materialised all around her, gripping crying and screaming people. There were more crying people in front of the platform archways. They were organised into four lines, with OMs marching up and down between them, holding guns that looked exactly like the ones the military used, with glowing buttons. The only difference was the yellow button was missing—the one used to stun people. *I guess they don't need it, not when they'd rather kill anyone who goes against them.* Hailey shuddered.

'Get in line for sorting. I've got other people to grab.' The OM who'd kidnapped her shoved her towards the line in front of platform 3, and then vanished.

Hailey clutched her heart pendant, her eyes combing the hall. She had to get out of here. Opposite her, about twenty yards away, was a door. It was the only way out. But two OMs stood on either side of it, the blue, red, purple, and white buttons on their guns glowing as they stood alert, ready to shoot down anyone who tried to escape.

'Keep the line moving.'

The butt of a gun nudged into Hailey's back. 'Sorry,' she mumbled to the OM glaring at her, and stepped forward to close the gap between her and the person in front.

Her gaze went back to the door; at the same time, a man in the line beside hers made a run for it. He made it all of ten steps before a jet of electricity shot into his back.

'AHHH!' he cried, collapsing to the floor.

The OM who'd fired his gun stood at the end of Hailey's line. 'Tisiphone,' he called out.

Ice water as cold as a Chione's powers trickled through Hailey's veins, stopping her heart. *Tisiphone? Why is he calling an Erinys's name?*

A few people screamed as a woman wearing a tattered red dress materialised beside the man's fallen body. *No. No. No. They can't be back.* Hailey's legs wavered. She'd put the Erinyes back to sleep in Tartarus—she'd used the wand on them. But here was one, very much awake. Tisiphone grabbed the unconscious man, her long black nails digging into his shirt, and then red mist enveloped them both like a cloud of blood, leaving behind a metallic scent.

'Anyone who attempts to escape or defies us in any way will be spending the rest of their years in Tartarus,' the OM who'd called the Erinys shouted. 'Now keep the lines moving.'

Nausea twisted Hailey's stomach. *Tartarus is open for business again. Does that mean Hades is awake too?* Her legs wavered even more, threatening to give out. What if he blamed her for killing Persephone? What if he wanted vengeance? Was he looking for her and her friends right now, wanting to finish what he'd started—killing them with a fireball?

Hailey didn't dare look towards the exit again. This wasn't a game. She couldn't just take a chance at escape and hope if she failed that she'd be allowed to live. She glanced at the lines instead, checking for familiar faces. None of her friends were there, nor her mum. *Please, Tyches, let her have escaped. Let Brennan have gone back for her.*

'Your turn,' an OM said to her.

Hailey had been so busy checking the crowd for her mum and friends that she hadn't realised she was at the front of the line now. She hadn't been able to see before what was happening up here, but now that she could, she almost collapsed in shock. Standing in front of her was Madam Grayson. Hailey glanced at the other three lines. There was Master Anderson, Madam Norwood, Sir Bliss. *So this is where the teachers disappeared to. They're prisoners. Thank the Tyches they're not dead.*

'Madam Grayson?' Hailey stepped up to her on shaky legs.

'That's far enough,' the OM standing beside Madam Grayson warned when Hailey was a few feet from her overseer. 'What's your power?' the OM asked.

'She's an Anemoi,' Madam Grayson said before Hailey could even open her mouth.

Hailey frowned, ever so slightly, and then realised that Madam Grayson had just saved her life. The gods knew about the prophecy —according to Nemertes. If Hailey had admitted she was a Zeus, then the OMs probably would have killed her on the spot. *Thank you*, Hailey mouthed to Madam Grayson, who didn't so much as smile. Her face was impassive, like she'd never met Hailey before.

'Hmmm,' the OM said, glancing at a clipboard. 'Let's give her to Aphrodite. She'd probably like a personal wind blower to keep her cool.'

An OM materialised beside her. 'Where to?' she asked.

'Aphrodite,' the other one said.

The OM's fingers locked around Hailey's arm. The world spun around her before she could even think about the fact she was about to meet an Olympian.

When the world reformed, Hailey braced herself, warmth flowing into her hands as she readied her powers. She expected to find Aphrodite in front of her. *Will she sense I'm a Zeus? Will she order the OM to kill me? Or will Aphrodite incinerate me with a fireball herself?*

Hailey's whole body sagged when no almighty goddess stood before her. Instead, she was staring at a palace lit by the moonlight. Its turrets and spires gleamed with rainbows, like Poseidon's palace, but this one was carved of mother-of-pearl.

'Not bad, right?' the OM said as she shoved Hailey through the double doors. Big glowing pink orbs floated beneath the ceiling, storeys above, lighting the entryway. It was long, leading towards a wide mother-of-pearl staircase. 'Hephaestuses and conjurers worked a straight twenty-four hours to get it built,' the OM said, the tip of her gun pressing into Hailey's back as she steered her towards the staircase. 'Every god has a palace now, in whatever part of the world they rule.'

Their footsteps echoed in the empty entryway.

'What part of the world is this?' Hailey dared to ask as she got close enough to the staircase to see the glass doors behind it. Not even the dim glow from the moon was enough to see what was out there.

'Australia. The Sydney Opera House had the best view, so we blew it up and built the palace in its place.' Hailey didn't need to turn around to know the OM was smiling—she was actually proud of the fact she'd been responsible for destroying an iconic landmark. 'Now stop right there,' the OM said the moment they walked past the staircase.

Is this seriously happening? Is my first trip to Australia really as a prisoner?

Bang. Bang. The OM stomped the heel of her boot on a mother-of-pearl floor tile directly behind the staircase.

Hailey jumped at the sudden noise. *What's she doing?*

Four of the 20-inch tiles retracted back like an electric window, revealing a staircase lit by pink lights imbedded in the mother-of-pearl walls. Flashes of Poseidon's dungeon swarmed Hailey. *No. Not again. Not another dungeon.*

'Move.' The OM jabbed the tip of her gun into Hailey's back.

Hailey clutched her necklace, her heart racing. *It's okay. Stay calm. Just do what she says.* She took the twenty steps slowly, inching down towards the door at the very bottom of them. She froze on the last step, not wanting to find out what was on the other side of the door. *A monster? Maybe I'm its dinner.* Automatically, she took a step back.

'You're not going anywhere.' The OM's gun jabbed into her back. 'If you try and run, I'll call an Erinys to take you to Tartarus, and trust me when I say that's not a place you want to go.'

Hailey didn't need the OM to tell her that. Images of a burning sky and standing in a dark hatch filled with water flashed into her mind. She shuddered. *I will never be a prisoner of the Underworld again,* she promised herself. *Never!*

'Open,' the OM said, and the gold door opened inwards.

Hailey braced herself. Would a minotaur charge out at her? Would it be a gladiator ring, where OMs and Aphrodite would watch as she battled a Nemean lion, or a chimera, to the death?

Oh, she thought when she stared inside. The room was half the size of her common room at Poseidon's Academy. There was no furniture. No paintings. Only a glowing orb of light beneath the ceiling, shining light over the sixteen people lying on the floor. Blankets were pulled over them; some people's eyes were closed as they slept, but most stared up at the light, shivering. *It's a prison,* Hailey realised with a gulp.

If the OM hadn't been behind her, she would have run. She would have run as fast and far away as she could so she didn't have to be locked up in another dungeon. But an Erinys taking her to Tartarus would be far worse than this place. *Hades is probably down there, waiting to avenge his wife's death.*

'In you go.' The OM's gun dug deeper into Hailey's back,

forcing her forward. The sour stench of body odour wrapped around her, wrinkling her nose. 'Better get some rest. You start work in an hour.' The door slammed behind Hailey.

Her grip tightened on her necklace, her thumb rubbing the heart pendant. *Don't think about the fact you're trapped in this room. That you're a prisoner. It's going to be okay. I don't know how, but it is. You're alive for now, and that's what matters.*

Blankets were stacked in a corner—the only luxury that seemed to be allowed down here. Hailey was definitely not sleeping. Not when people were still being dragged from the island and assigned to gods. *Are my mum and friends okay? Or are they going to be marched through that door soon?*

Hailey started pacing, walking back and forth in front of the door. Moss that smelled like fresh rain covered the ground. It was soft and squishy beneath Hailey's bare feet. *I'm guessing a Demeter grew it.*

Not a single person lying on the floor stirred; it was like they were afraid to move without permission.

How did I get here? How did the Olympian Mysteries find our island? Everyone who knew about it was living on the island, or in a parallel world... It had to be a Hecate using a locater spell, Hailey realised. *Medusa.* None of them had thought about that possibility. They'd all been worrying about the gods and wanting to hide from them, not remembering that the Mysteries were working with them and that they probably had some very powerful Hecates that could use magic to track them down. But why would they have cared about where they were? They weren't doing anything. Weren't plotting an attack. *Maybe I should have left with Kallie.*

Hailey jumped aside as the door opened. *Please don't be Mum. Please don't be Mum.* A girl stumbled into the room, tears streaming down her face. It wasn't her mum, but she recognised that black hair with rainbow colours shimmering in it. 'Zara?'

Zara's puffy eyes locked on to Hailey as the door slammed

behind her. 'Hailey? Thank the Tyches.' She launched herself at Hailey, crying into her shoulder. 'I'm so scared. I don't know what to do.'

'It's okay. Everything is going to be fine,' she said, almost grinning. The Tyches had truly sent some good luck her way by sending Zara here. She was an Iris—she could get them out of there. She'd been a first year at the Academy—before Poseidon had sent a tsunami to flush everyone into the sea. Hailey had seen glimpses of her on the island, but they hadn't spoken. 'What happened?' Hailey asked, stepping back to look at Zara's red blotchy face. 'Why didn't you use your powers to get away?'

Zara sniffed and wiped her sleeve across her nose. 'I wanted to help everyone else first.' Her voice was thick. 'I was letting as many people step into my rainbow as I could. I never saw the woman coming up behind me…' She sniffed again. 'And then I appeared at a tube station as someone was shouting about the Erinyes taking us to Tartarus if we tried to escape. I was too scared to use my powers after that.' She shuddered.

'It's okay,' Hailey said, rubbing her quivering shoulder. 'You did the right thing. But there are no OMs in here, you can use your powers now and get all of us out.'

Zara glanced around, checking to make sure there really were no OMs in there with them, before nodding. 'Okay.' She waved her arm in an arc. Nothing happened. 'That's weird.' She tried again. Still nothing. She frowned at her hand. 'I don't understand. My powers aren't working.'

'You really think they'd leave us unguarded if we could still use our powers?' a guy who looked in his early twenties said from where he was lying on the floor a few feet away.

'Leave them alone,' a woman who looked as old as the Academy's nurse, Madam Mendem, snapped from beside him. 'We all tried when we got here.' She stayed lying on the floor, but cast her gaze towards Hailey and Zara. 'Our powers don't work in this room. This whole place is like a giant neutralising bracelet.'

'Shhh,' someone hissed. 'Dreaming is the only time I get to escape this horrible place.'

The woman gave Hailey and Zara a sad smile. 'There's no escape, girls. Only death or a transfer to Tartarus.'

13

PRISON LIFE

ailey stood outside with Zara, the both of them now wearing tunics that looked like pillowcases someone had cut arm and head holes in. The OM who'd collected them this morning had given them the outfits to replace their pyjamas, as well as sandals. They stood with three other prisoners, their backs to the glass doors that led into the palace's entryway. What had once been a huge area paved with tiles that stretched out to the water was now a pile of dirt. A pearl pathway cut through it, leading towards a temple, where columns positioned into a rectangle held up a marble roof. Beneath the roof, a mother-of-pearl statue of Aphrodite gleamed, waiting to be worshipped. And behind it, where high-rise buildings had once stood, marking the CBD, was rubble.

Three OMs stood around Hailey and the others, watching, waiting to see if anyone would make a run for it. If the OMs had been standing in a line together, Hailey would have thrown a gust of wind at them while Zara created a rainbow to get them the Tartarus out of here. But the OMs were spread out in opposite directions. She could only aim her wind in one direction at a time, and she doubted the OMs would stand around while she took them out one by one. Escaping would have to wait. They'd only get one chance to do it, and failing would mean death or imprisonment in Tartarus.

'Aphrodite would like a garden surrounding her temple,' the OM standing in front of them said. 'You're a Demeter, boy, aren't you?' He directed his gaze at a guy who looked about sixteen; he hugged his arms, quivering. He nodded. 'Speak up,' the OM shouted.

'Yes, sir,' he said, eyes on the ground.

'Good. Aphrodite would like a rose garden that stretches out as far as the eye can see,' the OM went on. 'The rest of you will plant the seeds, and this Demeter will grow them.' He tossed five brown paper bags on the ground; one split open, spilling seeds over the dirt. 'Everyone get planting. Now,' he growled when no one moved.

Hailey bent down, grabbing the bag that had split open. She ran her fingers through the dirt, trying to scoop as many seeds as she could back into the bag.

'Should I create a rainbow now?' Zara whispered in Hailey's ear, reaching for the bag beside Hailey's.

'No,' Hailey whispered back, casting a quick glance at the OMs, who were spread out even further now. 'They'll attack us the second you move your arm in an arc. It's too risky. We have to wait. Now go and start planting seeds,' she said, sending Zara away as she clasped the tear in the side of her bag. She peeked inside at the hundreds of seeds. *These will take all day to plant.* The sun was already so hot, beating down on her, sending sweat trickling down her back.

'Hurry up,' an OM growled, stopping in front of Hailey; it was the same OM who'd brought her here during the night, 'or I'll call an Erinys.'

'Sorry,' Hailey mumbled, and dug her nails into the ground, clawing a hole. She dropped a seed into it and smoothed the dirt over the top.

'What are you doing?' the OM demanded.

'Planting the seeds, like you said,' Hailey replied with a frown.

'You're an Anemoi, aren't you?'

Hailey gulped. 'Yes.'

'So use your wind to spread the seeds out.'

'Oh,' was all Hailey could think to say. She straightened from the ground and stared at the other prisoners. All of them were using their powers.

A teenager a few years older than Hailey was throwing handfuls of seeds into the air. Before they could drop to the ground, he waved his other hand and the seeds shot out in every direction, scattering over the earth. Another teenager was pressing her hands to the dirt. Cracks stretched out from her palms, shooting across the barren plane as if an earthquake had just ripped tiny fissures in the ground. The teen girl picked up the bag of seeds beside her and began dropping them into the dozens of snaking cracks. The Demeter stood by Aphrodite's temple and raised his arms. Dozens of green shoots sprang up in front of him, growing and expanding into bushes with blooming pink roses.

Not far from him was Zara, using her powers to create rainbows. They stretched across the field, their multicolours shimmering as she threw seeds into them. *They're letting her use her powers.* If Hailey could get close enough, maybe they could jump into a rainbow and get out of there. And then she spotted the OM right beside Zara, their hand on the trigger of their gun.

'Hurry up,' the OM in front of Hailey barked. 'Are you daft?'

'Sorry,' Hailey said, and tipped the bag's contents into her right palm, letting the paper bag fall to the ground. *Now what? Anemois blow wind from their mouths; if I create wind using the sky, the OM will know I'm a Zeus. And then I am so dead... Just fake it. Come on, you can do this.*

Hailey stretched out her right hand and aimed her other

hand at the seeds in her palm. She sucked in a breath, her heart doubling in speed as the OM watched her, her hand hovering near the trigger of her gun. *You've got this. Come on. Make it look real.* She blew out the breath as warmth shot from the fingertips she had aimed at the seeds. A breeze blew them from her palm, spraying them across the earth as she continued to exhale. Blowing and blowing until every last seed was gone.

'I've never seen an Anemoi use their hands when creating wind,' the OM said, narrowing her eyes at Hailey.

Medusa. Be careful, the voice in her head warned. 'It helps me direct the wind,' she lied.

The OM's gaze narrowed even more, eyeing Hailey up and down, before she finally shrugged. 'Whatever works,' she said. 'Aphrodite doesn't want thorns on her roses, so get to work on cutting them off.' She held out her hand, a pair of pruning shears materialising on her palm.

Hailey's jaw dropped when she gazed at the hundreds upon hundreds of roses blooming—shooting up from the ground with spindly leaves and then thickening to bushes with varying shades of pink roses blooming open. It was a Herculean task to cut all the thorns off—there were only five of them, and there had to be at least a thousand rosebushes. *Are they planning to work us to death?*

'Okay,' Hailey said. What else was there to say? The OMs were in charge. She was a prisoner. She couldn't refuse, or argue, not without consequences. She'd do anything to stay out of the Underworld, because if she ended up there, her life would definitely be over.

Hours passed, and Hailey's stomach grumbled, her back aching. She trimmed at the thorns, her pruning shears now sticky with sap. Cuts that stung like papercuts covered her hands, oozing blood, from where the thorns had torn at her skin. She didn't know how much more she could take of this before she passed out. She hadn't had anything to eat or drink today. Her mouth was as dry as the sands of Egypt, and her skin was red with sunburn as the unrelenting sun beat down on her. It was a battle not to swipe her hand and send a cloud to cover it, or a rainstorm to blow in and cool her down. The harbour's water looked so tempting to jump in. She licked her parched lips, imagining dipping her hands into the still blue water and drinking until her throat no longer burned.

'You can have a five-minute break,' the OM closest to Hailey said. She held out her hand, and a plain white bread roll appeared in it. She tossed it to Hailey. 'Lunch,' she said, and conjured another bread roll, throwing it at one of the other prisoners.

Hailey stared at the bread roll, her stomach rumbling. *This is it?* She needed real food—a piece of meat on the roll, or at least some cheese. Her stomach rumbled again. *It's better than nothing, I guess.* She bit into it, tearing off a chunk of the soft bread and barely chewing it before swallowing. The pit in her stomach only seemed to grow by the second. *Please, Tyches, let them feed us dinner at least*, she thought as she bit off another chunk of bread, savouring every bite until it was gone. She picked the crumbs off her shirt and licked them off her dirty fingers. She was still so hungry, she'd eat the roses at this point.

Bells rang like a wind chime caught in a breeze.

'Worship time,' one of OMs said.

Everyone stood up from between the rosebushes and walked towards the temple. Hailey followed them, not wanting to find out what would happen if she hesitated. She knelt in front of Aphrodite's statue, the ground hard beneath her knees; the mother-of-pearl glimmered with rainbows as Hailey stared at the goddess. *Is this what you want? To see us suffer?* she wanted to ask the statue.

'We hail thee, Aphrodite, great goddess of love and beauty,' the other three prisoners said, bowing their heads as Hailey and Zara exchanged frowns.

'Join in.' The butt of a gun slammed between Hailey's shoulder blades, forcing her to bow lower.

'We hail thee, Aphrodite, great goddess of love and beauty,' Hailey said through gritted teeth, copying the others as they repeated the same line over and over again.

* * *

Hailey sat back in the dungeon, drinking the stew she'd been given for dinner straight from the bowl. It was cold, and mostly broth rather than vegetables, but she didn't care. She just wanted the gnawing in her stomach to stop.

'I don't know if I can do that again,' Zara said from beside her, wiping the back of her hand across her mouth. 'My entire body is aching.' She sniffed, tears welling in her eyes.

'It's okay,' Hailey said, putting an arm around her shoulders. 'It won't be forever. Just a little while.'

'You best put any ideas of escape from your mind,' the woman who'd told them that this place neutralised powers said. She sat, leaning against the wall next to Hailey and Zara. 'Anyone who tries is always caught. The lucky ones are killed on sight. The unfortunate ones are sent to Tartarus. This place is like the Elysian Fields compared to that place.'

Hardly, Hailey wanted to scoff. She'd been to the Elysian Fields—they were a paradise. And this place, with the way the OMs treated them, wasn't far off of the treatment in Tartarus, with humans forced to work in a mine—when they weren't being tortured.

'I don't want to go to Tartarus.' Zara sniffed, cuddling into Hailey's shoulder. 'I want to go home. I want my mum.'

'Me too,' Hailey said, wondering where her mum was right now. *I hope Brennan rescued her. I hope she's not a prisoner of some other god. Where did the others go? One of the other islands the dematerialises had scouted out? Wherever they are, please, Tyches, let them be safe.*

The door opened, and Hailey expected to see another person hauled inside, but instead an OM stepped in. This one had blonde hair braided into a crown, and was young—maybe eighteen years old. Hailey didn't recognise her—*how many OMs live in this palace?* 'Someone has made a horrible mess in the dining hall. I need a volunteer to clean it.' Everyone's eyes dropped to their bowls. Hailey was too slow and met the OM's gaze. 'You.'

Hailey's entire body ached, even her eyeballs hurt, and her hands stung, but she pushed to her sore feet, ignoring the pain that shot down her back and into her legs. 'I'll be back,' she told Zara, who looked up at her with red wet eyes.

Hailey followed the OM outside and gazed up the stairs, cringing. She didn't think she had the strength to walk up them, let alone clean a dining hall.

The dungeon door closed behind her.

'Wait,' the OM said when Hailey moved to take the first step.

Hailey turned back to her with a frown. 'Sorry, do you want to go first?'

'No. I need to talk to you, and here is the safest place to do so.' She cast a quick glance up the stairs.

Hailey's frown deepened. 'Talk to me?' The OMs revelled in ordering people around, watching them suffer, so it made no sense to Hailey that one wanted to have a conversation with her. And then realisation hit her like a fireball to the stomach. *Has she worked out who I am? Does she know I'm a Zeus? I have to get out of here.* Hailey was seconds away from knocking the OM over and running back into the dungeon to grab Zara.

'We've never officially met, but I've known you for the past three years,' the OM said, making Hailey hesitate. 'My name's Tamzin, and I'm the Morpheus who's been sending you dreams.'

14

OPERATION ESCAPE

'What?' Hailey's mind was reeling. *Dreams?* 'Wait, by dreams do you mean dreams about monsters and beanstalks?'

Tamzin nodded. 'Yep, those dreams.'

Hailey's legs wavered; she put her arm out, pressing her hand against the smooth pearl wall to keep from collapsing. Those dreams, the ones that had haunted her at Poseidon's Academy… they were sent by a Morpheus? All this time, she'd thought it was her subconscious messing with her. But it had been an actual person. *Why? What was the point in any of them?*

'You were never very good at listening,' Tamzin said, her back to the dungeon's closed door. 'I even sent you a dream about the ambush, and you didn't do anything. Do you know how much I risked sending that dream?'

'You mean the dream about nereids coming out of the sea?'

'Yes. I made it as obvious as I could.'

Hailey blinked. 'How was I supposed to know that it had come from a Morpheus? How was I meant to know any of the dreams had come from someone? They were just dreams. Why didn't you just appear in my dreams and tell me what you wanted me to know?'

Anger flared in her like a fire potion. The person standing in front of her had known about the wand, and about Hades and the Erinyes kidnapping people back when Hailey was in first year. Tamzin had let all those people get kidnapped and tortured for months. And the island, she'd known about the ambush. If she'd just come out and told her, Hailey could have evacuated everyone before the Mysteries had showed up. She wouldn't be trapped in this dungeon with Zara. She'd be with her mum and friends. Safe.

'It's not that simple,' Tamzin said, casting her eyes up the empty staircase. 'There are always people watching—there's someone in the Mysteries who can walk into a Morpheus's dreams, and they do it all the time. I had to send you dreams in code, more or less. I risked so much in your first year when I sent you that dream telling you the wand was responsible for the missing people.' She shook her head. 'I still can't believe no one caught me for that. But Hades would have woken the other gods if I didn't do it. I had to take the chance.'

'How did you know? How did you know about all of that stuff before it happened?'

'I'm an Apollo too. I had visions about that stuff happening.'

Hailey frowned. 'But the first weird dream I had in first year was months before anyone went missing. Apollos can't see that far into the future, can they?'

'Not usually.' She adjusted the shoulder strap of her gun, the gun's multi-coloured buttons glowing brighter in the dimly lit stairwell. 'It's kind of a long story, but when I was at the Academy, the Powers teacher, Master Quinn, used to give me potions to help me sleep. I didn't know it then, but he was in the Olympian Mysteries.' The lights embedded in the mother-of-pearl walls glowed bright enough to show the betrayal on Tamzin's face. 'His job was to recruit new members for the

Mysteries.' She hugged her arms, shivering, as if remembering something horrible. 'Those sleeping potions he was giving me were actually power-amplifying potions brewed by a Hecate as strong as the original goddess of witchcraft. They grew my powers enough that I can now see months into the future, instead of hours.'

'Wow.' *Potions exist that can amplify someone's powers?* Hailey had never heard of such a thing.

'Anyway, I had a vision one day about Master Quinn taking me to meet the Mysteries. I told Amathia, and she got in contact with the Government. They recruited me as a spy. Amathia couldn't let Master Quinn stay at the school, though, so she made up an excuse about wanting a Unique teacher to take the position of Powers teacher and that she had to let him go. He wasn't happy, but he didn't want to blow his cover. And that's how I ended up here.'

'Whoa.' *What else was there to say? The Mysteries had infiltrated the Academy... They'd been recruiting students, not to mention sneaking them potions to grow their powers... What would have happened to me if that OM spy had still been the Powers teacher when I'd arrived at the Academy? Would he have killed me as soon as he'd learned I was a Zeus? Or would he have tried to recruit me instead? Thank the Tyches Tamzin learned the truth about him.* 'So, if you're a spy, does that mean you're here to help me escape?'

'Not yet, but soon.' Her gaze glanced back up the stairs. 'I have to be careful. Like I said, the Mysteries are looking for spies. I can't do anything to make them suspicious of me. When I can, I'll create a diversion so you can escape.'

'And the others too?'

'No.' Tamzin's voice was firm. 'If I let everyone go, then I'll definitely be caught. You are the most important person in this world right now. I'll only risk my life for you.'

'Because of the prophecy? General Killian told me the

Government want nothing to do with me. They don't care about prophecies.'

'Well, as an Apollo, I'm all about prophecies,' Tamzin retorted. 'I can't speak for the one told after the gods' demise, but I can say that you're a key piece to defeating the Olympians.'

'What does that mean? Have you seen something?' That crushing weight of the sky that had been lifted off her shoulders when General Killian had told her the Government wasn't interested in her came crashing back down. *I thought I was free.*

'I haven't had a specific vision. I just know that you're important. And you being stuck here is a bad thing.'

'Well, I'm not leaving without Zara. I don't care how important I am to anything.'

Tamzin blew out a breath. 'Fine. I'll see what I can do about helping her too.'

'When?' Please let it be tonight; Hailey couldn't endure another day of labour.

'I don't know. I have to wait for the perfect time when it won't look suspicious. It could be tomorrow, it could be next week.'

The thought of living the day she just had over and over again made her want to give up. 'Can't I just attack you now and escape with Zara? That won't look suspicious—not if I really do attack you.'

Tamzin's finger hovered above the trigger of her gun. 'Your powers won't work down here. You'll have to get upstairs to use them, and there are Mysteries everywhere. They'd shoot you before you even made it to the top of the stairs. Please listen to me when I say this, Hailey.' Her eyes were serious. 'You'll only get one chance. That's it. If you mess it up, it's over. You have to be patient.'

As much as Hailey wanted to knock her over and make a run for it, she was right. If the Mysteries caught her, it was game over. And without her powers, she couldn't fight any OMs she crossed paths with upstairs—not unless the front door was open with a clear view to the sky, which was highly doubtful. 'Okay,' Hailey said, pain burrowing deeper into her muscles at the thought of staying for another day of hard labour. 'I'll wait.' She took a step towards the dungeon's closed door.

'Where are you going?'

'Back inside.'

'No. There really is a mess in the dining hall that needs cleaning.' Tamzin shrugged. 'Sorry, it was the only way I could talk to you in private without anyone else seeing. Come on, it'll only take an hour or two to clean.'

* * *

Days passed by. Days of tending to Aphrodite's rose garden… cutting thorns, watering, fertilising—any mindless task the OMs could think to assign Hailey and the others with. By day four of her imprisonment, Hailey was seriously considering making a run for it. Of risking death so that she might have the chance of freedom, of a decent meal that actually filled the ever-growing pit in her stomach. And water. Oh, how she dreamed of drinking enough water to wash away the endless dryness of her throat. She'd all but given up on Tamzin. She hadn't even seen her again since that night. If she wasn't going to get her out, then Hailey would rescue herself.

She was polishing the statue of Aphrodite, running a rag up and down the mother-of-pearl arm, while she stared at the three OMs patrolling. Two were lost among the rosebushes, marching up and down them as they watched three prisoners spray roses with a potion that would keep away bugs. The third OM was behind Hailey, his eyes combing the field of roses as he held his gun.

Zara was two yards away, scooping pellets of Demeter Feed onto the rosebushes' roots. The OM behind Hailey was more focused on the others than her. If she lifted her arm, she could create a lightning strike at the other end of the garden. With any luck, it would light the roses on fire. In the chaos, her and Zara could escape before anyone had a chance to shoot them.

'You.'

Hailey's gaze snapped away from Zara with a gasp, thinking an OM had just read her mind, but her breathing calmed when she saw it was Tamzin stomping towards her from the palace.

'Aphrodite wants a fire lit,' Tamzin said, a smirk on her face as she stopped in front of the statue. 'Your Anemoi powers can help you light it.'

The OM standing behind Hailey laughed. 'Great idea. I wish I'd thought of that one.'

'I also need someone to help in the kitchen. Maybe that one over there.' She pointed to Zara. 'That's the Iris, right? She can use her rainbow to deliver food.'

'You.' The OM pointed at Zara; she froze, her face draining of colour. 'Go help in the kitchen.'

'Both of you follow me.' Tamzin turned on her heels and marched back towards the palace.

'Hailey, what's happening?' Zara asked as she ran to catch up. 'Where are we going?'

'It's okay,' Hailey whispered as they followed the path through the garden of roses. 'This is it. The escape.'

Tamzin led them through the palace's glass doors—the ones directly behind the entryway's staircase. She stopped a few feet from the floor tiles that hid the staircase to the dungeon, and turned to them. 'I'll call someone else to take you to the kitchen.'

'Wait, what?' Zara stammered. 'I thought we were escaping.'

'Shh,' Tamzin hissed, glancing around the empty entryway. 'Not at this very moment.'

'Why? I could create a rainbow right now,' Zara said, reaching out her arm.

'Don't.' Tamzin grabbed Zara's wrist and yanked it down. 'If you two escape while I'm meant to be watching you, then my cover is blown. My mission is too important for that.'

'So then how are we escaping?' Hailey asked.

'I've had a vision about something happening. Soon. It'll create a big enough distraction to draw all of the Olympian Mysteries. Anyone who escapes while we're distracted is the collective's fault.'

'How will we know when?' Hailey asked. 'What's the distraction?' *Why does Tamzin have to be so cryptic?*

'You'll know. Trust me on that. When it happens, create a rainbow to take you to the front of the palace,' she told Zara. 'There are huge rosebushes growing near the palace's doors—you can hide behind them. Hailey, you'll have to get outside and meet her there.'

Hailey's heart was beating faster and faster as she thought about all the things that could go wrong: Hailey might not realise when the distraction—whatever it was—was actually happening and miss her chance to escape... an OM might catch her running out of the palace and shoot her... an OM might catch Zara using her powers and shoot her... 'This all works out, right? You've had a vision about us being okay?'

Tamzin shook her head. 'I don't know. I haven't had a vision about this. Only about something happening to draw all of the Olympian Mysteries—even I don't know what it will be. I just saw all of us running towards something.' Her eyes shot up and her face turned impassive, almost stone-like. 'Darrian.'

An OM stomped towards them from around the staircase. 'Yes?'

'Take this one to the kitchen.' Tamzin nodded at Zara. 'She's an Iris, so she has permission to use her powers to transport food. But if she attempts to step into the rainbow, kill her, or send her to Tartarus. Your choice.'

A wicked smirk spread across his face. 'Oh, I hope she makes a run for it.' His finger tapped on his gun's trigger. 'It's been days since I've shot someone. Come on, let's go.' He grabbed Zara by the wrist and pulled her away.

Zara glanced back at Hailey, her eyes wide. *It'll be okay,* Hailey mouthed, and prayed to the Tyches that she was telling the truth.

'And you're off to see Aphrodite,' Tamzin told Hailey.

Hailey's heart skipped a beat. 'What? No.'

'Yes. Now, come on.'

'I-I-I can't.' Hailey's legs rooted to the ground. 'She might sense what I really am. She'll kill me.'

'The Olympians can't sense what power someone has,' Tamzin said. 'Come on, don't look so worried. Aphrodite's one of the nice ones.' She grabbed Hailey's arm and tugged her forward, leading her to the front of the staircase.

Reluctantly, Hailey followed Tamzin up them, her legs trembling with every step. She was about to meet an Olympian. One of the most powerful gods who had ever lived. The video of the gods' return flashed into her mind. They had taken down the military like it was nothing. No effort at all. They had so much power, and Hailey didn't think humans had seen the half of it yet.

They reached the top of the staircase and wandered down a hallway lined with paintings of Aphrodite... Aphrodite standing on a giant scallop shell in the sea, Aphrodite holding the apple of discord, Aphrodite lying on a chaise lounge...

Will Aphrodite kill me if I don't light the fire fast enough? Will our escape plan be over before we've even had a chance to run?

Tamzin stopped outside a pair of gold doors decorated with enough pearls to fill ten treasure chests. She lifted her fist to knock.

Run! a voice in Hailey's head yelled. *Run now before Aphrodite sees you! Get outside!*

'Enter.'

Hailey glanced back towards the staircase—it was only

fifteen yards away. She could sprint for it and run downstairs. There were no OMs currently guarding the entryway; she could make it outside, and then use her powers to fight off anyone out there. But that would mean leaving Zara behind.

'Move.' Tamzin's voice was stern; her face turned back to stone as she shoved Hailey through the open doors.

Too late.

The sweet perfume of roses wafted over Hailey as she entered the room. And what a room it was. Varying shades of pink and red roses grew over the walls and dangled from the ceiling. A scallop-shell bed big enough to fit five people in it rested against the wall to Hailey's right, covered in silk sheets and pink pillows. On the wall across from it gleamed a mother-of-pearl fireplace stacked with logs. A chaise lounge and two armchairs sat in front of the fireplace. And there, standing across the room, not ten yards from Hailey, was Aphrodite, staring out a window. Blonde curls fell to her waist, woven through with gold thread that made her hair sparkle.

'This one will light a fire for you,' Tamzin said. 'I will be outside if there are any issues.' She closed the door, trapping Hailey inside.

Aphrodite didn't even turn around. She just stared out the window, acting as if she hadn't even heard Hailey and Tamzin come in. Something gold in her hand gleamed. *A locket.* Aphrodite rubbed her thumb over it, looking out at the Sydney Harbour Bridge. *Whose picture is inside the locket? Hephaestus's?* Hailey remembered a memory of Amathia's that she had shown their Ancient History class. Hephaestus was recovering from his fall from Olympus and Aphrodite had come to visit. Hephaestus had sent her away, but Aphrodite hadn't wanted to go—she'd searched for him to make sure he was okay. *Maybe she had loved him?*

Hailey so badly wanted to ask Aphrodite what had happened to him, and Hestia. Why those were the only two Olympians who hadn't made a reappearance. *Are they dead? Imprisoned? Hiding?* But she didn't dare open her mouth. She walked towards the fireplace, kneeling down in front of it. *How am I supposed to do this?* She spotted a mother-of-pearl lighter beside her knee and picked it up, flicking the lid open. *Please let me be a natural at this.* She aimed it at the logs, pressing the button on the side of the lighter. *Click.* A fireball the size of an olive shot out, sparking against the logs before puffing into smoke.

Tartarus. I need my wind to grow the flame. Hailey glanced at the wall to her right. It had five windows. Four of them were closed. The fifth one was the only open one, and it was the one Aphrodite was currently staring out of. *She'll definitely feel my wind whip past her if I use my powers. Too risky.*

Hailey focused back on the fireplace, aiming the lighter at the logs again. *Click. Click. Click.* Three fireballs shot at the logs, at the same time, Hailey blew, trying to grow the flames enough that the logs caught fire.

'AH!' she cried out as a fireball the size of a grapefruit blasted into the logs, exploding them into pink crackling flames.

Hailey stumbled back with a gasp, crashing onto her back. She blinked, staring up at Aphrodite. Power radiated from her, crackling the air as Hailey gazed into the goddess's violet eyes.

'The Mysteries enjoy torturing you humans, don't they?' Aphrodite said. 'I've told them a hundred times I am perfectly capable of lighting my own fireplace, but still they send someone every day. I suppose they are hoping I'll lose my temper and kill them.' She reached a hand down to Hailey, her gold bracelets jangling as they slipped down her wrist. 'It's all right. I won't harm you.'

Hailey hesitated. An Olympian—one of the same ones who had attacked her world only days ago—was offering to help her up. *This has to be a trap, right? If I take her hand, she'll cackle and throw me into the fire, won't she? What choice do I have? I'll never make it to the door before she hits me in the back with a fireball.*

With a trembling arm, Hailey clasped Aphrodite's hand, tensing. Waiting for the moment the goddess would strike. Power pulsed beneath her skin like a heartbeat. The goddess pulled, yanking Hailey back to her feet before taking a step back from her, as if sensing Hailey's terror.

'Thank you?' Hailey said, confused.

'I don't actually want any of this.' Aphrodite's eyes drifted around the room, over the hundreds of roses blooming over the walls. 'Zeus is the one who wants it for all of us. He even charged the Olympian Mysteries with being as cruel to humans as possible.' She paced back to her window, her pink gown flowing behind her, and gazed outside again.

Hailey just stood there, the pink flames crackling in the fireplace. She opened her mouth, not sure what would come out, and then snapped it closed when a cloud of dark red mist swirled beside Aphrodite's bed. *The Erinyes!* Hailey braced her legs, ready to bolt for the door, but it wasn't an Erinys who materialised. The man who appeared looked like an ancient warrior, wearing a combination of black armour and leather. A sword was strapped to his back, and a ruby-hilted dagger dangled at his waist. *Ares!*

Evil and cruelty radiated off him, sending chills down Hailey's spine as he stepped towards Aphrodite. 'No need to keep pining for me. I'm here now.'

Aphrodite spun around, recoiling as he reached out to touch her, acting as if his arm were a slimy octopus tentacle. 'What are you doing here, Ares?'

'I missed you,' he said, trailing his fingers up her arm. 'I thought you might be lonely in this big palace of yours.'

Oh, Medusa, Hailey thought, taking a step back. *Please let me gain the power of invisibility, or fall through the floor. Please let me out of this room.*

'I told you to stay away from me.' Aphrodite blinked out of existence, rose petals falling where she'd been standing. 'I will never forgive you for what you did to Adonis,' she said, re-appearing by the doors.

'He was a human,' Ares snapped, whirling around to face her. His eyes fell to the locket in her hand; a mocking smile curved his lips. 'Still crying over him, are you?'

Oh, Tyches, please get me out of here. Where's that distraction?

As if sensing her thoughts, Ares's gaze snapped to Hailey as she coward by the fireplace. 'What are you doing in here, human?' A fireball as black as his eyes materialised in Ares's hand.

'Stop!' Aphrodite ordered him, crossing the room to stand in front of Hailey, blocking her from the god. 'She was lighting the fireplace before you materialised in. Haven't you heard of knocking?'

Ares growled at Hailey, his eyes burning with loathing. She gulped, waiting for him to launch the fireball at her. Aphrodite was an Olympian, which meant the fireball wouldn't even singe her skin. Hailey would be the only one to burn.

Ares's hand snapped closed, crushing the fireball; wisps of smoke escaped between his fingers. 'Get out of here before I change my mind about sparing your life.'

Hailey ran for the doors as fast as someone being chased by a six-legged cheetah. She ripped one open, closing it behind her as she leaned her back against it, gulping in air. *I'm alive. I'm alive. I'm alive.*

'Are you okay?' Tamzin stood in front of her.

Slowly, Hailey pushed away from the door, her legs shaky. 'Ares showed up.'

'That means that—'

'FIRE!' someone shouted from downstairs. 'FIRE!'

'This is it!' Tamzin said as the acrid smell of smoke tainted the air. 'You know what to do.' She raced down the hallway, towards the staircase, before Hailey could even say thank you.

Hailey followed after her, slowing her pace when she

reached the steps. She glanced down at the entryway. Smoke clouded the air, but as far as Hailey could see, there weren't any OMs running around down there. *You can do this. Just be careful.* Hailey snuck down the staircase, the smell of smoke growing with every step. She pulled the top of her tunic up to cover her mouth and nose against the smoke as it burned her throat and nostrils.

She dared to look around to the glass doors. They were open, smoke billowing in from outside. Everything was on fire —all of the rosebushes up in flames. Dozens of OMs were spread among the chaos, trying to extinguish the flames. Hailey watched a Chione shoot flurries of snow from her hands, freezing the flickering flames. Another OM conjured bucket after bucket of water, tossing each one over the burning roses. The flames were spreading faster than the Mysteries could put them out. *Who did this?* And then she saw them: two prisoners standing in front of Aphrodite's temple, which had been spared so far. But there should have been three. *Someone is missing. They must have done this. They must have had a secret second power to create fireballs and used it to burn the roses so they could escape.* It was the only explanation Hailey could think of. *Please, Tyches, let them have gotten away. And please let me get away.*

Hailey pressed her tunic tight against her mouth, her eyes watering as she walked through the smoke, heading towards the doors. She pushed them open, reaching one arm towards the sky as she braced herself for OMs to charge at her. But there was no one standing guard outside. *Thank the Tyches.*

She dropped her arms, gulping in fresh air that calmed the burning in her lungs as she turned to her right, where rose-bushes as tall as Hailey grew in front of the palace. Relief and overwhelming joy rushed through her when she saw Zara crouched behind the nearest bush. Zara smiled, and moved to come out of her hiding spot when someone said, 'Well, well, what do we have here.'

Hailey's blood froze when she heard that voice, and even Zara was smart enough to stay hidden. *No. It can't be.* She turned around, her jaw dropping.

Venus stood before her, the twins—Nerissa and Cleo—at her side. Grins lit their faces, making them look like an arachne who'd returned home to find a golden hind caught in its web.

'Venus?' *What in Tartarus is* she *doing here?* She looked like her usual perfect self, with her face as pretty as a porcelain doll's, and her blonde curls pristine—not a single strand of hair out of place. The twins were the same—as beautiful as nymphs, and their loose dark curls immaculate. *They're definitely not prisoners.* 'Why are you here?'

'I live here.' Venus's chest puffed up. 'When Aphrodite saw how powerful I was, she just had to have me.'

It was only then that Hailey noticed what the three of them were wearing: black catsuits. *They're dressed like the Mysteries!*

Venus's grin widened. 'You haven't worked it out yet, have you?'

'Worked out what?'

'We joined the Olympian Mysteries.' Her violet eyes sparkled —eyes the same colour as Aphrodite's. 'Who do you think burned everyone's clothes and stole the travelling necklaces?'

'The Olympian Mysteries. They used spelled travelling necklaces to get in and out of the palace.' *Didn't they?* That's what Hailey and her friends had figured out, after they'd discovered Stetho—the gorgon kidnapping students. She'd told them the Mysteries had given her a necklace to get around the palace, so Hailey had assumed that meant the Mysteries had travelling necklaces to move around the palace too.

'No, they didn't. They had us, and a few others.'

Us? Others? 'What are you talking about?'

'Before Amathia banished her sisters, Nemertes came to me and asked if I'd like to have a hand in awakening the gods, and that I would be rewarded if I did so.' Her chest puffed up even more, pride beaming from her. 'Of course I said yes. Do you remember that little sea-monster attack?'

She would never forget it. A giant octopus and a sea-serpent had broken into the grounds when her friends had been outside. She'd almost been pulled into the sea and drowned—not to mention eaten. 'The one where you left me to die?'

'Yes, that one.' She giggled, like it was a harmless prank she'd pulled on Hailey, rather than something that had almost led to Hailey's death. 'That was a distraction. Nemertes knew Amathia would banish her for unleashing Poseidon's Plague, so she told me that when the monsters attacked next year, that meant I was to go to the back of the palace. That's where Nemertes was waiting. So while you were busy fighting a giant octopus, we and the other OM recruits were safely at the back of the palace, receiving our instructions from Nemertes.'

'You almost killed everyone in the entire school!' Hailey had always known Venus was cruel, but she never would have thought she was evil, at least not to the point where she was willing to kill people.

Venus shrugged. 'As long as I was getting warming potions and protected from the gorgon, I didn't care.'

'Better others die than us,' Nerissa said.

'And we clearly made the right choice,' Cleo added. 'We get to live in a palace, while you live in a dungeon.'

The twins giggled.

'How exactly are *you* here?' Venus crossed her arms, showing off her hot pink nails. 'Zeus wants you dead more than anyone else, yet you're living as a slave in Aphrodite's palace.' Hailey said nothing. 'Oh, you lied about your powers. They don't know the truth about you, do they?' Her smile darkened. 'Oh, how Zeus will reward me when I tell him exactly who you are. But first, you need to be punished for trying to escape. Tisiphone,' Venus called.

15

RETURN TO TARTARUS

Hailey reached towards the sky, warmth flowing up her arms, but it was already too late. In the blink of an eye, Tisiphone appeared in a mist of red. Memories of the Underworld flashed through Hailey's mind like a bolt of lightning, one after the other… the bridge across the endless abyss, the hatch of darkness, the room of fears… The terror of those memories snatched the air from her lungs, and she gasped, clutching her chest.

The Erinys's blood red eyes met Hailey's, and a wicked smile curved her face. 'You,' she rasped.

Pain blasted through Hailey's head before she could even think of begging the Erinys for forgiveness. She screamed, her nails digging into her scalp, trying to claw out the burning pain. *No. Not again!* she begged, collapsing to her knees as she plunged into a memory. She expected to see her dad, to have to re-live his death over and over again like she had in the Under-world. But this was a different memory.

She stood back in Auckland's CBD. Her past self was standing in front of her, with her back to Hailey, and her friends on either side of her. *NO!* Hailey wanted to scream when she saw what her past self was staring at—an enormous temple, and a line of people closing in on her. But Hailey couldn't speak. She couldn't even blink. She was frozen there, forced to watch the memory re-play.

'We're going,' Brennan said, holding out his hands for Past Hailey and her friends to take.

No. I don't want to see this again! The burning pain in Hailey's head intensified, setting her brain on fire.

A fireball slammed into Lexa's chest.

NO!

The pain in Hailey's head vanished, taking the memory of Lexa dying with it. She blinked, sunlight streaming down on her. She was back outside the palace, lying on her back. Her head was turned to the right, her gaze on Zara hiding behind the rosebushes. Zara's eyes were as wide as a full moon; she began to reach for Hailey. *No*, Hailey mouthed. They had no hope of escaping now that the Erinys was there. There was no point in both of them being caught.

Sorry, Zara mouthed back, tears in her eyes, and then the world disappeared in an explosion of red.

'Hailey!'

Hailey blinked when the world reformed, the smell of rotten eggs choking her. Iron bars greeted her, and behind them was Kora.

'Ow!' Hailey cried as Tisiphone's clawed hand gripped Hailey's arm, the Erinys's long black pointed nails stinging her skin. She shoved a neutralising bracelet onto Hailey's wrist, the gold band tightening like a shackle.

'*Dazatr*,' Tisiphone rasped.

The bars creaked and moaned, sliding open. Tisiphone shoved Hailey inside the cell, where flaming torches flickered on the stone wall. 'Hades will be glad you are here.' Tisiphone's wicked smile returned as the bars slammed shut, and then the

Erinys was gone, vanishing in a puff of red mist that left a lingering smell of blood behind.

'Hailey.' Kora flung her arms around her, squeezing. 'They got you too.'

'Kora, I can't believe you're down here,' Hailey said, pulling from the hug and studying her, double checking that Kora was really there and not a figment of her imagination. Her pink-streaked blonde hair was covered in so much dirt it looked brown, and she wore a tunic exactly like the one Hailey had on —*seems to be the standard attire for prisoners.* 'Did they catch you on the island too?'

Kora nodded. 'I was helping get people to the dematerialisers, and then the Mysteries...' She gulped. 'I'm so glad you're alive.'

'Where's everyone else?' Hailey glanced around the bare cell, which was about the size of her bedroom. 'I thought there'd be more people down here.'

'There are.' Kora scratched at her arm with fingernails caked in dirt. 'They're in the mine.'

Hailey frowned. 'But not you?'

Kora's eyes dropped to the dirt ground. 'I won the lotto.'

'Lotto?'

'Yeah,' Kora said, rubbing at her arm again. 'The Erinyes pick someone everyday who doesn't have to work in the mine. They're trying to turn us against one another—make us resent the person who doesn't have to work.'

Just when Hailey thought the Erinyes couldn't be more cruel, they do something like that. 'I—'

'I was hoping they wouldn't catch you,' a voice as dry as a dust storm rasped.

Hailey glanced to her left. In the cell beside theirs, separated by a wall of bars that stretched from the floor to the rock ceiling, sat a woman, slumped against the stone wall that ran along the back of the cell. Her platinum hair had turned grey with dirt, and the pale blue gown she wore had lost its sparkle. 'Amathia!' Hailey gasped, rushing towards the bars. She dropped to the ground, dirt puffing up as she wrapped her hands around the warm metal, peering at the nereid who had run Poseidon's Academy. 'What are you doing down here?'

Amathia's lips were cracked, and her turquoise-coloured eyes had lost their shine, now looking like dull gemstones. 'Nemertes told Poseidon that I was the one who betrayed the gods to Nikolai.' Every word was strained, like it hurt. 'He put me down here so I could die of water deprivation for my crime.'

Of course, Amathia needs the sea. Without water, she'll die. 'How long do you have?'

'Not long now. Maybe a few more days.'

'No.' Tears glistened in Hailey's eyes. 'You can't die. You have to help us stop the Olympians.'

'It is too late for me. I failed this world.' Her eyelids slipped closed.

'Amathia!' Hailey reached through the bars for her.

'Don't,' Kora said from behind her. 'She's just sleeping. Let her rest.'

Hailey turned to Kora. Tears glistened in her eyes too. 'But nymphs don't sleep.'

Kora shrugged. 'I guess they do when they're dying.'

Hailey watched Amathia's chest rise and fall with shallow breaths. *She's alive, for now.* Thinking about it, Hailey didn't know why she was so upset about Amathia only having a few more days, because right now, at this very second, Tisiphone was telling Hades Hailey was alive and in his dungeon. He'd be here soon to kill her, or he'd send for Zeus to do it. Either way, she wouldn't live to the end of the day. *Please, Tyches, let Zara have escaped. At least let* her *live.*

'So how did you get down here?' Hailey asked Kora, pushing to her feet. *Don't think about the fact you're about to die. Just keep distracted.*

'The Mysteries assigned me to Ares after I was captured.' She hugged her arms, her skin growing paler. 'I used my powers to heal one of the other prisoners. The Mysteries found out and sent me here, to Tartarus.' She leaned her back into the corner of the cell, a flaming torch flickering near her head. 'Tartarus? Can you believe that?'

'I've been here before,' Hailey admitted. *What's the point in secrets anymore? Everyone already knows about the gods still being alive.*

'What?'

'Back in first year, back on Killer Island when I fought the griffin, Demi raided its nest and found a wand.' Hailey clutched her heart pendant necklace. *That's where everything went wrong. That's what started all of this—the gods returning.* 'It had a spell with it that woke up Hades, Persephone, and the Erinyes. When we figured it out, we came here to stop them. I guess there wasn't much point to that.' All of what they'd gone through that first year had been for nothing. The Olympians had come back anyway. *But how? What did the Olympian Mysteries find that helped them resurrect the gods?* She'd ask Hades when he came. At least she'd know the answer before she died, not that it would help anyone.

'Wow. I would be annoyed that you didn't invite me, but after being a prisoner here, I don't think I would have liked coming very much.'

'Hades is going to kill me.' Hailey leaned her back against the bars, the metal warm.

'What?' Kora pushed away from the corner. 'Why?'

'We accidentally killed his wife.' *How will he do it? Will he throw a fireball at me and watch me burn like my friends and I watched Persephone burn? Or will he take me to some horrible room of tortures and kill me slowly?* She shuddered, her stomach twisting. 'I don't want to die.'

'There's something you need to know, the bra—'

Black mist as dark as a moonless night swirled outside the bars. And then he appeared. Hades. Dressed in black robes that emphasised his sallow skin. 'YOU!' he roared, and flicked his hand. *BANG!* The bars slid open with such force it was as if a Heracles had used all their might to open them.

Hailey backed into the corner, just as Hades curled his fingers towards himself. 'Come.'

An invisible force gripped Hailey and flung her forward, tossing her to land at Hades's feet.

'Hey!' Kora cried.

Hades flicked his hand again. The bars slammed shut before Kora could slip through the opening.

Hailey couldn't move. Terror, heavy and suffocating, pressed down on her, pinning her to the ground. *I'm going to die. I'm going to die. I'm going to die,* her voice repeated in her head again and again. Her fingertips tingled with pins and needles, urging her to use her powers, to save herself. But there was no sky down here. And even if there was, she had a neutralising bracelet on. She was powerless.

'Up,' Hades hissed. The invisible force returned, yanking Hailey to her feet and holding her in place, like an invisible barrier around her body, as Hades stared at her with black eyes that burned with enough hate to kill her on the spot. The Erinyes were a yard behind him, their red eyes reflecting the fire burning in the torches on the walls as they watched.

One of Hades's hands was stretched towards Hailey, his telekinetic powers keeping her from moving. In his other hand, a black fireball burned. 'My wife is dead because of you. It is only fitting you die the same way.' He reached his hand back.

'Hailey! No!' Kora screamed as Hailey squeezed her eyes shuts.

Please let it be quick.

'Not so fast.'

Hailey's eyelids flicked open, and her jaw dropped when she

saw who was standing by Hades, gripping Hades's arm to keep him from flinging the fireball. Her dress was emerald green—the same colour as her eyes—and she wore a crown of red poppies on her brown hair. *Demeter!*

'Persephone was my daughter. I'm the one who gets to exact vengeance,' Demeter growled at Hades. She dropped her hand onto Hades's palm, his fireball puffing into smoke.

'Of course, Demeter.' Hades bowed his head as the goddess of harvest released him.

The invisible force kept Hailey pinned in place. *This is it. This is my only chance to save myself.* 'I didn't kill Persephone,' Hailey pleaded. 'Hades did—with a fireball.' If she could convince Demeter that Hades was responsible for her daughter's death, then maybe, just maybe, Demeter would kill Hades and give Hailey a little more time to work out how the Tartarus to get out of there.

'She's lying.' Something flared in Hades's gaze—*is that fear?* 'Humans will do anything to save themselves.'

'Yes, they will,' Demeter agreed. She raised her hands. Two vines covered in thorns sprang up from the dirt like snakes burrowing up from the earth. They slithered towards Hailey, wrapping around her ankles and curling up her legs.

'Ahhh!' Hailey cried out, the thorns stabbing into her skin like barbed wire.

'You killed my daughter.' Demeter glared at her with eyes as poisonous as deadly nightshade.

Hailey gritted her teeth against the thorns' stabbing pain as they curled around her, tighter and tighter, biting into her skin like teeth. She opened her mouth to plead one final time that she hadn't killed Persephone, but her words fell away when the vines snaked around her throat. She froze, her heart hammering as she waited for them to tighten and strangle her to death.

Demeter aimed her fingers at the vines, hate and loathing

radiating from the goddess like heat from a raging fire. 'This is for Persephone.'

Lightning struck the ground beside Demeter. 'STOP!' A man appeared in the flash of light.

Demeter kept her eyes on Hailey, the hate in them growing with every beat of Hailey's heart, like her very existence was an insult to the goddess. 'She killed Persephone, our daughter.'

'Unhand her, Demeter. I will not ask you again.'

Demeter's hand shook, and for one terrifying second, Hailey thought she was going to do it—going to kill her. She braced herself for the pain of the thorns stabbing deeper into her throat.

'Fine,' Demeter huffed, dropping her hand.

The vines fell from Hailey like limp octopus tentacles, landing on the ground and sinking back into the earth. Tiny holes peppered her skin, blood oozing from them. Hailey didn't even notice. Her gaze was on the man beside Demeter. Power poured from him like a beaming sun, making the air crackle. 'Zeus,' the word was a whisper as it escaped from her lips. With the invisible force that had been holding her in place gone now, it was a struggle for Hailey to keep from collapsing as she faced the King of the Gods—the most powerful of all the Olympians, and the god she shared her powers with.

'Yes,' he said, eyeing her up and down with eyes as blue as her own. 'One of the Olympian Mysteries that serves Aphrodite informed me that the only human in the world with my powers was down here.'

'I didn't know it was her, Zeus. Otherwise I would have called for you,' Hades pleaded, standing on Demeter's other side.

'Silence,' Zeus snapped. 'Is it true, do you possess my powers?'

Careful. Be very careful. 'I'm an Anemoi.' Her voice shook.

'We will see about that.' Zeus raised an arm towards the ceiling of rock and crushed his hand into a fist.

Hailey frowned. *What's he doing?* And then realisation hit her like a cyclops's fist to the stomach as she watched Zeus's eyes darken to grey, and then black.

'You're lying.' Zeus's arm dropped back to his side. 'I just created a storm above the surface, and your eyes changed colour. An Anemoi would not be governed by the sky.'

'I can't shoot lightning from my hands,' Hailey blurted out. By the luck of the Tyches, maybe Zeus wouldn't kill her if he didn't see her as a threat. Maybe he'd let her live down here as punishment, and then she could figure out a way to escape—if Demeter or Hades didn't kill her first, but she could worry about them later. Right now, Zeus was the biggest threat. 'I'm not the one the prophecy speaks of. I have barely any power.'

'Kill her, Zeus,' Demeter hissed. 'She killed our daughter.'

'I didn't,' Hailey said quickly. 'Hades killed her. It was an accident—his fireball ricocheted and hit her—but he's still the one who killed her. And he wasn't going to wake you up,' she added to Zeus. If she could turn the gods against one another, maybe they'd forget about her. Maybe they'd leave to battle it out and she could escape. 'He wanted to rule the world on his own.'

Zeus whipped around to the King of the Underworld. 'Is that true?'

Hades opened his mouth, and then closed it. Defiance washed away the fear lingering in his features. 'Yes,' he said. 'I could have woken you up when I returned, but I didn't feel like taking orders.' Loathing burned in his black eyes. 'We are brothers, but you have always treated me like a lesser god. You banished me here, to the pits of the earth, while you and our siblings ruled over the world. I wanted to enjoy some freedom first, before awakening you.'

'You delayed our plans,' Zeus growled, lightning flickering on his fingertips. 'You will be punished for that.'

'Do what you will with me. This life holds no joy without

Persephone by my side. I would rather join her in the afterlife than stay as your puppet.'

'Very well.' Zeus threw his arm out. Quicker than Hailey could blink, a lightning bolt shot from his palm and blasted straight into Hades's chest.

Hailey's jaw dropped as the King of the Underworld hit the ground, the hole in his chest smoking.

'NO!' The Erinyes, who'd been content watching the scene so far, rushed towards Zeus like enraged demons, their talons extended like knives, ready to slash the King of the Gods.

With the effort it would take to shoo away a fly, Zeus flicked his hand at them, lightning shooting from his fingers this time. The Erinyes collapsed in an instant.

Dead. Hades and the Erinyes are all dead. Just like that. And I'm next.

'Now her,' Demeter said, pointing at Hailey.

Zeus turned back to her, eyeing her up and down again as her entire body shook. He scoffed. 'I highly doubt you are the one the prophecy speaks of. So feeble. Can you even wield my powers? Or is blowing around wind the best you can do?'

Hailey opened her mouth to say something. To beg for her life. But no words came out.

'Ah, you are afraid,' Zeus said, the flickering torchlight bouncing off his crown of gold leaves. 'With good reason. Because whether the prophecy speaks of you or not is irrelevant. A human having my powers is not something I will tolerate. I am the only Zeus in this world.' Zeus's hand shot out so fast Hailey didn't have time to blink, let alone run for her life. His palm glowed with white light, only for a second, and then a lightning bolt shot out, ploughing into Hailey's chest.

Pain tore through her, so intense and hot that it was like she was exploding—her body tearing itself apart. And then it was gone. Darkness swallowed her. *Am I dead? Is this what death is? Lingering in darkness?* If she'd been in her body, she would have cried. She would have screamed. But she didn't have a body here. *I don't want to be dead.* She didn't want to leave her friends and family behind. She wanted to find her mum and make sure she was okay. Her mum would be all alone now that she was gone. And where were her friends? She never even got to say goodbye. *I don't want this. I don't want to be dead. I should have tried harder. I should have been a better Zeus. I should have let those teachers train me to be a weapon instead of running away. Maybe then I'd have been strong enough to escape from Zeus, or at least escape from the Mysteries so Zeus never found me. I'm sorry I didn't try harder.*

'Hailey,' the voice cut through the darkness like a beam of light. 'Hailey, please wake up. Please, Hailey. This world needs you.'

Hailey opened her eyes, staring up at Tartarus's rock ceiling. She blinked. *How am I alive?* One of her arms was above her head, and someone was squeezing her hand. With a gasp she sat up, tearing her hand free as she turned to find Kora sitting behind the bars of her cell.

'No!' Hailey reached for her chest where the lightning had struck her. A hole was burned into her tunic, the fabric singed around it, but there wasn't so much as a cut on her skin. 'No, Kora. It's a mortal wound. You'll die.'

'I know,' Kora said, her voice weak as blood spread out on her tunic in the same spot Zeus's lightning had struck Hailey. 'I'm not important to this fight.' Her skin paled before Hailey's eyes, draining of all colour as if a lamia were sucking her dry. 'You're the one who will end the war. You're the one who matters.'

'No. I won't let you die for me.' She reached through the bars, gripping Kora's shaking hand. The gold neutralising bracelet no longer shackled Kora's wrist; it was beside her, in the dirt—and so was the one Hailey had been wearing. 'Give me the injury back.'

'It doesn't work like that.' Her voice was barely a whisper. 'I'm happy to give my life for yours. We had some fun adventures.'

'No, Kora. Please.' Hailey gripped Kora's hand tighter, tears flowing down her cheeks. 'Please, give me the injury back. Please. I don't want you to die.'

'Too late,' she mumbled. Her head lolled backwards, her limp hand ripping from Hailey's grip as Kora hit the ground, blood spilling from her chest onto the dirt.

'NOOOOOOOOOO!' Hailey screamed, and reached through the bars for Kora, to shake her, to bring her back. Lightning exploded from her hand like a jet of electricity, blasting into the back wall of Kora's cell, sending hunks of rock and dust scattering everywhere.

'What the...?' Hailey drew her hand back, staring at it. Electricity sparked on her fingertips, and power pulsed inside her hand like a heartbeat. *Use me. Use me,* each pulse urged. 'I *am* the one the prophecy speaks of.' She'd feared gaining the power to shoot lightning her entire life. She'd run away from the prophecy, of the idea that she would be the one who would have to defeat the gods. But here she was, lightning pulsing through her veins, and all she could think was *Yes, let it be me. I will destroy every last one of them.*

16

REBELLION

'D*azatr*,' Hailey said, the bars creaking as they slid open. She slipped inside the cell, dropping down beside Kora and squeezing her friend's cold hand. 'You shouldn't have healed me.' Tears dripped from her eyes onto Kora's pale face. 'I don't want anyone dying for me. Come back, Kora. Come back.' Sobs tore through her as a heavy weight settled on her chest like a knoxen trying to crush the air from her lungs.

'Medusa! What happened?'

Hailey's head whipped to the open cell door. Riley stood there, his mouth open as he stared at Kora's lifeless body. 'Is she…'

'She's dead,' Hailey said, the last word cutting through her like a knife.

'How?'

'It's my fault.' Hailey sniffed, wiping a hand across her wet face. 'Zeus came here to kill me—he shot me with lightning—but Kora healed me. She's dead because of me.' A fresh wave of tears gushed from her eyes like a tidal wave, and she gasped in tiny breaths of air, trying to breathe past the crushing weight on her chest.

'It was her choice,' Riley said, dropping to his knees beside Hailey and wrapping his arms around her. 'It wasn't your fault. The gods are responsible, and the Mysteries. Nobody else.'

Hailey sobbed into him until she had no tears left to shed. She sniffed, pulling back and finally looking at Riley. His eyes were red, tears glistening in them. 'Where did you come from?'

'The mine.' Smudges of dirt covered his face, and crumbs of rock littered his hair. 'The Erinyes just disappeared—they never leave us alone. When they didn't come back, I volunteered to check out the dungeon, to see if they were here, and if they weren't, to go back to the mine and get the Tartarus out of here before they came back.'

'They're dead,' Hailey said, her throat aching.

The Erinyes lay outside the bars, their bodies next to Hades's. 'Zeus, I'm guessing?'

Hailey nodded.

'Guess that means we're free.' His tone was flat, his words empty as his gaze flicked to Kora.

'There's something I don't understand.' Hailey was in no rush to leave. She didn't even think she could stand. Grief pinned her to that floor, glued her beside Kora. She couldn't leave her friend down here alone, not in this horrible place. 'How did she get the bracelet off, and mine too?'

'They didn't set them correctly.' Riley stayed beside her. 'The Erinyes just shoved them on our wrists, thinking they'd stay locked if they didn't set a release date. What they didn't know was that without a release date, the bracelets don't properly lock. Amathia told us we'd be able to take them off by saying "release" in Goldarin. We've been waiting for the right moment to strike though.' He swallowed. 'Kora picked now.'

Amathia! Hailey had forgotten all about her. Her head snapped towards the bars that separated Hailey's cell from hers. She was still propped against the wall, her eyes closed. Her chest rose and fell with shallow breaths. *She's still alive, just sleeping.*

She must be close to dying if she could sleep through everything that just happened. 'We have to get Amathia to water. She doesn't have long left.'

'Okay, I'll...'

Riley's words fell away as a voice carried down the hallway of cells. 'I can't believe we get stuck on Tartarus duty.'

'Where is everyone anyway?' another voice asked. 'These cells are all empty.'

'Probably in the mine,' a third voice said.

'So why did you materialise us here then?' the first voice demanded.

'I thought they'd be in the dungeon. Come on, I'll take us there.'

Hailey and Riley sat in silence, their bodies tense, waiting to be discovered. But the voices didn't return.

'I think they're gone.' Riley blew out a breath. 'I guess Zeus fessed up to killing Hades and the Erinyes and sent the Olympian Mysteries down here to take over. I need to help the others fight them—this is our chance at freedom.'

'No, it's too dangerous.' Hailey didn't want anyone else to die.

'If we don't, we'll be prisoners forever, and we'll all die.' He pushed to his feet. '*Oatvatnaeat.*' His gold neutralising bracelet expanded to double its size and slipped from his wrist. A shudder tore through Riley the moment the bracelet hit the ground. And then another. And another. It was like he was having a seizure, and then an exact replica of him stepped out of his body.

'Don't worry, we've got this.' Charlie winked at Hailey. 'Let's go.'

'No,' Hailey called after them, but they were already gone, their footsteps echoing down the hallway of cells. She wanted to run after them. To dash into that mine and send her lightning streaming through every last OM. But her legs didn't move. She didn't have the energy to stand up, let alone kill however many OMs were in the mine. And she didn't even know how to use her new power, not really. What if she accidentally killed Riley, or one of the other prisoners?

'Hailey.' The voice was a croak.

'Amathia?' Hailey crawled towards her, dragging her body across the dirt. 'We need to get you to the sea.' She stopped in front of the bars, gripping her hands around them as she peered through at Amathia's frail body.

'I saw what Zeus did.' Her cracked lips stuck together as she spoke. 'I saw what Kora did, too, before I passed out. You can't blame yourself.'

'She died for me. Zeus killed me, not her.'

'She made her choice.'

'Only because she thinks I'll defeat the gods. But I'm not strong enough. Zeus has already killed me. I can't defeat all of them.' As much as Hailey wanted to run around the world and kill every last Olympian, she wasn't so stupid to think that having the power to shoot lightning made her invincible. Zeus could still strike her down. Any one of the Olympians could. She was no hero—at least not the one that everyone wanted her to be: the great and mighty human Zeus who faced the gods without fear and destroyed them with a flick of her hand.

'Not alone, no,' Amathia croaked. 'But you're not alone. This world will stand behind you.' Amathia reached through the bars and squeezed Hailey's hand, her grip as weak as a 200-year-old mortal's.

'I'm afraid.' She didn't want to die, but she also didn't want to turn her back on the world, not when she'd been given this power. Yes, she'd run from it. Yes, she'd never wanted any part of this war. But now that the military had failed, and her friends were dying, she had to step up. But what if she wasn't strong enough? What if she let down the entire world?

'You cannot escape your destiny.'

There was that word—*destiny*. Oh, how she hated it. Amathia had said that exact same thing to her back in first year, after Hailey had admitted how much she hated being a Zeus, and had only come to Poseidon's Academy to escape from the sky and her powers. *Guess I didn't do a very good job. Well, Fates, it looks like you managed to catch up with me after all.*

'Come on, we need to get you to water. If I am to defeat the gods, I need you beside me to help.' Hailey's grip tightened on the warm metal bars as she pulled herself up on shaky legs. If she didn't do something—at least try and fight—then Kora's death would be for nothing. 'I'll make your death count,' Hailey said as she walked past Kora's body and slipped out of the cell.

'*Dazatr*.' The door to Amathia's cell creaked, sliding open. Hailey moved towards Amathia's hunched body in the corner. She wrapped her arm under Amathia's shoulders and hauled her to her feet.

'If you can get me to the Acheron River, I'll be able to regain my strength.' Amathia's feet dragged on the dirt as she took baby step after baby step towards the open cell door.

'You're a nereid not a naiad. You need the sea.' Hailey kept a firm grip around Amathia as they shuffled into the hallway of cells.

'The sea flows into the Acheron. I can follow it from the Underworld.' She was walking as slowly as a sloth. At this rate it would take them days to get out of the dungeon and up to the river. Plus, they'd need to get past Fifth: the three-headed monster dog that kept anyone from leaving the Underworld. And what would they find in the mine when they got there? *Are the Mysteries slaughtering everyone right now?*

Hailey froze as someone materialised in front of them. They'd only managed to walk a yard from Amathia's cell. *Please don't be an Olympian Mystery.* 'Here, let me help.'

'Lila!' Hailey almost collapsed in relief when she recognised the girl's blue-tinged hair—she was a fifth year at the Academy, at least she had been before Poseidon had kicked the school population out. 'Thank you.' Hailey reached for her hand, tingles dancing up her arm the moment their fingers touched. Black mixed with flaming torchlight swirled around her, and then she was standing on a rotting dock in a huge circular cavern lit by flaming torches. Rocks hung from the towering ceiling like icicles, waiting to slice through the air and crush anyone unfortunate enough to be standing below, and the smell of rotten eggs was doubly as strong here.

Hailey shuddered when she stared at the black river before her, which was so still it looked like obsidian. Her mind flashed to sinking beneath the water, to feeling like a complete failure who could do no right. 'Are you sure you should go in there?' Hailey asked Amathia as the nereid stepped away from her grip. 'It's the river of woe—it makes you want to die.'

'Only if you're human.' Amathia inched over the crumbling planks of wood to get to the end of the dock. 'I'll be fine.' She fell into the water, hitting the surface face first, and then sinking beneath the blackness.

'Will you be okay to get back?' Lila asked. 'I need to help the others lock up the OMs, and explore the Underworld.'

'Does that mean you fought the Olympian Mysteries and won?' Hailey asked, voice eager to hear that everyone was safe.

She nodded. 'Yeah. Riley and Charlie came charging in and yelling it was time. The Mysteries didn't know what was happening until after we'd all taken off our neutralising bracelets. There were only five of them and over a hundred of us—they basically surrendered straight away.'

'Thank the Tyches.'

'So you're good to get back then?'

'Yeah, thanks for the lift.'

Hailey turned back to the water as Lila vanished, watching the still surface. *Come on, Amathia. Where are you? How long will it take her to swim to the end of the river and into the sea? Where even are we in the world? Is the Underworld at the bottom of the sea, like Poseidon's palace?*

Does it really matter? We're in charge now. They didn't need to escape from the Underworld anymore. They'd taken it over. With the Erinyes dead, no one would be calling for them to collect humans that weren't being perfect slaves. As far as the gods were aware, the Olympian Mysteries were running the Underworld now. All Hailey and the others would have to do was pretend to be them—dress in those black outfits they wore. *There are so many Mysteries, the gods will never remember who they actually put in charge down here.*

No one else will ever have to suffer the torturous gaze of an Erinys, or be tortured by Hades. Zeus killed all of them, like it wasn't even an effort. Can I do that now that I have the power to shoot lightning? Can I kill a god?

Hailey stared at her palms. How was having lightning supposed to help her defeat them? Zeus had the same powers, only a thousand times stronger than Hailey's. She definitely couldn't kill him with lightning. But maybe the other gods? And how was she meant to do that, go back into the world and hunt them down so she could blast them with lightning and hope it killed them? *Why couldn't the prophecy be more specific?—like... Only the one born with the powers of Zeus, who can shoot lightning from their hands, will be able to defeat them. And this is how they'll defeat them...*

'I've been searching for you.'

Hailey whipped around, her palms shooting up. Warmth flowed down her arms and into her hands, electricity sparking on her fingertips. 'Aphrodite?'

The goddess stood before her, beauty radiating from her like sunlight as she stared at Hailey with violet eyes. 'You. You were at my palace.'

Hailey's hands were still out, the warmth of her powers trapped inside them, waiting for her to unleash her lightning straight at the goddess. 'What are you doing here?' Hailey asked, torn between testing her powers to see if they could kill a god and letting Aphrodite speak. She'd been nice to Hailey. Not like Ares. If it had been him standing in front of her, she wouldn't have hesitated to shoot a hole right through him.

'I've been searching for you,' Aphrodite repeated, the sparkle in her blonde curls dulled by the dimness of the torch-lit cavern. 'I've been searching for the mortal Zeus. One of the Olympian Mysteries was boasting about how she'd discovered you and summoned Tisiphone to take you from my palace.'

The hairs on the back of Hailey's neck stood on end, and the electricity dancing between her fingers sparked and crackled. 'Did Zeus send you to check if I was really dead? Are you going to take me to him so he can kill me again?'

Aphrodite shook her head. 'No. Of course not. I want to help you.'

'How?'

'I—'

Water splashed across Hailey, the lightning sparking between her fingers hissing and smoking as Amathia landed between her and Aphrodite, two of the docks' rotten planks snapping. 'Get away from her!' Amathia growled at the goddess. Her dress sparkled like the iridescent scales of a fish once more, and her platinum blonde hair gleamed—practically glowed—as she stood tall. It was as if she were a phoenix reborn.

'No, it's okay,' Hailey said, dropping her hands. 'I want to hear what she has to say.' If an Olympian wanted to help her, she wasn't going to say no—providing it wasn't a trap.

Amathia didn't move. Her body was tense, waiting to pounce on the goddess. She stared at her, as if trying to read her mind, before finally saying, 'Very well,' and stepping aside. 'But if you betray us, I will drown you in the Acheron River. You have my word on that.'

'It's nice to see you again, too, Amathia,' Aphrodite said,

voice calm. 'I believe the last time we crossed paths was when you took me to your underwater cave to see Hephaestus.'

'He didn't trust you. I don't think I should either.'

'You're wrong. He did trust me. That's why I'm here.'

'Are you joining our side?' Hailey didn't dare get her hopes up that the goddess would say yes. She couldn't exactly think of a reason why Aphrodite would want to join humans against her own kind.

'I've always been on your side.' The gold bracelets on Aphrodite's wrists glowed in the flickering torchlight. 'My kin do not know that though.'

'Why would you help humans fight your own kind?' Warmth still tingled in Hailey's hands. She wasn't so stupid to let her guard down—this could all still be a trap. If Aphrodite said the wrong thing, or made one wrong move, Hailey would test her new powers out on her. For all she knew, this could be a distraction while the Olympian Mysteries took back control of the Underworld and the goddess would kill her the second she got the all clear that the human rebellion had been quashed.

Aphrodite's gaze flicked to the river of black water behind Hailey and Amathia. Sadness lingered in her violet eyes. 'I never agreed with the way the others treated humans—with the joy they gained from such cruelty,' she said, her eyes returning to Hailey. 'Mortals were always kind to me. I even fell in love with one—Adonis.' She pressed her fingers to the locket around her neck—the same one Hailey had seen her staring at when Hailey had been in Aphrodite's room. 'Zeus forced me to marry Hephaestus as punishment, and sent Ares to kill Adonis.' She swallowed, her hand dropping from the locket. 'I was never brave enough to stand up to my father and tell him what I thought, as you heard, Amathia, that day in the cave.'

'So what made you change your mind?' Amathia's body was still tense, ready for an attack.

'Hephaestus.' A ghost of a smile lingered on her pink lips.

'Before the Great Battle, Zeus summoned the Olympians and told us that if the battle did not go in our favour, he had a plan to save us. Before we departed to fight, Hephaestus spoke with me. He told me that Zeus's backup plan involved Hecate, and that Hephaestus knew exactly what spell she had created to save us, and that it would require a volunteer to sacrifice themselves by absorbing the Olympians' powers and staying behind to die. He'd already spoken with Hestia—another Olympian loyal to humans. She agreed to be the sacrifice, having long become tired of her immortal life,' Aphrodite said. 'Hephaestus told me he was going to volunteer too. Or at least make it look that way.'

Hailey listened to Aphrodite like she were an oracle telling her her future. *This is it. This is the story of how the Olympians survived. And the answer to how humans can have Olympian powers when the Olympians never died—it was because they transferred their powers to Hestia, and when she died, all of the powers she'd absorbed fell to humans.*

'You see, long before the Great Battle ever took place, Zeus asked Hecate to create a spell that would save the Olympians, if humans ever turned on us,' Aphrodite continued. 'She designed a spell that could freeze us until we were awakened—she poured the spell into tiny orbs of light—but for it to work, she needed something to contain the magic. She asked Hephaestus to craft two boxes, so he knew of Zeus's survival plan before any of us. He told me that he planned to take a light after the rest of us were frozen and hide himself away in his workshop.'

Hailey had so many questions swirling around in her head... *how do gods transfer their powers to each other? Can humans do the same thing? How did Zeus and the other gods re-gain their powers if they gave them up?* She bit her lip to keep from asking them, not wanting to interrupt the goddess.

'The lights to awaken us were spelled to find each of us, so Hephaestus would awaken when the rest of us did,' Aphrodite continued her re-telling. 'The other gods would never know he survived. He made a deal with Hestia to transfer all of the Olympians' powers to her so that he could live. He said he needed me, too, and to go to his workshop when I awoke so we could find a way to save humankind. That girl who came to us —Cady—'

'Cady?' Amathia's eyebrows shot up. 'What about her?'

Aphrodite frowned. 'She awakened us. I thought you knew.'

Hailey's jaw dropped. *Cady, the shyest girl at the Academy, brought back the Olympians?!* Never, in a million years, would Hailey have ever guessed it was her who'd betrayed all of humankind. 'How?'

'With a gold seed spelled to take anyone who swallowed it to Olympus,' Aphrodite explained. 'Before she ever found the seed, Poseidon's nereids enlisted her to find a way to Olympus's palace and awaken us.'

Gold seed? Hailey gasped. *The gold seed Demi brought back from the griffin's nest! Cady saw it back at the Academy, just before we found out the travelling necklaces had been stolen and we couldn't go home. That seed could take a person to Olympus?* For two years, Hailey had had a ticket to Olympus sitting in her drawer, hidden under her underwear. Once again, her stupid decision to go to Killer Island back in first year haunted her. If she hadn't gone there, then she never would have fought the griffin, Demi never would have stolen the pouch of gold seeds, and Cady never would have used those seeds to go to Olympus and wake up the gods. *This whole time I've been trying to stop people from waking up the gods, but I basically handed over the golden ticket to bring them back.*

Hailey stumbled back a step, her stomach twisting.

Amathia gripped her arm with slender fingers before she could fall into the river. 'Are you all right, Hailey?'

'It's my fault.' Hailey gulped. 'Cady took that seed from me. I didn't know what it did though; otherwise I would have—'

'It doesn't matter.' Amathia's fingers remained on Hailey's

arm, her grip firm to keep Hailey from collapsing. 'Cady, my sisters, they would have found another way to go to Olympus. You cannot blame yourself. What's done is done.'

Hailey slowly nodded. *The nereids are persistent, that's for sure. They never would have stopped searching for a way to awaken the gods. But still, I had a hand in bringing the Olympians back. I owe it to this world to do everything I can to undo what's happened. Why, why, why did I go to Killer Island? That cursed place has brought nothing but evil.*

Amathia's hand dropped from Hailey's arm as her turquoise-coloured eyes focussed back on Aphrodite. 'What were you saying about Cady?'

'She told us of the prophecy, about a Zeus defeating the gods—she didn't tell us who the Zeus was though.'

Well, at least Cady didn't completely throw me under the stampede of chimera. She could have handed Zeus a photo of Hailey, and he could have had every Olympian Mystery searching for her. It still didn't make up for the fact that Cady was the reason the gods were back. *What drove her to do something so stupid? To condemn the world like that? What did the nereids promise her?*

'I told Hephaestus, and he tasked me with finding the Zeus and bringing them to him.' Aphrodite's gaze turned to Hailey. 'I've been searching everywhere for you, and you were in my palace the whole time.'

'Well, not the whole time,' Hailey said, barely being able to comprehend how ironic it was that while she'd been living in Aphrodite's palace, praying to the Tyches never to cross paths with the goddess—lest Aphrodite sense her powers and kill her—Aphrodite had been looking for her, to help her. 'So what can Hephaestus do?' Hailey wasn't ready to completely believe Aphrodite and let her guard down; she still had no reason to trust the goddess.

'He's the god of fire and metalworking,' Aphrodite said simply. 'He created weapons to help the Olympians defeat the

Titans. And now he's creating a weapon to help humans defeat the gods altogether.'

Hailey's knees buckled with relief. *Yes, yes. A weapon! That's what we need.* So far, their best human weapons had done nothing against the Olympians. They were defenceless against them. But if Hephaestus was crafting them a super weapon, then they at least had a chance of destroying the gods.

'I believe Hephaestus would do that,' Amathia agreed, 'but you have no proof that any of what you have said is true. How can we trust you when you are an Olympian?'

'I swear on the River Styx that everything I have said is the truth. I wish to help humans defeat my kin. I have no love for my family. They are cruel and merciless. They have taken everything from me.' Aphrodite's fingers brushed against her gold locket.

Hailey believed her. She heard the hate in her voice... the sadness, the betrayal. She really did want to destroy her own kind. And Aphrodite had protected her when Ares had tried to kill her. She wasn't like the other gods.

'And if I'd wanted to harm you, I could have killed you when your back was turned,' she added to Hailey.

'Take me to him.' If Hephaestus had some big gun that vaporised Olympians, she'd happily go into battle against them.

'I can't.' Aphrodite's shoulders slumped just a little. 'I think Ares is tracking me. He won't sense me down here though— magic protects this place,' she added quickly when Hailey's heart skipped a beat. 'I can't risk leading him to Hephaestus. And Hephaestus can't risk leaving his workshop to come here— if he is discovered, the battle will be over before it has begun.' She met Amathia's gaze. 'Do you remember how to get there?'

Amathia nodded.

'Good. Travel there as soon as you can. He'll have a plan by now.'

17

WAITING

'What are we waiting for?' Hailey asked, turning to face Amathia. A pile of rose petals rested on the ground where Aphrodite had been standing; they vanished a heartbeat later. 'Let's go.' She never imagined she'd be so eager to meet a god. But if Hephaestus was really on their side, he could end all of this. There'd be no more killing. No more enslavement. She could find her mum and her friends. The world could go back to how it was. The sooner that happened, the better.

'We should wait until tomorrow.'

'Tomorrow? The gods or the Mysteries could figure out we're not prisoners down here anymore. They could kill us at any moment. We can't waste time.'

'We also can't be foolish and rush into something without a plan.'

'Do you think Aphrodite was lying and it's a trap?' *Please don't say yes. This is our only chance. Please don't let it be a ruse.*

Amathia shook her head, her waist-length blonde hair brushing against her dress. 'No. I believe Aphrodite is one of only two gods we can trust—Hephaestus being the second. I never once heard a story of her harming a human, and that day in the cave, when she visited Hephaestus, I saw the hatred she held for her father over what he had done.'

'So why can't we go there now?' Hailey could almost feel the Mysteries closing in on them. *Do they have an Apollo who's had a premonition about what's happening in Tartarus? Are they rallying forces to charge in here?*

'Because his volcano is in the ocean—that's the oceanids' territory.' Amathia trailed a hand over her bare neck, where her teardrop pendant had once hung—the same pendant Nemertes now wore. 'By now all nymphs will know of my betrayal. They will not let me pass through their waters, especially not with a human.'

More evil nymphs. Great. 'Why do we have to swim through the ocean? Can't we just get a dematerialiser to take us?'

Amathia shook her head. 'Hephaestus designed his island to block anyone from materialising in—anyone but himself. Crossing through the ocean is the only way there.'

Well, that sucks. 'Can't you avoid the oceanids? The ocean is a big place, how would they even know you were swimming in it?'

Amathia tapped her collarbone. 'It's true, they would have to spot me to know I was there. But they patrol the ocean. While there is a chance we may not cross paths with them, there is also a chance that we will. And that is a chance I do not wish to take.'

'What will going tomorrow instead do?' *Aside from waste time and increase our chances of getting caught here,* she added to herself.

'Give us a better chance of passing through unseen. The oceanids love the sunrise—the time of day when the sea sparkles and changes colours. They are all above the surface when it happens.'

'So we leave at sunrise?'

'Yes.'

'What if a god or someone from the Mysteries comes down here before then?' *What if they're on their way right now?*

'As you humans say, we will battle that minotaur when we cross paths with it. But for now, I believe we are safe. Zeus killed Hades and the Erinyes, so he knows they're no longer in charge. As long as we dress like the Mysteries, anyone who comes down here will think we are one of them.'

Please, Tyches, let us stay alive until tomorrow. Please.

* * *

Hailey lay on her back on the bright green grass in the Elysian Fields, staring up at the violet-blue sky as fluffy silver clouds floated through it. Ethereal music that sounded like a choir of sirens singing drifted through the air, and the crisp scent of freshly cut grass mixed with the sweet smell of fruit and blooming flowers filled Hailey's nostrils as she lay there, beside a river that curved its way through the Fields.

She spared a glance around. The Fields seemed to go on forever in every direction—a paradise stretching on and on. A diamond path weaved its way through the vibrant green grass, breaking off into several directions.

The one Hailey was closest to led to a magnificent garden, where sunflowers, tulips, pansies, and dozens of flowers that sparkled like jewels bloomed in dazzling colours. Pomegranate, apple, cherry, and fig trees—and so many others—were mixed in among the flowers, the plush silk cushions at their bases offering a comfortable place to relax. A languid river curved its way through the garden, tracing its path from a glistening waterfall.

Another path led to an open area ringed with round tables draped in thin silk cloth, circled by elegant chairs. Banquet tables offering a sumptuous feast of meats, vegetables, cheeses, and desserts were mixed among them.

Hailey's eyes followed another path. When she'd first been here, it had led towards a marble temple bordered by polished pillars. Now, it was nothing but rubble, the prisoners of the Underworld having destroyed it. *Hades definitely won't miss it—no point in worshipping the dead.*

The final path led to a palace constructed of pure gold; it glinted and gleamed in the sunshine. That's where everyone currently was—or at least the people not pretending to be OMs and prisoners out in Tartarus. The first time Hailey had been here, she'd wanted to run to that palace. To see what wonders lay inside. And now that she actually had the freedom to go into it, she didn't want to. She didn't feel like she had a right to. Not when Kora and Lexa were dead, and so many other humans. Why should she get to live in luxury while the rest of the world suffered? She shouldn't even be in Elysium, but she'd wanted to see the sky, even if it was fake. Her gaze returned to it, and she reached a hand towards it, waiting for warmth to flow up her arm and into her fingertips. But there was nothing, not even a tingle. The sky was an illusion. She dropped her arm, electricity pulsing in her hand like a ticking time bomb waiting to explode.

She smiled at the thought of facing Zeus, of seeing the look on his face when he realised she was still alive. And when she used Hephaestus's weapon on him. *Would it kill him? Or just wound him? Well, if it only wounds him, it'll give me enough time to cut off his head or something. Surely that would kill an immortal, wouldn't it?* If Pandora were around, Hailey would have asked her. Her immortality was different to the Olympians though. She actually died when she was killed, at least for a little while. But the Olympians didn't appear to even get injured.

'I'll figure it out, Kora. I promise. I'll kill him. I'll kill all of them. I won't let your death be for nothing. I'll prove to you I was worthy.' A tear slid down her cheek as her heart squeezed. 'You shouldn't have done it though. I don't want anyone giving their life for mine.' Her father had done the same thing when she was eight—diving in front of a falling branch that had been heading straight for her.

If she could, she'd take it all back. She'd let her dad live. She wouldn't let Kora trade her life for hers. And she would have jumped in front of that fireball to save Lexa. But it was done now. As much as Hailey hadn't wanted anything to do with this battle against the gods, she no longer had a choice. She was partially responsible for them being back, which meant she was partially responsible for all of the people they'd killed. It was her responsibility to make things right, and to ensure Kora's death wasn't for nothing. She had to do everything she could to destroy the gods. She had to be worthy of what people had sacrificed for her.

And now that Hephaestus was on their side and creating a weapon to kill the gods, they actually had a chance. *What will the weapon be? A gun that shoots silver bullets? No, that's lycaons. Well, bullets that kill gods?*

'Hailey!'

Hailey propped herself up on her elbows, her jaw dropping when she saw who was running towards her from the Elysian Field's entrance tunnel. She leapt to her feet, running onto the diamond pathway that cut through the grass towards the tunnel. 'Demi!' She sprinted towards her best friend, pulling her into a hug the second she reached her.

'I thought you were dead.' Demi squeezed her, as if making sure Hailey was really there and not a shade lingering between worlds. 'Zeus said he killed you.' Tears glistened in her green eyes as she stepped back.

'Hailey!' Aaron bolted towards her from the entrance tunnel with Hermes-like speed, Alec in tow. He wrapped his arms around her, Hailey tensing as something twisted in her stomach.

You're just relieved he's okay, she told herself, ignoring the weird feeling in her belly.

More arms wrapped around her as Alec caught up, forming a group hug. 'Are you okay – Hailey?' he puffed out as they broke apart.

'Yes.' Tears blurred her vision. Her friends were here. They were alive. *Thank you, Tyches.* 'How did Zeus tell you I was dead? How are you here?'

'First off, why are you dressed like an Olympian Mystery?' Demi asked, eyes combing over Hailey's black cargo trousers and top. 'Are you a spy?'

'No, I'm not a spy. Zeus left the OMs in charge down here, and we're pretending to be them so we don't get caught.'

'The rebels have control of the entire Underworld?' Aaron's face lit up, like he'd just been told they were the current rulers of the world.

Hailey nodded. 'Yeah. Now, tell me about how you're here. What happened to you after the island? How did Zeus tell you I was dead?'

'He went on the news.' Demi pulled her phone from her pocket, placing it on her palm. 'Here, its playing on repeat. Show the news.' She touched the pair of gold wings on the phone's glass screen, gold light shining up from the symbol and morphing into a 15-inch screen. Zeus was standing in front of a long table with seven empty chairs—*that's where the Government was sitting when they told the military to stand down.*

'I know that some of you have been holding out hope that the human who stole my powers would save you.' A shudder tore through Hailey as Zeus's eyes stared directly into the camera. She pressed a hand to her chest, remembering the searing pain of his lightning shooting through her. 'I am well aware of the ridiculous prophecy that speaks of this human defeating my kin and me. I have consulted with Apollo, and he has confirmed that this prophecy is nothing more than a fable.' Lightning flashed in Zeus's blue eyes. 'But for those of you who are foolish enough to believe in such fairy tales, I have regretful news for you. I am now the only Zeus in this world. The Mysteries arrested the human who possessed my powers, and I killed her. She is dead. Nothing can stop us now.'

Demi slipped the phone back into her pocket. 'So he didn't kill you? It was a lie?'

'Not exactly.' Hailey hugged her arms, the centre of her chest tingling. 'He shot me with a lightning bolt.'

Aaron cocked an eyebrow. 'How did you survive?'

'Are you an immortal now too?' Alec asked, his eyes widening with wonder.

Hailey shook her head, her gaze dropping to the sparkling diamond pathway. She couldn't bear to look at her friends' faces when she told them. She didn't think she could handle seeing the pain in their features as they learned the truth—that someone else they cared about was dead. 'Kora healed me before I died.'

'Oh, thank the Tyches she was there,' Demi said. 'Where is she now? In the palace?' Her gaze locked on to the gold palace in the distance.

'Demi, wait.' Aaron grabbed her arm before she could run towards it.

Tears burned Hailey's throat. 'She's dead.'

'What?' Hailey didn't need to look at Demi to know that her face had just shattered.

'It was a mortal wound.' Alec's voice was barely above a whisper.

Hailey nodded, tears slipping from her eyes and landing on the diamond pathway. 'She gave her life for mine.'

'No, she can't be gone,' Demi protested. 'Where is she? It's not funny, Hailey.'

Hailey sniffed, finally looking up to meet her friends' rheumy eyes. 'I'm sorry.'

'No. She's not dead.'

'Why don't you take Demi to the waterfall,' Aaron suggested to Alec.

Alec nodded numbly, steering Demi away, but Hailey could still hear her crying, and her protests that it wasn't true.

Tears streamed down Hailey's cheeks, thick and fast. 'I didn't want her to do it.'

'It was her choice.' Aaron put a hand on her arm, squeezing.

'How will I tell her parents, and Tahlia?' The grief returned with crushing force. She couldn't face them. She couldn't tell them she was the reason Kora was dead. They'd hate her. They'd never forgive her.

Aaron squeezed her arm tighter. 'It wasn't your fault, Hailey,' he said, sensing her thoughts. 'And you won't have to tell anyone else what happened to Kora. Not everything is your responsibility.'

The guilt squeezed tighter and tighter, slowly crushing her to death like an anaconda constricting around a golden hind. She dug her nails into her palms, forcing her mind to focus on the stinging pain. *Stay here. Keep it together. Focus. If you fall into this bottomless pit of guilt and regret, you'll never come back out.* People had sacrificed themselves for her. She had lightning now. No matter how much she wanted to, she couldn't sit around crying and feeling sorry for herself, not when people were out there dying. *I have to be a soldier. A warrior. I have to be the Zeus everyone needs. I have to be strong.*

With a deep breath, Hailey pushed the pain away, forcing it out of sight like a gust of wind blowing away a cloud. She wiped at her swollen eyes. 'How are you here? How did you know how to get to Tartarus? Where's my mum?' she asked, suddenly realising that Evonee should have been there with them. *Where are all the parents?*

'There was another ambush.' Aaron ran a hand through his messed-up hair, his gaze shifting from Hailey's, like he was ashamed to look at her. 'That night the Mysteries attacked us, the night they took you, those of us who escaped went back to Poseidon's Island—it was the only other safe place we knew… About an hour later, the Mysteries showed up there.' Aaron swallowed, his hands clenching into fists. 'I wanted to fight them, but my mum said I had to get everyone to safety.' His gaze returned to Hailey's, guilt lingering in his eyes. 'All of our parents stayed behind to distract the Mysteries so that the rest of us could escape.'

Hailey's stomach dropped. All this time she'd managed to keep it together because she'd kept telling herself her mum was okay. That she got away. 'What?! They took my mum?'

'I'm sorry, Hailey.'

Hailey's legs wavered, giving out; she dropped to her knees on the hard ground, her head spinning. *How is this happening? My mum's gone.* The tears returned, streaming down her face as she gasped in tiny breaths.

Aaron dropped down beside her, putting his hand on her quivering back. 'She'll be okay.'

'You can't know that. What if she's with someone like Ares?' She remembered the cruelty that had seeped off him like the stench of death seeps off a corpse.

'Don't go down that road,' Aaron warned. 'You could spend a lifetime thinking about all of the what ifs. None of that matters. Only what we do now does. We have to focus on fixing things. We can't do that if we're busy crying.'

His words hit her like a fireball to the stomach. But he was right. She could sit here crying and thinking about all of the horrible things that might be happening to her mum, but that wouldn't fix anything. *I have to be strong. I have to be a warrior,* Hailey reminded herself.

'You're right.' She sniffed, and wiped her black sleeve across her face. The best thing she could do for her mum, and everyone else in the world, was get to Hephaestus tomorrow and pick up whatever weapon he'd been working on. Then she would hunt the Olympians down, one by one, and free all of their prisoners. *I'll find you, Mum. I promise.* 'So everyone else who escaped is here too?'

Aaron nodded. 'Yeah. They're waiting by the Acheron River for us to give the all clear.'

'Is Zara with you? Did she find you?' *Please say yes, please say that she somehow managed to work out where you were and she's safe now.*

'That's the Iris, right, the first year?'

Hailey nodded. *Please say yes.*

He shook his head. 'Sorry. She wasn't one of the survivors, but her friend… Lacey, I think her name is, is with us.'

Be a warrior, Hailey repeated to herself. *Don't start freaking out again. She got out. She'll be okay. She's smart.* 'So how did you get here?' Hailey asked, distracting her mind from racing through all of the horrible things that might have happened to Zara.

Aaron glanced towards the entrance tunnel, twenty yards from them.

Hailey followed his gaze. Brennan stood in front of the tunnel, his hands in his pockets as he stared at the grass. Vibrant-coloured flowers with petals that sparkled like sapphires, rubies, and emeralds grew on the inside of the tunnel behind him, and spread out over the walls on either side of it.

'Brennan,' Aaron called him over.

Keeping his eyes lowered, he walked towards them. 'I didn't mean to interrupt,' he said, slowly raising his eyes to meet Hailey's. 'Are you okay?'

No, not really. But I have no choice but to act like I am. 'Yeah. How did you get here?'

'This is going to sound really weird, but I had a dream.' His eyebrows knitted together, as if trying to remember every detail perfectly. 'I dreamed that I travelled across the sea, passing over islands until I came to the mouth of a cave shaped like a skull. It was the entrance to the Underworld, and then I woke up and everyone was talking about how you were dead. That Zeus had killed you in Tartarus.' He rocked back on his heels, his hands still in his pockets. 'I thought it was crazy, but I said I had a dream about where the Underworld was, and then Demi demanded I take her there—here. I can't believe my dream was right.'

'Tamzin,' Hailey said with a smile.

Brennan frowned. 'What?'

'Tamzin is a Morpheus and an Apollo. She's a spy in the Mysteries. She sent you that dream so you would find me. And together, we can kill the gods.'

18

FINDING HEPHAESTUS

'Show us,' Demi said when Hailey had finished telling her, Alec, and Aaron about everything that had happened since she'd been taken from the island. 'I want to see.'

The four of them sat by the waterfall. Moss grew over the mountain of rock in front of them. The waterfall tumbled down it, the mountain's rocky ledges splitting it into a series of mini-waterfalls that spilled into the pool of water beneath with the soft rushing sound of falling rain.

Hailey aimed her palm at the water, its surface glittering like blue topaz in the imitation sunlight. Warmth rushed into her hand, her palm glowing bright white a second before a lightning bolt blasted from it. *Hiss.* An explosion of water shot into the air like a bomb had just detonated beneath the surface.

'Medusa!' Demi gasped, water spraying across her face.

'Abah.' Alec gaped, his jaw almost hitting the ground.

'Whoa.' Aaron stared at the water as it crackled and sparked. 'You just became the most powerful human in the world. It doesn't change anything,' he added, focusing his gaze on Hailey. 'You don't have to do anything with your new power. You don't have to fight the gods.'

'I want to.'

Aaron frowned. 'What do you mean? I thought we agreed that's the military's job.'

'Too many people have died. Kora gave her life so that I could live. I can't dishonour her memory by doing nothing, especially after I got this power.' Lightning sparked on her fingertips. 'I've spent my whole life running from that prophecy. Praying to the Tyches it wasn't talking about me, because I felt like a massive failure as a Zeus. But I'm glad it's me.' Anger burned in her like a Hecate's flaming potion. 'The Olympians are destroying our world. They've enslaved our friends and family—even killed them. They're not going to stop. But with this power, I have a chance to win against them now.'

'Hailey, I'm the first one to rush into a battle,' Aaron said, his voice serious, 'but I don't think the Tyches will be on our side this time. We don't know how your new power works—if it's strong enough to kill an Olympian. And even if it is, the Olympians could kill you before you get close enough to shoot them with lightning. Our best plan is to let General Killian handle things.'

'There's something they don't know.' Hailey glanced around. A few people sat on the cushions in the garden, others wandered down the diamond pathway towards the gold palace, but none of them were close enough to hear Hailey and her friends' conversation. She lowered her voice anyway, not wanting to risk anyone overhearing the secret she was about to reveal. 'Aphrodite came here looking for me,' she said, the rushing sound of the waterfall quieting her words to a whisper.

'Aphrodite?' Demi gasped. 'Did she want you back as her slave?'

'No. She said I had to find Hephaestus. That he secretly used the same magic the other Olympians did, and that he's at his workshop building a weapon to fight the gods with. He wants me—the Zeus—to go to him so he can give me something to help kill them.'

'Seriously?' Demi's eyes practically popped out of her head. 'Like a secret spy mission? That's so cool! I'm so in!'

'Did she say what type of weapon?' Alec asked, finally recovering from the shock of Hailey's new power. 'Something capable of draining the Olympians' powers? Something that stuns them? Something that—'

'She didn't say,' Hailey cut him off.

'How do we know this isn't a trap?' Aaron crossed his arms, looking more sceptical than anything else. 'A way for the Olympians to get rid of you once and for all?'

'Zeus thinks I'm dead, and if Aphrodite had wanted to kill me, she could have done it while she was here,' Hailey explained. 'Amathia says we can trust her—and Hephaestus.'

'I don't know, Hailey.' Aaron stared at the waterfall as it cascaded down, thoughtful, like he was running a series of scenarios through his head. 'Why would they turn on their own kind? It doesn't feel right to me.'

'Don't you remember that memory Amathia showed us in Ancient History class?' Demi said before Hailey could. 'Hephaestus went all crazy and was going to trap the Olympians in thrones, and Aphrodite sounded like she wanted to help, but she was scared. Which I totally get. Zeus is the craziest most terrifying person to ever live.'

'And Aphrodite was nice to me, before she knew I was a Zeus,' Hailey added. 'I think she's one of the good gods.'

'I don't know.' Aaron shook his head. 'There's too much that can go wrong. They're our enemy. We shouldn't trust them.'

'You don't have to come.' Hailey wasn't going to waste time trying to convince him when it didn't matter anyway. 'Only I need to go. I'm done hiding and waiting for other people to fight the gods. This has to end.'

Aaron blew out a long breath, dropping his arms to his sides.

'You're right... We can't hide in the shadows anymore. I'm still not convinced this isn't a trap, but better we risk our lives than someone essential, like General Killian.'

'Wait. What? Risking our lives?' Alec stammered. 'But Hailey said—'

'It's not a trap,' Hailey reassured him before his skin could pale anymore.

'We'll see,' Aaron muttered.

* * *

Hailey wrinkled her nose against the stale stench of body odour as she walked into the mine—a colossal circular pit with twenty tunnels carved into its walls. Pickaxes clanged against rock as fifty or so people wearing torn and dirtied tunics mined precious metals and jewels from the glittering walls. Carts brimming with rubies, emeralds, and other jewels squeaked as the miners pulled them away to polish the jewels. Five people dressed in black stood among the miners, watching them.

'Work faster than that. Put your backs into it.'

'Shut up, Riley,' Charlie muttered, slamming a pickaxe into the wall, sending a spray of dirt and rock over his face.

Riley grinned as he strode past him, tapping the gun hanging from a strap around his shoulder. 'Have to make it look real if the *actual* Mysteries or Olympians drop by.'

Hailey hated to see people working in the mine, but they'd all agreed that the only way to keep control of the Underworld was to make it look like it was business as usual, should an OM drop by, which meant taking turns pretending to be prisoners.

'Ready?' Brennan drew Hailey's attention back to him and her friends, standing beside her. He held his hands out to them.

'Good thing you're here,' Demi said. 'Otherwise, we'd have to face Fifth—and he is one angry monster dog thing.'

'Yeah, I remember,' Alec said with a shudder.

They joined hands, the cavern swirling into shades of blackness mixed with swirls of red, green, and blue. When the world reformed, Hailey was standing in front of the Acheron River, the smell of rotten eggs drenching the air. Amathia was already there, on the rotting dock, staring at the foul water.

'We don't have to jump into the river, do we?' Demi hugged her arms. 'I didn't like how it made me feel last time.'

'No, we won't be going in the river.' Amathia turned towards them, her blue dress sparkling. 'Brennan, as you brought the others here, could you take us out?'

Brennan nodded. 'Of course.' He held his hands out, everyone linking back together. One floating sensation later, and they were standing on an island the size of Aphrodite's dungeon. It was basically a pile of sand, with a couple of palm trees. The sea stretched out around them.

'Thank you, Brennan.' The sun rose behind Amathia, on the horizon, painting everything in an amber glow. 'I'll ask you to wait here for us.'

Brennan frowned. 'You don't want me to come with you?'

'The more who come, the more dangerous it is. Please wait here.'

His gaze met Hailey's, the uncertainty in it questioning whether that's what she wanted. The more friends she had going with her, the more safe she would feel, but his powers wouldn't work out there, at Hephaestus's workshop, so there was no point in putting his life in danger. She nodded, mouthing *it's okay*.

'All right,' Brennan agreed, uncertainty still lingering in his voice. 'I'll stay.'

'Now what?' Demi stared at the sea, the water as blue as topaz. 'Do we have to swim there? How far is it? I can't see anything but water.'

'Far,' Amathia said, a wave rolling over her feet. 'But I'll get us there quickly. Join hands.'

Hailey took hold of Amathia's outstretched hand, and clasped her other hand with Demi's. Her heart raced as she thought of all that could go wrong—*what if the oceanids catch us? Can I use my lightning in the water without electrocuting my friends?*

'Medusa, I am so excited,' Demi squealed, her feet sinking into the sand as she bounced on her toes. 'I've never travelled by nereid before.'

'Me neither,' Alec said. His skin was pale, but curiosity glistened in his eyes—the wonder of discovering something new. 'How fast will we go? How many miles per hour do you travel? How long will it take us to reach the volcano?'

'Stop asking boring questions,' Demi snapped. 'And Amathia did take you through the sea last year.'

'I was unconscious. It doesn't count,' Alec huffed.

'Enough,' Amathia interrupted, voice calm 'When I say jump, take a deep breath and jump, and whatever happens, don't let go of anyone's hand. Jump.'

Hailey sucked in a breath, filling her lungs until they felt like they would burst, and leapt towards the water. She expected to sink into it, but the moment she touched it, Amathia's hand tugged hers and Hailey torpedoed through the sea as fast as Hermes using his superspeed. The coral reefs blurred into rainbows as she shot past them. She squeezed Amathia's hand tighter, not wanting to find out what would happen if she let go —*abandoned in the sea to either drown or become dinner to a sea-monster?*

Just when Hailey thought she couldn't take another moment of shooting across the sea, her head popped above the water. She'd expected to be greeted by a giant wall that stretched into the sky, but instead found herself staring at open water. There was no mistaking the divide though. A strip of water as wide as a road stretched lengthwise in front of Hailey, its deep blue shade a clear contrast to the misty blue colour of the sea and ocean on either side of it. It was as if the Protogenoi—the primordial gods of creation—had taken a paintbrush dipped in royal blue varnish and swiped it through the middle of the sea and ocean to create a divide.

'I think I'm going to be sick,' Alec groaned, his face tinged green.

'If you vomit, I'll kill you,' Demi warned him.

'Shut up,' Aaron hissed as they floated in the water. 'We're near the ocean.'

'Oh, right, the oceanids,' Demi said, lowering her voice. 'I'll still kill you if you vomit, though, Alec,' she added.

'Now what?' Hailey asked. The sun was pushing through the sky, painting everything in its golden light.

'We move as quickly as we can,' Amathia said, 'and hope the oceanids are watching the sky and not the water.'

They slipped through the divide, which was as blue as the spilled ink from a pen, before joining hands again.

'What happens if the oceanids catch us?' Alec asked, his eyes darting around, searching for lurking nymphs.

'Nothing good,' Amathia said before everything blurred again.

Hailey's heart pounded in her ears. She couldn't see anything at this speed. *What if the oceanids are swimming after us? I wouldn't know. Will Amathia see them? Will she be able to escape from them while dragging the four of us along? Or will she have to tear her grip from ours to fight the oceanids and hope we don't drown?*

Please, Tyches, let us make it safely to the volcano, Hailey prayed. *Please don't let me have to find out if I can use my lightning in the water without electrocuting everyone.*

The ocean stilled, Amathia jolting to a stop. For one terrifying second, Hailey thought it was because the oceanids had found them, but then she saw it...

19

HEPHAESTUS'S WORKSHOP

A sunken island floated before her—a rainforest under the water. Amathia tugged Hailey's hand, and the five of them stepped onto the island's sandy ground, tingles prickling Hailey's skin as she passed through the force field that protected this place from flooding with water. Not a single drop of water clung to her—to any of them—thanks to Amathia's water-repelling nymph powers.

'Whoa,' Demi said, for once lost for words.

'This is… This is…' Alec's jaw dropped open, unable to finish his sentence.

Hailey couldn't even form words. A rainforest stretched before her, and in its centre sat a volcano—an actual volcano—with steam rising from its top, casting the greenery in mist. The ocean stretched over the island like a dome of water, a force field holding it back. *It's just like Poseidon's Academy—another world under the water, only this is an entire island.*

'Everyone be on alert,' Aaron warned, his hands already up, waiting to summon his force field at the first sign of danger. 'This could be a trap, remember.'

'Right,' Demi said, tearing her eyes from the volcano. 'Um, I don't see anyone. If it was a trap, we would have been ambushed already, right?'

'They could be watching us. Waiting.' Aaron's gaze scanned the rainforest, his eyes passing over palm trees, bamboo, ferns, and orchids.

'Maybe this was a bad idea,' Alec squeaked, standing behind Aaron for cover.

'I don't believe it's a trap,' Amathia said, voice calm, 'but you are wise, Aaron, to be on alert, just in case. Hephaestus,' Amathia called out.

Aaron whipped towards her. 'What are you doing?'

'We can only enter the volcano if Hephaestus brings us inside,' Amathia explained. 'Hephaestus,' she called again.

'If it is a trap, you're giving away our position.' Aaron's gaze combed the trees, his palms outstretched, ready for an attack.

A flame as tall as a palm tree shot up in front of them, its heat washing over Hailey like a blast of hot air. A man with dark hair to his shoulders stepped from it, an orange fireball in his hand.

Hailey's heart skipped a beat, her legs rooting to the ground. *Oh no, Aaron was right about it being a trap.* Lightning sparked on her fingertips as she stretched her arm out, ready to find out if her new power could kill an Olympian.

'Amathia!' Hephaestus gasped with relief. He crushed the fireball in his hand, smoke seeping out between his fingers. 'I am so glad to see you.'

Amathia smiled, her skin practically glowing. 'And I you.'

Hailey exhaled, her heart calming as she dropped her arm. *Not a trap. Just a cautious god.* Aaron kept his palms up, not yet ready to let his guard down.

Hephaestus's gold eyes moved to the four of them. He frowned. 'Why have you brought humans here?'

'This is Hailey.' Amathia nodded towards her. 'She's the

Zeus, and these are her friends… Demi, Alec, and Aaron. Aphrodite told us to come here.'

'The Zeus.' A smile as bright as the sun lit Hephaestus's face as his eyes locked with Hailey's, staring at her like she was a piece of treasure he'd spent his whole life searching for. 'Thank Tyche. Everything comes down to you.'

'No pressure,' Hailey muttered.

'Um, so you're really Hephaestus?' Demi asked, eyeing the god up and down. 'Like the god of fire and metalworking we learned about in school?'

'I don't know what you've been taught about me, but I am Hephaestus.'

'I… I…'

'Ignore him,' Demi said, cutting off Alec's attempts at speaking. 'He can't handle meeting celebrities.'

Hephaestus frowned. 'Celebrities? I am unfamiliar with that word.'

'It's not important,' Amathia cut in. 'Could you please take us to your workshop and show us what means you have created to defeat the Olympians.'

'Of course,' Hephaestus said, and lifted his hand.

'Wait!' Aaron yelled, his palms still up. 'How do we know you're not taking us somewhere we can't fight you—somewhere where our powers don't work? Or somewhere where you can easily kill us?'

'Seriously, Aaron?' Demi rolled her eyes. 'Stop with the trap stuff. He could kill us right now if he wanted to.'

Kindness lingered in Hephaestus's eyes—the same kindness Hailey had seen in Aphrodite's—as he met Aaron's gaze. 'I swear on the River Styx that I will protect you while you are here. I want nothing more than to protect the humans of this world and see my kin's tyranny ended.'

'We can trust Hephaestus, Aaron,' Amathia said. 'You have my word on that.'

Aaron kept his palms up, staring at Hephaestus as if trying to read his mind. 'Fine,' he gave in. 'Take us to your workshop. It's not like we have much of a choice.'

Hephaestus waved his hand. Flames shot up around Hailey, their heat tingling her skin. The warmth was nothing compared to what hit her when the flames disappeared. Air as hot as hydra's fire washed over her as she materialised in Hephaestus's workshop. Floating orbs of light, like the ones at Poseidon's Academy, lit the gloomy space, casting light over the metal strewn across the floor and on wooden tables. Shields, helmets, and weapons ran along the walls, all of them rusted and looking a few millennia old.

'Medusa, it must be a thousand degrees in here,' Demi gasped from beside Hailey.

'That is the price of having a secret workshop inside a volcano,' Hephaestus said, materialising in front of them with Amathia.

'It's not going to erupt, is it?' Alec asked, sweat beading his forehead.

'Not unless I want it to,' Hephaestus assured him.

'Aaron, you can put your hands down now,' Amathia said. 'As you can see, there's no one else here. This isn't a trap.'

Aaron's palms were in front of him, separating Hailey and her friends from Hephaestus and Amathia. He dropped them. 'It doesn't mean no one is coming,' he mumbled.

'So what's this weapon you have for us?' Demi asked. 'Is it this?' She grabbed something that looked like an oversized silver torch from the nearest table. 'Will it turn the Olympians into gold sparks?' She pointed it straight ahead; Alec scrambled from her path, metal chinking under his feet as Demi poised her finger in front of the button on the torch-looking thing's base.

'No, that's not it,' Hephaestus said as Aaron plucked the item from Demi's hand and placed it carefully back on the table, as if it were a grenade that might explode. 'I haven't actually created the weapon yet.'

'What?!' Demi exclaimed.

Hailey's mouth popped open, and she had to bite her tongue to keep from exclaiming her shock too. The whole point in them coming here was to pick up a weapon to kill the gods, and Hephaestus hadn't even started on it yet. *Maybe there really is no hope for us.*

'I can't create it without Zeus's lightning,' Hephaestus said, his eyes landing on Hailey. 'That's why I asked Aphrodite to find you and get you here. I need your powers to create the weapon.'

'My powers?' Hailey frowned. 'I can't give you my powers, can I?' If that was something she was capable of, she would have given them up years ago.

'I don't mean literally give them to me.' Hephaestus stepped back, revealing the forge behind him; flames danced inside it. 'Shoot your lightning into the fire.'

'Um, okay,' Hailey said, not sure what that would achieve— other than to burn a hole through the forge. She reached her arm towards it, sweat glistening on her skin as warmth flowed into her hand. She pushed it out like the sun pushes out rays of heat. *CRACK!* A blinding streak of lightning shot into the forge. The flames quadrupled in size, exploding outwards, like a bomb had just detonated, before shrinking back. Hailey blinked as she stared at the flames, thinking she must be imagining things, because the fire was no longer orange. White flames flickered, and in them sparked electricity like mini streaks of lightning. 'What the…?'

'Whoa, that's so cool.' Demi ran up to the forge, watching the fire flicker with the lightning.

'The flames absorbed her powers,' Alec said, running a hand through his sweaty hair, gobsmacked. 'How?'

'I used my powers to create fire capable of absorbing

powers,' Hephaestus said simply. 'And I may have had Hecate spell the forge before I brought it here.'

'Incredible,' Alec said, mouth still open.

'How long will it take you to create the weapon?' Aaron asked. 'We don't have much time—things are not going well out there.'

Hephaestus threw a fireball at the forge. Demi leapt back as the flames exploded, shooting embers over the metal floor. The fire burned even whiter, the lightning sparking even more. 'It will take at least a week—most likely longer. I am sorry.'

'That long?' Hailey's shoulders slumped, her stomach twisting tighter. *What will the world look like by then? Will the gods have destroyed everything?* Her mum was out there somewhere, a prisoner. *What if she doesn't have a week? What if the god who has her kills her before then?*

'It is not an easy task to create something powerful enough to subdue the King of the Gods,' Hephaestus said, blasting another fireball at the forge to keep it burning hot. 'There will be much trial and error.'

'We appreciate all you are doing for us, Hephaestus,' Amathia said, placing a hand on his broad shoulder. 'We will return when it is ready. How will you get word to us?'

'Aphrodite gave me these.' Metal clanged beneath Hephaestus's boots as he strode to a table, limping with his right leg, which was clearly still injured from when Zeus had thrown him from Olympus a millennium ago. He shoved aside scraps of metal and held up a handful of Hermes stamps. 'I can send you a letter. Where are you residing?'

'We—'

'Wait,' Aaron cut Amathia off. '*This* could be the trap. He could be using us to find out where the other rebels are.'

'Seriously, Aaron, you are way too paranoid.' Demi rolled her eyes. 'We're in the Elysian Fields.'

'Demi!' Aaron scolded her, sweat running down his muscled arms.

She shrugged. 'What? He's the only chance we have, Aaron. If he's lying about creating a weapon, then there's really no hope for us anyway.'

'I'm not lying,' Hephaestus said, hurling another fireball at the forge. Hailey could barely breathe it was getting so hot.

'I think perhaps it's best that we send you a letter to check on your progress,' Amathia said, holding out her hand for a stamp. 'While I hope that the Elysian Fields will remain our residence, these are fickle times. Anything could happen, and we cannot risk your letter being seen by the wrong person.'

Hephaestus nodded, beads of sweat slipping down the back of his neck. 'Yes, that is a wise plan. You can write me in a week, and tell me of where you are residing so that I can write back straight away as to whether or not I have completed the weapon.' He reached his hand to Amathia's, dropping a stamp into her palm. His fingers lingered for a moment. He cleared his throat, pulling his hand back. 'Um, I do have something I can give you now though.' He shoved aside more scraps of metal, sending them clanging to the floor. He turned back to them, a hunk of quartz crystal the size of Aaron's fist in his hand. 'This will show you anyone in the world you want to see. I stole it from Hecate while the other gods were fighting in the Great Battle. I thought it the best way to spy on my kin when we awakened, but I believe it will be of greater benefit to you.' He held it out to Hailey.

It was as heavy as a bag of drachmas as she rested it on her palm. 'Can it show me my mum?' she asked, staring at the crystal's rough edges.

He nodded. 'Yes. All you need do is speak her name and think of her.'

Hailey inhaled, imagining the vanilla-turpentine scent of her mother, picturing Evonee in her head, smiling and laughing as she spilled flour and drizzled egg goo all over the kitchen bench while making Hailey pancakes. 'Evonee Woods.' The rock shimmered like a rippling lake, and then her mum was there, her image reflected back at Hailey as though she were staring at a fortune teller's crystal ball. 'Mum.' Hailey touched the crystal, trailing a finger over its bumpy edges.

Evonee held a jug as she stood, statue still, behind a woman seated at the head of a table. The woman wore an elegant gold breastplate over her white dress, and a spear rested against her chair. *Athena!*

The goddess of wisdom and war waved a hand over her cup, and Evonee stepped forward, pouring gold liquid from the jug. 'She's okay.' Tears streamed down Hailey's cheeks as she watched her mum fill Athena's cup to the brim. 'She's okay,' she repeated. *It's not as good as her being free, but at least she's alive, and she's with Athena, which is a lot better than Ares.*

'I want to see my parents too,' Demi said, grabbing the crystal from Hailey.

'That's enough for now,' Amathia said, her voice scratchy and her lips dry. 'I know you are all eager to see your parents, but you can do so when we are back in Elysium. I can't bear this heat for much longer.'

'Fine,' Demi muttered.

'I'll take that.' Aaron snatched it from her hand. 'I have pockets—you don't. We can't risk you dropping it if the oceanids attack us,' he added before Demi could argue. 'So if we asked this rock to show us Zeus, it would?' Aaron asked Hephaestus, turning the crystal over in his hands, staring into its many faces.

'Yes.' Hephaestus nodded. 'But it won't tell you exactly where in the world he is. It will only show you him.'

Aaron's shoulders dropped a little, disappointment creasing his face as he slipped the crystal into the pocket of his cargo trousers. 'Better than nothing, I suppose.'

'So what else have you got for us?' Demi asked, peering around.

The flames crackled as Hephaestus tossed another fireball at the forge. *What is it, a thousand degrees in here now?* 'Nothing. That's it.'

'Seriously? You've been down here for how long and you've done what?'

'Demi, do not speak to him like that,' Amathia scolded, sounding a lot like Madam Grayson.

'Because he's an Olympian?'

'Hephaestus is risking everything to aid us.' Sweat poured down Amathia's face, her skin flushed. 'If the other gods knew he lived, they would kill him. He is betraying his entire race for us. Have some respect.'

'Sorry. But I really thought there'd be more weapons.'

'I'm not sure what the Hephaestuses of your world are capable of, but I cannot create powerful objects instantly. It takes time, especially when it comes to weaving magic into something—I am not Hecate, after all.'

'Okay, I get it.' Demi crossed her arms. 'It's hard work. I'm sorry.'

'So what happens if someone finds you before you finish making this weapon?' Aaron asked, his hair wet with sweat. 'Your underwater island is in the oceanids' territory. One of their patrols could find it, then what?'

'The oceanids don't travel out this far, that's why I picked here,' Hephaestus said, another fireball glowing in his hand. He tossed it at the forge, sending more heat rising in the already boiling room. 'And even if they did find it, they would have no reason to believe that I was inside the volcano building weapons. As far as the Olympians are concerned, I perished with the other gods. Finding the location of my workshop would be nothing more than a curious discovery for them,' he explained. 'And if their curiosity led them to explore the volcano, I could erupt it, giving me enough time to flee with the weapon.'

'Ooh, can I be here when you erupt the volcano?' Demi asked with eager eyes.

'I'm not planning on doing that. It is merely a failsafe.'

'We should let you return to work,' Amathia said, covered in so much sweat she looked like she'd just gone for a swim. 'Thank you again for all you are doing.'

'Yes, thank you,' Hailey said. She wasn't happy that she had to wait another week for the weapon, but Hephaestus was risking so much. Without him, Hailey wasn't sure what chance humans had of taking down the gods. And he'd given her a way to see her mum. She could keep an eye on her now and make sure she was okay until all of this was over.

'Can you wave your hand and send us back to the Elysian Fields?' Demi asked, wiping a hand across her sweaty forehead.

'No, I can't.' He threw another fireball at the forge. The air was so hot now that every breath burned Hailey's lungs—it was like being back under the lava sky that burns above Hades's palace in Tartarus.

'Why?' Amathia asked.

'I'm not powerful enough. Aphrodite snuck me ambrosia after we were awakened, but it was only enough to restore my powers. The risk of her returning with more was—is—too great. That is why it will take me longer to build the weapon.'

Demi scratched her wet hair. 'What does ambrosia have to do with anything?'

'It makes the gods more powerful, doesn't it?' Alec asked, his eyes on the metal floor, not daring to meet Hephaestus's gaze. 'Humans believed that eating ambrosia would give them powers, but it also strengthens powers, doesn't it?'

Hephaestus nodded. 'Yes.'

'How are...' Alec gulped, his eyes still on the floor. 'How are you able to keep from dying if no one is worshipping you?'

Hephaestus smirked. 'That would be Aphrodite. She has dedicated part of her territory to me and set up temples in my honour for humans to worship at. She told the other gods it was to honour the sacrifice I made so that they could live.' His smirk grew. 'They are all so self-important they are not the least bit suspicious.'

Wow, Aphrodite is one clever goddess. Thank the Tyches she's on our side.

'So what do we do now?' Aaron asked, his arms crossed, sweat glistening on his skin. 'The sun will have finished rising by now, which means the oceanids will be back on patrol. How are we meant to get past them?'

'With that item you thought was a gun that turns us Olympians into sparks,' Hephaestus said, his eyes shifting to Demi.

'So it *is* a gun.' She snatched the torch-looking thing from the table, knocking scraps of copper and silver to the ground in the process.

'It's a net gun,' Hephaestus explained. 'It will trap them long enough for you to escape.'

'I'll take that.' Aaron pulled it from Demi's grip before she could hit the button on its base and release a net.

'Hey. I got it first.'

'I'm the one who actually knows how to shoot a gun. This isn't a game, Demi. We could die if we make one mistake.'

Demi sighed. 'You're right, but when we get back to the Elysian Fields, I want to test it out—maybe have some fun with the Mysteries.'

'And how are we supposed to breathe if the oceanids attack us?' Alec asked, a slight shake to his voice. His eyes only lifted enough to look at Hephaestus's chest.

'I have something for that too.' Hephaestus moved towards the forge, throwing another fireball into the electrified flames, which were so white now they were practically invisible. A chest the size of a suitcase rested beside the forge, next to a giant pair of tongs. Hephaestus threw the lid open and started tossing out things that Hailey actually recognised—a conjuring plate, a phone, a travelling necklace, and then he pulled out a snorkel made of blue steel.

'That's a Poseidon snorkel,' Alec said. 'It filters oxygen from water.'

'Yes. Aphrodite brought me an assortment of items so that I could study the technology of this new world.'

'Um, small problem,' Demi said. 'There's one of those, and four of us. Are we supposed to share it if we get attacked?'

'I'll make more.' Metal chinked under Hephaestus's boots as he moved towards a table covered in an assortment of rocks— gold, silver, quartz, malachite, and dozens more. He picked up a hunk of steel from the table, clutching it in his fist as he squeezed the snorkel in his other hand. The rock melted like ice-cream, steel dripping from Hephaestus's closed hand before the silver liquid solidified. The steel stretched out into a pipe, the bottom of it curving up into a mouthpiece.

'Whoa, that's so cool!' Demi exclaimed, dashing forward to snatch the newly formed snorkel from Hephaestus. 'I forgot that some Hephaestuses can duplicate items,' she said, turning the snorkel over in her hand, examining every inch of it to make sure it was all there.

A twinge of pain shot through Hailey's heart at seeing Hephaestus use his powers, and she touched the necklace her dad had crafted for her. How she wished he was here. *He would have loved to meet Hephaestus, the god who had given him his powers.*

'Now you'll be able to breathe underwater if anything should happen,' Hephaestus said, handing them each a snorkel.

'Thank you again, Hephaestus,' Amathia said, her voice so dry it sounded as if her throat were full of sand. 'We are incredibly grateful.' Her eyes locked with Hephaestus's, their gazes lingering.

Demi nudged her elbow into Hailey's ribs and nodded to the two of them with a grin. Hailey grinned back. Apparently, Amathia and Hephaestus were more than just friends, or they wanted to be. *That must be why he gave her that necklace, the one that granted her immortality—the one Nemertes was now wearing.*

'Can I ask one thing,' Alec said, his eyes finally moving to meet Hephaestus's.

'What is that?'

'If you cared about humans, why did you make bows and arrows for Artemis and Apollo that never missed their targets?' His voice shook ever so slightly. 'They killed entire families with those weapons.'

Hephaestus smirked. 'Not everything is what it seems. I did craft those weapons to never miss their targets, but I also crafted them to knock out any human they touched, and to heal any wounds. I had to borrow a couple of powers for that one, but you have my word that the twins' weapons have never killed a human. I created them only to appear that way, at least long enough for the twins to be satisfied and vanish.'

'Oh,' Alec said. 'The history books never mentioned that.'

'I should hope not, or the twins would have tossed their bows and arrows aside for real ones.'

'That's enough questions for now,' Amathia said as Alec opened his mouth to ask something else. 'We must leave and allow Hephaestus to begin work on his weapon.'

'Send me a letter in a week and I will inform you of my progress.' Hephaestus waved his hand.

Flames shot up around Hailey and the others, and then they were back in the rainforest, standing beside the force field that held back the ocean. Cool air washed over her like a wave on a hot summer's day. She breathed in, the air cooling down her burning lungs.

'Is it safe for us to go back?' Aaron stared into the ocean, his finger resting on the net gun's button, ready to shoot if he spotted an oceanid. But there were only fish swimming about. 'Should we wait until tomorrow?'

'Swimming in the ocean is never safe,' Amathia replied. 'We cannot stay here though. Brennan is waiting for us, and we need to be in the Underworld in case something goes awry. Make sure you have that weapon at the ready, Aaron. Okay, snorkels in.'

Hailey closed her mouth over her snorkel's mouthpiece, the steel's metallic taste biting into her tongue. She took Amathia's hand, and grabbed Alec's trembling one with her other. She hadn't expected to go back through oceanid territory. She'd thought Hephaestus would give them a lift home. *What if the oceanids catch us?*

'Hold on tight.' Amathia tugged Hailey through the force field.

Tingles pricked her skin, and then she was zooming through the ocean, coral reefs and fish a blur of rainbow around her as Amathia rocketed through the water. Hailey didn't like not being able to see—not knowing if the oceanids were around. *The ocean is a big place; the chances of a patrol spotting us are minuscule*, she reassured herself, just as Amathia's hand ripped from hers.

20

OCEANID TERRITORY

There were three of them. Three oceanids wearing flowing dresses that shimmered like mother-of-pearl. Seashell crowns perched on their heads, and they each rode a sea-creature the size of a horse. The salt water stung Hailey's eyes as she squinted to see them. One was riding a sea-slug. Another sat on a turtle's back. And the third rode an electric eel.

The one on the sea-slug charged for Amathia. The two of them vanished into the ocean, becoming blurs too fast to follow as they zipped around the rainbow reefs.

Hailey swished her arms back and forth and kicked her legs in circles, treading water as she closed her lips as tightly as she could around the snorkel's mouthpiece. The Poseidon snorkel filtered the water, sending only oxygen down the tube for her to breathe in. She barely had time to even freak out about how they were going to survive this when the oceanid riding the turtle charged for her and her friends.

Aaron aimed the gun, and fired. A net shot from the gun's tip, wrapping around the oceanid like a blanket of strangulation seaweed. The turtle escaped out from under her, swimming away as the oceanid sunk towards the ocean floor. The third nymph was faster. Her electric eel shot forward before Aaron could re-aim the gun. The oceanid's hand swiped out, knocking it from his grip. She reached towards him, an evil grin on her face like the one Nemertes wore every time she tried to kill Hailey.

Seaweed wrapped around her wrists like snakes before she could lay a finger on him. Demi's hands were out, growing the seaweed from the ocean bed below to wrap around the nymph like rope, holding her in place as she shrieked and thrashed about.

The eel shot out from under her before any of the seaweed could touch it. Unlike the turtle, it wasn't fleeing. It charged straight for Hailey, who was a little way back from the others. Its body wrapped around her before she even had a chance to realise she was being attacked. It squeezed around her like a python, pinning her arms so she couldn't use her powers. And then its whole body lit up. Hailey tensed, waiting for the eel's electricity to shoot through her, but instead of pain, her skin hummed and tingled, absorbing the electricity like a sponge absorbing water. It thrummed in her body, building and building until she couldn't take it anymore.

'AHHHH!' she cried, the electricity exploding from her in forks of lightning. The eel's squeezing body fell limp, and it slipped off her, falling to the bottom of the ocean to join the oceanid trapped in the net.

'Hailey,' Demi called, the snorkel and water muffling her voice as she, Alec, and Aaron swam up to her.

'You okay?' Aaron's muffled voice asked as he pointed to her and then gave a thumbs up.

She nodded, her body tired and aching, like every ounce of energy had fled her in that explosion of electricity. She needed a nap. A really, really *long* nap. She glanced around for Amathia. Without her, they'd never make it back to the island Brennan was waiting on, or even back into the sea, for that matter. 'We need to find Ama—' A hand grabbed her arm. Her head swung around as her arms shot up, ready to shoot her lightning. She sighed. 'Amathia.' The third oceanid was nowhere in sight. *Thank the Tyches.*

The five of them linked back up, Amathia wasting no time in rocketing back through the ocean.

'What in Tartarus was that?' Demi asked as they re-surfaced at the divide. 'I didn't know you could do that, Hailey. It was like you exploded.'

'I didn't know I could do it either.' Hailey tossed her Poseidon snorkel in the water, the tube of steel sinking beneath the surface as some of her energy returned. 'It was like my body absorbed the eel's electricity and then shot it at it.'

'Wow,' Alec gasped, taking out his snorkel. 'Your body is like a conductor. That means—'

'Enough talking, we need to get back before the oceanids find us,' Aaron snapped.

'I must say, as fascinating as this new discovery about your powers is, I agree with Aaron that we must leave,' Amathia said, stretching her hand out to Hailey again.

Hailey took it, and the five of them crossed through the inky blue water barrier before speeding through the sea.

* * *

'Hailey, wake up. Hailey.'

Hailey's eyes flew open, and she shot to her feet, warmth burning her fingertips as electricity crackled.

'No, it's okay. Don't use your powers,' Demi quickly said.

Hailey's heart slowed, and the warmth in her fingertips dissolved. She stared at the cushions on the grass, and then up at the pomegranate tree blooming sweet-smelling fruit above her. *That's right, I came here for a nap after we got back, while the* others filled Brennan in on what happened with Hephaestus. 'What's going on? What time is it?'

'It's only been a few hours since you passed out,' Demi said. 'But something amazing has happened.' She was grinning from ear to ear.

The military launched another attack against the Olympians and won, and now we don't have to do anything. 'What?'

'You have to see. It'll be so much better that way. Brennan can take us.'

Hailey hadn't even noticed him standing a yard back from Demi. He smiled at her, his cheeks flushing as their eyes met. 'Oh, hi, Brennan.' She turned her gaze back to Demi, who was bouncing on her toes. 'Are our parents back? Has someone killed a god?' They were the only amazing things she could think of that would make Demi so excited.

Demi's smile faltered. 'No. Nothing that big. Come on, you have to see. You'll love it.' She grabbed Hailey's hand and tugged her towards Brennan.

The bright greens, pinks, and purples of Elysium swirled around her before she even had a chance to ask where they were going. Flaming torches flickered on the rock walls as Hailey materialised in a hallway of cells. *Why are we in the dungeon?* All of the cells around her were empty, but Amathia, Aaron, and Alec were standing outside of one, along with a teenage girl and boy Hailey didn't recognise.

'What's going on?' Hailey asked as she walked towards them.

'See for yourself,' Amathia said, stepping aside to reveal who was inside the cell.

Hailey's jaw dropped. 'Venus!' Glaring at her from behind the bars was the very person who had sent Hailey to Tartarus. The same person who had told Zeus who she was— she'd basically signed Hailey's execution.

'You!' Venus hissed. 'You're supposed to be dead. Zeus killed you.'

'He tried,' Hailey said, marching up to the bars as fury as hot as a Hecate's bubbling cauldron boiled in her. 'Kora is dead because of you.'

Venus shrugged, admiring her pink nails. 'I don't even know who that is.'

Lightning sparked on Hailey's fingertips, and she lunged for the bars, stretching out her hands to strangle Venus. Someone grabbed her arm before she could, and she whipped around to Aaron, glaring at him.

'Don't let her provoke you.'

He's right. She's trying to make me angry. Deep breath. Just breathe. Hailey inhaled and exhaled, the anger burning in her easing enough that she could turn back to Venus's grinning face and not shoot her full of lightning.

'She's worth more to us alive,' Aaron added. 'We were just interrogating her.'

'Trying to,' Venus scoffed. 'But it won't work. I'm loyal to the Olympian Mysteries, and the Olympians.' Her chest puffed up. 'I'm basically the goddess of love and beauty—the same as Aphrodite. She'll probably send Ares to rescue me, and he'll kill all of you.'

'As if Ares cares about a human,' Aaron snapped back at her. 'You're nothing to the Olympians.'

'How is she here?' Hailey asked before Venus could open her mouth to hiss a retort.

'Us.'

Hailey turned her attention to the two people she didn't recognise, standing to her left. They looked at least eighteen. The girl looked like a full-on warrior, with a sword sheathed on her back, throwing stars hanging from a belt, and a dagger strapped to each leg. 'I'm Nova, and this is Mute.' She pointed to the guy beside her. His face was indifferent; he didn't even bother smiling, just stared with a stoic silence. 'I call him that because he doesn't talk,' Nova added.

'You are the coolest people ever,' Demi said from Hailey's right. 'I wish I'd been there when you tackled Venus.'

'And I hope I'll be there when Ares runs his sword through you.' Venus grinned.

'No one knows where she is. And no one cares. Her threats are empty.' Nova focussed her attention on Amathia. 'We brought her here as an offering to let you know we come in peace.'

Aaron narrowed his eyes, his posture arrow-straight, ready to jump into battle mode. 'How did you know where to find us? Why did you think we'd want Venus? How do you know who she is?'

Hailey gulped. In her excitement at seeing Venus behind bars, she'd never stopped to question how these two strangers had found them in Tartarus. *Is this a trap? Are they in the Mysteries? Are the Mysteries already here, in the mine, battling everyone?* Warmth rushed into her hands.

'At the risk of sounding crazy, I had a dream.'

Hailey clenched her fists, holding her lightning at bay. 'Go on.'

'I was in New York when the gods returned.' Nova's voice shook.

'Ugh, I do not want to be bored by your life story,' Venus sniped, retreating to the corner of her cell and leaning against the stone wall.

'I was with my family,' Nova continued, ignoring Venus. 'We were...' She gulped, tears glistening in her blue eyes. 'I saw the lightning coming straight for us—it was like the sky was full of electricity. And then I was somewhere else.' She smiled at Mute, who didn't even blink. 'Mute grabbed me before the lightning hit—thank the Tyches that the random stranger standing right behind me on the street was a dematerialiser. We were living in the ruins—had ourselves a nice abandoned house that was only missing a few walls.' She fidgeted with her left armguard, which ran from her knuckles up to her elbow. 'Anyway, I had a dream last night, and this chick showed up in it and told me to come to Aphrodite's palace—told me where it was and everything. Mute materialised right outside, and I took out the two guards.' She trailed her fingers over the ruby hilt of the dagger strapped to her right leg. 'And then the Morpheus chick from my dream came out of the doors with this one.' She pointed at Venus, who was admiring her pink nails in the light from the burning torch above her. 'She told us how to get here, and that if we brought you this Aphrodite, you'd let us stay.'

'All those loyal to the human race are welcome here.' Amathia smiled.

The warmth in Hailey's hands dissipated like steam rising into the air. *It was Tamzin. She sent them. They're not with the Mysteries. Thank the Tyches.*

'You've totally earned yourself a bed in the gold palace,' Demi said. 'Anyone who managed to lock Venus in a cage deserves nothing less.'

'I'm happy to interrogate her,' Aaron volunteered, his posture straightening even more as he turned to Amathia, tucking his hands behind his back. 'My dad trained me in interrogating enemies.'

'That won't be necessary,' Amathia said. 'Venus is merely a human. The Olympians would never trust her with any information of worth.'

'That's not true.' Venus's gaze snapped up from her nails. 'They trust me.'

'Leave her.' Amathia turned her back on the cell. 'Perhaps time in Tartarus will do her well to think on her transgressions.'

'You're on the losing side, Amathia. I don't care who I sacrifice, as long as I survive,' Venus hissed as Hailey and the others joined hands with Brennan. 'I'll kill you for locking me up here!'

* * *

Hailey was lying on her back in the garden, staring up at the violet-blue sky. Red, yellow, pink, and purple tulips bloomed around her, and fallen pomegranates lay near her head. They were so close. So close to this all being over. Once Hephaestus had made the weapon for her, she'd kill every last god—minus Aphrodite and Hephaestus, of course. *Maybe I won't even be the one who has to kill them. Maybe the prophecy only mentioned a Zeus because Hephaestus needed their powers to make a god-killing weapon.* Maybe she could hand it over to General Killian and sit back while the military did their job. *That would definitely be the better option—not having to go up against the Olympians. But if only I can use the weapon, I'll take them on. I'll destroy them for everything they've done—for everything they've taken from me... my home, Lexa, Kora, my mum. And Venus had a hand in all of that too.*

Venus, an Olympian Mystery? She'd always loved tormenting people, but joining a psycho cult and helping them bring back the gods was next level. She was the one who'd released a gorgon in the Academy, and the one who'd helped the nereids try and freeze Hailey and the other students to death. And she'd sent Zeus to the Underworld to kill her. *Maybe I should have let the wand kill her back in first year,* Hailey thought, remembering how Hecate's wand had tried to coerce her into shooting a death spell at Venus. If Venus had died, then she never would have joined the Mysteries, the nereids never would have recruited her, and maybe none of this would have happened. *But then there's Cady. Cady is ultimately the one who released the gods. Why? What did Nemertes say to her to convince her to do something so stupid?*

'Hailey, why don't you come into the gold palace?' Demi asked, dropping down on a cushion beside her.

Hailey shuffled into a sitting position, leaning her back against the trunk of a pomegranate tree so she could face Demi. 'I don't want to. Not when people are dying out there.'

'You don't have to punish yourself for something you can't help.'

Maybe I could have helped… maybe I could have done more to save more people. 'Did you see your parents?' Hailey asked, nodding to the crystal in Demi's hand.

'Yeah.' Demi trailed her fingers over it. 'They're serving Artemis. They seem okay, for now.'

'That's good,' Hailey said. 'What about everyone else's parents, are they okay?'

Demi nodded. 'Alec's parents are locked up in a room somewhere. Aaron's dad is still in the Academy's dungeon, and his mum is actually living there, too, as a servant to Poseidon—I guess because she's a siren. At least they're together, kind of.'

'Hopefully Poseidon and the nereids don't figure out she's his wife,' Hailey said, having no doubt that they'd use that as another means to torture Jake.

'I want to ask the crystal to show me Jayden.' Demi's fingers trailed over the crystal's rough edges. 'But I'm scared.'

Hailey frowned. 'Why?'

Demi swallowed. 'You heard what Aphrodite said. Cady woke them up. Jayden is with her. Which means he's our enemy. What if he's torturing someone for information? Or killing people? I don't want to see that.'

Hailey reached a hand out to touch Demi's. 'It's Jayden. He would never hurt anyone.'

'Then why did he do it?' Tears glistened in Demi's eyes, turning them a brighter shade of green. 'Why did he betray us?'

Hailey hadn't really thought about it. She'd only been focused on Cady's betrayal, but the two of them were together, which meant Jayden had at least known about what she'd done —that she'd woken up the Olympians. And he'd chosen to run off with her, so he was on the Olympian's side. *That makes no sense. Jayden wouldn't even let Demi take a jewel from the Academy's grounds, as if he'd suddenly join the Olympians and help them enslave humankind.* 'Maybe he's pretending,' Hailey offered. 'Maybe he's a spy—maybe he's trying to figure out a way to stop the

Olympians by pretending to be on their side.' It was the only explanation that made sense to her.

'Let's find out,' Demi said, fixing her eyes on the crystal. 'Show—'

'Demi.'

Demi's head snapped behind her. Aaron was marching towards her with Alec, the two of them following the diamond pathway from the Elysian Field's entrance tunnel. 'We need that crystal to see what the gods are doing. It's not a toy. It's a tactical advantage.'

'First I want to see Jayden.'

Aaron opened his mouth to say something and then closed it. 'Okay. He's probably with the Olympian Mysteries, so we could learn something by looking at him too.'

'Show me Jayden Daniels.'

The four of them crowded around the crystal, peering at its many faces as it rippled and then revealed their former best friend.

He was standing in a bedroom that looked ostentatious enough to belong to a prince. Cady was with him. Tears streamed down her face as he waved his hands at her, his face red. Hailey had never seen Jayden angry, let alone furious. But that's what he was. Cady grabbed his arm. Even though there was no sound, she could clearly make out Cady shouting the word 'Please' as she tried to pull him towards her. He ripped his arm away, shaking his head before storming off.

'That didn't look good,' Alec stated the obvious.

'Wish this stupid thing had sound.' Demi shook the crystal. The image of Jayden walking down a hallway vanished, and the crystal's transparent surfaces glittered back at them.

'It doesn't look like he's on their side after all,' Hailey said, assuming that might have been what the fight was about— convincing Cady this was wrong or something, and her disagreeing.

'Maybe, or maybe they were arguing about something unrelated,' Aaron countered. 'At least we know he's safe. Time to see what the gods are up to.' Aaron grabbed the crystal from Demi, resting it in his palm. 'Show me Zeus, King of the Gods.'

The crystal rippled again. Hailey's heart raced as Zeus's bearded face appeared. And then the crystal was falling, dropping to the soft grass as ten people wearing ski masks burst through the Elysian Field's entrance tunnel, guns raised.

INTRUDERS

'The Olympian Mysteries!' Demi exclaimed. She, Hailey, Alec, and Aaron bolted to their feet.

'Hands behind your head,' one of the intruders shouted as he and the other nine closed the distance between them and Hailey and her friends.

Hailey stretched out her arms, electricity crackling on her fingertips as Aaron raised his palms, shielding them with his force field.

'Wait.' The man at the front of the team stopped, a few yards short of Aaron's barely visible force field. 'Lower your weapons,' he instructed the others.

'Olympian Mysteries!' someone shouted, running down the diamond pathway towards the gold palace. 'Olympian Mysteries! Olympian Mysteries!'

'Barrows, go and stop him bef—'

Too late. Before the OM could get the rest of his order out, a dozen people charged from the gold palace. Some wielded swords. Others held fireballs. But most were empty handed as they sprinted towards the intruders, waiting to get close enough to use their powers.

They didn't get within twenty yards before an OM hit a yellow button on their submachine gun. Yellow light blasted towards the people charging from the palace, ploughing into them like a force field. They collapsed in an instant, weapons clattering, and fireballs hissing to smoke.

'I know those guns.' Demi grinned, stepping closer to the intruders.

Aaron dropped his hands. 'Dad?'

The people in black pulled off their ski masks. Hailey grinned along with Demi, expecting to see Jake and the rest of PET. But they weren't there. She only recognised one person—General Killian. She let her arms fall to her sides, her electricity fizzling out as she breathed a sigh of relief. *The Mysteries haven't found us.*

'He's still MIA,' General Killian said.

Aaron's hands tucked behind his back, his posture straightening and his feet snapping together. 'Sir, I apologise. I didn't realise it was you.'

'Help the others secure the perimeter and call in the rest of the team,' General Killian ordered the soldiers behind him. There was a mumble of 'yes, sir's, and then they dispatched, marching back through the entrance tunnel. General Killian stepped towards Hailey and her friends, a few fallen cherries getting crushed under his boots. 'One of my undercover operatives sent me a dream of the Underworld on fire, and through the flames I saw a cave shaped like a skull. I took it to mean that the Underworld was no longer ruled by Hades and the Erinyes, so I put together a team to come and investigate.' His eyes snapped to Hailey; creases stretched across his forehead. 'Zeus said he killed you.'

A stab of pain shot through Hailey's chest. 'An Asclepius saved me.'

'She can shoot lightning now,' Demi blurted out. 'Did you come here to take her with you when you fight the gods?'

'Lightning you say?' the general mused, curiosity sparkling in his eyes. 'Can I see?'

The old Hailey would have refused. Would have said she wanted no part in this battle. But the new Hailey, the one who craved vengeance, threw her arm towards the Elysian Field's entrance. Rocks and singed flowers spewed over the grass as lightning blasted a hole into the wall beside the tunnel.

'Incredible.' The general rubbed his chin, staring towards the smoking hole twenty yards away. 'You are the first Zeus in history to ever possess that power.' He turned back to Hailey. 'Perhaps the prophecy does have some truth to it.'

'I'm happy to help in any way I can.' It was an offer Hailey never thought she would ever make, not when it involved facing the gods. 'Hephaestus is creating a weapon right now that can kill the gods.'

'Hephaestus?'

'I'll explain everything to you, sir,' Aaron said, the unconscious people on the diamond pathway and grass starting to twitch, before diving into everything that had happened since they'd last seen the general on the island.

'Well, you have been up to a lot since we last crossed paths,' General Killian said when Aaron was finished. 'This place will make a great base.' He nodded as he stared around, his gaze drifting towards the gold palace. 'As long as we can keep fooling everyone and letting them think the Olympian Mysteries are still in charge down here.'

'Is that why you came?' Aaron asked. 'You were looking for a new base?'

'No, not exactly. We're ready to attack.'

'You don't want us to help you, do you?' Alec was as pale as a full moon.

'Only if you want to,' General Killian said. Moaning sounded as those stunned on the ground began to rouse, their bodies jerking. 'Our spies in the Mysteries informed me that every day the gods are building more temples. With each one they build, they grow more powerful. If we have any chance of stopping them, we need to destroy their temples, or as many of them as we can.'

'Look, I'm all in for any plan that involves kicking the gods' arses,' Demi said, 'but won't they feel us destroy their temples, and then come and kill us?'

'Yes.' General Killian nodded. 'From everything we know of the Great Battle, the gods are connected to their temples. If we burn one, they will feel it. That is why we need to burn as many temples at once as we can so the Olympians don't have enough time to attack.' He swallowed, the scar slashed across his neck stark in the bright sunlight. 'And that is why I came here. For my plan to succeed, I need more people than I currently have. I've come to ask for volunteers.'

'We totally volunteer.' Demi clapped her hands together. 'I would love the chance to burn down some temples.'

'I don't know.' Alec gulped. 'It sounds really dangerous.'

'Where are your parents?' General Killian gazed around, as if expecting to find them hiding behind one of the fruit trees. 'I would prefer adults, and I'm sure they wouldn't want you anywhere near a fight.'

'The Mysteries took them.' Anger swelled in Hailey. 'They're prisoners now.' *And I'll do anything it takes to destroy the gods—I'll burn every one of their temples myself if I have to.*

'We'll help you, sir,' Aaron said, posture still straight. 'We'll do whatever it takes to kill the gods.'

* * *

'Does everyone know their mission?' General Killian asked.

They were still in the Elysian Fields, standing by the garden. The people the military had knocked out with their guns were awake now, and more people had joined them from the gold palace, as well as Tartarus. Everyone willing to help was divided into twelve teams of five, with each team having at least one military person. Riley, Charlie, and Amber were with one team. Brennan and Tahlia were in another team—the one standing right beside Hailey's. Tahlia was one of the people who'd originally escaped the Mysteries during the island ambush. She'd come to the Underworld with Demi, Alec, and Aaron, and all of the other survivors. Hailey's stomach twisted with guilt, and pain stabbed at her chest as she briefly met Tahlia's gaze. Aaron had told her about Kora. About how she'd saved Hailey. Hailey had fully expected her to never speak to her again—she was the reason, after all, why her best friend was dead. But she'd found Hailey straight afterwards and told her it wasn't her fault. That she would have done the same thing if she'd been in Kora's position. That Hailey had nothing to feel guilty about. *Nothing to feel guilty about? I wish that were true.*

'Um, do I get a gun?' Demi asked, standing directly in front of General Killian. 'I feel like we should all have guns.'

'These are military-grade weapons,' the general told her, tapping the submachine gun strapped around his shoulder. 'No, you may not have one. You'll have to rely on your powers.'

'Well that sucks,' Demi huffed, crossing her arms.

'As I was saying, each team has a dematerialiser. If you come under attack, the dematerialiser will bring your team straight back here. We don't want any casualties.'

'Won't the temples be guarded?' Tahlia asked, standing beside Alec, who was as white as a Thanatos's victim. 'The last time we went near one of their temples, there were Mysteries.' Her voice quaked.

Hailey bit back tears. *Stay strong. What happened to Lexa won't happen again. The military are on our side this time. We have a plan.*

'Our spies in the Mysteries have taken care of that for us. All the temples we are striking will be unguarded,' General Killian said, the Elysian Field's ethereal music drifting through the air, soft as a whisper. 'If there are no more questions, prepare to disembark.'

The military person assigned to Hailey's group held out his hands.

'You don't have to go if you don't want to,' Aaron said, noticing Alec's trembling.

Alec took a deep breath, and then another. 'No. I want to. I want to help. I want to fight.'

'Then let's go burn some temples to ash,' Demi said.

The Elysian Fields swirled from existence as Hailey linked up with Demi, Alec, Aaron, and the military guy. When the world reformed, she was standing on a beach. A temple the size of her common room at Poseidon's Academy loomed before her, decorated with jewels, shells, and pearls, just like Poseidon's palace, only here the walls were stone instead of crystal.

Hailey inhaled the salty sea air, the steady cadence of waves rolling onto the shore calming her nerves just a little. *Breathe in. Breathe out. You're safe.*

'Everyone stay behind my force field,' Aaron said, his palms out in front of him as his head swivelled from side to side, searching for any threats.

'What happened to them?' Alec asked, nodding towards the two Mysteries slumped on either side of the archway into the temple.

'Our spies did their job,' Military Guy said, the multi-coloured buttons on his gun glowing like the jewels on the temple's walls. 'They were instructed to use a sleeping potion on all the Mysteries guarding the temples. Stay here. I'll check inside.' He raised his gun and stepped around Aaron's force field, slipping through the temple's archway. 'All clear,' he said a heartbeat later.

Hailey blew out a breath she hadn't realised she'd been holding. *It's okay. This isn't like the time Lexa died.* The four of them walked inside. The giant space was bare—except for a marble statue of Poseidon holding a trident.

'Wow,' Demi said, strolling up to the statue. Polished jewels and jewellery glittered in baskets, and candles burned at Poseidon's marble feet. 'Since we're burning this place down, might as well save the jewels.' Demi scooped up a handful of sapphires, slipping them into the pocket of her black cargo trousers.

'There's no time for that,' Military Guy snapped. 'We have to strike each temple as quickly as possible before the Olympians come. Everyone outside.'

Demi shoved one final handful of jewels into her pocket before shuffling outside with Hailey and the others.

Military Guy dragged the two soldiers a few yards from the temple, before pulling a vial off his utility belt. Blue liquid swirled through with red gleamed inside the glass. He threw it through the temple's archway. *Crack.* The glass shattered, and before Hailey could even blink, flames shot up, sending a wave of heat rushing over her skin.

'Cool!' Demi exclaimed, the flames reflecting in her green eyes. 'Can I blow up the next temple?'

'This isn't a game,' Military Guy said. Smoke wafted around the five of them. He held out his hands. 'Let's go.'

The next temple they appeared outside of looked exactly the same as the one before, with its stone walls glittering with jewels. The only real difference to this new beach was that the sun was setting, painting the sky and sea blood orange.

'Wait here,' Military Guy ordered. 'We wasted time at the last temple when you followed me in.' He disappeared inside for a few heartbeats before coming back out. 'All clear.' He pulled another vial from his belt, tossing it through the archway. *Crack.* Flames shot up.

'What are you checking for?' Demi asked, the heat from the fire beading her forehead with sweat.

'Our mission is to destroy the temples, not kill the Mysteries —I'm checking for any unconscious bodies inside. Now join up.'

Hailey reached for Military Guy's hand. 'AH!' she screamed, snatching her hand back. A tentacle as thick as a tree trunk curled around Military Guy's waist. And then he was gone. Dragged up into the air. Hailey whipped around, her legs wavering when she saw what was in the sea. A monster stood three storeys high on a serpent tail. Tentacles hung from its body like gangly arms, thrashing just above the water. It's face, round and smooth, was basically a giant mouth, crammed with rows of razor-sharp teeth.

Hailey had seen this monster before, in one of Amathia's memories. It had destroyed an entire city. *A kraken!*

'NO!' Demi screamed, the kraken throwing Military Guy into its mouth.

The kraken roared so loud the earth quaked.

Aaron's hands shot up as one of the monster's tentacles lunged for them. He was a second too slow. The tentacle wrapped around Demi's waist, the monster yanking her. *BANG.* She slammed against Aaron's force field. The tentacle slammed her against the force field again and again, like a child trying to make a square peg fit through a round hole.

'Let her go!' Alec shouted. He clawed at the tentacle, grey slime oozing between his fingers, and yanked, ripping the tentacle clean off.

Black blood spilled over the sand like ink squirted from a squid. The kraken roared, the smell of its rotting-flesh breath washing over Hailey.

Demi gulped in air, black blood dripping from her hair and down her face. 'Thank – you.'

BANG! Two tentacles slammed against Aaron's force field, sending ripples shooting across it.

Aaron grunted, his hands dropping half an inch. 'We need to get out of here.'

'Would help if – we knew – where we were,' Demi puffed out.

The monster's tentacles slammed against the force field a second time.

'We'll have to run,' Aaron said, face red and voice strained. The tentacles slammed against his force field again and again. 'When my force field breaks, just run.'

'No.' The word came out before Hailey even realised she was saying it. 'We won't make it.' Aaron's hands shook—he'd be too exhausted to even try and run—and Demi looked about ready to pass out; judging by the way she was holding her ribs and gasping in air, Hailey was guessing she had a few broken ribs, maybe even a punctured lung. 'I can kill it.'

'With your lightning?' Demi grimaced, clutching her side.

Bang. Bang.

'It's a monster, Hailey,' Alec said. 'It would take—'

'I can do it. There's no other way.' She and Alec might have a chance of escaping, but there was no way in Tartarus she was leaving Demi and Aaron behind to die.

Aaron dropped to his knees, blood dripping from his nose. His palms stayed out, his hands shaking more and more with every passing second.

Please, Tyches, give me the strength to do this. Hailey stretched her palms towards the orange sea. Sparks crackled on her fingertips. 'Drop it, Aaron.'

His hands fell.

Time slowed down. The kraken's tentacles launched towards them; at the same time, Hailey poured all of her anger into her hands, like her anger was volts of electricity feeding into her powers… Her mother was a prisoner. Kora was dead. Lexa was dead. Zeus had tried to kill her. The Olympians were taking over the world. They were destroying everything. Killing every-one. She screamed, letting her anger free with her lightning as two lightning bolts shot towards the kraken. The bolts blasted straight through its head like laser beams; the monster's entire body sparked and smoked, even the water bubbled. And then it dropped. Just like that. It fell into the sea—a giant black puddle oozing out like spilt oil as its dead body floated on the surface.

'Hailey, you did it!' Demi shouted.

Hailey's arms turned as heavy as lead weights. Her energy fled from her like a wave retreating back into the sea. The world spun into a haze of orange, and then she was falling backwards, her eyelids sliding closed.

22

—————

TRAITOR

Hailey blinked her eyes open, staring up at a gold ceiling. 'Where am I?' she mumbled, sitting up.

'You're awake.' Demi sat on a chair beside her. Her hair was wet, and her clothes fresh—not a single drop of black blood on them. 'You're in the gold palace.'

Hailey frowned, pushing herself into a sitting position. A fire crackled in the fireplace across from the four-poster bed she was in. A chest of drawers sat against one wall, with glass perfume bottles that looked centuries old scattered across the top of it. 'How did I get here?'

'Well, you passed out after you killed that huge monster— that was incredible, by the way.' Demi pushed a strand of wet hair from her face. 'Alec said it was because you overused your powers, or something, and drained all your energy. We thought we were totally stranded and that Poseidon would send another monster to kill us, but then Brennan showed up and saved our arses.'

'Why did Brennan show up?' She glanced around the empty room. 'Where is everyone else? Are they okay?' Lexa lying dead on the ground with a hole in her chest flashed into her mind. Her parents crying. Screaming. *Please no. Not again.*

Demi gulped, her eyes dropping a little. 'Everyone got ambushed, Hailey. Each team managed to destroy the first temple, but the Olympian Mysteries attacked them at the second one—or, if people were really lucky, like us, a monster came for them instead.' Her words were empty, tired, all of her usual humour gone.

Hailey jumped out of bed. 'I need to see Tahlia and the others.' Tears burned her throat, already assuming the worst—that she had more names to add to the list of friends she'd lost.

Demi hopped up, putting her hands on Hailey's shoulders to keep her from running from the room. 'It's okay, Hailey. Tahlia is fine,' Demi said quickly. 'It was the soldiers that died,' she added. 'Most of them sacrificed themselves so everyone else could get away.'

'General Killian?'

'He's alive. That's where Alec and Aaron are. Come on.'

Hailey followed after Demi, walking down a gold hallway filled with doors. *It's Lexa all over again. This time was meant to be different—this time was meant to be safe. We did the right thing—we followed General Killian's orders instead of running off into danger on our own. But still, people died. How many?* Her stomach twisted as she followed Demi down a staircase. *Are my friends battling for their lives right now? Are there enough Asclepiuses to heal everyone?* Hailey gulped. *I can't lose anyone else. I can't.*

They reached the entryway, Demi leading her through a set of double doors. The scene hit her like a fireball to the face. Judging by the vastness of the room, and the lights that glittered beneath the ceiling like stars, this place was once a ballroom. Now, it was a hospital. People lay on the ground, blood pooling on the gold ornate tiles as those uninjured flitted from person to person, pressing bandages to wounds, and tucking pillows under heads.

'Riley!' He was lying right near the open doors, three gashes running across his bare chest. Hailey dropped to his side. 'Are you okay?'

His skin was as pale as the sand on Poseidon's Island. 'Yeah, I'll be fine when it's my turn to be healed.'

'What happened?'

'Artemis sent a sphinx after us.' His words were quiet, barely above a mumble. 'It got in a lucky hit before our dematerialiser got us outta there.'

'Where are the Asclepiuses?' Hailey glanced around. Three people lay slumped against the right wall. Gashes covered their faces, arms, legs—blood soaked through their clothes. They looked just about ready to bleed out, but as Hailey watched, their skin knitted back together, their wounds healing closed. *It'll be a while before they're in any shape to heal anyone else.*

'Here, drink this.' A guy who looked like he was in his twenties kneeled beside Riley, holding a vial out to him. 'It's a healing potion I brewed—or more like a "keep you alive long enough to be properly healed" potion.'

Riley downed the vial of amber liquid the boy handed him. 'Thanks,' he mumbled, before his eyelids fluttered closed.

'I added a sedative to it,' the Hecate said to Hailey. 'You can't feel pain if you're asleep.' He shrugged and ambled off to help the next person.

'Come on, Hailey. We need to join the others,' Demi said.

She squeezed Riley's hand, his fingers ice cold. 'You're going to be okay.' She swiped at a rogue tear and pushed to her feet, taking in the room of injured people. *How did this happen? It was supposed to be simple: destroy the temples and leave at the first sign of danger... It's done. Asking why isn't going to change anything. Focus. Find General Killian.*

'They're over here.'

Hailey followed Demi to the far-right corner, weaving around the people lying on the floor. She stepped over pools of blood, which slowly receded like puddles of water drying up under the sun as the palace's self-cleaning magic kicked in.

Alec and Aaron sat beside General Killian. A pillow was tucked under his head, and his gun rested by his right arm. Blood soaked through his torn shirt—*looks like the same wound as Riley's. They must have been on the same team.*

'I'm glad you're okay, Hailey,' Aaron said as she and Demi sat down opposite him and Alec.

'How did this happen?' she asked, focusing on General Killian lying in front of her.

'We were ambushed.' The general pressed a hand to his bleeding chest. 'I thought if we attacked fast, they'd never catch us—that by the time the Olympians felt one temple being burned, we'd already be at the next one. But not a single team made it to the third temple.' Blood oozed from between his fingers.

'I'm going to see if one of the Asclepiuses is ready for more healing.' Alec gulped, his skin tingeing green as he stared at the blood seeping from the general's chest. 'That doesn't look good.'

'Do you think they knew about the plan, sir?' Aaron asked as Alec darted away.

'It's possible.' General Killian grimaced, pressing his hand tighter to the wound. 'We have spies in the Olympian Mysteries, so the Olympian Mysteries could have spies within the military.'

'Or they turned one of your spies, sir,' Aaron added.

'So what do we do?' Demi asked. 'How do we find out who it is? I doubt anyone will admit it if we just ask them.'

'We interrogate everyone,' Aaron said, face fierce, like he was ready to start bashing people's heads together until he found the spy. 'If there's a traitor here, I'll find them. You can trust me, sir.'

'No.' General Killian's voice was growing weaker by the second. 'We have no proof there's a spy, and if there is, it wouldn't be anyone here. Otherwise, they would have told the Mysteries where we were hiding. They'd have attacked by now and put an end to the rebellion once and for all.' He swallowed, a trickle of blood leaking from the corner of his mouth. 'I'll need to cut off communication with my operatives.'

'What does that mean?' Hailey asked.

'It means we're currently dead in the water.' More blood trickled from the corner of the general's mouth. 'We can't plan anything, not when we have no one on the inside feeding us information. We'll have to wait until Hephaestus finishes that weapon for you, and then come up with a plan from there.'

'You didn't tell anyone about him, did you?' Hailey's heartrate doubled in speed. *If the spy knew about Hephaestus, then the Olympians would find him and kill him.*

General Killian shook his head. 'I didn't tell anyone. Make sure you don't either. He's our last hope at ending all of this.'

* * *

'You have to see this,' Tahlia said, running into the ballroom.

Everyone had been healed now, and most people had left to go back to their rooms, but a few—like Hailey and her friends—had stayed, being too exhausted to drag their bodies up the stairs. It had been a long two hours of sitting with the injured, tending to their wounds, and basically keeping them alive long enough for the overworked Asclepiuses to heal them.

They sat in the middle of the room, their legs splayed out in front of them as their brains tried to process everything that had happened that day.

Tahlia ran up to them with her phone, a screen showing the news hovered above it. 'Zeus just came on.' She dropped to the floor, holding her phone out so they could all watch.

Hailey stared at the video, her body tensing. She clutched a hand to her chest, cringing as she remembered the burning agony of his lightning blasting through her. The sting of her nails digging into her skin focussed her mind, keeping her grounded in the moment. *You're okay. You're okay. You're okay.*

'What is this?' Demi asked.

Zeus was standing in the same room he had been the last time he'd appeared on the news—the one with the black background and a long table. This time he wasn't alone. Behind him, just in front of the table, four people knelt with pillowcases over their heads.

'I don't know, but it doesn't look good.' Tahlia gulped.

'By now everyone should be watching this,' Zeus finally said. 'Many of you have succumb to us, accepting my kin and me as the rightful rulers of this world. But there are still those of you who continue to fight. To try and destroy us. My patience is wearing thin. These four are the most recent humans to defy us.' He flicked his hand behind him; the pillowcases flew off the four prisoners' heads, as though an invisible person had yanked them off.

Hailey's gaze flicked over the people unfortunate enough to be kneeling behind Zeus. The first was an old man—maybe eighty, the next was a woman who looked about her mum's age, another woman knelt beside her, and then there was… *No! It can't be!* Hailey blinked, waiting for the fourth prisoner's face to change, because the person she was currently seeing couldn't be there. Her friend couldn't be seconds away from execution.

'Jayden!' Demi exclaimed, reaching a hand towards the image floating above Tahlia's phone, her fingers stretching towards him and passing right through the screen. 'No.' She drew her hand back, shaking her head. 'Not him.'

He was at the very end, on the left. His eyes wild and shooting around, trying to work out where he was, or maybe how to escape.

'I… I…' Alec stumbled, and then gulped.

'These four humans betrayed us,' Zeus continued. 'I hereby sentence them to death.'

'NO!' Demi screamed. 'NO! We have to save him.' Her gaze shot to Hailey, Alec, and Aaron, tears welling in her eyes. 'We need to go now! We need to get a dematerialiser. Where's Brennan?'

Aaron was pale—Hailey had never seen him pale before, not even when they'd been imprisoned in Tartarus and tortured. 'We don't know where Jayden is.' The words were quiet, reluctant.

'No!' Tears streamed down Demi's face. 'We can't let him die. Brennan!' she shouted.

Hailey hugged her arms around Demi, squeezing her best friend as she shook and cried. Doing nothing to save Jayden went against everything in her. *What choice do we have? We have no idea where he is, and even if we did, Zeus would kill us the second we appeared.*

'Who is that?' Tahlia pointed to the screen.

Hailey let go of Demi to look back at the video. Zeus now stood at the side, next to the old man, facing the line of prisoners. A woman stood beside him. Pure white hair draped down her back, falling to her waist. Her skin was as pale as someone who had never seen the sun. Hailey's first thought was that she was a lamia —a vampiric creature who fed on the blood of humans. But then she reached a hand towards the prisoner kneeling closest to Zeus.

'No. Please don't do this,' the old man begged. She brushed her fingers across his cheek, her fingertips barely touching his skin. He gasped, his eyes bulging as he pressed a hand to his chest, his nails clawing at his skin. He gasped again and again, the colour draining from his face with every feeble attempt to breathe. And then he collapsed, his face hitting the floor.

'A Thanatos!' Alec gasped.

Nausea twisted Hailey's stomach into knots as the woman moved to the next person.

'We can't let him die!' Hair clung to Demi's tear-streaked

face. 'We need to go. Where's Brennan? I need to find him.' She sprinted off. 'Brennan!' she screamed, hurtling through the ballroom's doors. 'Brennan!'

Hailey wanted to go after her. To hold her and tell her everything would be okay. But she couldn't move. She was rooted to the spot, her eyes locked on the screen as she watched the second victim collapse, and then the third. And then it was Jayden's turn.

He didn't beg like the others had. He raised his head high, not making eye contact with the Thanatos as she stretched out her long fingers, running them down Jayden's cheek. He gasped like the others had, his skin growing paler, like a lamia was draining the life from him. And then he hit the ground.

The nausea in Hailey's stomach swelled, stretching into her throat. She ran off to the corner, vomiting. Her best friend since preschool was dead. Killed. Just like that.

'Let this be a warning of what will happen to anyone who betrays us,' Hailey heard Zeus's voice say, right before Hailey collapsed to her knees, her body shaking as sob after sob ripped through her.

Jayden is dead. Dead! Never coming back. Yes, he'd run off with Cady. Abandoned them. Betrayed them. But he was still her friend. Still the person she'd grown up with. Still the person who'd protected her from other kids when they'd bullied her about her powers. He was the one who'd always reassured her. Told her not to worry. And now he was gone.

An arm wrapped around her shaking shoulders. Aaron didn't say anything, just hugged her to his side, holding her as a monsoon of tears ran down her face.

* * *

'It's going to be okay, Demi,' Hailey said, running a hand down her best friend's back as she cried into a pillow on the four-poster bed Hailey had been sleeping on only three hours ago.

'He's gone, Hailey. It's never going to be okay,' she said, voice muffled by the pillow. She turned her head to look at Hailey. Pieces of hair stuck to her wet face. 'I never got to say goodbye. He just disappeared, and then we saw him with Cady. Now I'll never get to talk to him and ask him why he did it. Why he helped her.'

'I—'

The bedroom door burst open. 'Hailey! Demi! You have to help me.' Nova staggered into the room, her hand pressed to her ribs, blood oozing from between her fingers and dripping onto the floor. Mute stood behind her, his face impassive.

'Medusa! What happened?' Hailey leapt up from the bed. 'Are the Mysteries here?' Warmth shot into her hands as her heartbeat tripled in speed, expecting a dozen OMs to rush in behind Nova.

'No. The Mysteries aren't here.' Nova grimaced, pressing her hand tighter to her bleeding side. 'Aaron came to me. He told me what happened to your friend Jayden. He wanted to get revenge, so he asked if I'd help him burn some more of the gods' temples.'

The knots in Hailey's stomach twisted tighter. *No. Please don't tell me he was that stupid. Not after what happened today.*

'He didn't want to get you involved, because you were both so upset,' Nova continued. 'I felt like getting some revenge, too, after the ambush, so I agreed. We figured the Mysteries would be celebrating their first attack on us, so they wouldn't expect a second one.' Mute stood perfectly still while Nova spoke, his face giving away nothing. 'We hit Zeus's temple. But the OMs showed up.' Nova gritted her teeth, blood continuing to drip to the gold floor. 'Mute got me out. But Aaron is still there. We need to help him—with your powers, Hailey, you'll be strong enough to fight off anyone.'

'We need to tell General Killian,' Hailey said, rushing for the door. That's who Nova should have gone to first, not her.

'I'll get Alec.' Demi's voice was raw as she stood up, but panic underlined her words.

'No.' Nova stepped in front of the door, blocking their path. 'We went out there without the general's permission. He's not going to risk more lives by sending out his team to find one person. He'll leave Aaron out there to die. We have to go. Before it's too late.'

Aaron, you idiot. Why did you do something so stupid? This all felt a lot like first year, when Kendra had run off to Killer Island and Hailey had gone after her instead of telling a teacher. And that had led to so much awful stuff. But there really was no time to get help. Aaron could be battling ten OMs right now, fighting for his life. If it were her or Demi in his position, he wouldn't hesitate. He'd charge in to save them, no matter the danger.

'Okay, let's go.' *Please, Tyches, protect us.* She held her hand out to Nova and Demi.

The room swirled around her like a gold tornado the second Nova touched Mute's hand. When it reformed, she was standing in a grassy field, with bushes spread about, and trees looming in the distance. Warmth burned her hands as she raised them, ready to test out her new power on the Mysteries. But the place was deserted. There was no temple, not even the smouldering ashes of one.

'Is this the right place?' Hailey asked, dropping her hands as she turned to Nova.

Nova's eyes swept across the grassy field. 'Yeah. The potion we used to destroy the temple was designed to leave no traces.' Her hand was still pressed to her side, blood dripping on the green grass. 'Have a look over there—behind those bushes.'

Nova jerked her head towards a cluster of bushes as tall as Hailey.

Hailey moved towards them, electricity sparking between her fingers. No one would take her by surprise. Not again. If Aaron was dead as well, she'd… *Stop. Aaron is alive. He's smart. He knows how to survive.* 'Aaron?' She stretched her hands towards the bushes, their branches scratching her skin as she pulled them apart. Nothing. She turned back to look at Nova. 'There's no one he—' Her words fell away when she saw Demi standing a yard from her, staring with wide eyes. 'Demi, what's wrong?'

Demi clawed at her back, trying to reach for something Hailey couldn't see, and then she turned around. A throwing star gleamed between her shoulder blades, two of its points stabbing into Demi's back. She turned back to face Hailey, dropping to her knees, her arms falling to her sides, giving up on trying to reach the star.

Instinct, and a tingling in her fingertips, kept Hailey from running towards her best friend. *A throwing star is stuck in Demi's back. A throwing star exactly like the ones clipped around Nova's waist.* Her eyes snapped to Nova standing a few feet behind Demi. Hailey couldn't get to her best friend, not without Nova attacking her too. 'You did this?'

Nova shrugged. 'Orders. Don't take it personally—actually, do. The whole reason the Mysteries asked me to kill her was to make you weaker.'

Demi was still on her knees, looking more shocked than anything. *She's safe for now. That tiny throwing star won't have done much damage. Just keep talking to Nova. Find out what the Tartarus is going on. Then get rid of her so you can help Demi.* 'What? What are you talking about?'

'Oh, I'm a spy.' A grin stretched across Nova's face. 'We both are.' She jerked her head towards Mute, who hadn't moved a single step. His face was as impassive as ever. 'The Mysteries sent me to gain your trust. To learn who you cared about the most, and to take them away from you.' Blood coated her hand as she dropped it from her side. Her top wasn't even torn. *The blood's fake.* 'You see, Zeus knows you're still alive. He decided it would be more fun to break you rather than kill you again. At least for now. I'm sure he'll get bored of this game and come for you when he's ready.'

What in Tartarus is happening?... Nova's a spy? Hailey had trusted her. Everyone had—even General Killian. *Nova was there when he revealed his plan about destroying the temples. She's the traitor. The one who sold them out to the gods and Mysteries. She's the reason every team got ambushed. She's the reason people died. And she just tried to kill my best friend. And she's just standing there, smiling, like this is all some sick twisted game to her.* Rage as pure and hot as a chimera's fiery breath consumed her.

'I'm going to kill you!' Hailey screamed, throwing her arm at Nova. She pushed her rage into her hand, her palm burning; lightning shot out, sparking towards Nova.

Nova dove from its path, somersaulting and landing back on her feet with the gracefulness of a gymnast. She grinned at Hailey. 'Missed me, little Zeus.'

Hailey threw her arm out again, another blast of lightning shooting for Nova. She dodged it with the ease of someone dodging a charging sloth. 'I'd love to stay and keep playing this game with you, little Zeus, but I made a promise to someone. Kill you later.' She ran towards Mute, stretching her arm out.

Hailey aimed her hand again, lightning blasting from her palm and shooting straight for Nova's back. She disappeared before it touched her, her and Mute vanishing in the blink of an eye.

'Hailey,' Demi mumbled.

'I'm here. I'm right here.' Hailey rushed to her, dropping to her knees beside her. 'I'm just going to pull out the star.' Demi grunted, her fingernails digging into the grass as Hailey pulled the star out. 'Okay, it's done,' Hailey said, tossing the star away.

Blood speckled the back of Demi's top, but not enough for Hailey to be worried about her bleeding to death. *It looks like Nova failed her mission. Thank the Tyches.*

'I just felt this pain in my back,' Demi said, shivering. 'I can't believe Nova was a spy. She must have been the one who told the Mysteries about our attack on the temples.'

'Yeah, it was definitely her. She—Medusa!' Dread spilled through Hailey like ice water as she realised something. Something she should have realised the second Nova revealed she was a traitor. 'If the Mysteries sent Nova to the Underworld as a spy, that means they know we're in charge down there, not them. They're probably attacking right now.' She could see it... the Mysteries materialising in, throwing fireballs, slashing swords—killing everyone. 'We need to get back there.' She launched to her feet, ready to sprint in any direction and start praying she crossed paths with a dematerialiser.

'Um, my legs aren't working.'

'Let me help you.' Hailey gripped a hand around Demi's wrist and tugged to pull her up, but Demi's knees stayed rooted to the grass.

'I can't feel my legs.' Demi's voice shook. 'Why can't I feel my legs?'

Hailey gulped, her stomach twisting tighter and tighter. 'It just looked like a cut—nothing deep enough to do any damage. I'll check again.' She dropped back to her knees behind Demi. Through the small tear in Demi's shirt, Hailey could see two cuts. Blood trickled from them, but not enough that Demi should be feeling anything other than pain... unless she was missing something. 'I'm just going to tear your shirt a little.' Hailey gripped the torn fabric and ripped. She choked down a scream when she saw it. The wounds were nothing—just two shallow cuts. But around them, Demi's veins were dark blue. The streaks of dark blue stretched over her shoulders and under her arms. She'd seen something like this before, when an arachne had bitten Aaron. She leapt up. 'I need to get help.' Her voice shook as she stared around the deserted field. There was nothing in the distance—no buildings, no houses. Only trees.

'What's wrong?'

Hailey gulped. 'It was poisoned—the star.'

'Oh.' Demi eased herself down to lie on the grass, her body quivering. 'I guess that's why I feel like a Thanatos's victim.'

'I'm going to find an Asclepius to heal you—or some of that green mush Pandora used on Aaron when the arachne bit him.' There had to be someone around somewhere. She'd go running into an Olympian Mystery base camp if she had to. 'I'll be back with help.'

'No.' Demi's hand latched around Hailey's ankle, her grip so weak Hailey could have easily pulled free. 'Don't leave me.'

'You'll die if I don't find an Asclepius.'

'It's too late.' Blood coated Demi's tongue as she spoke, spilling out of the corners of her mouth. 'There's no one around here—Nova would have made sure of that.' Demi's grip tightened ever so slightly on Hailey's ankle as she stared up at her. 'I don't want to die alone, Hailey.'

Hailey looked around again, searching for anyone—for any sign of life out there besides them. But there was nothing. *I'm such an idiot for not seeing this was a trap when we first materialised here. Is there even such a thing as a potion that destroys the ashes of what it burns? Even if there is, I should have realised that the gods would never build a temple in the middle of nowhere. What point's a temple if there's no one around to come and worship at it?*

'Please stay with me.' Demi's hand squeezed a fraction tighter, her fingernails turning blue. 'Please don't leave me. Please. Please, Hailey. Stay.'

If Hailey did leave to find help, her only real plan would be to pick a direction and run in it, praying to the Tyches she got lucky enough to find someone who could heal Demi. And in that time, her friend would be here, alone and scared. And staring at Demi now, seeing the blood trickling from her mouth and the shallow breaths rattling her chest, told Hailey that her friend wouldn't live long enough for her to find help. *I can't leave her. Not like this. Not when she's begging me to stay. Be strong, Hailey. You have to be strong for Demi.*

She swallowed down the tidal wave of tears waiting to gush forth, her throat burning. *Be strong.* 'Okay, I'll stay.' She dropped back on the ground, shifting Demi's head to rest in her lap. 'Someone will probably rescue us soon anyway. Aaron or Alec will notice we're missing and work out where we are—they're probably getting a Hecate to cast a locator spell right now.' *More likely they're battling the Olympian Mysteries, fighting for their lives. Please, Tyches, protect them. Please let Tamzin have sent someone a dream and told them about the impeding ambush.* Praying was the only thing Hailey could do for them. She couldn't get to the Underworld. And right now, she needed to focus on Demi. She had to trust her friends to save themselves. 'We'll be fine. Someone will be here soon.'

Demi's hand was as cold as a Chione's powers as it gripped Hailey's. 'You don't have to lie to me. I know I'm going to die.' Blood trickled over her bottom lip. 'Promise me you'll find my parents, and you'll look after Annabelle.'

Rogue tears ran down Hailey's cheeks, a lump lodging in her throat. 'I promise.'

'Please remember that you're stronger than you think.' Demi's voice was weak, her breaths growing shallower and shallower. 'You're an awesome Zeus, no matter what anyone says.'

'Please don't leave me,' Hailey begged her, squeezing her hand tighter, as if that would stop Demi from passing over to the afterlife. 'I need you. Please, Demi. I can't do this without you.'

'Yes, you can.' Demi's eyelids fluttered. 'You're going to kick the Olympians' arses. You're going to save the world.' Her voice was barely a whisper.

'I need you.' Hailey squeezed her hand tighter and tighter. 'Please stay with me. Please.'

'Sorry.' Her head rolled to the side, blood spilling onto Hailey's trousers as Demi's hand turned slack.

'No! Demi! Don't leave me!' Hailey screamed, shaking her. 'Don't leave me! Asclepius! I need an Asclepius! Help! Help! Please!'

23

EMPTY

The ground was hard beneath Hailey as she lay on the grass beside Demi. She stared at the sky, watching the clouds float past. Pain pounded in her head, and her throat was so dry it felt like she'd swallowed a mouthful of sand. But she barely noticed any of that. Empty, that was how she felt. Like something had been ripped from her when Demi had died.

Hailey had no idea how long she'd been lying there—long enough to cry a century's worth of tears, at least that's what it felt like. She kept waiting for Zeus to show up, or someone from the Mysteries. She almost wanted them to. She didn't want to live in a world where her best friend was dead. *It should have been me. Nova killed Demi to get to me. And she did it because that's what Zeus wanted. This is his doing. He wants to destroy me. Well, you succeeded. My mum is gone, you killed Jayden, and now Demi, and possibly Alec and Aaron... I can't stand it.*

Grief pressed against her like the weight of the sea, pinning her to the grass. She couldn't move. She didn't think she'd ever move again. All she could do was lie there and stare at the sky.

'Medusa! Demi! Hailey! What happened?'

Hailey tried to open her mouth, to say something. Anything.

But it was like her jaw had been glued shut.

Aaron appeared above her. He shook her. 'Hailey, what happened?'

Her eyes stayed on the sky. She couldn't even smile with relief to see that he was still alive. *Is this how a gorgon's victim feels? Watching the world around them but not being able to move, to do anything? A prisoner in their own body?*

'Is she okay?' Alec appeared above her, too, his voice hesitant, like he was afraid of the answer.

'She's in shock,' a voice Hailey didn't' recognise said. 'We need to get back. Now.'

'But Demi. She's...' Alec's words choked off.

'We need to get back,' the voice repeated. 'Link up.'

A hand touched her arm. She didn't even flinch. The sky swirled into a mess of blue and white as tingles rushed through her body. And then she was looking at a ceiling that had light streaming down from it like sunshine. She blinked, the new surroundings helping to free her from her body's imprisonment. 'Where am I?' Her voice was rough, like sandpaper.

'An underground bunker,' the unfamiliar voice said.

Hailey winced as she sat up, the pounding in her head intensifying. To her left stretched a long table surrounded by twenty chairs. *I know this place. This is where General Killian took us after the military surrendered to the gods.*

The unfamiliar voice belonged to a woman. Pins that looked as sharp as knives stuck from her black bun, and scars marred her arms. She was one of General Killian's people. Hailey stared at her like her life depended on it. She didn't want to look at Demi beside her. She didn't want to see the tears in Alec's and Aaron's eyes as they felt for a pulse and shook her.

'What happened in the Underworld?'

'There was an attack,' the woman said.

'Where is everyone else?' Hailey staggered to her feet, pressing a hand to her head to still her headache. 'Where's Brennan? Tahlia? Riley?' She stepped towards the closed door beside her. She couldn't lose anyone else. If she did, she was certain she would shatter into a million pieces.

The woman blocked her path, holding her palms up to calm Hailey down. 'It's okay. Your friends are here. I'm Colonel Jia Liu.'

'I want to see them.'

'Not right now, Hailey,' Aaron said from behind her, his voice hollow. 'Trust me when I say they are some of the few people still safe. We need to know what happened to you. What happened to Demi.'

Hailey gulped, finally turning around to look at her best friend. Alec was next to her, tears streaming down his face as he held Demi's limp hand. Dried blood stained the corners of her mouth, and her dark skin looked almost grey. *No. Demi can't be dead. It's not possible. I have to bring her back. There's still a chance.* She turned back to the woman, ready to bowl her over if she didn't let Hailey past her. 'We have to heal her. We need an Asclepius.'

'It's too late,' Jia said.

'Get an Asclepius!' Hailey screamed. 'Now!' Electricity sparked on her fingertips.

Jia nodded. 'Okay.' Her voice was soft, soothing. 'I'll get one. You just sit here with your friend.'

Hailey turned back to Demi, dropping to her knees beside her. 'It's going to be okay. I'm going to bring you back.'

'No! Don't!' Aaron shouted.

Something blasted into Hailey's back, slamming into her like Aaron's force field. Darkness consumed her. And then white light washed it all away. She closed her eyes against the brightness. The smell of salt rushed up her nostrils, and the steady cadence of waves rolling onto a shore filled her ears. She opened her eyes to a sunny sky, waves washing over her bare feet as she stared out at a glistening blue sea. *What in Tartarus…?*

Footsteps sloshed against the wet sand behind her. 'I thought you might like this setting.'

Hailey's head snapped to the person now at her side. 'Tamzin!' She looked so different, wearing shorts and a tank top instead of the black clothes the OMs wore. 'I barely recognise you in that outfit.'

Tamzin grinned, her braided crown of blonde hair looking golden in the sunlight. 'Yeah, well, black was never really my colour. Plus, I'm not exactly in the Mysteries anymore.'

The water was cold on Hailey's feet as wave after wave rolled onto the shore. 'What do you mean?'

Tamzin stared out at the sea, her eyes on the horizon. 'Nefertari worked out I was a spy—she's the leader of the Olympian Mysteries.'

'Medusa. Are you okay? Are you in a dungeon right now?'

She shook her head, her blonde hair sparkling in the sunlight. 'I had a premonition right before they came for me.' She swallowed, finally turning her gaze to Hailey. 'I'm so sorry they used me to trick you into letting them stay in the Underworld. I had no idea… not until it was too late.'

Tricked? Too late? What's Tamzin talking about? And then it all came back. Pain stabbed through her heart. Demi was dead. Because of Nova… Nova who they'd let walk right into the Underworld and run free all because she'd told them that Tamzin had come to her in a dream and told her where to go. *Idiot. You should have known she was lying from the start. Tamzin has always sent you cryptic dreams, but Nova said Tamzin actually appeared to her and told her where to go, and I didn't even question it. And now Demi's dead, and more people would have died when the Mysteries attacked the Underworld.*

'I can see what you're doing,' Tamzin said. 'Beating yourself up isn't going to change anything. Learn from your mistakes.'

'But—'

Her gaze shot back to the sea; the sun was starting to dip in the sky, falling towards the horizon. 'Time's almost up. I just came here to say that I'm sorry I couldn't stay.' She glanced back at Hailey, the sun dropping lower and lower, painting the sky a deep orange. 'Now that Nefertari knows I'm a spy, she'll be tracking me. It's too dangerous for me to be at the bunker. But I dropped you off a present.' She reached out, squeezing Hailey's wrist. 'Don't lose hope yet.'

The sun disappeared below the horizon, darkness stretching across the sea and reaching for Hailey. 'Tam—' She blinked her eyes open. She was lying on the bottom bunk of a bunk bed. 'What happened?' she asked, sitting up.

'Good. You're awake.' Another bunk bed rested against the opposite wall. Aaron stood up from the bottom bunk. 'Colonel Liu stunned you.'

Hailey frowned, throwing her legs over the side of the bed. 'Why?'

Dark circles coloured the skin under Aaron's eyes, making him look like he hadn't slept in days. 'She was scared you couldn't control your powers, at least while you were so emotional.'

'Emotional?' Grief slammed into her like a charging minotaur. 'Demi! Where's Demi?' Hailey leapt up.

'Wait.' Aaron held his hands up to stop her from running for the door. 'You need to tell me what happened first. We need to know how Demi… We need to know what happened. You only have to tell me. I can tell everyone else.'

Hailey didn't want to remember. She didn't want to relive Nova's betrayal. To relive Demi… The knife stabbing into her heart twisted. But Aaron deserved to know the truth. Demi was his friend too. And she had to know what happened in the Underworld. How he managed to escape. If everyone made it out alive… 'Okay, I'll tell you.' She dropped back onto the bed. 'But I want to know what happened in the Underworld.'

Aaron plunked down beside her, his hand resting next to hers on the bed's grey blanket. 'Deal.'

'Nova came into Demi's room,' Hailey began. 'She said you were angry after Zeus killed…' She swallowed around the lump in her throat. 'She told us you asked her to go with you to burn one of Zeus's temples.'

Aaron's fingers pressed into the blanket, his nails scrunching up the fabric. 'She used me to trick you?'

Hailey nodded. 'She said the Olympian Mysteries attacked. She got away, but you didn't. She told us we needed to go back for you.' Her voice shook, and pain squeezed her heart like a cyclops's crushing fist. 'When we got there—wherever there was —Nova hit Demi in the back with a throwing star.' The lump in her throat expanded to the size of an apricot. 'I thought she'd be okay—it was only a cut. But it was poisoned.' Tears clouded her vision. 'I wanted to get help, but she didn't want me to leave her. I'm sorry. It's my fault she died.'

'No, it's not.' Aaron wrapped an arm around her shoulders. 'Nova tricked you. She tricked all of us. I can't believe she used me to hurt you.' Anger lined his words.

'She was my best friend.' Hailey squeezed her heart pendant, the metal cold. 'I can't let her be dead.' *This world is filled with magic. I can bring her back—I'll do whatever it takes… battle a dragon, swim through a river of fire, trade my life for hers. Anything.* 'We need to find a gorgon and get its blood.' *That's how Amathia brought Demi back after Stetho killed her. Why didn't I think of it before? Why wasn't I out there searching for a gorgon after Demi died instead of lying on the grass feeling sorry for myself?*

'That won't work,' Aaron admitted slowly as Hailey jumped up from the bed. 'She's been dead for too long.'

'Fine, then a Hecate strong enough to mix a necromancy potion.'

'Necromancy doesn't bring back the dead. It only resurrects them for a short period.'

'Well then we can keep using the potion on her until we find something more permanent.'

Aaron pushed to his feet with a sigh. 'It wouldn't be her, Hailey.' His eyes were red. 'It would be something dark. Demi wouldn't want that.' He put a hand on Hailey's shoulder. 'We need to let her rest in peace.'

Hailey shrugged his hand off. 'Why are you so willing to let her go? She was your friend, don't you care about her?'

He flinched like she'd hit him. 'Of course I care. I—' He combed a hand through his unruly hair. 'I just know I can't change what's happened, and if I stop to let myself think about the fact Demi is gone, then I don't think I'll be able to come back from that.' The circles under his eyes seemed to darken even more. 'We're still fighting a war. There's an entire world that needs us. We have to honour Demi by staying strong and continuing the fight. That's what she would want—and Jayden too.'

Hailey dropped back down on the bed, her legs shaky. He was right, but she didn't have any strength left—she wasn't like him. She wasn't a soldier. She didn't know how to cut off her emotions, how not to care that someone was dead. 'I'm tired of fighting. Everyone keeps getting killed because of me. It's not safe for anyone to be my friend, or to even know me. That's why Nova did it. She said the Mysteries want to destroy me—take away everyone I love. You should save yourself now.'

Aaron put an arm around her as he sat back down. 'I'm not going anywhere. I will stay by you. Always. I promise you that much.'

Hailey wiped at the tears leaking from her eyes. 'Tell me why we're here.' Maybe if they stopped talking about Demi, the pain trying to crush her to death would ease off. Maybe she'd forget about the emptiness.

Aaron let his arm drop from Hailey's shoulders. 'Nova brought back friends.' He rubbed the back of his neck. 'The

Mysteries materialised in. They attacked the gold palace and freed the OMs in Tartarus's dungeon. Nova got Venus out. I'm guessing Venus was in on the plan from the beginning—kind of like a trojan horse.' He shook his head. 'I should have known something was up. I should have seen that Nova was playing us.'

"I made a promise to someone"... that's what Nova said before she dematerialised with Mute. Something clicked into place for Hailey. Something so obvious she couldn't believe she hadn't figured it out before. 'Medusa! Nova is Venus's sister.'

Aaron frowned. 'What?'

'She's her sister. Think about it... Kora told us back in first year that Venus's sister was an Ares. Nova even looks like Venus —minus the curls and violet eyes. After she'd admitted to being a spy, she told me she had to go because she'd made a promise to someone. She must have told Venus that if she played along and pretended to be a prisoner, Nova would free her. I can't believe we didn't figure it out.'

'You're right.' Aaron gritted his teeth, shaking his head. 'Why didn't I see it? I should have seen it. I messed up—the both of them even have astrology names.'

'We've been too trusting.' They hadn't exactly interrogated Nova and Mute when they'd shown up—they'd just let them straight in, all because they'd brought Venus with them, and because Nova had told them Tamzin had sent her a dream. *So stupid.* 'We can't trust anyone anymore. At least no one new.'

'Agreed.'

'So what happened with the Mysteries? How did you and everyone else get away?'

Aaron sighed. 'Well, we didn't all get away. I actually never really had a chance to fight.' His shoulders dropped, and he stared at the floor, like he was too ashamed to meet Hailey's eyes. 'I was looking for you when they came. Brennan and I both were. We were in Demi's room when the screaming started. We ran into the hallway. General Killian was running down it, heading for outside. He stopped long enough to tell us to evacuate and threw a travelling necklace at us. I went to run after him, to help him in the battle, but Brennan grabbed me before I could, and the necklace brought us here.' His shoulders sagged even more. 'I begged him to take me back. If I'd joined the fight, then maybe a few more people would have been able to escape.'

Hailey rubbed her hand on his back. 'You'd probably be dead if you'd stayed.'

'Maybe.' He shrugged. 'Anyway. The military swarmed us as soon as we arrived. They picked up pretty quickly that General Killian was in trouble, though, and Brennan took them to the Underworld. They brought back as many people as they could. But almost everyone was taken.'

'Annabelle?'

He shook his head.

Hailey's heart pulsed with pain. 'I promised Demi I'd take care of her. I can't even do that right.'

'We're going to get her back,' Aaron promised. 'We're going to rescue everyone who was taken. I'm going to make up for not fighting in that battle.'

I'll find her, Demi, your parents too. I promise. 'What about Amathia?'

'I don't know what happened to her. She's not here.'

'How did you find me?' Hailey asked before she could dwell on what fate might have befallen Amathia and the others captured.

'Brennan was smart enough to grab Demi's pillow before he got us out of there. A Hecate used some of the hair on it to cast a locator spell.' Aaron finally looked up at her, his eyes full of shame. 'I'm sorry it took so long to find you. If I'd been faster with the spell, maybe there would have been enough time to save Demi.'

'There's only one person to blame in all of this. Zeus.'

Hailey's lightning thrummed in her veins. 'This is all a game to him—torturing humans and making them suffer as much as possible is his entertainment.' He needed to be stopped, now more than ever. If Hailey crumbled, like she wanted to do so badly, he would win. There would be no one left to stand against him. The military was relying on her to go back to Hephaestus and get the weapon he was working on. That was the only way to end this. The only way to honour the dead's memories. Demi would be ashamed of her if she saw Hailey sitting on a bed feeling sorry for herself. She had to push her emotions aside, just like she'd done with Kora. *Be a warrior. Be a warrior. Make Zeus pay.*

'We can't sit around blaming ourselves,' Hailey said, squeezing her heart pendant. 'We need to be strong for Demi, and everyone else who's given their lives, or are enslaved.'

Aaron nodded. 'We're the only hope the world has left.'

'Let's not disappoint them then. But first, I need to say goodbye to my friend.'

When Hailey walked into the briefing room, she couldn't even see Demi. The chairs that had lined the long table were against the walls, a crowd of people surrounded it instead—Alec, Tahlia, Brennan, Riley, Charlie, and Lacey among them. Hailey walked towards them, everyone parting to make way for her. Tears spilled from her eyes when she saw her. Demi was lying on the table, the ceiling's shining light streaming over her unmoving body, casting her in a golden glow.

'I'm so sorry,' Brennan said, staring at the floor, unable to meet Hailey's teary gaze.

Tahlia squeezed Hailey's arm. 'We'll give you time alone.'

'Sorry,' everyone muttered, their heads low as they headed for the door.

'Wait, Lacey,' Hailey called, a tiny flicker of hope sparking in her. Lacey was a Hermes who could see the dead. *Maybe she can see Demi.*

She turned back to Hailey, sadness creasing her face. 'I'm sorry, but I can't see her,' she said before Hailey could even ask.

'Oh.' Her words hit Hailey like a fireball to the stomach. 'She might still show up, right?' Maybe if Demi could tell Lacey she was okay, then the emptiness in Hailey would go away, and the pain stabbing her heart would stop. *Maybe.*

'Yes,' Lacey said, her fingers twisting through one of her twin ponytails. 'It's possible she's somewhere else right now, or she could be here. Watching, not wanting to show herself to me. I'll let you know if she does though.'

Hailey nodded. 'Thank you.'

Lacey slipped out the door, leaving Hailey alone in the room. She took Demi's cold stiff hand in hers. 'I'm sorry this happened to you. You were the best best friend anyone could ask for.' She sniffed, fresh tears pooling in her eyes. 'I really don't know how I can do this without you. You've always been fearless, and that fearlessness helped give me courage.' A tear rolled down her cheek. 'All I want to do is curl up and cry, but if I do that, I'll never get back up again. I can't let the Olympians destroy this world. I can't sit around feeling sorry for myself. There's too much at stake.' She swallowed around the lump in her throat. 'So I'll make you a promise right now... I promise I'll be strong. I'll keep fighting. I'll make sure Nova pays for what she did to you. I'll find your family, and I'll kill the gods.'

'I can help with that.'

Hailey whipped around, her eyes narrowing when she saw who was standing in the doorframe. 'It can't be.' She blinked, waiting for the person's face to morph into someone else's. But it stayed the same. 'You... I saw you die.'

Jayden grinned. 'Don't believe everything you see.'

24

REUNITED

'It *is* you!' Hailey rushed towards him, wrapping her arms around him. She half expected him to be an illusion, but he was solid. 'You're real. How are you real?'

Jayden pulled from the hug. Normally, his black hair would be perfectly styled, with way too much gel. But it was flat now, and long enough to reach his ears. And his face... he looked liked he'd aged ten years in the month since she'd last seen him. 'Callista saved me,' he said.

Hailey frowned. 'Who?'

'Me.' A girl who looked around eighteen years old stepped into the room, moving to Jayden's side. Black gloves stretched up past her elbows, emphasising her pale skin and white hair.

Hailey gasped and jumped back. Warmth surged into her hands as her palms shot up, aiming them directly at the girl. 'You're the Thanatos! You're the one who killed all those people.'

'Hailey, stop. It's okay.' Jayden moved in front of Callista, his voice calm. 'She's on our side. She helped me escape.'

Hailey hesitated. 'We've been tricked before. That's how Demi died.'

Jayden stumbled back a step, bumping into Callista as she

coward behind him. He reached for one of the chairs against the wall, his fingers gripping the top of it as he steadied himself. 'Demi's dead?' His eyes moved past Hailey, to the table. His jaw dropped. 'Demi!' He ran towards her, shaking her. 'Demi, wake up. I'm back. Wake up.'

Hailey kept her palms raised at the Thanatos. Warmth tingled in her hands, her lightning letting her know it was there when she needed it. 'She's dead, Jayden.' Her eyes stayed on Callista, watching her as she stood in the doorframe. 'Because of the Mysteries. The same people you were helping.'

'I wasn't helping them... At least not by choice,' Jayden added.

'What do you mean?' Hailey didn't dare turn around to face him. All Callista would have to do was touch Hailey, and she'd be dead. 'Are you a spy?'

'No,' Jayden said. 'I'll explain it soon. But first we need to save Demi.'

The tiniest prickle of hope fluttered in Hailey's chest—a beam of light no wider than her pinkie finger stretching into the emptiness consuming her. 'Save her? You can do that?'

'Yes, if you let Callista past you.'

Hailey stared at the Thanatos. The girl on the TV had been terrifying—walking from person to person and ending their life with a brush of her fingertips. But the girl in front of her was anything but: her eyes were cast down, and she hugged her arms, like she was actually scared of Hailey. *Cady used to look like that—scared and meek—and she was the one who woke up the gods. I can't trust her. I can't... but what if she can bring Demi back? It's worth the risk—I'd try anything to bring Demi back. And it's not like she can kill Demi again.*

Hailey dropped her arms, the warmth and tingling in her hands ebbing. 'Okay, help her.'

Callista kept her eyes on the ground, shuffling past Hailey to stand on the opposite side of the table to Jayden.

'How can you save her?' Hailey asked, moving to Jayden's side. 'Your powers kill people.'

'My powers can also bring people back.' Callista gazed at Demi's lifeless body; strands of her wavy brown hair hung over the table's edges. 'But there's a price.'

'What? You want money?' Disgust lined Hailey's words.

'No, I—'

'I'll take care of it,' Jayden said, clasping a hand on top of Demi's.

Callista narrowed her ice blue eyes. 'Are you sure?'

Jayden nodded. 'I'll pay it. Just bring her back.'

'All right.' Callista tugged on the fingertips of her right glove before peeling the glove down her elbow and off her hand. She did the same with the left glove, placing them both beside Demi. She stretched her milky white arm over Demi's chest, stretching her fingers towards Jayden.

'No!' Hailey shouted. 'Her touch kills.'

'Not always.' Callista's hand was inches from Jayden, waiting for him to take it.

'It's okay, Hailey. I promise.' Jayden squeezed Demi's hand, as if reassuring her it was going to be okay, that she wouldn't be dead for much longer, and then he clasped his fingers with Callista's. Hailey expected him to drop dead, like he had in the video. But nothing happened.

So a Thanatos's touch doesn't equal instant death? Interesting. 'Why do you need to hold Jayden's hand?'

'Bec—'

'Because she needs to touch someone living to call back the dead.'

'Um, yeah,' Callista said, frowning at Jayden. 'Touching someone living helps focus my powers. Now for your friend.' Callista's other hand hovered above Demi's. She looked at Jayden, unsure.

He nodded. 'Do it.'

'As you wish.' Blue light glowed from Callista's palms the second she touched Demi. The light spread up Demi's arms and into her chest; it flowed down to her stomach, and then into her legs, until her entire body was glowing like fluorescent blue coral.

Hope sliced through Hailey's grief like a Nemean lion's claws slicing through metal. She hadn't dared believe Callista could bring Demi back. After all, her powers were designed to kill, not resurrect the dead. But something was happening. It was like she was pushing life back into Demi. 'It's working,' Hailey said, already smiling, waiting for Demi to sit up. 'Yes, it's working.'

The light dimmed like the dying flame of a candle. Callista stumbled back a step, the blue light vanishing altogether. Jayden tightened his grip on her hand, steadying her as he moved around the table to stand beside her.

Hailey stared down at Demi, a flood of happy tears waiting to pour down the second her best friend opened her eyes. But they remained closed. She didn't so much as twitch. 'Why didn't it work?' Hailey demanded. Callista rested her head against Jayden's chest, his arm around her to keep her from falling. 'Try again.'

'It – worked,' Callista puffed out, her out-of-breath words making her sound like she'd just run up a flight of stairs. 'It takes – time. Her spirit has to – find its way back to her – body. She's been dead – a day, so it will take longer than if – she'd only recently passed.'

'How long?' Hailey pressed.

'Tomorrow.'

'You need to lie down.' Jayden held Callista firm to him. 'Where's a bed?'

'I'll take her.'

Hailey's head whipped around. Tahlia stepped forward from the doorframe. Alec and Aaron stood there, too, watching silently. 'Were you watching the whole time?'

'We got here during the glowing light show,' Tahlia said, striding past Hailey and moving around the table towards Callista, who was pulling her black gloves back on. 'Here, let me help you.' Tahlia put her arm around Callista, careful not to touch any of her skin.

Alec scampered away from the door as the girls approached, giving Callista a wide berth and joining Hailey at the table. 'Will she really come back?' He stared at Demi's grey-tinged face.

Jayden nodded. 'I promise.'

'But will it be her?' Alec chewed his lip, not taking his eyes off Demi. 'She won't be a shade or anything?'

'She'll be her old self—the same crazy Demi.'

'Here's another question for you, what are *you* doing here?' Aaron asked, still by the door. 'How did you get here? How are you alive? Why were you with the Mysteries? Why did Zeus have you executed?'

Jayden sighed like someone who didn't have the strength to speak another word. 'I spent the last three hours answering those questions from the military. Did you know that? That I arrived this morning expecting to find you, but instead I found the military and got thrown into an interrogation room?'

'No, I didn't know you were here,' Aaron said, crossing his arms, indifferent. 'The military had every right to interrogate you. You were with the Mysteries, and then you suddenly showed up here after we were attacked and driven from the Underworld.'

'I wasn't with the Mysteries—well, I was, but I wasn't, not really.' Jayden shook his head, leaning his hands on the table. 'I don't even know where to start. Will you at least let me try and explain?'

'I want to know what happened,' Hailey said. 'But I don't want to leave Demi.'

'And I don't want a possible traitor wandering around our

bunker on a reconnaissance mission.' Aaron shot Jayden a pointed look.

Jayden put his hands up in surrender. 'All good. We can talk here.' He scooted around the table, to their side, and dropped to the cement floor, crossing his legs. Hailey and Alec joined him, facing their backs to the table. It reminded Hailey of being back at Poseidon's Academy, and how they would sneak into each other's dorms and sit around planning how to stop the nereids. *So much for that*, Hailey thought. After all they'd been through, the nereids had still managed to resurrect the gods.

'Joining us?' Jayden asked Aaron.

Aaron leaned his back against the wall beside the door, his arms still crossed. 'Nope. I'm going to stay here in case you make a run for it. The military will be keeping an eye on the Thanatos—Tahlia has probably already knocked her out with sleep dust. But I'm going to be watching you.'

'That's fine, do what you have to do.' Jayden's voice was casual, indifferent to Aaron's hostility. 'So, it all started last year, before the end-of-year holidays,' he began. 'Cady found me in the grounds one day when I was studying. She was holding a goblet. She said she'd made me a drink to say thank you for standing up to Venus for her. I didn't really think much of it, and I just drank it. Everything after that is a bit blurry.' He furrowed his brow, like he was trying to remember something. 'I just remember always wanting to be with her. I did everything she told me to. When she said not to spend time with you anymore, I stayed away, as much as I could. I didn't know why, I just felt like I didn't have a choice... And then Amathia sent everyone home for a week after the gorgon incident.' He took a steadying breath. 'I didn't know I'd never get to come back to the Academy, that Cady wouldn't let me. She said it was too dangerous. That she'd resurrected the Olympian gods and Poseidon would take back his palace. It was like I didn't even care. Can you believe that... after everything we went through to keep the gods dead, I was suddenly okay with them being alive?' He shook his head, baffled. 'She told me she was in the Olympian Mysteries and that we were moving to their headquarters. That's where I've been this whole time. In their castle. I haven't been helping them though. Just living there, feeling like I was trapped in a dream—or more like a nightmare.'

So many questions swirled around Hailey's head... *Did Cady drug Jayden? With what? Where are the Mysteries headquarters? How did he get here? Where's Cady? Why did she do it? Why did she awaken the gods?* Hailey kept her mouth closed, though, the cement floor cool beneath her as she listened to Jayden's every word.

'And then a few days ago, Cady said she had to tell me something,' Jayden continued. 'That she'd done something really bad and couldn't live with it anymore... She'd given me a love potion.' He curled his lip, disgust lining his features as he dropped his eyes to the ground, like he couldn't bear to look at Hailey and the others anymore. 'Nemertes gave it to her in exchange for her helping wake up the gods. Cady was afraid to tell me how she really felt about me, because she didn't want to risk me not liking her back and losing me as a friend, so she gave me the potion.' He looked up again, his gaze hesitant as it met Hailey's, and then shifted over Alec and Aaron. 'I've been under a love spell since the end-of-year holidays. That's why I stopped being friends with you. Not because I wanted to, but because I was spelled to. You have to believe me on that.'

The desperation, the sadness, the betrayal in his eyes told Hailey he was telling the truth. When the year had started, Hailey had thought he was acting like a jerk because he suddenly had a girlfriend and had forgotten Hailey and the others existed. But he'd been under a spell that whole time, and she hadn't even noticed. *I'm a horrible friend.*

'Cady said she wanted to know that it was real—that I actually loved her,' Jayden went on, not giving anyone enough time to interrupt and say they were sorry for not helping him. 'So she gave me an antidote to the potion. It was like I'd been stuck in a dream for months and had finally woken up. I was so angry. I couldn't believe what she'd done. She'd taken away my freewill. She'd woken up the gods. She'd doomed the world. And I'd watched.' Jayden shook his head again, pain and anguish lining his features. 'I tried to get out after that, to come and find you, and to find my parents—Cady didn't bother bringing them to the Mysteries headquarters. I have no idea where they are.' He swallowed. 'Anyway, I wanted to make up for what I'd done—standing by the Mysteries while they helped the gods take over the world—so I tried to kidnap their leader: Nefertari. I figured they'd be lost without her, and the military could get information from her.

'But I got caught—before I ever got anywhere near her.' He shuddered, hugging his arms around his stomach. 'That's why Zeus ordered my execution. You see, Callista lived in the castle, too, but not by choice. The Mysteries kidnapped her so they could use her as their executioner. We talked sometimes, back when I was under Cady's spell. We weren't exactly friends, but I think she saw that I was a prisoner, too, even if I didn't realise it at the time.' A sad smile crept across his face. 'Anyway, apparently Zeus left, and an OM materialised in to take care of our bodies. Callista used...' He trailed off, swallowing. 'Um, she took care of them and brought me back.' His hands squeezed tighter around his stomach. 'And then another OM materialised in. She said her name was Tamzin and she was on our side and could take me to you, Hailey.'

So that's what Tamzin had meant when she said she'd dropped off a present.

'She used a travelling necklace to bring us here, and then she left, right before the military surrounded Callista and me, and we spent hours being interrogated.'

'You were under a love spell that whole time?' Guilt

squeezed Hailey's heart like a fist. 'I'm so sorry. I should have known. I should have done something to help you.'

'Same.' Alec's shoulders were slumped, guilt creasing his face. 'I'm sorry too.'

'You couldn't have known.' Jayden's hands dropped from his stomach. 'A love spell that strong is pretty impossible to come by. Nemertes found someone as strong as Hecate herself to brew it, all so she could manipulate Cady.' He dropped his head. 'I still can't believe she did all of this.'

'So people are dead and enslaved because your girlfriend wanted you as her boyfriend?' Aaron was still beside the door, silent fury pouring off him.

'I know. It's insane.' Jayden combed a hand through his hair. 'She also did it because she wanted the gods to take back their powers—that's what she thought would happen if she brought them back.'

'What, and then they'd be on their merry way?' Aaron scoffed. 'How can anyone be that stupid? Our parents are slaves, Demi and about a million other people are dead because of her.'

Jayden's gaze flicked to Demi's body; tears glistened in his eyes when he turned back to Hailey and the others. 'I know, but she wasn't thinking. She never wanted any of this. She's not evil.'

'You said she wanted the gods to take their powers back,' Alec said, his voice meek. 'Can they do that?'

Jayden shrugged. 'I have no idea. As far as I know, they haven't taken anyone's powers.'

Aaron pushed away from the wall, his eyes narrowing in on Jayden. 'You said you could help. How?'

'I can help you take down the Mysteries. The most powerful Hecate in the world is their leader—she's the one I tried to kidnap. She brews potions that increase people's powers. She can even see the future. She's the reason the Mysteries are so formidable. Without her, the cult would be at a loss. And without the Mysteries to support them, the Olympians would have a much harder time trying to control the human race. It would at least give us a chance to fight back.'

'I'm sure there's another leader waiting to take her place,' Aaron countered, arms still crossed.

'Of course, but none as powerful as her,' Jayden said. 'And if you blow up the Mysteries' castle, then that'll weaken the cult even more—they may never be able to recover from the loss of losing their leader and their headquarters.'

'And how exactly are we meant to do all of this?' Hailey asked, cold seeping through her trousers from the cement floor, her butt starting to go numb. Jayden was talking like it would be an easy task, but he'd been on the OM's side, more or less, and had managed to get himself executed. So how were the four of them—five when Demi was back—supposed to invade a stronghold and take down an entire cult?

'We do nothing.' Jayden leaned back on his hands. 'I told the military everything I know, and I gave them my and Cady's travelling necklaces—they're the only way to get into the castle.'

'So for once we can let someone else risk their lives?' Alec heaved a giant sigh of relief, like he'd just been told he'd never have to worry about a single thing for the rest of his life.

'I'm going to confirm your story. Don't move.' Aaron pointed a finger at Jayden, who raised his hands in surrender.

'I'm not going anywhere.'

'I won't be long,' he told Hailey, his footsteps echoing down the hallway as he strode from the room.

Do nothing? Let the military handle it? Hailey couldn't deny her relief to hear that. Her past encounters with the Mysteries had been terrifying, to say the least. They were all so strong—*I guess because of the power-boosting potion their Hecate leader is handing out.* Taking them all down was definitely a job for someone with a Tartarus of a lot more training than Hailey and her friends had. The military did this kind of stuff all the time—at least, she assumed they did. With Jayden's inside information, she had no doubt they'd be able to pull off a raid. *Maybe they'll even come across Nova and Venus and throw them into a dungeon never to see sunlight again. Or, better yet, blow them up with the castle.*

'There's something else I need to tell you.' Jayden's gaze shifted to Alec. 'The Olympian Mysteries headquarters are actually the TripleAS headquarters—at least they were.' He swallowed. 'Your parents are there, Alec, and a few other people we know.'

Alec's spine shot up. 'Really? They're in the TripleAS headquarters? The crystal only showed me them in a room. I didn't know where it was.'

'I'm not sure what crystal you're talking about,' Jayden said with a frown, 'but that's where they are. Locked up in the dungeon. I told the military all about it. They'll rescue everyone imprisoned there.'

Tears glistened in Alec's eyes. 'Thank you.' He launched at Jayden, wrapping his arms around him. 'Thank you so much.'

A grin spread across Hailey's face. By tomorrow, the military would have kidnapped the OM's leader, rescued Alec's parents, destroyed the Mysteries stronghold, and Demi would be alive. *Blue skies.*

25

THE PRICE

'Hailey?'

Hailey's eyes flew open. She was lying on the bottom bunk of a bed, dim light filtering down from the ceiling. 'Demi?' She glanced across at the other bunk bed. Joy as bright and pure as sunlight blasted through her when she saw her best friend sitting on the edge of the bottom bunk. 'Demi!' Hailey leapt up, rushing the few steps towards her best friend and wrapping her arms around her. Tears poured down her cheeks. *Demi's back. Demi's back. She's alive! Thank you, Tyches! Thank you!*

'Hailey, you're crushing me,' Demi gasped out.

'Sorry.' Hailey pulled back, wiping strands of wet hair from her face.

'It actually worked.' Aaron stepped into the room from the hallway, where he'd been keeping guard. 'You're back. Thank the Tyches.'

'Are you really back though?' Alec was on the top bunk of the bed Hailey had been sleeping in. His back was pressed into the corner of the wall, creating as much space between him and Demi as possible. 'Are you you, or are you a soulless version of Demi?'

Demi frowned. 'What are you talking about, Alec? Have you been drinking ambrosia wine?' Her gaze flicked between him, Hailey, and Aaron, her frown deepening. 'What's going on?' She glanced around the room. 'Where am I?'

Hailey dropped down beside Demi, having no idea how you were supposed to tell a person that they'd died and been brought back by a Thanatos. *Quickly?* 'Um, you died, Demi. Nova killed you. Do you remember?'

'I died? Again? Wow, that's becoming a real habit of mine.' She combed a hand through her straggly hair. 'The last thing I remember is Nova saying she needed us to help Aaron.' Her eyes shot to Aaron by the door. 'Thank the Tyches you're okay. She said the Olympian Mysteries ambushed you.'

'That never happened.' A muscle in Aaron's jaw tightened, hinting at the anger burning within him.

Demi's frown somehow got even deeper. 'What?'

'It was a lie.' Rage flickered in Hailey like a fireball. She would find Nova; she would make her pay for what she'd done to her best friend. 'Nova tricked us so that she could kill you. And then she went back to the Underworld with the Mysteries and attacked.'

'Medusa! Where's Annabelle?' Demi jumped to her feet.

'They took her.' Aaron's shoulders slumped, his gaze falling to the cement floor. 'I'm sorry, Demi. I should have gotten her out. I failed.'

Tears glistened in Demi's eyes. 'No, not Annabelle.' She sunk back onto the bed, her body sagging.

'We're going to find her,' Hailey promised, wrapping an arm around Demi's shoulders. 'We're going to rescue all of our families.'

Demi wiped the back of her hand across her eyes and sniffed. 'Where's the crystal? I need to see her.'

'I'll get it for you.' Aaron didn't lift his eyes, shame keeping them pinned to the floor. 'It's the least I can do.'

'I'll come too.' Alec scurried down the bunk bed's ladder and out of the room after Aaron, moving so fast you would have thought an arachne was after him.

'What if they killed her?' Demi's voice was barely a whisper.

'The Mysteries don't kill kids—at least not ones as young as Annabelle.'

'Wait.' She turned her gaze on Hailey, tears making her emerald eyes all the more brighter. 'You said I died. How am I back? Did you use gorgon blood again? Where did you even find a gorgon?'

Hailey shook her head, the hint of a smile creeping onto her face. 'No, not gorgon blood. Jayden came here.'

'He's dead, Hailey. We saw him die.' More tears streamed down her face.

Hailey's smile grew bigger. 'He did die, but the Thanatos brought him back. He brought her here with him, and she saved you—apparently Thanatoses can bring back the dead.'

Demi stared at Hailey, like she was waiting for Hailey to say it was all a joke and Jayden was still dead. 'You're being serious?'

Hailey nodded, her grin widening. 'Yes, he's here.'

Demi pressed a hand to her mouth. 'Thank the Tyches.' More tears streamed down her face. 'Can I see him? Where is he?'

'He slept in one of the other rooms. I'll—'

'Jayden wanted me to say he's sorry.'

Hailey's gaze shot to the door, to Lacey standing there, chewing her lip. 'About what?'

Lacey fiddled with one of her ponytails, curling the end of it around her fingers. 'That he won't be able to help you battle the gods.'

Hailey frowned. 'What do you mean? Why? Where is he?'

'Yeah, I want to see him.' Demi pushed to her feet, wiping at her eyes.

'You can't.' Lacey swallowed, chewing on her lip so hard Hailey was sure she'd draw blood.

Unease coiled in Hailey's stomach, a bad feeling settling over her like an electric storm about to hit. 'Lacey, what's going on?' she asked, standing up too.

Lacey's gaze dropped to the floor. 'He's dead.'

'No, he's not. He came back. He was here last night,' Hailey argued, the unease in her stomach coiling tighter. She ignored it. Jayden was alive. She hadn't dreamed that. And she'd hugged him, so he couldn't have been a shade. He was alive. 'Where is he?' she demanded. *What kind of sick practical joke is this?*

Lacey's eyes finally lifted, settling on Hailey. She saw the torment in them—the hesitation and pain. Hailey had never thought about how difficult being a Hermes would be, how the power to speak to the dead meant they would also have to tell people that their loved ones had passed away and then watch those loved ones shatter into a million pieces. *But that's not the case now, because Jayden is alive.*

'There was a price to bring back Demi.' Lacey's voice was quiet, barely a whisper.

'What's going on, Hailey?' Demi stared between Lacey and her. 'You said Jayden was alive again.'

'He is,' Hailey reassured her. 'Callista—the Thanatos— wanted money to bring you back. Jayden took care of it.'

Lacey bit her bottom lip again, blood dotting it. 'That wasn't the price... The price was a life. It's the only way to bring someone back from the dead—a life for a life.'

Hailey shook her head, her stomach turning as bile rose into her throat. 'No. Jayden didn't say anything about that.' *Lies. Lies. Lies. Why is Lacey lying?* 'Where is he?' Anger coated her words. 'This isn't funny, Lacey.'

'Enough of this.' Demi pushed past Lacey, bursting into the hallway. 'Jayden,' she called.' Jayden, where are you?'

Hailey followed after her on shaky legs. *Lies. Lies. Lies. Jayden is alive.* 'He's in this one.' She strode to the door next to the room her and Demi had just come out of. She lifted her fist to knock.

'Just open it.' Demi shifted Hailey aside, pushing the handle down and throwing the door open. 'Jayden! You're back!' She ran over to the bottom bunk against the right wall. Jayden was asleep, dim light filtering down from the ceiling. 'Jayden.' She shook him when his eyes didn't open. 'Wake up.'

Hailey stayed where she was in the doorframe, her feet rooted to the floor. Jayden looked like Demi had—his lips tinged blue, his chest still. He was dead.

'He's not going to wake up.' Lacey stood at Hailey's side. 'He said he couldn't let you die, Demi. He doesn't want you to feel sad or guilty. This is what he wanted. He'd give his life up for yours a million times over.'

Jayden's dead. How is Jayden dead? He'd just come back. After being away from them for so long, he'd finally come back. Tears burned Hailey's throat. She swallowed them down, pressing a hand to the doorframe as her legs wavered. *Be strong. Keep it together. Do not let this break you. Do not let Zeus win. You are a warrior.*

'He's not dead,' Demi snapped, shaking him more ferociously. 'Wake up, Jayden.'

'I'm sorry.'

Hailey glanced over her shoulder to Callista. Her skin looked sickly in the hallway's dim glow. Lacey moved from beside Hailey, Callista slipping through the door and walking towards Jayden.

'It's what he wanted.' She placed a gloved hand on his arm.

Demi didn't flinch away from her. She showed no fear, despite the fact she was standing beside someone with the power to kill her with a single touch. 'You're the Thanatos. Bring him back! Now!'

'I can't.' Callista's voice was meek, her words lined with

regret. 'He gave his life for yours. It's not possible to bring him back, not without killing you.'

'Then kill me.' Demi held her hand out to Callista. 'I'm the one who died, not him. He shouldn't have given his life for mine. It's not fair.'

'No!' Hailey said, her hand still pressed to the doorframe. This was all too much—watching Jayden die, then Demi, then Jayden coming back, then Demi coming back, and now Jayden being dead again. She couldn't take the yo-yoing of life and death anymore. She couldn't watch Demi give up her life for Jayden's. She would have stopped Jayden from doing this yesterday if she'd known what Callista had meant by there being a price. She never would have let him sacrifice himself, not when this had all happened because of her. 'I'll give my life for his.' Hailey stepped forward, forcing her wobbling legs towards Callista. She'd given Hephaestus her lightning; he was creating a weapon right now to destroy the gods. He never said she would have to be the one to wield it, which meant anyone could probably use it. She—her powers—weren't important to this world anymore.

'Jayden loved you.' Lacey's word stopped Hailey in her tracks; she turned back to look at her, having forgotten about the fact that Jayden—his shade, anyway—was in the room with them. 'He loved both of you. He wants you to live.'

'No. He doesn't get to make that choice. Kill me!' Demi grabbed Callista's shoulder, gripping on tight as if touching the Thanatos would be enough to trade places with Jayden.

'I'm sorry.' Callista stepped away from her, pulling her gloved hand back from Jayden's arm. 'Jayden made me promise I would let him stay dead. That's a promise I plan to honour.'

'NO!' Demi unleashed a scream as loud as Natasha's.

Hailey ran to her, wrapping her arms around her best friend and holding her tight as sobs shook her. Hailey stared at Jayden's unmoving body through blurry eyes. She'd only just gotten him back, and now he was gone again. And this time, he wasn't coming back.

* * *

'Are you sure you want to be here?' Hailey asked Demi, squeezing her hand.

The two of them, along with Alec and Aaron, stood outside the door to the briefing room. The door was closed, muffled voices coming from the other side.

Strands of hair stuck to Demi's wet face as she nodded. 'Yes.' Her voice was raw. 'I need to know that Jayden didn't die for nothing. That the military are going ahead with the plan. Plus, I can't be in that room anymore.' She shuddered. 'Especially not with that Thanatos in there now.'

Hailey squeezed Demi's hand again. 'Okay.'

After sitting with Jayden and crying for what felt like a century, Hailey and her friends had decided to find out what the military were planning to do about the Mysteries. When they were going to strike. When they would be one step closer to killing the gods. Mostly, they wanted a distraction—even a brief one—from the grief of losing another friend.

'Why haven't they left yet?' Alec bit his lip, staring at the door. 'My parents are in a dungeon.' He began pacing. 'They should have left to rescue them by now. They shouldn't be sitting around in a meeting.'

Aaron reached his hand out, lightly gripping Alec's shoulder to stop his pacing. 'This is normal. They're infiltrating the Mysteries headquarters; they have to be smart and come up with a plan of attack before they go anywhere near that castle. I bet they're finalising everything right now and will be heading out soon.'

Alec nodded, resuming his pacing as Aaron's hand dropped from his shoulder.

The muffled voices continued to drift from the room. *How will they infiltrate the Mysteries headquarters?* Hailey wondered. Jayden might have given them travelling necklaces to get inside without being detected, but they'd still need to move around a castle swarming with OMs. *They're the military. This is literally the type of thing they deal with on a daily basis—at least I think it is.*

'I'm going to ask to go with them.' Aaron broke the silence.

'What?' Hailey, Demi, and Alec all said at the same time.

'They're infiltrating the OMs home base. They'll need all the personnel they can get,' he said. 'And I can make sure your parents get out safe, Alec.'

'No.' The word was out of Hailey's mouth before Aaron had even finished his sentence. She'd already lost too many people she cared about. She wasn't risking losing someone else, especially when there was no reason for Aaron to go. The military hadn't asked for their help, so in her opinion, that meant they had things under control.

'We can't lose you too.' Demi's voice was thick, on the verge of tears again.

'It's too dangerous,' Alec agreed, pausing his pacing. 'I want my parents back more than anything, but not at the cost of you getting yourself killed.'

Aaron raked a hand through his hair, messing it up even more. 'My dad's trained me for this type of thing. I know what I'm doing. It won't be—'

'No,' Hailey said again, tears threatening at the very thought of him leaving with the military. She grabbed his arm, clutching his wrist as though holding on to him would stop him from going. 'Please. Don't go. For me. Don't go.'

'I…' He stared into Hailey's eyes, her gaze full of desperation. He swallowed. 'Okay. I won't go.'

'Thank you.' She hugged him, squeezing him tight, her stomach quivering with… *relief? That's definitely relief. He's my best friend. I don't want to lose him, that's all.* Hailey pulled away, the musky scent of body spray mixed with sweat tickling her nostrils, as the briefing room's door opened.

Fifteen military personnel marched out, sparing Hailey and her friends confused glances before disappearing down the hallway.

Aaron took the lead into the briefing room. Jia stood at the head of the table, folding up a map; two obsidian travelling necklaces rested beside it, their wings glittering in the light streaming from the ceiling.

Jia straightened, frowning at Hailey and her friends. 'Aaron? What are you all doing here?'

'Jayden's dead, ma'am.' Aaron's voice was flat.

'What?!' She pulled a handgun from her belt, from beside a set of throwing knives. 'Are the Mysteries here?'

'No, ma'am,' Aaron said quickly when Jia moved to run for the door. 'It was the Thanatos—apparently Jayden volunteered to give up his life to bring Demi back.'

Demi sucked in a breath beside Hailey, slowly blowing it out.

'Oh.' Jia clipped the gun back onto her belt. 'I'm sorry for your loss. But we're about to leave for the mission he left us with.'

'That's why we're here, Colonel,' Aaron said, his posture arrow-straight and his feet together. 'We wanted to know that his plan was going ahead. How are you planning to capture the OM's leader?' His eyes drifted to the folded map on the table.

'We're not.' Jia picked up the map, tucking it into her trousers. 'Things have changed—we're blowing the whole place up instead.'

'No!' Alec yelled. 'My parents are in there. You have to rescue them.'

'I'm sorry, but it's too dangerous,' Jia said, her voice impassive. 'I can't risk the lives of my team to save a couple of people. Not when the stakes are so high. There are always casualties in war.'

Hailey couldn't form words. The military was going to just blow up the castle and all the innocent people trapped in the dungeon. Jia didn't even look like she cared that she was about to murder Alec's parents. *How can they be so ruthless?*

Jia picked up the travelling necklaces from the table. 'Now, if you'll excuse me, I've got a castle to blow up.'

'No. I can't let you do that, ma'am.' Aaron stayed where he was in front of the door—they all did.

Jia stopped ten feet from them, the black travelling necklaces dangling from her hand. 'I'm ordering you to move.'

Aaron raised his palms.

'Aaron Wynton, you will let me past right now, or you will never gain the honour of joining the military, I promise you that much.'

'I'm sorry, Colonel, but I'm not willing to give up on Alec's parents and all of the other innocent people in the dungeon.'

Jia hit a button on her watch. 'HEL—'

Aaron threw his palms forward, Jia's cry for help cutting off as she flew backwards, right over the table, and slammed against the concrete wall.

'I'm so sorry,' Aaron repeated, kneeling beside Jia's unconscious body.

'What's going on—Medusa, what did you do?'

Hailey, who'd been frozen since the moment Aaron had lifted his palms, regained control of her body. Tahlia had squeezed past her, Demi, and Alec. She stared at Jia lying on the floor, Aaron beside her, scooping up the travelling necklaces.

Running boots hitting the cement floor echoed towards them.

'We don't have time to explain, Tahlia.' Aaron's words were rushed as he straightened from the floor, the travelling necklaces clutched in his hand, and Jia's map tucked into his trousers. 'We need you to hold them off. Please.'

The sound of running boots was getting louder and louder—

they were mere yards away. Hailey's heartbeat tripled in speed, waiting for the military to rush into the room and see what they'd done.

Tahlia only hesitated for a second. 'Okay.' She sucked in a breath, dashing into the hallway.

'Hey, what are you do—'

Thump. Thump. Thump.

'I can hear more coming,' Tahlia yelled from outside. 'I don't know if I'll be fast enough to use my sleep dust on all of them. Whatever you're about to do. Do it quickly.'

What are *we about to do?* Hailey hadn't really thought about it. She was still recovering from the fact Aaron had just knocked out Jia.

'Is everyone ready?' Aaron joined them back by the door.

'Aaron, what did you do?' Alec gulped, staring at Jia's unmoving body, finally finding his voice. 'We're going to be in so much trouble. We'll probably go to prison for the rest of our lives.'

'She was about to kill your parents.' Aaron's voice was calm; his hands weren't even shaking. 'Is that what you really wanted?'

'No, of course not. But—'

'This is the only way to save them.' His eyes shifted to Demi, who looked as shocked as Hailey felt. 'The only way to fulfil Jayden's plan, because the military aren't going to—they're going to use what he told them to kill innocent people.'

'Take her down. Now!' someone shouted, their voice sounding like it was coming from the end of the hallway.

'We're running out of time.' Aaron held out one of the travelling necklaces to Hailey, Demi, and Alec. 'Now, I'm going to that castle, and I'm going to kidnap that Hecate, and I'm going to rescue everyone in that dungeon. I'm going to honour Jayden's memory. Who's with me?'

How is this happening? Only minutes ago Hailey had thought the military had everything under control. That she'd get to sit on the side lines for a change and let them handle things. But here she was, the military's current leader unconscious on the floor as Hailey debated whether or not to risk her life by breaking into the OM's base. Not that there was much to debate. Alec's parents' lives were on the line. There was nothing she wouldn't do to save her own mother, and that same rule applied to her friends' families.

'I'm in.' Hailey grabbed the necklace.

'I can't let you have all the fun,' Demi said, her voice flat. 'Plus, this is a really stupid idea, and stupid ideas is where we thrive.'

'Take her dow—' Another shout came from the hallway, cut off by a *thump*.

Everyone turned their eyes on Alec, who was practically chewing his lip off. 'They're my parents. Of course I'm going.'

Please, Tyches, let us survive this. Hailey lifted the necklace.

'Wait!'

Her hands paused, holding the necklace over her head, as Brennan burst into the room.

'I don't know where you're going, but take me with you. I can help.' He reached a hand towards Hailey. 'I can keep you safe.'

Hailey's eyes flashed to Aaron's, only for a second. Just long enough to see the hesitation in them—the fear that she might say yes, that her saying yes would actually mean something. Something more than her just agreeing to let Brennan help. Something she didn't want to admit to, or even contemplate. 'Sorry, not this time.' She dropped the necklace over her head at the same time Aaron did, the two of them joining hands with Demi and Alec.

She only saw the devastation on Brennan's face for a second before the room swirled around her and she was somewhere else.

26

THE CASTLE

Hailey's hands shot up, lightning sparking on her fingertips. She was in the bedroom she'd seen Jayden and Cady arguing in, when she'd been watching them in Hecate's crystal. It was almost as big as Aphrodite's room had been, with a silk sofa and armchair resting in front of a fireplace, wood stacked inside, waiting to be lit. A chandelier glittered above the four-poster bed, lighting up the window-less room.

Hailey had expected Cady to be there, but the room was empty. *Thank the Tyches.* She dropped her hands.

'All clear,' Aaron said, dropping his own hands, deactivating his force field. He pulled the travelling necklace over his head, Hailey doing the same. He slipped both of them into the pocket of his cargo trousers.

'So this is where he's been the whole time.' Demi ran a hand over the bed's green and cream silk quilt. 'I can't believe Cady had him under a spell. I should have known. I should have seen it.'

'None of us saw it.' Guilt squeezed Hailey's heart. When her friend had needed her most, she'd turned her back on him. If she'd worked out he was under a spell, then Cady never would have taken him to the Mysteries, and he'd probably still be alive… but Demi would be dead. *Stop. You need to stop blaming yourself for everything. Just focus.*

'The fact we all missed it, shows how powerful the Hecate we're here for is,' Aaron said. 'Without her, the Mysteries will lose a lot of their power.'

Demi turned away from the bed, rage lighting her face like a candle lighting a jack-o-lantern. 'I'm going to make sure she never brews anything again. Let's get the harpy.'

'Let's check Jayden's map and see where her quarters are.' Aaron pulled the map from the back of his trousers and unfolded it, lying it flat on the bed.

'Wait, we're getting my parents first, aren't we?' Alec asked as Hailey and Demi stepped forward to stand on either side of Aaron.

Aaron turned around to Alec, his shoulders raised and back, standing as tall as a soldier. 'We have to be tactical. We need to go after Nefertari first so—'

'No. I want to save my parents!' Alec exclaimed as loudly as he dared. 'That's the only reason I came here.'

Aaron put a hand on Alec's shoulder. 'I know. And I promise you, we will rescue them. But if we go to the dungeon now and get caught, there won't be a second chance to take down Nefertari. I know you don't care about kidnapping her,' he added quickly when Alec opened his mouth to argue, 'but we have to think about the bigger picture. Right now, the world is enslaved, and the first step in reversing that is taking down the Mysteries. And to do that, we need to remove their leader. For now, your parents are safe, and they'll stay that way until we go down and rescue them.'

'I don't know.' Alec chewed his lip. 'What if we get caught going after Nefertari? She'll be well-guarded. And she's probably got spells protecting her.'

All true. But what other choice did they have? They needed to get rid of the Mysteries—or at least weaken them enough that it also weakened the gods too. This was a way to buy more time for the human race until Hephaestus finished building the weapon.

'I wish I could tell you that everything will be fine,' Aaron said, his hand still on Alec's shoulder. 'But I don't know that it will be. We have insider information though—we've got a map from Jayden. We can come up with a plan that will help us complete our mission. But we need to do it quickly. Cady could come back at any minute. So you need to ask yourself, what would your parents want you to do... Save them? Or help save the world?'

Alec blew out a breath, his shoulders dropping. 'Save the world.'

'And we'll save them too. I promise. Come on, let's work out what we're doing.' Aaron turned back to the map, Alec moving to stand beside Hailey.

The map was more like a blueprint, with hand drawn layouts of the castle's three floors—with the dungeon consisting of the entire basement level. Hallways and rooms were all labelled. One room was circled—it was on the first floor and labelled "Nefertari's Hecate room".

'We need to get downstairs,' Aaron said, pointing to the circled room, which branched off from the entryway.

'They'll be guards down there for sure,' Alec gulped, voice shaking. 'How will we get past them?'

'With a distraction.' Aaron slipped his hand into his pocket and pulled out a vial the size of a small perfume bottle.

Demi squinted at the shimmering red and black liquid inside it. 'Is that a potion?'

'Yeah, it's an exploding potion—I pulled it off Jia when I grabbed the map and travelling necklaces. I thought it might come in handy.'

'If we set that off, it'll lead the Mysteries straight to us,' Hailey said, stating what she thought was a very obvious flaw in the plan.

'We're not going to be in here when it goes off.' A smile tinged Aaron's words. 'This potion has a timer.' He flipped the vial upside down, revealing a tiny black screen as wide as Hailey's thumbnail. 'We'll set the timer, sneak down the hallway and hide in one of the rooms closer to the stairs. Then, when everyone runs up to find out what the explosion was—and deal with putting out the fire—we'll go downstairs and grab Nefertari.'

'She's a witch,' Alec pointed out. 'If she's as powerful as Jayden said she is, then she could kill us with a death spell, or turn us into pigs.'

'I'll have my force field up so any spell she throws at us will ricochet. And if she does fight us, then, Hailey, you might have to use your lightning—just enough to injure her so we can use the military's travelling necklaces to go back to the bunker and drop her off. And then we'll go back for your parents, Alec.'

Aaron made it sound so easy—like nothing could go wrong. But Hailey didn't even know if she could shoot lightning at a person without killing them. *If I'm going to practise using my powers on anyone, the person in charge of a murderous cult is the best choice.*

'Let's do this already,' Demi snapped, folding up the map. 'Set the potion.'

Aaron tapped on the black screen on the bottom of the vial three times. The tiny screen brightened to white. 'Activate potion in five minutes.' Tiny black numbers appeared on the screen, counting down... *5:00, 4:99, 4:98.* 'It's set.' Aaron threw the vial on the bed and grabbed the folded map from Demi, tucking it back into his trousers. 'Let's go.'

The four of them snuck towards the door, Hailey's heartbeat quickening as Aaron leaned his ear against it. *Come on, there's a bomb ticking down in this room. We need to get out. How long is left now? What if there's someone outside? Can Aaron pause the countdown until the hallway is clear?*

'I don't hear anything,' Aaron said after a few heartbeats. He pushed the door handle down so slowly it was like he was moving in slow motion. He pulled the door open a crack, peering out. 'All clear,' he whispered, the four of them slinking into the hallway. Pots, vases, and statues lined it, reminding Hailey of Alec's mansion.

They moved as quickly as they dared, not making any sound as they crept along the hallway, moving past doors until they neared the twin staircases that led downstairs. There was a door across from the closest staircase. Aaron pressed his ear against it, listening.

Hailey gulped, her eyes darting to the staircases, and then towards the hallway that continued further down, and then back down the hallway they'd just come from. *Come on. We're too out in the open here. Anyone could spot us. How long is left on the potion? Come on, Aaron!*

Aaron straightened from the door and held his hand up at Hailey, Demi, and Alec, signalling for them to wait. He cracked the door open, peering inside.

Come on. Come on. Come on. There's a bomb about to explode.

Aaron pushed the door wide enough for him to slip through. Hailey held her breath, waiting for someone to shout out; instead, the door opened all the way, Aaron standing in the frame and waving for them to come in. The breath rushed from Hailey's lungs as they closed the door behind them. *We're okay. We're safe. Everything is going to plan.* None of them dared speak as they waited for the potion's timer to run out. The room they stood in was exactly like Jayden's, but this one was messy, with black clothes strewn all about, and knives, axes, and swords littering the floor. *I so don't want to meet the person who lives here.*

'How much longer?' Demi whispered, the four of them crowded in front of the closed door.

'About a minute,' Aaron said. 'Now shhh.'

That minute felt like an hour to Hailey. She kept waiting for someone to burst inside, to see them, and to shout out that there were intruders. What would they do then? *Fight? How many OMs are in this castle? Dozens? Hundreds? Maybe there's not that many. Most of them would be terrorising humans, wouldn't they? Maybe they only come back here at night. Wherever here is. Maybe —BOOM!*

The castle shook, shouts erupting as smoke wafted under the door. Hailey stiffened, listening to the shouts and running footsteps getting louder and louder until they were right outside the door. *Please protect us, Tyches.* The sound quietened, disappearing down the hallway.

'Be on guard,' Aaron warned, pulling the door open and lifting his palms.

Smoke billowed into the room, burning Hailey's nostrils and throat. She followed Aaron and her friends into the hallway, the smoke so thick she could barely see anything. She pressed a hand over her nose and mouth, her eyes watering as she crept towards the nearest staircase.

Aaron peered over the banister, his palms still raised. 'Entryway looks clear,' he whispered, taking the lead downstairs.

The smoke eased with every step Hailey took, her eyes and nose stinging less and less until she reached the bottom. Normally, you'd expect there to be a door to outside in the entryway. But where there should have been a door was a wall trimmed with gold. Adding to the fact Hailey hadn't seen a single window yet, she was guessing this place had been designed with no way to enter, or exit, without a travelling necklace. Without one, the whole place was basically like one big dungeon.

'This is it.'

Hailey turned around. Aaron was staring at a set of double doors between the two curving staircases. Words were carved into the oak: *Do NOT enter unless invited in. You have been warned.*

'Do you think there's a monster on the other side?' Alec squeaked from beside Hailey.

'We can fight a monster,' Demi said from Hailey's other side. 'We're experts at it now.'

There was something Hailey was more afraid of than a monster. 'What if there's an alarm?'

On the floor above, people were still shouting, and the smoke was growing thicker and thicker, gradually stretching down to the entryway like a dense fog.

'We just have to take a chance.' Aaron's palms stayed up. 'It's dumb, I know. If we do set something off, though, we put the bunker's travelling necklaces on straight away and get the Tartarus out of here. Now, come on, be ready.'

Hailey lifted her hands, warmth flowing into them as Aaron opened one of the doors. She stiffened, waiting for a screecher alarm to blare, but the only sound was the shouts from upstairs.

Aaron slipped through the door, Hailey following behind him. Her hands shook, her heart hammering, expecting to find Nefertari standing over a boiling cauldron, chanting spells—or an army of OMs charging towards them. But they were in another hallway—a really weird one lined with ornate-framed mirrors that stretched from the floor up to the eight-foot-high ceiling.

'Why are there so many mirrors in here?' Demi asked, closing the door to the entryway. 'There has to be at least fifty.'

'It's spooky.' Alec shuddered, staring at his reflection in one.

'I don't know.' Aaron's eyes combed the two walls of mirrors. 'Let's go slow. Stay behind me.'

Hailey gulped, her fingertips tingling. Something felt very off about this place. *They're just mirrors. It's some sort of weird decoration*, she reassured herself, creeping behind Aaron as he edged down the hallway, heading towards another set of double doors at the very end.

Movement caught the corner of Hailey's eye. Her head snapped to her right, electricity sparking between her fingers. Her reflection greeted her.

'What is it?' Demi hissed, coming to her side.

'Nothing. Just my reflection.' The tingling in her fingertips increased, warning her of nearing danger. *I know there's danger— the Hecate must be right through those doors, twenty yards ahead.* She started up after Aaron again, taking only a few steps before Demi called out.

'Hailey!'

Hailey whipped around, expecting to find an OM racing towards them. But the hallway was empty. *Completely* empty. Demi and Alec were gone! 'Demi? Alec?' A chill stretched down her spine, making her hairs stand on end. Something was very wrong here. 'Aaron, somethi—' she began to say as she turned back towards him, but her words fell away when she saw that he was gone too. 'That's not possible,' she said aloud, her hands shaking. 'He was just here. They all were. Guys? Where are you?' Hailey spun around, left and right, eyes searching for her friends. *I must be imagining things. They have to be here.* Only her reflection stared back at her. *No. They have to be here.* 'Demi? Alec? Aar—'

Hands latched on to Hailey's shoulders and yanked her backwards. She braced herself to be smashed into a mirror. Instead, her body tingled with pins and needles. The hands on her shoulders lifted, but before she could turn around to face her attacker, a man appeared in front of her. He grinned, raking a hand through his black hair, mussing it up like he was checking himself out in a mirror.

Hailey stepped towards him, raising her sparking hands.

Thump. Her head bumped into something—like an invisible wall or a force field. 'Ow,' she yelped, rubbing her forehead.

The man's grin widened. 'That never gets old.'

Hailey rammed her fist against the invisible wall. 'What did you do?'

'Did you think the mirrors were mere decoration?' he drawled. 'I trapped you in one of them, just like your friends. Now if you'll excuse me, I need to tell the others about your arrival. I'm sure Zeus would love to order your execution.' He turned, walking away.

'No!' Hailey threw out her hand, lightning blasting from her palm.

Crack!

Hailey fell forward, shattered glass cutting her hands and knees as she hit the ground on all fours. She barely noticed the pain, too distracted by the screecher alarm now blaring. She didn't even have time to stand up before six OMs surrounded her, pointing their guns. The alarm cut off, leaving Hailey's ears ringing as she crouched frozen on the floor. Her brain trying to catch up with what had just happened.

The man who'd trapped her in the mirror stood in front of her, the other OMs on either side of him. 'That was stupid,' he said. 'Now you'll have seven years bad luck for breaking a mirror—good news is you won't live that long.'

Do something! Hailey lifted her bleeding hands, feigning surrender. Warmth poured up her arms as she prepared to fill the room with lightning. It spread to her fingers and—*click.* An OM shoved a neutralising bracelet on her wrist, cutting off Hailey's powers before she could even create a spark.

27

REUNION

The world swirled around Hailey, reforming into a bare white room the size of Hailey's bedroom back home. Two people were inside, sitting on the padded floor.

'Mum! Dad!' Alec shouted, running towards them.

'Alec!' Amelie wrapped her arms around her son, tears spilling from her eyes as she hugged him, Alaric joining in, squeezing his family tight.

Demi and Aaron stood beside Hailey, along with two OMs.

'I recognised him as your son,' the OM on Hailey's left said. Grey peppered his dark hair. 'I thought you'd like to spend some time together before his execution.'

'Execution?!' Alaric exclaimed, breaking the hug apart. His glasses were gone, and his hair greasy. 'Darius, you are not executing my son! Or his friends!'

'It's out of my hands. Their infiltration has already been reported. Zeus will use them to make another example.'

'I—'

Darius and the other Mystery vanished, leaving Hailey, her friends, and Alec's parents alone in the door-less and window-less room.

'Alec, what are you doing here?' Amelie asked, holding her son's face in her hands, staring at him like he might disappear at any second.

'We came to save you,' Alec admitted.

'And capture the leader of the Mysteries—'

'What a stupid idea,' Amelie burst out, cutting off Demi. She dropped her hands from Alec's face. 'You are children. You can't just materialise into this castle and expect to kidnap the most powerful Hecate in the world. If it were so easy, someone would have already done it.'

'There has to be a way out of here,' Aaron said, dragging his hands down the white walls. 'A secret door or something. Help me look.'

Hailey moved to the adjacent wall, sliding her hands over it. She didn't dare listen to the voice in the back of her head telling her this was pointless. That she wasn't going to find a button or secret lever on smooth walls. But not doing anything wasn't an option. She would not stand idly by and let Zeus execute her. Not again. She would fight, even with this stupid neutralising bracelet on her wrist.

'There's no way out.' Regret lined Alaric's words. 'The only way in or out is a travelling necklace or a dematerialiser.'

'Or portaling in.'

Hailey whipped around, catching the briefest glimpse of a woman in black falling from the ceiling before she landed on the ground.

'Got you!' Aaron shouted, grabbing her from behind, wrapping his thick arms around hers, pinning them. 'Let us out.'

'I'm here to help,' the woman said, not bothering to fight against him.

'No,' Demi gasped, her jaw dropping as she walked up to the OM. She stared into the woman's face, blinking. 'It can't be. It can't be you.'

The OM smiled. 'It is, Demi. It's so good to see you again.'

'Who is this, Demi?' Aaron's grip stayed tight around the OM.

Demi gulped, gawking at the woman like she was a shade. 'That's my aunt. Elena.'

'Your aunt?' Hailey frowned. As far as Hailey knew, Demi's aunt had given her up for adoption after Demi's parents had died in a robbery. She lived in America. But with her hair wavy like Demi's, and having the same skin tone and facial features, there was no denying the similarities between them. *What in Tartarus is going on?*

Demi continued to stare, face dazed. 'How are you here?' Her eyes dropped down and then back up, taking in Elena's black clothes. 'You're in the Mysteries!' She stepped back, shaking her head. 'Why? I don't understand.'

'There's no time to explain,' Elena said. 'I don't know how long it will take before Zeus comes here—or orders you moved somewhere else to await your execution. We have to hurry.'

'No.' Demi shook her head again. 'I want answers. I want them now. I haven't seen you in eleven years. I don't even remember you—the only reason I recognise you is because of the family photo album I have. Now tell me, why are you in the Mysteries?'

Elena's eyes combed the room, running over every person in there, like she was looking for someone to stand up for her, to agree that they needed to go. But no one said a word. Hailey was too shocked, her mind trying to grasp what the Tartarus was happening. How Demi's long lost aunt was standing in the dungeon with them right now.

'Okay. Fine. I'll give you the quick version. Can you at least tell your friend to let me go—my arms are going numb?'

'Let her go.'

'Demi, I—'

'Let her go,' she repeated, cutting Aaron off.

'If you make a move, I'll take you down,' Aaron warned, stepping back from Elena.

'Thank you,' Elena said, rolling her shoulders.

'Explain.' Demi crossed her arms, the look on her face telling Elena that she better have one Tartarus of an excuse to explain her abandoning Demi and why she was now in the Mysteries.

'The Mysteries recruited me when I finished school,' Elena began, talking quickly. 'They won me over with their spiel about how powers don't matter in the Olympian Mysteries—everyone is equal. As an Other, I'd been bullied my entire life, made to feel inadequate. So I went to one of the Mysteries' meetings. They made me feel special, so I kept going back.' A ghost of a smile tugged at her lips, like she was remembering a fond memory. 'I never told your mum, Demi, because I knew she would disapprove. I was happy there, at the start—I had friends. We would do silly things like worship statues of the gods. I didn't think it would work and that it was just a laugh. So I joined in.' The smile vanished. 'And then when I was twenty-three, the Mysteries said I was going to help them rob a museum. That was too far for me. I didn't want to break the law, so I told them no. They threatened to kill my entire family if I didn't.

'I was so upset I went to Charlotte, your mum, crying. I told her everything. She said I couldn't do it. I couldn't go. But I told her I had to, to keep her safe. You were only four at the time. I didn't want anything to happen to you. Or my sister, or my parents.' Tears glistened in Elena's eyes. 'It was my mess; I had to clean it up, and if I got caught and went to jail, then that would be on me too. Your mum begged me to stay, but I left. I met the others at the museum like we'd planned. One of the other members set off an exploding potion in the building next door to the museum. It drew everyone out, and we got to work on stealing as many artefacts as we could.'

Her shoulders dropped. 'But two people snuck in—your

parents, Demi. They found me, tried to get me to leave with them. I was going to as well. I opened up a portal, and then…' She gulped, tears spilling down her cheeks. 'And then one of the others I was with killed them. Right in front of me. They jumped through the portal I'd opened for your parents, and they dragged me with them. Just left Charlotte and Elijah there.' She wiped away her tears, sniffing. 'Your mother put me down as your legal guardian, should anything happen to her and your father. You weren't safe with me though—or with your grand-parents. So I sent you away, to England, to be adopted and have a new life. But I was trapped in the Mysteries. They said they'd kill my parents if I betrayed them, and that they'd find you and kill you too. So I stayed. And I did everything they asked me to.'

'That's how my parents died?' Demi's voice was thick, tears welling in her eyes. 'The Mysteries killed them?'

'Yes. Because of me. I'm so sorry.'

Demi sucked in a breath, blowing it out slowly before sucking in another. She swallowed, wiping her eyes. 'That's a lot to take in.'

Hailey moved to her side, squeezing her best friend's hand. She could only imagine how she was feeling. Learning that the aunt who'd abandoned you was trapped in the Olympian Mysteries and that a cult had murdered your parents wasn't something anyone was equipped to deal with.

'Now we need to get you out of here.' Elena pulled a water canteen from her belt.

'Wait.' Demi stopped her. 'We came here to kidnap Nefertari—'

'Demi, don't give away anything else,' Aaron warned, standing behind Elena, ready to tackle her if needed.

'She's my aunt. I trust her.'

'Going anywhere near Nefertari is too dangerous.' Elena shook her head. 'You've already learned that. I'm taking you out of this castle.'

'No.' Demi's voice was firm. 'We risked everything for this plan—if we don't finish it, my friend Jayden's death will have been for nothing. If you want to make up for what you did to my parents, then you'll help us.'

Elena winced, like Demi had slapped her. 'I—' She swallowed. 'Okay. I'll help you. Release all bracelets in this room.'

Click. Click. Click. Click. Click. Click.

Hailey's bracelet expanded on her wrist and slipped onto the floor. Warmth rushed into her hands, her powers returning.

'You can't do this, Alec. None of you can,' Amelie said, rubbing her red wrist. 'It's too dangerous. We're all going back to wherever you came from.'

'Mum, you have to trust me,' Alec said. 'I have to do this. I promised my friends I would help them. We're doing it to save the world.'

'No. I can't lose you,' she said, pulling him close.

'You won't. I'll come back.'

'Please don't go, son.' Alaric joined the hug.

Pain squeezed Hailey's heart as she watched the three of them. She missed her parents so much. She'd have given anything for them to be there with her. To hold her. To tell her they loved her. But her dad was dead, and her mum was a prisoner.

Elena unscrewed the lid on the canteen and tipped it over. Water spilled out, pooling on the padded floor. She clipped the canteen back on her belt and crouched down, running her hand over the puddle, spreading the water wide. The water shimmered like a reflective pool, rippling, and then Hailey was staring down at a woman grinding herbs in a mortar and pestle. 'Anyone who's coming, we need to move now.'

Alec pulled away from his parents. 'I'm sorry, Mum and Dad.'

'Alec, no!' Amelie cried, reaching for him. Alaric held her, tears in his eyes.

'Jump.'

No one hesitated. The five of them jumped into the puddle. Hailey fell through the floor, her stomach somersaulting as she braced herself to smash onto the ground. But she landed softly, right behind Nefertari.

THE HECATE

Woodsy herbs mixed with the sweet scent of flowers wafted around Hailey. The room reminded her of the Hecate room at Poseidon's Academy, only triple the size. A wooden table, almost as wide as the room, stretched lengthwise in front of Nefertari. A cauldron bubbled beside her, green mist seeping from it as she continued grinding herbs in the mortar and pestle. Rosemary, sage, sandalwood, belladonna, Nemean lion fur, volcanic ash, and about a hundred other ingredients littered the table and lined the shelves that ran along the walls. Potion bottles were spread among them, various coloured liquids shimmering inside.

'I was expecting you.' Nefertari didn't turn around—she didn't even stop grinding her herbs.

'Then you'll know what happens next.' Aaron's palms were up. 'We don't want to hurt you. Come quietly.'

Nefertari dropped a pinch of the herbs she'd been crushing into the cauldron. It bubbled more, green mist wafting out.

'Stop that,' Aaron warned.

'As you wish.' Nefertari finally turned around.

Hailey gasped, stumbling back half a step. Her eyes were

neon blue—a stark contrast to her black hair, which had gold beads braided into it. Thick black eyeliner emphasised her eyes even more. She looked like an Egyptian queen—back when Egypt had a monarchy, centuries ago—with her jewel-embellished white dress fit for royalty.

'I must say, I am disappointed in you, Elena.' Nefertari's eyes landed on her. 'I thought you were happy here.'

'Enough,' Aaron barked, palms still up, his force field the only thing protecting them from the Mysteries' leader. 'Open a portal, Elena.'

Elena pulled the canteen off her belt.

'That won't be necessary. None of us are going anywhere.' Nefertari's hand shot out, smacking the bubbling cauldron off the table. Green liquid splashed across Aaron's force field, sending ripples streaking across it.

'Nice try, but—AHHH!' Aaron's hands shook, his force field rippling more and more.

'Aaron, what's wr—Medusa!' Hailey cursed, seeing the blisters popping up over Aaron's hands.

'Aaron, your hands!' Demi shrieked.

'It burns,' he hissed, grinding his teeth together and dropping to one knee.

Green liquid dripped down his force field, sizzling on the ground.

'Drop your hands, Aaron.' Alec's voice shook. 'The potion is absorbing into your force field—into your powers.'

'Too – dangerous,' he ground out. Sweat poured down Aaron's face, the blisters on his hands spreading up his arms like someone was pouring boiling water over his skin. He was being cooked alive.

'Drop them.' Hailey grabbed the parts of his arms that weren't burned yet, forcing them down.

Hailey didn't even get a chance to ask if he was okay. Nefertari struck the second his force field was down.

Quicker than Hailey could blink, Nefertari threw a vial at Elena. It exploded against her shoulder, blasting her backwards.

'Elena!' Demi rushed to her aunt as she hit the ground, Elena clutching her burned and bleeding shoulder.

'Kalrkakat.'

Flames shot up, Hailey stumbling back as their heat washed over her, tightening her skin and burning her lungs. A wall of fire stretched across the room, not burning anything, just separating Hailey and her friends from Nefertari.

'We can't let her get away,' Aaron hissed through clenched teeth, pushing to his feet. 'Ahh,' he cried out, his red and blistered hands and arms shaking.

'You're hurt. Stay here. We'll take care of her.'

'No, Ha—'

'Come on, Alec, Demi,' Hailey cut Aaron off. There wasn't time to argue. Nefertari was probably already at the doors, about to run into the hallway and call for backup. They didn't have their travelling necklaces anymore—the OMs had taken them before they'd tossed Hailey and her friends in the dungeon. And Elena was currently passed out—*I hope she's only passed out.* There was no escape. The only thing they could do now was fight—or at least stop Nefertari from calling more OMs in here.

Alec grabbed Hailey's hand, stretching out his other one for Demi as she left her aunt's side to join them. The wall of fire burned in front of them, its heat tightening Hailey's skin.

'I hope I can do this.' Alec gulped before blowing out a breath.

An airy feeling rushed into Hailey's hand, and up her arm, spreading through her entire body, making her feel as though she were made of wind. Coolness swept over her, the flames' heat vanishing.

'Okay. Go.' Alec's voice was strained.

Please, Tyches, let this work. Hailey stepped forward with

Demi and Alec. She tensed, waiting for the flames to burn her, but she passed right through them, like they were nothing more than an illusion. She almost stumbled straight back into them; Nefertari wasn't running towards the doors like Hailey had thought she would be. She was standing two yards from them, her hand stretched out in front of her mouth. She blew, puffing black powder from her palm into Alec's face.

The heat from the flames pressed against Hailey's back, the airiness that had filled her fading away.

'And what exactly was that supposed to do?' Demi said, scorn lacing her words.

Nefertari grinned. 'Ask your friend.'

'I-I-I…'

'Alec, what's wrong?' Hailey asked. He was still phasing—his body all blurry.

'I can't change back.' He stared at his hands, his skin almost translucent.

'What did you do?' Demi demanded, taking a step towards Nefertari.

Nefertari didn't move. She just stood there, grinning, like this was all a game to her. 'I suppose you could say I took away his option to turn off his powers—at least for a little while. For now, your friend is nothing more than a shade.'

'Fix it!'

'Or what? There are no plants around here for you to play with, little Demeter. You can't hurt me. None of you can.'

'Wanna bet?'

'Demi, don't,' Hailey warned, the serious tone in her voice keeping Demi from charging at Nefertari. For all they knew, she had more of that black powder—more spells or potions that she could throw at them if they got too close. But Hailey didn't need to get close to take her down. Warmth poured into her hands, lightning sparking on her fingertips. She held her palm out at Nefertari, forcing her arm not to shake. Not to give away how truly terrified she was. 'You're going to fix what you did to Alec, and then you're going to come with us. Don't make me hurt you.'

Nefertari's grin widened. She opened up her arms, the jewelled bracelets on her left wrist chinking against one another. 'Go on then, give me your best shot.'

'I will.' Hailey's voice shook just a little. She hadn't used her powers on a human yet—she'd tried with Nova, but she'd missed her. She didn't know what damage she could do. What if she blew off Nefertari's arm? What if the lightning missed and ricocheted, hitting one of her friends instead?

'Do it, Hailey,' Demi cheered her on.

'Yeah, maybe you should.' Alec's voice was meek as he stood beside Hailey, still out-of-phase. 'I don't want to be a shade the rest of my life.'

'Come on, I won't fight you,' Nefertari taunted, her arms still open. 'Don't you want to prove to everyone what a powerful Zeus you are? To show all of those who mocked you for being weak, for not being worthy, that you are strong. Or are you as pathetic as they all believe you are?'

Rage bubbled in Hailey, consuming her like a pit of lava. *I am powerful. I am worthy.* Lightning shot from her palm, heading straight for Nefertari's leg. Nefertari's right arm swooped down to block it. Hailey waited for her to scream out and fall over, but the lightning didn't hit. Well, not exactly. The red gem in Nefertari's cuff bracelet absorbed the lightning, sucking the electricity into itself and glowing bright red, like the lightning had charged it. *What the...?*

Nefertari held up her right arm, showing off her bracelet to Hailey. 'I thought this might come in handy. It absorbs energy, you see,' she explained. 'But what's truly special about it is that it can also expel energy.'

The red gem glowed brighter, and before Hailey could even understand what Nefertari meant, lightning shot from the ruby, blasting straight into Hailey's left shoulder. 'AHHH!' Hailey screamed, stumbling back a step, almost falling into the wall of fire as her hand clutched at her burning shoulder.

'Hailey!' Demi and Alec both shouted.

She gasped in tiny breaths, trying to breathe through the pain pulsing in her shoulder and spreading down her arm.

'That's it!' Demi launched. Arms stretching out as she dove for Nefertari.

Nefertari jumped back, her hand disappearing into a pocket in her dress before throwing something that looked like dried vines on the ground. Demi hit the floor with a growl. *'Lodau,'* Nefertari said as Demi leapt back up.

The vines slithered to life like snakes, rooting into the ground and growing, wrapping around Demi's ankles as she tensed her legs to spring at Nefertari again. 'What the Tartarus?!' Demi shook her legs, trying to free herself from the coiling vines.

'Demi.' Alec rushed to her, his hands clawing at the vines snaking around her. But his fingers passed right through them.

'Get this off me!' Demi wriggled, the vines stopping their coiling as they reached her shoulders, having pinned her arms to her sides.

'Struggle all you like, the vines won't release you,' Nefertari said from in front of Demi. Alec continued trying to grab the vines, his hands passing through them, and Demi, again and again. 'You know I could kill you all,' Nefertari said, her neon blue eyes sweeping over the three of them. 'In fact, it would bring me great joy after all of the trouble you have caused my followers, and the gods. But, alas, Zeus wants the honour of executing you.'

Hailey continued gasping in tiny breaths of air, her shoulder and arm feeling like they were on fire. *Just breathe. Just breathe. It's not over yet. Zeus isn't here yet. There's still time. There's still a chance. Just breathe.*

'Go to Tartarus!' Demi hissed, wriggling her shoulders.

'Actually, you know what, I *can* kill one of you.' A dark smile tugged at Nefertari's red lips. She pulled a dagger from her gown, the emerald hilt glinting in the fire's light. 'You're supposed to be dead.' Her eyes locked on Demi. 'One of my followers was meant to kill you. I'm not sure how you survived, but that's something I can fix.'

'No!' Alec yelled, grabbing for Nefertari, for the knife. She stepped straight through him, like he was made of mist, raising the dagger, its glinting point aimed straight for Demi's vine-covered chest.

'NO!' Hailey screamed, power rushing through her entire body like an electrified wave. The pain in her shoulder vanished, her hands sparking. She stretched her fingers towards Nefertari. *This is the person who ordered Demi's death. She's responsible for everyone who's died—Lexa, Kora, Jayden. She's responsible for my mum being a prisoner. This Hecate is the reason the gods are back. She helped resurrect them. She helped them take over the world. And she's helping them maintain power—helping them keep the human population enslaved. So much death. So much pain. All because of her. No more!*

Hailey's hands glowed white, lightning streaking from her fingertips. Ten jets of electricity shooting straight for Nefertari. Terror seized her face, the dagger dropping from her hand as she crossed her right arm over her chest, the ruby in her bracelet glinting, glowing bright red as it absorbed one of the lightning bolts. But the other nine hit their mark, striking Nefertari in the chest, her arms, and her stomach. The impact sent her flying backwards across the room, straight into the closed doors.

'Demi, are you okay?' Hailey used her good arm to hook her fingers into the vines and pull.

'Yeah, just get me out of this stuff.'

Hailey ripped at the vines, snapping them apart like a

Nemean lion clawing through a tree, freeing Demi's arms and legs.

'Thank you.' Demi sighed in relief, rubbing at her scratched-up arms. 'Your shoulder looks really bad.'

Hailey spared it a half-glance. Her shirt was burned, the flesh visible underneath a combination of red and black. Pain began pulsing in it again, spreading down her left arm. 'It's fine.'

'She's dead.' Alec, still out-of-phase, stood beside Nefertari's unmoving body six yards away. His eyes were locked on her, watching wisps of smoke rise from the nine lightning-strike wounds.

Dead? The word hit Hailey like a cyclops's fist to the stomach. She'd just killed someone. But she hadn't meant to. She'd just wanted to save Demi. To save all of her friends. She gulped, her legs wavering. She wanted to kill the gods, and she'd tried to kill Nova. But she'd never stopped to think what killing someone actually meant—that she'd be taking away someone's life. Taking them away from people who cared about them.

She pressed a hand to her mouth, tears spilling from her eyes as she dropped to her knees.

'Hailey, what's wrong?' Demi's arm was around her, shaking her.

'I didn't mean to,' Hailey said through tears, guilt pressing against her. *Dead. I killed her. I killed someone. I'm no better than the gods, than the Mysteries.*

'You saved my life. Don't you dare be sorry.' Demi's arm was tight around her shoulders, hugging Hailey to her side. 'By killing her you've saved so many people. You did the right thing.'

Hailey sucked in breaths, trying to breathe against the tightness squeezing her chest. *The right thing. I did the right thing... but I killed someone.*

'What happened?' Aaron's voice asked.

Hailey didn't turn around, she hadn't even noticed the heat

from the wall of fire cut off. She knelt there, tears flowing down her cheeks as she stared towards Nefertari's corpse, and Alec standing above it. *I did that. I killed her.*

'Is Hailey—'

'She's fine. Nefertari is dead,' Demi said, her arm still around Hailey.

'Alec, what's wrong with you?'

'She hit me with a potion—I can't change back.' Alec's voice was quiet, on the verge of tears.

'We'll figure it out. We need to go. Mysteries could come in here at any second.'

'Come on, Hailey.' Demi helped her up, putting Hailey's good arm around her shoulder. She steered her around to face where the wall of fire had burned. It was gone now, not a single trace of its existence left—the floor wasn't even singed. A numbness spread through Hailey, cutting off her tears and leaving her feeling empty, as they stepped towards the table covered in potions and herbs, and the fallen cauldron; Elena stood on the other side, smiling with relief when she saw Demi.

'Elena! You're okay.' Demi's pace quickened towards her aunt, Hailey stumbling to keep up.

'Your friend found a healing potion,' Elena explained as they manoeuvred around the table to reach her. 'He also found one to put out the fire.'

'Is there one to fix me?' Alec asked, joining them with Aaron.

'We'll figure it out,' Aaron said again, and patted Alec on the shoulder—he tried to anyway, his hand passing straight through him. 'Sorry.'

'Jump.'

A puddle of water stretched across the ground in front of Elena, through it, Hailey could see the briefing room in the bunker. She jumped with Demi and her friends, falling through the air for a few heartbeats before she landed on the briefing room's table.

'Put your hands up.'

Two soldiers stood by the open door, their guns pointed directly at Hailey and her friends. Hailey raised her hands, cringing as pain blasted down her left arm.

'It's okay, it's just us,' Aaron said, his hands raised beside Hailey. Alec, who'd been standing next to him, had fallen through the table—or more like passed through it, with the table coming up to his waist as he stood inside it, his feet on the floor.

'Yeah, we just completed your mission for you,' Demi said from Hailey's other side. 'We took out the Mysteries' leader— you're welcome.'

Hailey's hands shook. *I killed her.*

'Colonel Liu, we need you in the briefing room,' one of the soldiers said into his watch, his gun remaining trained on Hailey and her friends.

They stood there, on the table, their arms raised with guns pointed at them.

'Come on, you know who we are,' Demi said, staying put for the moment.

'Yes, you're the four teenagers who attacked me and committed treason,' Jia said, entering the room.

'Colonel, we wanted to help.' Aaron kept his hands up. 'We couldn't let you kill Alec's parents. We wanted to try Jayden's plan first.'

'That wasn't your call.' Fury lined Jia's words. 'You're not a member of the military—lucky for you too; otherwise you'd be facing a court-martial.'

'Please, there isn't much time,' Elena said from beside Demi. 'I have to go back and rescue everyone in the dungeon before the Mysteries discover their leader is dead.'

Jia narrowed her eyes. 'Who are you?'

'The person who helped kill Nefertari.'

'She's dead?'

'Colonel, please. We'll explain everything, just please let her go back to the dungeon. Alec's parents are waiting. Once they're safe, Elena will take you to the castle to blow it up.'

Jia narrowed her eyes even more, as though trying to read Elena's mind. She turned back to the two soldiers; she nodded, and they lowered their guns. 'Okay, go,' she said to Elena. 'You can all get down now.'

Hailey clutched her left arm to her chest as she lowered it, clenching her teeth against the pain and letting Aaron help her down from the table. Elena unclipped her canteen, pouring a puddle of water on the cement floor and kneeling down. She pressed her fingertips to the water, ripples spreading across the puddle before calming to reveal an image of Alaric and Amelie pacing their dungeon cell.

'I'll be right back.' Elena jumped into the puddle, the water evaporating to nothing a heartbeat later.

'What did you do?' Jia demanded.

Hailey didn't even hear Aaron's response. She just stood there, feeling empty. *I killed someone. I killed someone.* She barely registered Elena landing back on the table, or Alaric's and Amelie's crying as they embraced Alec—*tried* to embrace Alec. More people soon followed, all of them crying like they couldn't believe they were finally free. She ignored the Asclepius who came over to her, who healed her shoulder. At some point, someone put an arm around Hailey and steered her from the room. She didn't even know who it was until they led her into one of the sleeping quarters, guiding her towards a bunk bed and sitting down with her.

'Hailey, you need to snap out of it.' Aaron's arm, still wrapped around her shoulders, shook her.

'I've never killed anyone before.' Hailey's voice was quiet, barely a whisper. 'Only monsters.'

'She *was* a monster.' Aaron was resolute. 'She's—she was—the leader of the cult who resurrected the gods. She was the one who helped them take control of our world. She's responsible for everyone who has died so far. You did the right thing—if you hadn't killed her, she would have killed Demi. And the military were planning on killing her anyway. You just beat them to it.'

Hailey swallowed, Aaron's words sinking in. *Nefertari was a monster. A murderer. A torturer. Just like the gods. And I'm going to have to kill the gods, aren't I? Isn't that the plan? Isn't that what I want? To destroy them for everything they've done? I did the right thing,* Hailey told herself slowly. *I did the right thing. Nefertari was a monster.*

'Hailey, you're okay. Thank the Tyches.' Brennan stood in the doorframe, his legs tensing, about to run over to her, but then his eyes shifted to Aaron, to his arm around her, and Brennan stilled, like he'd been rooted to the spot. 'Sorry, I didn't mean to interrupt.' He raked a hand through his hair. 'I heard you were back and wanted to make sure you were okay. What happened?'

'We dealt a lethal blow to the Olympian Mysteries,' Aaron said. 'Once all the prisoners are rescued, Colonel Liu and her team will be blowing up the Mysteries headquarters.'

'Wow, that's incredible.' He stared at Hailey, who was looking at her lap, still trying to process everything. 'Are you okay, Hai—'

'Hailey!'

Hailey's eyes snapped up then, relief banishing away the guilt shredding her insides. 'Pandora!' She jumped up, wrapping her arms around her friend as Pandora ran to her.

'Elena just brought her through,' Demi said, coming into the room with Alec, who was solid again, a gold neutralising bracelet gleaming on his wrist.

'I'll leave you alone,' Brennan muttered, Hailey not even noticing him leaving.

'What happened to you?' Aaron asked, standing up from the bed.

Pandora pulled back from Hailey. Her waist-length strawberry blonde hair was grimy and knotted, and the flecks of gold in her blue eyes sparkled as tears welled. 'I tried to rescue your dad and his team after they got captured,' Pandora told Aaron as the five of them stood in a circle. 'But Nemertes caught me.' Her voice cracked. 'She took me to Poseidon, and he sent me to Zeus to deal with.' She shuddered. 'He said he was glad I was still alive, and that I would be his weapon again.' She hugged her arms, her nails torn like she'd been clawing at something—*probably the walls of her dungeon cell.* 'He sent me to the Mysteries to keep locked up. They forced me to drink a potion that amplified my powers.' Tears slid down her cheeks.

Hailey's throat burned with her own tears. She could easily guess what had happened next—what Zeus had made her do.

'They dropped me in the middle of a city full of people and took my neutralising bracelet off before vanishing and leaving me there.' She hugged her arms tighter, more tears falling. 'I didn't want to hurt anyone. I tried to hold my powers in. But the potion made them so strong... They all died. I couldn't stop it.'

Hailey wrapped her arms around Pandora's shuddering body, Demi doing the same. 'It wasn't your fault,' Hailey said, starting to feel okay with killing Nefertari. *She really was a monster—no better than the gods. She was responsible for thousands of people's deaths. By killing her, I've probably saved lives, isn't that what matters more?*

Hailey, Demi, and Pandora stood there, hugging and crying, while Alec and Aaron stood awkwardly by, watching—or more like Aaron stood awkwardly by while Alec pressed a hand over his nose and mouth, trying not to breathe.

'Have you already given us Poseidon's Plague?' Alec's hand muffled his words.

The girls pulled apart, wiping their eyes. 'No. I've got this on again.' She held up her arm, a gold neutralising bracelet glinting on her wrist.

'So your powers are definitely turned off?' Alec pressed.

Pandora nodded, sniffing.

Alec dropped his hand, just as someone else entered the room.

'Ava?' Hailey said.

Ava pushed her purple-framed glasses up her nose, her eyes on the ground, and her dark hair as grimy and knotted as Pandora's. 'I'm so sorry. You have to know that. I didn't mean for any of it to happen. I didn't have a choice.' Her words were rushed, her gaze remaining on the ground, like she couldn't bear to meet Hailey's eyes.

'What are you talking about?' Demi asked. 'What did the Mysteries make you do?'

Ava's eyes snapped up then, locking on to Demi. Ava's legs wavered, and she reached a hand out to the doorframe, holding it for support. 'You're alive! How are you alive?'

Demi gulped. 'Jayden gave his life for mine.'

'Wait, how do *you* know about that?' Aaron crossed his arms, eyeing Ava up and down, as if trying to read her mind. 'I'm guessing Elena just brought you back from the Mysteries' dungeon. How did you know Demi died?'

Ava took a deep breath. 'Because I'm the one who ordered her death.'

AN UNEXPECTED VISITOR

Hailey sat on the bottom bunk bed, with Demi and Ava on either side of her. Alec and Aaron sat on the bunk bed across from them, and Pandora had just left, wanting to give them privacy.

'Okay, we're sitting down like you wanted,' Demi said, looking over at Ava on Hailey's other side. 'So what did you mean you ordered my death?'

'The Mysteries captured me on the island—my parents too.' She twisted her grimy dark hair around her finger and chewed her lip. 'When they found out that I could send thoughts to people, they sent me to the Mysteries headquarters.' She shuddered. 'They gave me a potion to make my powers stronger so that I could receive thoughts as well, and also send thoughts over long distances—like to the other side of the world.'

Is that all Nefertari did? Force innocent people to drink a potion to grow their powers so she could use them as a weapon? She'd done the same thing to Tamzin and Pandora. How many other people did she use like that? Did she force to do horrible things?

'All I'd need to do was think of a person and then I could

instantly send them a message, and they could send me one back,' Ava continued.

'Why didn't you send us a message?' Aaron asked. 'You could have given us information about the Mysteries. We could have used it to take them down sooner.'

'Because they were watching me,' Ava explained. 'Every hour, an Athena would come into my cell and look into my mind to make sure I hadn't used my powers to send any messages without their permission.' She hugged her arms. 'They said if I betrayed them—if I ever tried to contact someone other than the person they were telling me to—they would kill my parents.'

'I'm sorry,' Hailey said, putting an arm around her. 'That must have been terrifying.' She couldn't even imagine how awful it would be to have the Mysteries telling her to do something that would harm others, and that they'd kill her mum if she didn't. She could already see where this story was going— why Ava felt responsible for what had happened to Demi. In her position, Hailey would have done whatever it took to keep her mum alive.

'I met Nova when I was there,' Ava continued. 'She told me she was about to start a spy mission, and that I'd be the one sending her messages about her mission, and that she'd send me back everything she learned to relay to the Mysteries.'

Anger and hate flared in Hailey at the mention of Nova's name. *Where is she now? Is she in the castle? The castle that Jia and her team are about to blow up? Is Venus with her? Are they both about to die? They deserve whatever they get. They're as bad as the gods.*

'She sent me a message about the attacks General Killian was planning on the temples,' Ava went on. 'I didn't tell the Mysteries at first. I kept it quiet. But then the Athena looked into my mind and saw it.' She dropped her head. 'They shot my dad for not telling them. It didn't kill him though. They wanted him to die slowly. They said they'd only heal him if I did every-thing they asked.'

'I'm so sorry.' Hailey rubbed Ava's shoulder. *Monsters. The Mysteries are all monsters.*

'My dad was in so much pain—he was going to die without an Asclepius. I wanted to save him, so when the Mysteries told me to send Nova a message to kill Demi, I did it.' Her eyes met Demi's, tears glistening behind her glasses. 'I'm so sorry. It was the only way they would heal my dad.'

Demi reached across Hailey, clasping Ava's hand 'It wasn't your fault.' Tears glistened in her eyes too. 'I would have done the same thing to save my dad.'

'And I would have done it for my mum too,' Hailey agreed.

'Same,' Alec said.

'Yeah.' Aaron nodded.

Ava sniffed. 'Thank you. I was scared you'd never forgive me.'

'It was the Mysteries, not you,' Demi said. 'And right now, I hope they're all burning.'

'Some of them are,' Jia said, walking into the room.

Aaron jumped up from the bed, his posture straightening. 'So it's done then, ma'am?'

'Yes. The exploding potions have just gone off—although I daresay many of the Mysteries will still escape using travelling necklaces. But they'll no longer have a place to congregate, or a leader,' she said. 'I can't condone your disobeying of orders, but I will say that your father would be very proud, and that one day you will make a great soldier.'

A smile tugged at Aaron's lips. 'Thank you, colonel.'

'Now, the reason I came here is because after you knocked me out and stole the travelling necklaces, someone showed up at this bunker.'

'Who?' Demi asked.

'I think it will be easier to show you. I spent two hours interrogating them, and I believe they are telling the truth. Come, they want to see you.'

'I'm going to find Riley and Charlie,' Ava said, giving Hailey and Demi a final hug before slipping out of the room.

Hailey followed after Jia with her friends, her mind trying to work out who the mysterious stranger was. *Is it Hephaestus? Maybe he finished the weapon early and came here to give it to me. But how would he know I was here? Why would he risk leaving his workshop when he said to do so would mean risking the other Olympians sensing him?*

Jia led them down another hallway of doors, pausing outside of one that said *Detention cell 3*. Where a door handle should have been was a small black screen the size of a sticky note. Jia pressed her thumb to it. *Click.* Jia pushed the door open, the five of them piling into a small room that only had a bed and a toilet. And on the bed sat someone Hailey had never expected to see again—at least not in this bunker.

Hailey blinked. 'Cady?'

'What is *she* doing here?' Demi demanded, fury lining her words. 'She's the one who woke up the gods. She's on the Mysteries' side. She killed Jayden.'

'Colonel, she's our enemy,' Aaron said, his posture still straight.

'I'll let her explain,' Jia said, squeezing between them and leaving the room, her footsteps echoing down the hallway.

Cady's head was lowered, her fly-away brown hair in her face. 'I'm sorry.'

'That's it? After everything you've done, you're sorry?' Demi's fury only grew, like a fire fuelled by an Anemoi's wind. 'Give us one reason why we shouldn't keep you locked up in here forever.'

Cady looked up at them through her hair. 'Because I can help you kill the gods.'

'You woke them up,' Hailey bit back. Cady was the reason

the gods were on the loose. *Yes, Nemertes manipulated her, but she hadn't forced her to find a way to resurrect the gods—that had all been Cady's choice.*

'Why do you want to kill them suddenly?' Aaron demanded, his arms crossed.

'Because it wasn't supposed to be like this,' Cady said, her voice meek. 'When Nemertes came to me, she said the gods would take their powers back and that the world would keep going on, but that humans would be equal again. That's all I wanted—for people with god powers to lose their superiority. For them to stop bullying me and Others.'

'Were you not paying attention in Ancient History?' Demi's words were sharp, like a dart from a sea-urchin bomb. 'Humans are the gods' slaves. That's why they created us. You can't be so stupid that you'd think they'd just take their powers back and leave us alone.'

Cady shrugged, more hair falling in front of her face. 'I don't know. Yeah, I guess it was wishful thinking. But I was desperate. I've been bullied my entire life—I couldn't take it anymore. I wanted it to stop.' She sniffed, wiping at her eyes. 'I did have second thoughts when I got to Olympus, but by then it was too late. I would have been stuck up there if I hadn't woken them.'

'What was it like?' Alec's eyes gleamed with wonder.

'Not now, Alec,' Aaron snapped.

'They were all in the throne room—frozen—and there was this box filled with lights.'

'Skip ahead,' Aaron said. 'To the part where you explain why we shouldn't let you rot in here.'

Cady pushed her hair from her face, her head rising ever so slightly. 'Because I want to help you kill the gods. They trust me, at least enough that I'm allowed to go to Olympus, which is also the one place where ambrosia grows—it makes them strong. Without it, they'd be weaker—maybe weak enough for neutralising bracelets to work on them.' Her words were rushed, like she was afraid Hailey and her friends would leave before she'd finished explaining her plan. 'I can burn their ambrosia so they have nothing left.'

'You could really just walk in and destroy it, just like that?' Aaron pressed.

'They let me walk around, as long as I stay out of their way—my chameleon powers help with that. If I had an exploding potion, I could set it to blow up the ambrosia trees.'

'Why now?' Demi demanded. 'Why not when they started killing people?'

'I was afraid,' Cady admitted, dropping her gaze. 'I didn't want to die. But then they killed Jayden.' She swallowed, tears glistening in her eyes. 'I left after that.'

'Jayden who you put under a love spell!' Demi practically yelled. 'You took away his freewill. How could you do that to him when he was always nice to you? He's dead because of you.'

Hailey put an arm around her best friend, trying to calm her. Hailey wasn't ready to trust Cady yet; for all she knew, this was another trap. But it sounded very promising. If they could weaken the gods by destroying their ambrosia, then maybe the military could hit the gods with neutralising nets again. Maybe they'd actually work this time and the military could lock the gods up until Hephaestus finished his weapon. *If this works, it could save a lot of lives. It would also mean I could get my mum back.*

'I know.' Cady's hair fell back in her face as her head dropped lower. 'I didn't want to lose him. It was selfish. And now he's dead.' Her voice was thick. She looked back up at them, her eyes peering through her hair. 'I want to make it right. I want to kill the gods—I don't care if I die doing it; it's what I deserve.'

'How did you get here?' Aaron asked, his arms still crossed.

'Someone named Tamzin found me and gave me a travelling necklace. She said if I used it, I could make everything right again.'

'If Tamzin sent her, we can trust her,' Hailey said, hope beginning to bloom in her like a flower opening, petal by petal. *This could work. This could really work. Did Tamzin have a vision about Cady destroying the ambrosia?*

'I need to meet this Tamzin.' Demi's words were cold—angry. 'Because she has some warped ideas about who to trust.'

'So you'll let me help you?' Cady asked, sitting up a bit straighter and leaning forward, eager to hear their response.

Hailey looked at her friends. Demi shook her head, Alec's eyes were still gleaming with curiosity, and she could only imagine he was thinking about what wonders Olympus held, and Aaron was thoughtful, like he was running a hundred different scenarios in his head.

Hailey didn't need to think it over for too long. *Cady joined forces with the Mysteries and woke up the gods, but Nemertes had preyed on her. She's kind of like Demi's aunt—she was manipulated into doing something and then had had no way out. Yes, Cady had the choice to tell Nemertes to jump in a volcano instead of teaming up with her, but after being tormented for so many years... what does that kind of pain and hate do to a person? Makes them desperate enough to do anything to make it all stop. Cady's a good person who has made some really bad decisions. And now she's trying to make it right.*

Hailey's hand dropped to Demi's, and she squeezed it. 'I know you don't want to trust her, but think about what Jayden would want us to do. He'd want us to help her, right?'

Demi sucked in a breath, blowing it out slowly. 'Yes,' she admitted through clenched teeth.

'I think we can trust her, Aaron,' Hailey said, focusing her gaze on him.

Slowly, he nodded. 'The final decision is Colonel Liu's, but I'll vouch for Cady.'

'Will you take pictures?' Alec asked Cady. 'Do you already have some? What kind of—'

'Alec,' Aaron cut off his rambling.

'Okay, Cady, we'll let you help,' Hailey said. 'But we're coming with you. So, tell us, how do we get to Olympus?'

Did you enjoy Hailey's latest adventure? Reviews are really important for newbie authors like me, so if you could spare the time to leave a review on your favourite book website, such as Amazon or Goodreads, it would mean so much to me.

ABOUT THE AUTHOR

Unlike Hailey, Sarah attended an ordinary high school, and a villain-free university—The University of Queensland—where she completed a bachelor's degree in writing and ancient history, and a master's degree in writing, editing, and publishing.

Prior to that, Sarah spent her younger years watching *Xena: The Warrior Princess* and *Hercules: The Legendary Journeys*, which sparked her interest in Greek mythology and saw her spend entire days by her bedroom window, waiting for a pegasus to swoop out of the sky and take her on an adventure worthy of Homer. When it was clear no pegasus was going to rescue her from her ordinary life, Sarah turned to writing her own adventures.

sarahavogler.com

www.ingramcontent.com/pod-product-compliance
Lightning Source LLC
Chambersburg PA
CBHW020559120726
47903CB00001B/305